About the Authors

Being an author has always been **Therese Beharrie**'s dream. But it was only when the corporate world loomed during her final year at university that she realised how soon she wanted that dream to become a reality. So she got serious about her writing, and now she writes the kind of books she wants to see in the world, featuring people who look like her, for a living. When she's not writing she's spending time with her husband and dogs in Cape Town, South Africa. She admits that this is a perfect life, and is grateful for it.

Nichole Severn writes explosive romantic suspense with strong heroines, heroes who dare challenge them and a hell of a lot of guns. She resides with her very supportive and patient husband, as well as her demon spawn, in Utah. When she's not writing, she's constantly injuring herself running, rock climbing, practising yoga and snowboarding. She loves hearing from readers through her website, nicholesevern.com, and on X, @nicholesevern

Scarlet Wilson wrote her first story aged eight and has never stopped. She's worked in the health service for twenty years, having trained as a nurse and a health visitor. Scarlet now works in public health and lives on the West Coast of Scotland with her fiancé and their two sons. Writing medical romances and contemporary romances is a dream come true for her.

Workplace Romance

Workplace Romance:
Be My Enemy

THERESE BEHARRIE

NICHOLE SEVERN

SCARLET WILSON

MILLS & BOON

First Published in Great Britain 2024
by Mills & Boon, an imprint of HarperCollins*Publishers* Ltd,
1 London Bridge Street, London, SE1 9GF

www.harpercollins.co.uk

HarperCollins*Publishers*
Macken House, 39/40 Mayor Street Upper,
Dublin 1, D01 C9W8, Ireland

ISBN: 978-0-263-32489-1

Printed and Bound in the UK using 100% Renewable Electricity
at CPI Group (UK) Ltd, Croydon, CR0 4YY

HER TWIN BABY SECRET

THERESE BEHARRIE

For Grant, who would pretend to be in a fake relationship with me so I could save face in a heartbeat. If we weren't already married, I mean. I love you.

For the online friends who've become my community. I didn't ever think you could exist, but I'm so grateful you do.

PROLOGUE

ALEXA MOORE HAD never thought the pressure her parents had put on her her entire life would result in this. She barely contained the squeal of excitement tickling her throat.

Her father was sitting beside her in the car, her mother at the back. Both were staring at their phones. They were either checking their emails, replying to emails, or writing their own emails. Leighton and Karla Moore were simple in that way. Work came first; everything else, second. They'd reconciled having a family in light of those priorities by treating their children as though they were work. That was why Alexa and her younger brother by a year, Lee, were raised to function much as their parents did: work was the most important thing. Being Leighton and Karla's children, they had to work harder than anyone else.

Who needed a loving, emotionally supportive family anyway?

But that wasn't for today. Today was for happiness and new beginnings. She wasn't stubborn enough not to acknowledge her parents' contribution to this moment. It was part of why she'd brought them with her. They were the ones who had suggested—instructed—her to start working as soon as she turned sixteen. They'd told her to give them half of what she earned, and because she was their child she'd asked them to help her invest the other half. On her graduation from her Honours degree in business, they'd gifted her with a policy they'd taken out with that money. It had been an impressive nest egg. And it had kept growing while she attended culinary school.

She'd got a bursary to study at Cape Town's Culinary Institute. She was lucky. If she hadn't, she would have had to use that nest egg and she wouldn't be able to move forward with her dream. Her parents had paid for her studies in business on the condition that she got distinctions for all her subjects. She had, though not easily, because she knew she'd already disappointed them by not taking the mathematics bursary an elite tertiary faculty had offered.

But her dream was her dream. A business degree helped her get to that dream—and helped her please her parents more than culinary school had. Their disappointment was worth it for this moment though. She had no student loans, four years of business knowledge, two years of culinary knowledge, and two years' experience in the industry. She was finally ready. This was the last step.

She pulled up in front of the property, letting out a happy sigh before she got out of the car. The brick façade of the building was as appealing as it had been the first time she'd seen it. As the first time it had encouraged her to take a chance on it.

'This is it.'

She clasped her fingers together behind her back to keep from fidgeting.

'This?'

'Yes.' She straightened her spine at the disapproval in her father's voice. 'It's an up-and-coming neighbourhood.'

'It looks unsafe, Lex,' Karla said.

'Oh, it's fine.' She waved a hand. 'You know how Cape Town city centre is. The fanciest road is right next to the dodgiest one. Besides, there are so many people around.'

As if proving it, a group of young people walked past them. They were most likely students; not exactly her target clientele. But everyone had to start somewhere, and students meant lecturers and parents and more mature people

who would come to the classy joint in the dingy neighbourhood for the feel of it. She jiggled her shoulders.

'I'm going to call it In the Rough, because this place is
a diamond in the rough.' She grinned. 'It's going to be—'

'Lee, darling!'

The world either slowed at her mother's exclamation, or
Alexa's heart was pumping alarmingly fast. Why was her
brother here? How much of what she'd said had he heard?
Would he use it against her?

'What are you doing here?' she asked, her voice cool,
a reaction to mitigate the heated emotions those questions
had evoked. She would not show them that vulnerability.
'I didn't tell you about this.'

'Dad did,' Lee said, taking their father's hand in a quick
shake. 'He told me about a week ago you were planning on
showing them a property. Gave me the address and everything, so I could check it out myself.'

'Why would you want to?'

'I can't check on what my big sister is doing with her
life?'

No, she wanted to answer. She would have, if their parents weren't there—they would disapprove. Somehow, after
years of trying and failing to obtain their approval, she still
wanted it. After years of her brother using that desire as a
weapon to compete with her, she was still offering it to him.

'To be fair, I'm not doing this with my life yet.' She was
trying to be civil, like she always did. Because she was still
trying to be a decent person with Lee, too. When would
she learn her lesson when it came to her family? 'I wanted
Mom and Dad to see this place before I put in an offer.'

'I know.'

'Did you want to see it, too?'

'Oh, I already have.'

She frowned. 'Why?'

'Because I made an offer.' He shoved his hands into

his pockets, his smile catlike. 'The owner accepted it this morning. This place is going to be mine.'

There was a stunned silence. Her parents broke it by asking Lee why he'd bought the place. Bits and pieces of his answer floated across to her. He wanted to secure the place as a surprise for Alexa. It was a smart business decision to invest in property, particularly in a neighbourhood that was fast becoming one to watch. If he and Alexa worked together, there was less chance of failure. The Moores could become a powerhouse in the hospitality industry.

Lies. Lies, all of it.

Lee spoke to them as fluently as he did his other languages. His linguistic skills were as impressive as her mathematical skills. He knew five of South Africa's eleven official languages; he also knew how to fool their parents. They thought he was a good, supportive brother when in reality, he was a master manipulator. All for the sake of winning a competition he'd made up in his head where they were the only competitors and he the only willing participant.

'Alexa,' Karla called. 'You're daydreaming, darling.'

She blinked. 'Sorry.'

'Did you hear what your brother did?'

'Yes.'

'Aren't you glad?'

'Why would I be glad?'

Her mother exchanged a look with her father. Leighton took the baton.

'Lee's made the smart decision here. It's not a buyer's market at the moment, so you might not have got the property. He has more capital, and more clout, so he had a better chance of being successful in the purchase.'

'He didn't know about the property before you told him,' she said numbly. 'And he only has more capital because he's been working longer.' In the business sector, which was more lucrative. Even her nest egg couldn't beat that. 'The owner said she hadn't had much interest in the six months the property's been on the market.'

'She did sound thrilled with my offer.'

She turned at the satisfaction in Lee's voice. When she saw it reflected on his face, her heart broke. This didn't feel like the other times. When he'd race to the dinner table, turn back to her and say, 'I win!' though he'd been the only one running. Or when he would bring a test home from school, announcing that he'd beat Alexa's mark from the year before.

This was more malicious. It was…uglier. And it proved that she would always be a target Lee would shoot at, no matter what the cost.

Unless she did something about it.

'I hope you find a tenant soon, Lee.'

'Wait!' he said when she started walking to her car. 'I thought you'd rent it?'

'So you can pop in whenever you want? Make your presence known in my business? Pull the rug out from under me when I think I'm safe?' She shook her head. 'I appreciate the offer, but you'll have to find someone else.'

'Alexa, you're being foolish.'

'No, Dad, I'm being realistic. But this is a great neighbourhood.' Her voice cracked, echoing her heart. 'He'll find someone to rent from him soon enough.'

'Darling, your brother only wants to help.'

She took a deep breath before offering her mother a smile. 'I know.' Even after he'd punctured a hole in her dreams and her parents were defending him, she couldn't be blunt. 'I can't take his help or I wouldn't be making the Moore name proud, would I? It's all about achieving things we can be proud of. I can't be proud of this.'

Another breath.

'You should go to the restaurant I booked for us tonight

with Lee. He deserves it.' She smiled at her family, well aware that it didn't reach her eyes. 'I hope you enjoy the food.'

She got into her car and drove away, leaving her heart and her dreams shattered behind her.

CHAPTER ONE

Four years later

'OH,' ALEXA SAID FLATLY. 'It's you.'

Benjamin Foster couldn't help the laugh that rumbled in his chest. 'Yes, it's me.'

Alexa Moore, owner of the elite Infinity restaurant, and the woman who probably hated him more than anyone else in the world, glowered.

'You need to stop following me.'

'I'm not following you,' he denied.

'Are you sure? You seem to be everywhere I am.'

'Because we're in the same business.'

Her eyes stopped scanning the room and settled on him. Sharpened. 'You're here to offer Cherise de Bruyn a job.'

He tilted his head. 'How did you know?'

'You think I didn't hear about Victor Fourie being poached from In the Rough?' She smiled, but it wasn't friendly. 'It's terrible when karma does her thing, isn't it?'

'I'm not sure why she would get involved.'

She gave him a look. He allowed himself a small smile.

'Fine, I do know.' A few seconds passed. Something cleared in his brain. 'You're here to offer Cherise a job, too.'

She responded by ignoring him. He shouldn't have wanted to smile. It seemed rude to since he was the reason she had to offer Cherise a job. She hadn't confirmed that was why she was there, but he was fairly certain. When the thought of being rude did nothing to deter his amusement—

apparently what his presence did to her tickled his funny bone—he turned to the barperson and ordered a drink.

'Can I get you one?'

'I don't want to owe you one, so no, thank you.'

He *tsk*ed. 'That's not very mature, Alexa.'

'Maturity is for the weak,' she muttered under her breath.

He didn't bother hiding his grin this time, but paid for his drink before he replied. 'I don't agree with that.'

'Why would you, Benjamin?' she said with a sigh. 'I said it. On principle, you can't agree with me lest *you* seem weak.'

'"*Lest*"?'

'It means to avoid the risk of.'

'I know what it means. I'm wondering why you said it.'

She sighed again, as though he were chopping up the last of her patience. Which was probably true. They'd known one another for eight years now. Or perhaps it would be better to say they'd known about one another for eight years. They didn't know one another, not by a long shot. They had only gone to the Culinary Institute together, the current venue of their meeting, and met on and off in the six years after that.

Whenever they did, they rubbed each other up the wrong way. It caused a friction so intense that sometimes Benjamin struggled to figure out how he felt about her. On the one hand, she never backed down, said interesting things like *lest*, and made him laugh. On the other hand, she was his greatest competition.

Who could be friendly with the competition?

Infinity was rated highly on all the important websites. He often heard whispers of the patrons of his own restaurant comparing In the Rough's food or ambience to Infinity's. It wasn't uncommon for patrons to do so; comments like that were part of the business. But her restaurant was the one he heard mentioned most frequently. It was also the one they preferred most frequently.

'Really?' she asked when he leaned against the bar. 'In this spacious, beautiful, but most importantly *spacious* place, you couldn't find someone else to bother?'

'Bothering you is more fun.'

Her reply came in the form of a glare. He smiled back, sipped from his drink, and didn't move. He did watch though.

She was right—the venue was gorgeous. It was nestled in the valley of one of the many vineyards in Stellenbosch. Bright green fields stretched out in front of them courtesy of an all-glass wall. The room they were in, usually a dining hall, had been transformed for the sake of the graduation. Chairs were set out in rows, a small stage had been erected on one side, and the opposite side housed the bar they were at. On the other side of the glass wall, accessed through a door on the side, were tables and chairs under tall trees.

He remembered sitting there many a lunch time when he'd been at the Institute. Hell, he remembered watching Alexa glower at him from inside the dining hall much in the same way she was doing now. He'd known even then that she was dangerous. How, he wasn't sure.

'What the hell is he doing here?'

The words weren't meant for him, but he heard them. When he followed her gaze, he saw the cause. Her brother, his business partner, was there. Benjamin didn't know why. Securing a head chef was more in line with Benjamin's responsibilities. But their partnership had evolved in the last four years, and their roles weren't what they initially were when they started working together.

Back then, Benjamin was the head chef and Lee's management company dealt with the running of the restaurant. Benjamin had since taken over some of those responsibilities, which was hard to do without a head chef. It meant that

Benjamin's time was still needed in the kitchen. For three glorious months after Victor Fourie had been persuaded to work for In the Rough, Benjamin had been able to explore more of the management side of things. As it turned out, he enjoyed running a restaurant more than spending all his time in the kitchen.

But Lee had been acting strangely when it came to this head chef thing. With Victor Fourie, Lee had actively encouraged Benjamin to go after the man even though he knew Victor worked for Alexa. It had started out harmlessly enough. They'd been out for drinks one night, discussing work, when the chef walked into the bar. It had seemed like a perfectly fair move to ask him to join them. After that night, Lee had told him to get Victor to take over some of Benjamin's responsibilities. Since it would take an immense amount of pressure off Benjamin, he'd done it, though he hadn't understood Lee's insistence. Now Lee was here…

'Ben!' Lee said when he saw them. His eyes flickered to his sister. Something Benjamin didn't like shimmered there. 'Fancy seeing you here.'

'Is it?' Benjamin asked, taking Lee's hand. 'I told you I was coming.'

'He has to pretend it's a surprise in front of me,' Alexa said, her voice emotionless.

He'd only ever heard her speak that way with her brother. He would have thought, after his and Alexa's antagonistic history, she would have aimed that tone at him, too. But when she spoke to him, her voice was icy, or annoyed, or full of emotion, none of which he could read. He found he preferred it.

'If he doesn't,' she continued, 'it would be clear that he's really here because of me.'

'Not everything I do is because of you, Alexa.' Lee said it smoothly, but Benjamin could feel the resentment.

'I wish that were true.'

Lee didn't acknowledge that Alexa had spoken. 'What I am surprised about is finding you two together.'

'Why?' Benjamin asked.

'Don't you hate one another?'

He looked at Alexa; Alexa looked at him. For a beat, they said nothing. Her expression changed then, going from icy cool to warm. His heart thundered in response to her hazel eyes opening. They grew lighter when they did, so that he could see the green flecks in the light brown. In a way no grown man should experience, Benjamin's knees went weak.

Her eyebrow quirked, as if she knew, though there was no possible way she could. But the show of sassiness pulled the side of her face higher, softening a defined cheekbone. It was an extraordinary juxtaposition to the other side of her face, which was untouched by the expression. It was still hard lines and sharp angles. That had never applied to her lips though, one side of which was now quirked up—much like her brow—in amusement. At him. He was amusing her.

Because he was admiring her full lips that looked as soft as dough. An interesting comparison, though not surprising since he regularly dealt with dough. What *was* surprising was that he wanted to mould that dough as he did in the kitchen. But with his lips instead of his hands, though he could imagine brushing a thumb over those soft creases...

He took a long drag from his drink, severely disappointed that it wasn't alcohol. He could have done with the shock, the burn of downing a whiskey. But no, he'd decided he shouldn't drink because he wanted a clear head when he spoke to Cherise.

How was this clear?

'Well, Lee,' Alexa said, her voice as smooth as the brandy he'd longed for. Or had he thought of whiskey? 'You know what they say: hate and love are two sides of the same coin.'

Lee's head dropped. 'What are you saying?'

'You don't know?' She turned to Benjamin. 'You kept your word. How lovely of you.'

Benjamin didn't know what was going on, but he understood he shouldn't say anything.

'There's no way you and Ben are dating.'

'You're entitled to believe what you want to, Lee. We don't owe you explanations.'

'You're dating her?' Lee asked Benjamin now. 'No. Of course not. You would have told me.'

'I asked him not to. Apparently his loyalties are divided now.' She wrinkled her nose. 'I shouldn't have said that. It was insensitive.'

She grabbed Benjamin's hand. Good thing he was still numb from shock, or he might have felt that explosion of warmth from the contact.

'I'm sorry, Ben.'

Their eyes met again. Nothing he could read on her face gave him any clues to her feelings. No plea that he play along; no acknowledgement that this was strange. Or maybe there were clues, but he couldn't recognise them.

Then she smiled at him. Her mouth widened, revealing strikingly straight white teeth. Those lips curved up, softening all the lines and angles of her face. Even her gaze warmed, though he had no idea why or how. It was a genuine smile that both stunned and enthralled him. He couldn't look away.

'Oh, you *are* together.' Lee's voice penetrated the fog in his brain. 'Wow. I can already see the headline in *Cape Town Culinary*: "Rival restaurant owners fall in love".' He paused. 'Maybe we should get the photographer to take a picture of you two now for the article? I'll call her over.'

Both of them wrenched their gazes away from one another to stare at Lee.

CHAPTER TWO

'I'D RATHER NOT,' Alexa said when she recovered from the shock. She set the water she'd been drinking on the bar, slid off the stool. 'If you'll excuse me, I think some fresh air would do me good.'

She looked at neither of them. Not the man who'd broken her heart too many times for her to count; not the man who'd helped her brother do it. Though now, of course, she was pretending that he was her boyfriend. She alone, because Benjamin had not once said a word about the elaborate tale she'd woven. He would now, of course. As soon as she was out of the way, he'd tell Lee that she was lying and they'd laugh at her.

Nausea welled up inside her. She hoped it didn't mean she'd throw up. She could already imagine Lee's questions: *Rough night last night, sis? Or are you pregnant?* He would laugh, she wouldn't, and he'd know something was up. The last thing she needed was her brother discovering her secret.

She soothed the panic the idea evoked by reminding herself that Lee's presence in the last four years had generally made her queasy. That could be the answer now, too. The thought calmed her. Remembering she'd been feeling surprisingly good these last months helped, too. She took a breath, exhaled slowly. She was one week away from entering her second trimester. Once she got there, she'd tell her parents, and there would be no chance Lee could tell them for her.

It might have been a little paranoid—but then, it might not. She had a brother who was intent on ruining her life after all. Telling their parents she was pregnant before she could was exactly the kind of thing he'd do. She wouldn't get the chance to tell them the story she'd practised since she'd decided to do something about her need for a family. Not the broken one she currently had, but a whole one. A safe one. A family she could actually trust.

As usual, the thought sent vibrations through her. Pain, disappointment prickled her skin. She stopped walking, bracing herself against a tree as she caught the breath her emotions stole. She didn't get the chance to.

'You haven't seen me in months and this is how you treat me?'

She closed her eyes, put all her defences in place, and turned. 'I thought you'd get the message.'

'What message?'

'I don't want to see you, Lee,' she told him. 'I don't want you in my life.'

Something almost imperceptible passed over his face. 'We're family. You have no choice.'

'I'm aware that we're family.' She took a deep breath. 'That's the only reason we've seen one another at all in the last four years. Mom and Dad have birthdays, and there are special days, like Christmas and…' She broke off. She didn't have to explain anything to him. 'Anyway, we have to see one another at those occasions. But not outside of them.'

'All this because I bought a building you wanted?'

'You know it wasn't only a building,' she snapped. Pulled it back. But it was hard to contain. It sat in her chest like a swarm of angry bees, waiting to be let out. She could *not* let it out. 'You've insisted on making this about you and me, but really it's about you. It's always been. I want to live my life without you. You can't seem to live yours without me.'

He smirked. 'You're putting an awful lot of importance on yourself.'

'No, you are.'

She meant to stride past him, but his hand caught her wrist.

'I assume you're here for a new head chef. What happens if you don't get one, Lex?' he asked softly. 'You can't keep running Infinity and its kitchen. You must be spreading yourself thin since your last chef left.'

'He didn't leave. You stole him. You and Benjamin stole him.'

'Which makes me wonder how your romance bloomed?' Lee's lips curved into a smile that broke her heart. Because it was mean, and so unlike that of the brother she'd once thought she had. 'Were you looking for revenge? Maybe you thought you could make him fall in love with you, then break his heart? Or maybe use your body to—'

'Lee.'

The voice was deep with unbridled emotion. Both she and Lee looked in the direction it came from. Benjamin stood there, watching them with a glower she'd never seen on him before. He was usually effortlessly charming, which had been one of the reasons she didn't like him. No one could be that charming, certainly not *effortlessly*. Her conclusion had been that he was a demon, or some kind of magical being sent there to test her patience. The test was going smoothly. Her results were not as positive.

His disapproval should have been aimed at her then, considering their history of battling against one another. But it wasn't. It was aimed at Lee. A thrill went through her before she stomped it down viciously. She did a few more jumps on it for good measure.

'Ben,' Lee said with a smile. He tended to reserve the vicious side of his temperament for her. 'Didn't see you there.'

'I thought as much. I doubt you'd be talking to Alexa that way if you did.'

Benjamin's eyes met hers. She wasn't sure how she knew

it, but he was asking her if she was okay. She angled her head. He looked back at Lee.

'You should probably get someone to help you if that's your perception of relationships.' He held a hand out to her. It took her a moment to realise he meant for her to take it. As if someone else were in her body, she did. 'Even so, I have to say I'm not thrilled with your implication. Alexa and I are in a healthy relationship. Neither of us is using the other. Unless there's something you want to tell me, Lex?'

Oh. He was keeping the pretence going.

Oh.

She shook her head.

'If I say something corny like "I'm using you for your addictive kisses", would you be mad?' he asked.

There it was, that effortless charm. It was kind of nice when it was being used for good. To help her instead of annoy her.

'You probably shouldn't say it, to be safe.'

He laughed. For a moment, it was just the two of them, amused at one another. A part of her wiggled with glee; another part told her to take a step back. This was confusing, and happening too fast. She wasn't even sure what 'this' was.

'Seriously?' Genuine confusion lit Lee's face. 'I thought this, you two, were a joke.'

'You were accusing Alexa of those things earlier and you thought this was a joke?' Benjamin's voice had switched from charm to ice.

Alexa cleared her throat. She didn't want this turning into a full-on brawl. Even if the prospect of seeing Lee punched brought her more joy than it should have. She was strangely certain that would be the outcome if she didn't intervene.

'Ben and I agreed to keep business and our personal

lives separate,' she told Lee. 'That's why no one knew about our relationship until today.'

'And you told *me*?' Lee asked. 'Now I know you two are lying.'

'You don't have to believe us, Lee.'

But she really wanted him to. Maybe that was why she went along with what Benjamin said next.

'He doesn't have to believe us, but why don't we show him why he should?'

When he looked at her, asked her permission with his eyes, she nodded. Told herself wanting to make Lee believe her was why she'd went along with what Benjamin did next. But all of that dissipated when he kissed her.

He'd never wanted to punch someone as much as he'd wanted to punch his business partner in the last few minutes. He wasn't sure if it was because Lee was acting almost unrecognisably, or if his instincts were tingling because he *did* recognise the way Lee was acting. It was the same way people in his past had acted. They'd need something from him, then act surprised, attacked, victimised when he asked them if they were taking advantage of his desire to help.

His instincts could also have been tingling because despite his past, he still wanted to help someone who needed him. It was clear Alexa did. It was his weakness, helping people. Not when the help was appreciated; only when the help was taken advantage of. He didn't know where Alexa fitted into that. It didn't keep him from kissing her though.

Not his best decision, though his lips disagreed. They heartily approved of the softness of Alexa's lips pressed against them. She smelled of something sweet and light; reminded him of walking through a garden at the beginning of spring. It felt as though he'd been drawn into that scene when her mouth began to move against his. His body felt lighter, as it often did after a long, dull winter and the sun made its comeback. He could easily imagine the two of them in that garden, surrounded by flowers, overcome with the joy and happiness a new season tended to bring.

The taste of her brought him sharply back into his body.

He hadn't intended on *really* kissing her. A quick meeting of lips was enough to convince her brother they were together—people who didn't like one another didn't kiss at all. He assumed. Before he started to kiss this woman he supposedly didn't like.

There was no time to think of it since his tongue had somehow disobeyed his desire to keep things simple. Instead, it had slipped between Alexa's lips, plunging them both into complicated.

But damn, if complicated didn't feel *good*. She was sweet, spicy, exactly as her personality dictated. The tangling of their tongues sent pulses through his body, settling in places that made him both uncomfortable and desperate. He used it as an excuse to rest a hand on the small of her back, pressing her against him. She gave a little gasp into his mouth as her body moulded against his, but she didn't pull away. She did the opposite in fact, reaching her arms around his neck and pulling herself higher so their bodies were aligned at a more pleasurable height.

It was that thought that had him pulling away. He wouldn't embarrass himself in public. More importantly, he couldn't embarrass Alexa. Both would happen if they didn't pull themselves together.

She didn't protest, lowering herself to her feet again, her gaze avoiding his. But then she shook her head and looked at him. Curiosity and desire were fierce in her expression, but it was the confusion that did him in.

Was it brought on by this little charade they were performing? Or was she surprised at the intensity of their kisses?

'Happy?' she asked.

He almost answered before he realised she wasn't talking to him. Good thing his brain had started working in time. He would have said something he couldn't take back if he answered. Something in the vicinity of a *yes and no* and maybe a few other statements.

Lee was watching them with a frown.

'You two really are together.'

'So you keep saying.'

'I mean it this time,' Lee said. His next words were directed at Benjamin. 'You've complicated things.'

No kidding. 'You didn't know about us for months.' *Because there was nothing to know.* 'We'll be fine.'

'I'm sure Cherise de Bruyn agrees.'

Benjamin thought that was a strange thing to say until he saw the jerk of Lee's head to the side. Cherise stood with her fellow graduates, watching the three of them with a bemused smile on her face. Considering he'd spoken to her first thing when he arrived, he was sure Alexa had, too. Now Cherise was watching the two people competing for her to work for them kiss, and was probably wondering what the hell would happen next.

To be fair, so was he.

CHAPTER THREE

ALEXA PAUSED AT her front door, wondering why she was doing what she was doing. No answer she came up with made her feel better about doing it, so she simply unlocked the door. She stepped aside to let Benjamin pass her, then closed it and resisted—barely—leaning her forehead against it. Alexa couldn't give in to her impulses any more. They were what had got her into trouble in the first place. If she hadn't pretended Benjamin was her boyfriend, she wouldn't be letting him into her home now to discuss the way forward.

It seemed particularly cruel that she had to do that here. Her home was *her* space. It was where she recovered from long, rough days. It was where she cried when the pressure of running a business got to her. It was where she remembered her complicated feelings when her sous chef had brought in her new baby.

Kenya had come in to show the baby around and had brought her mother, too. There had been so much love between the three of them. Alexa had watched it, her heart breaking and filling at the same time. When Kenya had handed her the child, that breaking stopped. She'd remembered all those times she'd thought family couldn't only mean competition and neglect. She hadn't seen examples otherwise, but she'd hoped. Then, between her studies, work, and her brother ruining her dreams, she'd forgotten that hope. Until she'd seen Kenya and her family. Until she'd held that baby.

She'd remembered that, once upon a time, her dreams

had included having a family. A warm, happy family with people who loved and respected one another. She thought about how she had no one to go home to at night. How the idea of dating and trusting someone so she could have someone to go home to made her feel ill. A new idea had popped into her head then. One year later, whoops, she was pregnant and there was no going back.

It wasn't so much *whoops* as going through vigorous fertility treatments and being artificially inseminated twice. But *whoops* was what she planned to tell her parents. Rather their disappointment that she hadn't been careful than tell them she didn't want anyone in her life who could hurt her the way they had.

She was clearly in a very healthy mental space.

'Nice place,' Benjamin said, breaking into her thoughts.

'Thanks.'

It was more invasive than she'd anticipated, having him look at her stuff. But they needed privacy, her place was the closest, and it was better to be here than at Infinity. There was more of her there, and with their baggage, it had felt wrong to take him there.

It wasn't that she wasn't proud of her home. Everything in it had been put there for a reason. The beige sofas were comfortable and expensive, the first items she'd bought for the flat. The restaurant had still been a baby, so it had taken most of her disposable income to buy them. She had slept on them for four months. They weren't as comfortable as a bed, but then, she hadn't been sleeping much anyway. She had been fuelled by the desire to succeed, and three to four hours of sleep were more than enough in those days.

The coffee table had come next, then the dining room set, both made from the most gorgeous stained wood. The fluffy carpet had been an indulgence considering she still hadn't had a bed, but filling the open-plan lounge and dining-room had been more important to her. It had made the flat feel like a home.

Her priorities had then shifted to her bedroom, which took her six months to complete. Last was her kitchen, separated from the dining room by half-wall, half-glass, with an opening on the right. The style somehow managed to give the impression of being open-plan, but offered privacy, too. She hadn't had the money to do what she wanted in the kitchen for the longest time, which was why she'd left it for last. Besides, she had everything she wanted at her restaurant, and that was enough.

After a year and a half, her kitchen was exactly what she had imagined it would be. Her appliances were top-of-the-range. Shelves were strategically placed all over the room; spices near the stove, fresh herbs near the window. Cupboards were filled with the best quality ingredients, and close to where they were needed. She'd added colour with fake plants, because her energy was mostly focused on keeping the herbs alive and there was too much competition for the light. And her utensils! Those were colourful, too, though pastel, which made her feel classy and grown-up. Heaven only knew why.

'I didn't expect it to be quite this…warm.'

She threw her handbag onto the sofa, shrugged off her coat. 'Because I'm so cold-hearted, you mean?'

'Not at all.'

'Then what did you mean?'

'It's just…' He looked around, as if to confirm what he was about to say. 'It really is lovely. Everything fits. It's like you selected each thing on purpose.'

'You didn't?' she asked. 'In your own home?'

'I don't have my own home.'

'What do you mean?'

'I live with my parents.'

She stared at him. She didn't know how long it was until his lip curled.

'You have an opinion on that?'

'No,' she replied. 'I don't.'

'You have an opinion on everything. Also, your face is saying something different.'

'You're right. I do have an opinion. But I don't want to share it.'

It was pure stubbornness, since sharing her opinion would have been the perfect segue into the questions she had. Why was he, a successful adult, still living with his parents? She knew he was successful because In the Rough was her main rival, according to reviews and social media, and she was pretty damn successful, despite the forces working against her.

It still smarted that they were succeeding with a restaurant that had been meant to be hers. The location, the property, the name—Lee had stolen it all from her. Then he'd gone and recruited Benjamin to work with him. Lee could have chosen *anyone* else. Actually, she was sure that Lee had specifically chosen Benjamin because the man annoyed her so much, though she wasn't sure how Lee would know that. Either way, Benjamin annoyed her more now that he was in cahoots with her brother. At least before, he'd annoyed her on his own merits.

He'd singled her out their first day at the Institute. She had no idea why, since she minded her own business. For some inexplicable reason, he'd decided she was partly *his* business, and he began to compete with her. She'd instantly recoiled; she had enough competition in life. She hadn't cut Lee out of her life and minimised her contact with her parents, only to replace them with a negligible man-child.

Now she had to work with the man-child.

'Would you like some alcohol?' she asked after a deep sigh.

His eyes flickered with amusement, contrasting the tighter lines on his face. 'Anything you want to give me is fine.'

She bit her tongue before she could reply. She hadn't thought of anything to reply with, but her tongue was often quicker than her brain. She didn't want to take the chance of saying something inappropriate. Such as how what she wanted to give him was another kiss to see if the spark she'd felt was a fluke...

She poured him a generous glass of whiskey from a bottle that was still three quarters full and settled on water and peppermint for herself.

'You're not having any?' he asked, accepting the glass from her.

She leaned back against the counter on the opposite side of the kitchen. 'I'm on an alcohol fast.'

'Why?'

She rolled her eyes. 'Does it matter?'

'You're annoyed because I asked?'

'Yes, actually. It's rude.'

Plus she didn't have a good answer for him. She hadn't anticipated him asking why she was fasting from alcohol. She should have known he wouldn't be polite and leave it at that though.

'Sorry.' His lips twitched. 'So...'

He didn't say anything more. She didn't speak either. The silence stretched between them like a cat in the sun. Then, as a cat would, it stared Alexa in the eyes, unblinking, until she sighed.

'This is what dating you is like?' She didn't wait for an answer. 'How disturbing.'

How she knew exactly what to say to get under his skin was what was really disturbing.

But then, disturbing seemed to be the theme of the night.

What with the fake relationship, the kiss, being in Alexa's home. He'd offended her by noting that her flat was homey, but he couldn't help but be honest. She'd done an amazing job turning what would have been a trendy, but not particularly special place into something he could imagine coming home to.

Well, not him, exactly. He had his own home. With his parents. Which she had an opinion on, but wouldn't tell him about because she was stubborn. He couldn't be upset by it since he was stubborn, too. If she'd asked why he still lived with his parents he wouldn't have told her.

Not that any of it was important now.

'Cherise saw us.'

'I know.' She drained her glass. Her gaze rested on his, before it rose to his face. Something about it made his body feel more aware. 'Would you like some more?'

He glanced at the glass. Empty. Strange. He didn't remember drinking from it. Except for that one time when he'd taken a long, deep gulp and—

Ah, yes. He remembered now.

'No, thank you.' Probably best with all the disturbing stuff happening.

'Tea, then? I'm making myself some.'

'Anything to avoid having a straight conversation with me?'

'What is this we're having, then?' she asked, filling the kettle with water. She took out two mugs, despite the fact that he hadn't answered her. 'A skew conversation? Diagonal?'

'Funny lady.'

Amusement flickered in her eyes. 'I try.'

'To annoy me, yes,' he muttered.

The amused light danced in her eyes again. He felt an answering light in his chest. He didn't care for it. It made him think the tables had turned.

'I know we have to talk about this.' She took out ginger from the fridge, sliced up some pieces and threw it in one cup. She looked over at him. 'Tea? Coffee?'

'Coffee. Please,' he added as an afterthought.

She began to make his coffee, expression pensive. 'I suppose I wanted to make the conversation easier. Less awkward. A discussion over hot drinks seemed like something that would help with that.'

His mother would like her, he thought before he could stop himself. Usually, he was more careful when it came to comparisons between his mother and people he wasn't related to. Hell, people he was related to, too. It tended to evoke protective feelings in him when he did. He blamed it on the fact that he felt protective of his mother, so when he recognised something akin to her in someone else, those feelings bled over. It had too often in the past, and he'd been hurt because of it. Which should have made him more careful. It usually did. Except now, apparently.

'How did I manage to upset you with that?' she asked, more resigned than curious.

'You didn't.' A lie. Or half-lie. He'd upset himself, but because of something she'd said.

Her eyes narrowed, but she finished his coffee, slid it over the counter towards him. She finished her own drink with a teaspoon of honey, then leaned back against the counter as she had with her water.

'Okay, so let's talk straight.' She bit her lip, then straightened her shoulders. 'I'm sorry for pretending you're my boyfriend. It was an impulse.'

'Why did you?'

She tilted her head, as if considering his question. Or perhaps considering whether she'd answer it.

'My brother is a jerk.'

He stared.

'You can't possibly not have noticed,' she replied at the

look. 'He's entitled, and competitive, and generally un-kind. I wanted to push him off a cliff. Since literally doing so would send me to prison, I settled for figuratively. You were the figurative.'

He took a minute to process that.

'He's normally a decent guy.'

'Maybe to you. But since you said normally, I think you recognised that he wasn't decent today.' She paused, her lips pursing. 'He normally isn't decent with me.'

Lee's behaviour today didn't encourage him to disagree with her. So he didn't.

'It's weird that you pretended *I* was your boyfriend. You hate me.'

'You were the closest person,' she said coolly, not deny-ing his statement. 'Also, you're his business partner. Best cliff.' She shrugged.

He took a steadying breath. He didn't like being used. He'd had too many instances of it in his life. His last girl-friend, his father's colleague, his cousin. Those were but a few, but they were the most recent. Remembering them had him steeling himself against Alexa's charm—or what-ever it was that kept him standing there.

'I don't like being used.'

'I'm sorry.' Her voice and expression were sincere. 'I'm sorry for putting you in a position to be used. For using you.'

It was that sincerity that had him saying, 'Apology ac-cepted,' when he wasn't entirely sure he meant it.

'Thank you.' There was a brief pause. 'So maybe now you can explain why you decided to go along with the cha-rade. Maybe you can apologise for that kiss, too.'

CHAPTER FOUR

THE EXPRESSION ON his face was comical. But, since she'd asked him a serious question, one she would very much have liked an answer for, she decided not to give in to the smile. To wait.

His expression became more comical. His mouth contracted and expanded, as if he were mouthing what he wanted to say, but not quite. Emotions danced in his eyes, though she couldn't put her finger on what they were. But really, it was that tick near his nose, which she'd never before seen, that amused her the most.

Still, she didn't smile.

'I thought… I mean, he was… I wanted to…'

His stammers made resisting the smile harder. It was strange. She had never before spoken with him long enough to have to resist any of her emotions. Usually, those emotions ranged from irritated to downright angry. Amusement generally didn't feature; not unless it was tainted with satisfaction. This wasn't. This was simply…amusement.

An alarm went off in her head.

'You wanted to *what*?' she asked, her words sharp, marching to that alarm.

He cleared his throat and met her eyes. His expression was now serious.

'I wanted Lee to stop acting like a jerk.'

'Well.' It was all she said for a while. 'You succeeded, just for a moment.'

'But at what cost?'

His eyes bored into hers, and her face began to heat.

Was he asking how she'd felt about that kiss? If he was, he'd have his answer in her blush.

Because it had embarrassed her, she assured herself. Her fingers lifted and slipped under the neckline of her dress. She lifted it, let it fall, sending air down her body, which had suddenly become clammy. For some reason, her skin was itchy, too. It was exactly how she felt on a summer's day in the kitchen. Hot and sticky, but satisfied at what she was cooking up.

Wait—satisfied? Where had that come from? What was happening to her?

Embarrassment, an inner voice offered again. She clung to it. Ignored the fact that her memories of that kiss, of how she'd felt much as she did now while he'd been kissing her, were vehemently disagreeing.

She took a deliberate sip of her tea. She'd put enough ginger in it that the flavour burned her throat. She relished it. Then met his eyes.

'A high cost,' she told him. 'It means Cherise thinks we're dating.'

He was watching her closely. She hoped to heaven he hadn't developed the ability to see into her head. 'And now she's confused about our opposing offers.'

'I tried to tell her the same thing we told Lee,' she said with a sigh. 'The whole "we're dating, but we're keeping our personal and professional lives separate" thing. I don't know if she bought it. She's certainly confused by it.'

'Me, too, to be honest with you.'

He gestured, asking if she'd like to have a seat in the lounge. She would have, desperately, since her body was aching from a day of standing. Her baby apparently didn't like that kind of strenuous activity. But it felt too intimate, sitting with him on the sofas she'd bought and slept on for months. A twinge in her back urged her to reconsider, and she spent hopelessly too long trying to decide. In the end, she strode past him without answering, as though it had been her idea all along.

Man, pregnancy was making her *stubborn*.

It was definitely the pregnancy. She didn't possess a stubborn bone in her body normally.

She sank into the sofa as soon as she sat down, a sigh leaving her lips immediately. His brows were raised when she looked at him.

'Why didn't you say something?'

'About what?'

'Needing to sit down.'

'I didn't need to.'

'So what you did now wasn't you finally relaxing and your body thanking you for it?'

'I have no idea what you're talking about.'

He shook his head, but the sides of his mouth were quirked. 'Stubborn isn't an appealing quality.'

'I don't care if you find me appealing.' She didn't give herself a chance to figure out why that felt like a lie. 'Besides, it's been a long day.'

'You get stubborn after a long day?'

'That's what I said, yes.'

'Is it because you're tired?' He was outright smiling now. Taunting her, really. 'Or is it a physical symptom? Aching legs, sore back, stubborn personality?'

'Yes.' It wasn't an answer, but it was all he'd get. 'Now— what are we going to do about Cherise?'

The smile faded, but the twinkle in his eyes didn't. He was sitting beneath the light fixture, which could account for that twinkle. But it didn't; she'd seen that twinkle before. It appeared whenever he was amused with her. It was frustrating to know. More frustrating was how attractive that amusement made him.

It danced in his brown eyes, crinkled the skin around them. That forced his cheeks up, which spread his full lips—lips she now knew had objectively impressive skills. None of that factored into how the angles of his face were affected. Warming them, softening them; perhaps a combination of the two. Either way, it dimmed his arrogance, that self-assured *I know I'm successful and handsome* edge of his. That edge was as devastating as it was irritating, particularly as it always seemed to be directed at her.

'What were you planning on doing about Cherise before all this happened?'

She snorted. 'Wouldn't you like to know?'

'Yes,' he deadpanned. 'That's why I asked.'

'You asked so you could outdo whatever I planned to do.'

'I wouldn't dream of it.'

'Like you wouldn't dream of stealing my head chef? Who was already working for me, I might add. Happily. For months.'

'That can't be true if he left,' Benjamin pointed out softly. 'It didn't take me much to convince him either.'

'Are you defending *stealing* my chef?'

'I didn't steal him. I…gave him another option.'

'You stole him,' she said flatly. 'Probably at the behest of my brother, because, as I mentioned before, he's a jerk.'

He hesitated, which gave her the answer. And disappointed her, strangely. Why, she wasn't sure. It might have been because he'd defended her in front of her brother and hadn't freaked out completely when she'd pretended he was her boyfriend. But one day's experience couldn't erase years of experience to the contrary. That experience had taught her that Benjamin Foster could be just as much of a jerk as her brother.

'I think you're on the right track though,' she powered on. If she did, it would help get him out of her house and she'd finally be able to rest. 'We do what we intended to do and let her make the decision as she would have without this complication.'

'We're not continuing the charade?'

She thought about it. 'We have two options, I suppose. One is that we do, but only verbally. If she asks, we'll talk about one another lovingly. Affectionately. Then, in a few months, we break up.'

'And the other option?'

'Tell her the truth. We were playing a joke on Lee.'

He went quiet for a few seconds. 'But if Lee finds out, we both look foolish. We'll have to answer why we were so…' he hesitated '…*invested* in proving we were together.'

'There's that,' she said slowly. She didn't want him to know she'd thought about that, too. Not to mention she hated the idea of Lee discovering the truth. He'd take such pleasure in it. He'd probably hold it over her head every time she'd have the misfortune of seeing him. 'There's also the implication that we're friends. Why would we play a joke on Lee if we weren't?'

'You're worried about people thinking we're friends, but not that we're in a relationship?'

'Well, yeah. At least there's a physical aspect to a relationship. People would think I was distracted from your personality because you look the way you do.'

He frowned. She could almost see his brain malfunctioning. Mostly because she was pretty sure that was what was happening to hers.

'Is that a compliment?'

'No,' she answered immediately.

But it was. She couldn't figure out why she'd said it.

She vowed there and then never to admit she found him attractive again. She wouldn't even *think* about his broad shoulders and full lips. He certainly wouldn't kiss her again either, so she'd have no reason to. And if she did think it— and he did kiss her—she'd remind herself there were high stakes involved.

She laid a hand on her belly, feeling the slight curve. At

this stage it could have been a good, generous meal as much as a baby, which amused her. She stroked her thumb over the curve, mentally assuring her child that she'd protect it. She paused when she saw him watching her.

What was it about being in his presence that made her lower her guard?

She moved her hand.

'Fine. We'll pretend to be together,' he said curtly. 'But only because Lee deserves to think it, after how he treated you.' He paused, as though something had just occurred to him. The frown deepened. He was scowling when he continued. 'We'll do whatever we intended to do with Cherise. I'll keep talk of our relationship with your brother to the minimum. We should both do that, to whoever we meet.' He downed the rest of his coffee and set the cup on the table. Stood. 'And in a few months, our fake relationship will end. It'll be as clean as this situation allows.'

'Er…yeah, sure.'

She set her own mug down, confused by the change in his temperament. But that was the least of her problems. She'd just realised her pregnancy wouldn't be a secret for much longer. People would have questions about the paternity of her baby. If she said it was Benjamin, she would be dragging him down an even more convoluted path. If she said it was some random guy as she'd planned to, people would do the calculations and accuse her of cheating on Benjamin.

Oh, no.

She really should have thought about this earlier.

'Benjamin, I think we need to talk about—'

'We've talked about everything already, haven't we?' he interrupted. His eyes were sharp, and she almost shivered from the intensity of them. So she just nodded.

'Great, then we don't have to see one another again for a while.'

'Okay.' Numbly, she followed him to the door.

'Thanks for the drinks.'

'Okay.'

'Good luck with Cherise.'

'Thanks.'

And then he was gone, leaving her to think about the extent of the mess she'd created that day.

The resolution he and Alexa had come to regarding their fake relationship went up in flames the moment he walked into In the Rough the next morning.

'You're dating my sister?' Lee asked, sitting arms folded at a stool in front of the bar. Apparently, he'd been waiting. 'What the hell, man? Do you have no boundaries?'

It wasn't early in the morning. In the Rough only opened from lunchtime, so generally he worked from home for a couple of hours when he woke up, then made his way to the restaurant at about nine. His staff would start trickling in then, too, most of them there by ten, and then it would be a bustle of activity until they closed at eleven at night. This morning, he'd been particularly grateful for the quiet so he could figure out what the hell had happened the night before.

One moment he'd been deciding whether to let Alexa's backhanded compliment slide, the next he was watching her stroke her stomach and his gut had clenched with need. It made no sense, but that gesture had seemed somewhat protective. It reminded him of the times he'd seen pregnant women do the same thing. Though Alexa probably wasn't pregnant, it had made him think about a life he'd never wanted. He was too busy taking care of his parents to even consider it.

Not that he minded; not in the least. His mother was lovely. Sharp and charming and the kind of mother who made sacrifices for her children. Except there were no children, only him. And that sharpness and charm and kindness didn't negate the strain of her illness.

They'd had no idea what caused it for a long time. His mother had been his father's admin help at the panel-beaters' company his father owned and ran. For ten years, almost, until she'd started complaining about the pain right after she'd had Benjamin. Aches that felt like they were all over, restricting her movement, making simple tasks hard to carry out. Doctors had prescribed ibuprofen, diagnosed her with the flu, told her she'd strained a muscle, or pushed too hard, or that she needed to take a break.

But even when she took a break, the pain would continue. Sometimes, if she stayed in bed and rested, it would make it worse. The doctors maintained they could find nothing wrong. It was the eighth doctor she'd gone to in four years who had diagnosed her with fibromyalgia.

His life hadn't changed dramatically, or at all, with that diagnosis. His father had simply sat him down and explained as best he could to a four-year-old that his mom was sick. Frank Foster had told Benjamin to try not to bother his mother as much when she was in bed. Maybe Benjamin could even help out a little more at home. He hadn't known the difference between that and what he'd done before, except now it came with the weight of verbal responsibility.

But she was his mother, and he wanted her to be happy. As he grew older, he thought having him couldn't have helped with his mom's pain. Because she'd made sacrifices for him at the cost of her own health, physical and mental, he would do the same for her. So he had. For the past twenty-odd years he had helped his parents. Now he cared for his parents. There wasn't really room for him to consider caring for anyone else in that situation either.

That pulse of need he'd felt with Alexa the night before? A fluke. There was nothing more to it. And he didn't engage with it any more because something more significant had occurred to him when he'd been talking with Alexa.

Now might be the time to confirm it.

'Did you hear me?' Lee demanded.

But maybe not before he'd had another cup of coffee.

'Mia,' he said to the tall woman behind the counter. 'Is the machine on?'

'You know it,' she replied with a sympathetic grin. It made him realise she'd heard what Lee had said. 'The usual?'

He unclenched his jaw slowly. 'No. Double espresso, please.' Her brows lifted, but she only nodded. He looked at Lee. 'Can you wait for me in the office? I'll be there in a second.'

'Mia, could you please add another cappuccino to that?' Lee said. 'And bring it to Ben's office when it's ready?' He shook his head. 'Or have someone else bring it. Sorry. It slipped my mind.'

Her smile didn't waver, but something on Mia's face tightened. It probably wasn't because Lee had been refer-ring to her disability—the limp that Benjamin hadn't once asked about because it was none of his business—but be-cause Lee had done so poorly. Benjamin wouldn't have expected it from him; Lee handled most things smoothly. Then again, he hadn't expected Lee to be a jerk to his own sister, so maybe he didn't know his business partner as well as he thought.

'Yeah, sure,' Mia said.

'Thank you.'

Lee gestured for Benjamin to lead the way. After one last glance at Mia to make sure she was okay, Benjamin walked away from the enticing smell of coffee to his office. It was a simple room. Not very big, but there was enough space for his desk and cabinet, and the large windows gave it an airy feel. Unfortunately, those windows looked out onto a car park with a busy Cape Town road just behind it. But that was the price he paid to be in a central location.

At least, that was what Lee had told him when he'd been courting Benjamin. Over the years, Benjamin had begun to believe him. Was he a fool to do so?

'This isn't your only business,' Benjamin noted, taking off his jacket and slinging it over the chair. 'Surely you have better things to do than to wait for me to talk about something that isn't business.'

'Except this affects our business,' Lee said with none of the charm, the ease Benjamin had once been privy to. 'Honestly, Ben. There are millions of women in South Africa, but you decide to sleep with my sister?'

'Watch it,' Benjamin growled, though he had no reason to defend Alexa. Apart from their fictional relationship. Which was not, as the title stated, real.

'She's already changed you,' Lee replied with a shake of his head. 'You weren't foolish before yesterday. Hell, the last time we spoke, you knew how important getting Cherise de Bruyn to work with us was. But now you're letting your head be messed around by your—'

'Be careful about what you say next.'

Lee's jaw tightened. 'This isn't going to work.'

'What isn't?' he asked coolly, leaning back in his chair. 'This partnership? Or my relationship with your sister?'

Lee opened and closed his mouth several times before he said, 'The relationship.'

'That hardly seems like any of your business.'

'It's literally my business.'

'No, my relationship has nothing to do with this business.' He paused when one of his waiters brought in their coffees. 'Alexa and I have been able to keep our relationship under wraps for months. It hasn't affected the way I've run things around here.'

'And yet here you are, snapping at me.'

'Because for some reason, when it comes to your sister, you change, too, Lee.' He downed the espresso. When it seared his stomach, he remembered he'd forgotten to eat breakfast. 'I don't like the way you treat her. I don't like the way you treat me when it comes to her.'

It was a warning.

'I thought this wouldn't happen.'

'What does that mean?'

'I thought working with someone who competed with my sister meant *I'd* be working with someone who competed with my sister.'

And there it was. Confirmation of his suspicions. When he told Alexa he wanted to continue the charade because of how Lee treated her, he realised there was more to it. It was because of how Lee had treated him, too. Lee had used him. Much as so many other people in his life had.

'My relationship with your sister doesn't have to affect the way we do things around here,' he said coldly. 'It won't for me. I'm perfectly capable of working with you and dating your sister. Since you two don't have a relationship, it shouldn't matter to you anyway.'

Lee's face was tight. Benjamin couldn't read what caused that tightness, or what was behind it. All he could see was a complicated mess of emotions. Since he had enough of those himself, especially after Lee's little bombshell, he didn't need to figure Lee's feelings out.

'We won't let your involvement with my sister affect the business.'

Benjamin gave a tight nod.

'What about our friendship?'

Benjamin didn't know how to answer that. He didn't trust Lee any more. How could they still be friends?

'See?' Lee said. 'You're already treating me differently.'

'I've explained why.'

He'd use Lee's treatment of Alexa as the scapegoat here.

He was sure she wouldn't mind. They were in this together after all.

Lee exhaled harshly. 'Fine. We'll just pretend you're not dating my sister.'

'What?'

His mother stood in the doorway, eyes impossibly wide.

'You're dating Benjamin Foster?'

Alexa's feet stopped working. That meant she was standing in the doorway of her office, frozen by both the words and the stare of accusation from Kenya.

'Who told you that?'

'You should have.'

'How did you find out?'

'A friend of mine was at Cherise's graduation yesterday.' Kenya leaned back in Alexa's chair. 'She asked me why I didn't tell her. Apparently, you and Benjamin were hot and heavy yesterday and it was the talk of everyone there. *And I didn't know.*'

'It hasn't been going on for very long,' she grumbled. *Like, less than twenty-four hours.* 'Besides, I didn't want people to know. It's new.'

And fake.

'Am I still people, Alexa?'

The question was serious enough to make Alexa blink. When she recovered from the shock, Kenya was watching her, waiting for an answer.

'I… I didn't tell anyone.'

Kenya stood, nodding slowly as she did. 'Yeah, why would you tell anyone? Least of all someone you've worked with for four years. Least of all someone who considers you a friend. Clearly that doesn't apply to how you consider me, does it?'

It would be so easy to get through this. If Alexa told Kenya the relationship was fake, contrived when she'd been desperate and in a panic to get away from her brother, Kenya wouldn't be upset with her.

She opened her mouth, but nothing came out. Not a single word.

What would happen if she told Kenya the truth? She'd look like a fool, for one. But Kenya might tell her friend, who might tell their friend, and before she knew it both her and Benjamin's reputations would be ruined. Not to mention that her brother would find out. And she couldn't face Lee's smirk when he heard she'd made up the entire thing for his sake.

'You can't even dispute it,' Kenya said, hurt thick in her voice. She strode past Alexa. Alexa wanted to say something, but her phone rang before she could. Picking up the landline, she barked, 'Yes?'

'Benjamin Foster's on the line for you,' came the voice of one of her waiters.

She bit back a sigh. 'Put him through.'

'Alexa?'

His deep voice was even more disturbing over the phone. Now she had to imagine his face. And for some reason it came without the arrogance that usually put her off.

'You called for me, didn't you?'

'Yes, I did, darling.'

'Darling? Really?' She looked behind her to ensure no one was there. 'You realise we're on the phone, right? No one else can hear what we're saying.'

'I'm here with my mother.'

'Your mother?'

'She'd like to meet you.'

'She'd like to… Wait, I'm missing something, aren't I?'

'Yes.'

It was the first time she felt as though he was answering her properly.

'Are you free for dinner tonight?'

'I'm not, actually. I'm working. As are you, considering we run restaurants.'

'I'm sure you can take an evening off for this *very important date.*'

She rolled her eyes. Belatedly, she realised he couldn't see her. She let the disappointment pass through her.

'Look, Benjamin, I don't know what's going on, but there's no way I'm going to meet your mother.'

'She would like to meet you.'

She could hear he was clenching his teeth.

'Is she giving you a hard time, Benny? Let me talk to her.' There was a short pause where Alexa could swear she heard Benjamin apologise. 'Alexa? This is Nina, Benjamin's mother.'

She closed her eyes. 'Hi, Nina.'

'Is it possible for us to meet?'

'Mrs Foster.' Alexa cleared her throat. 'I, um, I'm not sure.'

'Be sure, dear.' There was admonishment there, but Mrs Foster spoke again so quickly Alexa barely had time to process it. 'This evening might be too soon, considering your commitments. How about tomorrow evening? Could you arrange for someone to take care of things then?'

'I…um… I…don't know…'

'I just wouldn't want to meet you at your restaurant, dear.' Mrs Foster gave a sparkling laugh. 'You'd have to come out and speak to me in front of your employees and… Well, I don't need to tell you how awkward that might end up being.'

'No,' Alexa said numbly. 'You don't.'

'So it's settled, then! I'll see you tomorrow.'

'I… Yes, you will.' She cleared her throat. 'Could you please put Benjamin back on the phone?'

'Of course.'

There was another pause, then a, 'Yeah.'

'I have an hour for lunch today and clearly we need to talk. Can you meet me at St George's Mall at one?'

'Yes.'

'It wasn't a real question, but I'm glad you agreed. It makes things easier.'

CHAPTER FIVE

'WHAT WERE YOU *THINKING*?'

It was the first thing Alexa said when she saw him. A bit rude, in his opinion, but he allowed it because she'd made a good impression on his mother. Nina had murmured her approval and patted his cheek in affection. All this came after she'd read him the Riot Act for keeping his relationship a secret.

'Hello, Alexa,' he said calmly. 'Would you like to have a seat at one of the coffee shops? It is lunch, after all. And I haven't had breakfast. A busy morning,' he added, taking her elbow lightly and steering her through the crowds of people milling about. 'What with speaking to your brother about our fake relationship, having my mother find out about it, and then, of course, my actual business, which is open, but why would they need the manager and acting head chef there for the lunchtime rush?'

'I have responsibilities, too.'

'And yet here we are, gallivanting in the middle of the day.'

'It's not gallivanting.'

But she said it under her breath. He took it as agreement. How could he not?

St George's Mall had once been a busy street in Cape Town, but it had been reimagined for pedestrians. Now people walked through the bricked area lined with green trees and yellow umbrellas without the bother of traffic. There were three men playing drums a little way away from them, a boy who couldn't be older than nine dancing to the beat. Tourists browsed through the stands selling jewellery and African-inspired crafts. Residents walked with purpose to get to where they needed to be, or stopped at one of the cafes to grab something to eat. Police presence was heavy, but quaint, since they monitored the area on horses.

It was one of his favourite places, just fifteen minutes away from his restaurant. It screamed with the vibrancy of Cape Town, which was one reason he loved his city. He wasn't sure why Alexa had suggested it, since it was further away for her than for him. Could she have been considering him? Or was she merely trying to minimise the chances of someone she knew seeing them together?

He would have related to that, except his mother already knew, so his father would, too, and they were the main people he cared about. It was too late for keeping secrets for him.

'Hey,' she said, snapping her fingers. 'Can we sit here? Or should I ask another time?'

'Sorry,' he muttered, and gestured for her to sit.

They took a few minutes to look at the menu. At least, he did. She'd glanced at hers quickly, then set it down and was now watching him.

'You must be thinking it's a pity you don't have X-ray vision with how you're staring at me.'

'Hadn't considered it before, actually. Just like I hadn't considered having to talk to your mother and be manoeuvred—quite expertly, I might add—into having dinner with your family.' She slapped her hand against her leg under the table. *'I'm not even your girlfriend.'*

He exhaled, hoping the nervous energy in his body would escape from his lungs. No such luck. It stayed in his chest, bouncing around as though it were being chased by a happy puppy.

'Let's get something to drink.'

'Why would you let your mother think we're in a rela-

tionship?' she asked, ignoring him. 'This turns something
that could easily be solved into something so much more—'

'Alexa,' he interrupted, his voice slicing through her
panic. 'Let's get something to drink. We can talk about it
afterwards.'

Her jaw locked, but she nodded. The waiter came over.
He ordered sparkling water—he needed a break from the
coffee. It was probably the cause of the nervous energy.
Probably—and Alexa got rooibos tea. When the waiter left,
Alexa stared wordlessly at him. To emphasise her displea-
sure, she folded her arms and leaned back.

He took a deep breath.

'My mother being under the impression we're together
wasn't my fault,' he said slowly. 'Lee ambushed me this
morning—' that was more aggressive than what Lee had
done; or maybe not '—and when he was talking about the
relationship, my mother walked in. I'd forgotten some papers at home and she thought I might need them.'

He could hardly be upset with her for being sweet.

'Anyway, she found out, and since I've never told her
about any of my relationships, she kind of latched on to the
information. I couldn't tell her it was a lie without…' He
grasped on to the first thing he could think of. 'Without
your brother overhearing it.'

'Couldn't you have told her when he left?'

'No.' Anger made the word choppy. 'She was excited. I
couldn't disappoint her.'

'People survive disappointing their parents.'

The words were so unexpected, so cool, his anger fiz-
zled.

'Is that what happened to you?'

'It doesn't matter.' Her features softened, but the lines
around her mouth were still tense. 'What's going to happen when she finds out we're not really together, Benjamin? You don't think she's going to be disappointed then?

You don't think she's going to hate knowing that you lied to her? That you don't have a girlfriend?' She blushed. 'I mean, I'm assuming. I don't care about your romantic—'

'Of course I don't have a girlfriend,' he said, affronted. 'Do you think I'd be pretending to be your boyfriend if I did? Do you think so poorly of me?'

She stilled, though her eyes, big and bright, remained steady. 'You want me to say no, but experience has taught me I can't say that without reservation.'

He had no reply to that. What could he say? But it left a bitter taste in his mouth that she thought that of him. He didn't deserve it. The only thing he'd done that was morally ambiguous was offer her chef a job at In the Rough. Even then he'd done things above board. Victor Fourie had accepted Benjamin's offer without a comment about what he'd left behind. In the same way he'd left In the Rough behind when he'd moved on a couple of months ago.

Then again, he could see why she'd have that opinion of him. He worked with her brother, a man she had no relationship with. A man who treated her poorly, and apparently went out of his way to do so. Lee had used Benjamin to that end, too, and he'd unwittingly become a tool to hurt Alexa with. Frankly, he was still working out how he felt about it. Especially since he'd considered Lee a friend until all this had happened.

His fake relationship had thrown everything into upheaval. Including his relationship with his mother. He wasn't proud of it, but he couldn't bear to break his mother's heart. Up until today, he hadn't even known his mother wanted him to be in a relationship. But the happiness in her voice as she questioned him about his girlfriend—his first, according to her—told him otherwise.

He couldn't tell her it was all fake. He loved her too much. And yeah, maybe he'd get over disappointing her. But in that moment, it hadn't even occurred to him.

The waiter interrupted his thoughts, and when the man walked away, he sighed.

'I'm sorry. About my mother. I wasn't thinking. Or I wasn't thinking properly.'

She held the mug in her hands as if to warm herself, though it was a typical summer's day.

'I've been there,' she murmured. Then she set the mug down and took her head in her hands instead. 'I was there—yesterday. Because of my stupid brother, I caused this mess and—'

She hiccupped. An actual hiccup that was most likely the precursor to a sob. His hand shot out of its own volition, grasping her arm and squeezing in comfort. A hand left her head and rested on his hand.

And just like that, he knew he was in trouble.

Of course, he'd known that before. The entire thing with Alexa was, as she said, a mess. But before, he'd still had some control over his actions. He wasn't helping her because she needed help. Well, not *only* because she needed help. He also wanted to help her with his own free will. The moment she showed him vulnerability, though, that free will had waved goodbye and jumped on the nearest plane to anywhere but his mind. Because now he wanted to help her because she *really* needed help. She was distraught, and things needed to be fixed, and he was the ultimate help when things needed to be fixed.

He'd done it with his mother and father for most of his life, more so as an adult. He'd done it with his last girlfriend. His cousins. Friends. And he would do it now, with Alexa.

He curled his free hand into a fist.

She was *crying*. In public. In front of him. Because she was pregnant and because she had to tell him the truth. It was terrifying.

She pulled away from his touch, comforting—disturbingly so—as it was, and reached into her bag for a tissue. She found one, mopped herself up, and sternly told her hormones she wouldn't stand for tears again. When she was certain they'd got the picture, she downed the rest of her tea, lukewarm now, because of the tears, and looked at him.

His expression was inscrutable. She didn't know if that made her feel better or worse. But she couldn't rely on him to make herself feel better. So she took a deep breath, held it for a few seconds, then let it out. It was shaky at best; hitched at worse. She did it again, and again, until it came smoothly. Then she said, 'I'm pregnant.'

He stared at her.

She cleared her throat. 'So, you see, you have to tell your mother the truth or she'll think the baby's yours and things will get more complicated.'

He still stared at her.

'I wouldn't have told you if I didn't have to. I went over it in my head a million times last night, and again, after that phone call with your mother.'

He didn't say a word. She pursed her lips when they started to shake.

No, she told the tears that were threatening. *I had you under control. You can't disobey me.*

'I didn't want you to know,' she said, thinking that speaking would distract her. 'I didn't want *anyone* to know until I had no choice but to tell them. No one knows besides you. Because somehow, my decision is now going to reflect on you.'

He kept staring, but his mouth had opened. She had to wait a while longer before he said anything.

'You're pregnant?'

She nodded.

'We have to tell people the truth.'

She clenched her teeth when the statement brought a

fresh wave of heat to her eyes. She would *not* cry in front of him. Not again.

'Okay.' Her voice broke as she said it. Damn it.

'They'll think the baby's mine, Alexa,' Benjamin said, his voice pleading. 'My mother and your brother and everyone else. We can't just break up then.'

'Why not?' she asked desperately. 'Who cares what they think?'

'I do.' His face was stern. 'It'll be my reputation on the line.'

'It doesn't have to be,' she said, desperation once again taking the wheel. 'You can tell them I cheated on you.'

'What?'

'Make me the bad guy.' She hated the thought of it, but it was her only option.

'You'd rather have everyone think you cheated than tell the truth?'

'I don't care what everyone thinks,' she said heatedly. 'If Lee finds out I made this up because of him…' She met his gaze. 'He took my property and my restaurant years ago and he had no reason to. If I give him this, it'll fuel him for years.'

'What do you mean, your property? Your *restaurant*?'

She scoffed. 'Please don't pretend you don't know what Lee did. It's an insult to you and me both.'

'I have no idea what you're talking about.'

He seemed genuinely confused. Though that could have as easily come from the news that she was pregnant as from this. She sighed.

'I found the building for In the Rough. Came up with the name, too, because of the neighbourhood. I was determined to turn that place—*my* place—into a diamond.' The memory of it curved her lips. 'I went through hundreds of listings to find it, and I was so excited because it was *finally* time. I'd spent eight years working towards that moment, and finally...' She trailed off when a wave of sadness crashed over her. 'Anyway, I was supposed to take my parents to see it. I mean, I did take my parents to see it. But I made the mistake of telling them where it was when I scheduled the event with them a week before. We always had to make plans in advance with them.'

She shook off the resentment that she'd had to schedule the meeting with her parents in the first place. Second, but not by much, was that they'd told Lee.

'They told Lee, and he bought it out from under me. He offered to rent it to me. I declined. He would have never allowed me to do what I wanted to do.' She waved a hand. She wasn't sure what it was meant to signify. 'And then I heard you two had become partners. It made sense. If my brother was the devil, I suppose I considered you a demon. My dreams had turned into my own personal hell.'

It was as funny as it was heartbreaking. She was sure the small smile she hadn't been able to resist conveyed both.

'I knew none of that.'

'Would it have changed anything if you had?' she asked, wanting to know.

A complicated array of emotions danced across his face. She supposed she could understand it. It was a good business decision to be a partner with Lee. He came with property, a smart name, business knowledge, and experience. He also came with baggage: her. She had no idea whether Benjamin cared about that, but what she'd told him now didn't reflect well on Lee regardless. Unless he shared Lee's opinion of her, and her brother's lack of scruples, in which case it wouldn't change anything.

But he wouldn't look this tortured if things hadn't changed for him, would he? Or was she grasping at straws, desperate for someone, anyone, to finally be on her side instead of Lee's?

'It's smart to be in business with Lee,' came the careful answer. 'He's a good businessperson.'

'You still think so after what I told you?'

The stare flickered. 'He's been good to me.'

She licked her bottom lip before drawing it between her teeth. Then she nodded. 'I suppose that's fair.'

Disappointing, but fair. But it helped sharpen her idea of him. She'd been faltering on what she thought of him because he hadn't deliberately set out to hurt her with the restaurant. But after what had happened with her chef, and now, with his opinion of Lee remaining unchanged... It was best if she didn't think he was someone he wasn't.

'If we tell my brother the truth, he'll use it against you, too,' she said.

His lips parted, as if he hadn't considered it. Or maybe he didn't believe it was possible.

'It's too complicated to continue this lie, Alexa.'

She exhaled. 'Okay.' It was time to leave. She needed to recover from all this in private. She needed to prepare, too. 'Give me a few days. It shouldn't make a difference for you, but it'll help me figure some things out.'

He gave a slow nod. 'Then I guess I'll tell my mother.'

'Let me.' She had no idea why she said it, but it was too late to take it back. 'I'll come to dinner tomorrow. I'll tell her I dragged you into this and that you were being the perfect gentleman. I'll explain to her what happened with my brother, and how you couldn't come clean with him near by. We'll make you come out of this smelling of roses.'

'Why?'

'It's the least I can do after the trouble I caused.' She took out money and tossed it on the table. 'Call Infinity with the details about tomorrow.'

She hoped he couldn't see her shaking as she walked away.

CHAPTER SIX

HE OFFERED TO pick up Alexa at her flat. Partly because his mother had taught him to be a gentleman, and partly because he felt bad about the way things had gone the day before. He blamed it on his shock. She was *pregnant*, and he was the only person who knew. It seemed significant. It shouldn't have. She hadn't told him because she wanted him to know, but because it made their lie infinitely more complicated. Though he wanted to help her, he couldn't see how to. And he'd disappointed her because of it. But rather her than his mother.

Nina's reaction to the news that he was in a relationship had been surprising. After her shock and the millions of questions that had come with it, she told him how happy she was that he was dating.

'You're always taking care of us, Benny,' she'd said. 'I was worried it stopped you from living your life. But now you have someone!' She had clasped her hands in glee. 'I can't tell you how much I've wanted this to happen.'

He could only imagine how she'd react if she thought he was having a baby. He was worried enough about telling her the truth.

He took a shaky breath and rang Alexa's doorbell. Tried to keep his jaw from dropping when she opened the door almost immediately.

She wore a light pink dress, cinched below her breasts and falling softly over her stomach. He thought it might be a wrap-around dress considering how the material crossed over her body, parting in a slight V at her legs, ending in two different lengths. The V revealed two gorgeous legs, toned, sliding down into heels that matched the exact shade of the dress. There was another V, though he kept himself from looking at that too closely, since it appeared at her chest.

He *had* looked closely enough to notice that her breasts had become fuller with pregnancy.

Not that he had anything to compare them to. He hadn't looked at her breasts before. He'd simply...noticed they were there. She was an attractive woman, and, since he was attracted to attractive women, he'd noticed. And now he noticed that her breasts were fuller. It was all scientific. There was nothing more to it.

He noticed the style of her dress was somehow both highlighting her pregnancy and hiding it. Or did he only think that now because he knew she was pregnant? She wasn't showing apart from the fuller breasts and the slightest curve of her stomach. The dress flattered her body shape, which even before pregnancy had been a glorious mixture of full curves and lean muscle.

She'd always dressed for her body. Sometimes in dresses that made her look demure and saintly; other times in skirts and shirts that made him think she wanted to torment every person in the room around her. Though this dress seemed to fit with her general style—flattering, understated, seductive—at the same time it somehow didn't. It was warmer, softer, though he'd bite his own tongue off before admitting it.

'Are you going to say hello or keep staring?'

He instantly blinked, as if his body was trying to tell her he wasn't staring. But that was undermined by the blush he could feel heating his face. It got hotter when he realised he hadn't looked at her face since she opened the door. If he had, he wouldn't have spent such a long time contemplating her dress or her style, but trying to get his breath back.

She'd left her hair loose. He couldn't remember ever seeing it that way before. It was long, wavy, flowing past her shoulders and stopping halfway to her elbows. She'd parted it so that most of the thick locks had settled on the right side of her face. The rich brown of it bled into the lighter brown of her skin, as if folding dark chocolate into milk chocolate for a deliciously sinful dessert. Just at the beginning stages, before they mixed and created a brown that was more like his own skin tone.

Her lips were painted the same colour as her dress, her checks dusted with some of that colour, too. Her eyes, which were watching him speculatively, were somehow more pronounced, more emotive than usual. He guessed that also had something to do with make-up.

'Keep staring, then,' she answered for him. 'Okay.' She reached behind the door to somewhere he couldn't see, bringing a coat back, which she handed to him. 'Could you at least make yourself useful, please?'

He took the coat without a word, stepping back when she closed the door behind her. Then she looked at him.

'Honestly, Benjamin, this is an overreaction, surely.'

'No.'

'No, it's not an overreaction?' she asked. He nodded. 'You've seen me dressed up before. Mixers at the Institute. Graduation. Ours and Cherise's.'

'Not like this.'

'This is because I'm pregnant and I didn't feel good in anything else.' She straightened her shoulders. 'I know it's probably more formal than tonight required. It's just... The shop assistant told me it suited me.' She lifted a shoulder, though it wasn't as careless as he was sure she intended. It was defensive. 'I thought the dress deserved more effort from other parts of me.'

'Your hair's loose.'

'It has been before.'

'I've never seen it loose before.'

She frowned. 'Well, it's not my preference.'

'I know. That's wearing your hair in a bun.'

'I... Yes.'

She lifted a hand, tucked some hair behind her ear.

'A ponytail would probably be your next option.'

Her lips parted.

'Either on top of your head, when you're working, or at your nape, when you're dressing up.' He had no idea why he was doing this. It felt as if he was seducing her. But surely seduction couldn't happen without him intending it? He kept talking. 'Sometimes you plait your hair in two, then twirl the plaits around your head and pin them like a crown.'

Breath shuddered from between her lips. He swore he heard her swallow. Then she said, 'Only in the kitchen.'

He lifted a hand, pausing before he could do what he wanted. 'Can I touch it?'

'Can you...? My hair?' she asked, her eyes dipping to where his hand hovered above the strands on her shoulder. He nodded. 'Okay.'

'You're sure?'

'Yes.'

She sounded annoyed that he'd clarified. It made him smile. So did the strands of her hair, which were curly and soft and just a little wet.

'I like it like this.'

'In that case, I'll wear it this way more often,' she said dryly. 'It's incredibly practical for someone who owns a restaurant.'

He laughed. Gave in to the urge to tuck her hair behind her ear as he'd seen her do earlier. 'I wouldn't say no.'

She exhaled. 'What are you doing, Benjamin?'

He dropped his hand, looked at her face. 'I don't know.'

'You do know.'

'No, I don't.' He smiled. Almost as soon as he did, the smile vanished. 'Except for right now. Right now, I'm contemplating how to get you to kiss me again. I'd say it's an appropriate response to how incredible you look.' He shook his head. 'I was staring earlier because I didn't have anything to say. You're so beautiful. And so is this dress…and your hair, your face…' He shook his head again. Offered her a wry, possibly apologetic smile. 'I'm sorry. I think the last couple of days have officially caught up with me.'

Her expression was unreadable, but she said, 'It's been a rough couple of days.'

'Yeah.'

'Because of me.' She paused. 'I'm sorry.'

'You don't have to apologise. You already have, anyway.'

'Right.' She leaned back against her door, which he realised only now she hadn't moved away from. 'This hasn't been easy for me either.'

'I know.'

'A large part of it is because you get on my nerves. A lot,' she added when he frowned.

'That seems uncalled for, considering I just gave you a bunch of compliments.'

'You want acknowledgement for that?'

'A thank you would be nice,' he muttered.

'You're right.'

'Sorry—could you say that again?' He patted his pocket, looking for his phone. 'I want to record it for posterity.'

'This, for example, is extremely annoying. But at the same time, I can't stop thinking about the kiss we had the other day.'

He stilled.

'Which gets on my nerves, too. An interesting conundrum. Am I annoyed because I'm attracted to you? Am I annoyed because you annoy me but I'm still attracted to you?' She exhaled. It sounded frustrated. 'I don't have answers, but I keep asking these questions. Then, of course, you do something decent, like pretend to be my boyfriend even though you have no reason or incentive to. You stand up for me in front of my brother, which I found disturbingly hot. In the same breath, you act stupidly, and tell your mother—your *mother*—that I'm your girlfriend. Which, tonight, we have to rectify.'

She shook her head.

'Honestly, Benjamin, these last few days have been the most frustratingly complicated of my life, and I'm an entrepreneur with a crappy family. And I'm *pregnant*, about to become a single mother. Complicated is the air I breathe. But you make things...' She trailed off with a little laugh. 'And still, I want to kiss you, too.'

It took him an embarrassingly long time to process everything she said. By the time he got to the end of it, the part where she wanted to kiss him, his jaw dropped. Trying to maintain his dignity, he shook his head.

'I don't need someone to kiss me out of charity. Especially not someone who thinks I'm annoying.' The more he spoke, the more indignant he felt. 'I'm only annoying because you're annoyed with everyone. Don't deny it,' he said when she opened her mouth. 'It was like that at the Institute. You had so many people trying to be your friend and you'd brush them aside. Draw into yourself. It's like no one was ever good enough for you.'

She tilted her head, the muscles in her jaw tightening and relaxing, one eyebrow raised. 'You're upset—and lashing out—because I called you annoying?'

'I'm not...' He clenched his teeth. 'This is exactly what I'm talking about.'

'Oh—was this you trying to be my friend? Is this me drawing into myself?'

'You know what?' he said, shrugging his shoulders in an attempt to shrug off the irritation. 'I don't need to do this.'

'No, you don't,' she agreed. 'You should have just kissed me like I asked you to and neither of us would be annoyed now.'

'When did you ask me to kiss you?'

She narrowed her eyes. 'You think I told you I've been thinking about our kiss for the fun of it? That I'm attracted to you because I was ranting?' She snorted. 'You spend an eternity staring at me, telling me you're trying to get me to kiss you, and when I give you permission—'

'That was *not* permission.'

'Yes, it was. I said, and I quote—'

'Shut up.'

'Excuse me?'

'You gave me permission?'

'I did. But if you think you can—'

This time, he shut her up by kissing her.

Apparently, he did think he could. And she wasn't mad about it.

Not about the way his lips pressed against hers with a force that had her pushing back against her front door. Not about the fact that they'd had a ridiculous argument that culminated in this kiss in the passageway of her flat. She had no idea what her neighbours thought. She liked the idea of them cheering her on. It wasn't what she'd be doing if someone was arguing near her flat, but she was uptight like that. Her neighbours generally seemed cool.

None of that mattered now, of course. Benjamin had teased her lips open—it hadn't taken much cajoling—and now their tongues were entwined, moving around one another like two loose strands of a rope longing to be tied. She blamed the inelegance of it on the passion. Their argument had fuelled it, though she suspected it was always there between them, simply because of who they were. She couldn't fault it when it created a hunger that could be sated like this. With his lips moving against her, allowing gooseflesh to take the place of her skin. With his tongue, sending heat to places in her body that had been cool for longer than she could remember.

As if he had heard her, Benjamin's hands began to move. They'd been on her waist, keeping her in place, she suspected. But now they skimmed the sides of her breasts, running along her neck, angling her head so he could kiss her more deeply. The throaty moan that he got in response was a soundtrack for his journey back down, although now he lingered exactly where she needed him to. His touch was gentle at her waist, his thumbs brushing her belly. She gasped. It was intimate, him touching her stomach like that. It felt as if he was claiming her. Her baby.

And that was more intense than when he reached her hips and pulled her against him, bringing the most aching part of her to where she needed him.

But that wasn't true any more. The most aching part of her was her heart now, his innocent caress of her stomach awakening things that she'd forced to sleep years ago. When he pulled back, she offered him a small smile of reassurance. It was okay, him kissing her. She was okay. She wasn't being threatened by the loneliness that always followed her. She wasn't overcome by the enormity of her decision to have a baby alone.

After the thing with Kenya and her baby had happened, Alexa had thought more seriously about having her own. She'd done so with her head *and* her heart. Her head had told her that she was thirty years old, and her ability to become a mother wouldn't always be as simple as it was now. It told her that her business was steady enough for her to take maternity leave, and that when she came back she'd be stronger for having had her baby. If her business took a knock, she was still only thirty, and she'd work her tail off—with even more incentive than usual—to make sure it was back on track.

Her heart had told her that she was ready. She'd spent her entire life examining what she shouldn't be as a mother; who she shouldn't be as a parent. She was ready to finally have the family of her dreams. Where support, love, inclusion were the norm. She wouldn't push her child to breaking point, or create an environment where her child felt they needed to compete for her love. No, she would create warmth and happiness. A home, as she'd done with her flat.

But that was before she'd lost her head chef. Now her business didn't seem nearly as stable as it had been before. And that was before this kiss with Benjamin. Suddenly she was thinking about whether she was robbing her child of having someone else to love them. If she was robbing herself of sharing the miracle of the life growing inside her; or the tenderness Benjamin had shown her.

'Hey,' he said softly, his thumb brushing over her cheek. 'It couldn't have been that bad.'

'What? No.' She shook her head. 'It's not—it wasn't bad.' She gave him that smile again. 'We should probably get to dinner.'

'Alexa—'

'I'm fine, Benjamin. I promise.' But she wasn't. She was promising a lie. 'We're fine, too.' That one she meant.

Because in her head, this would be the last kiss. Tonight would be the last night they spent together. Soon people would know their relationship was fake, a joke. Lee would know—but she would survive it. She would go on to court Cherise de Bruyn and focus on getting the chef, as she should have from the beginning. No one would distract her. Not even Benjamin.

At least that way, though her heart seemed to be unsure of her decisions, her head wouldn't be.

CHAPTER SEVEN

'REALLY, MOM?' SAID Benjamin when they walked in. 'You haven't even said hello but already you have baby videos out?' His mother gave him a bright smile in return, and he couldn't even be mad. He rolled his eyes though. Looked at Alexa. 'Go ahead. Clearly my mother would like to start the evening with embarrassment.'

Alexa walked past him, wearing a smile more genuine than the last few she'd given him. He didn't know if he was relieved or annoyed. Neither. Both.

'I'm going to be very disappointed if there are no videos of him running around naked,' Alexa said. 'It's the only level of embarrassment I'll accept.'

'Well, then, you're in luck,' Nina Foster said with a smile.

'It's lovely to meet you, Mrs Foster.' Alexa held out a hand.

'I've already told you my name is Nina.' His mother ignored Alexa's hand, instead pulling her in for a hug. Alexa accepted with a small laugh. Benjamin released a breath he didn't realise he'd been holding. When his mother pulled back, she said, 'You can call me Aunty Nina, dear.'

At that, Alexa grinned. 'Perfect.'

'I take it Dad's in the kitchen,' Benjamin said to distract himself from the troubling warmth in his chest.

'Yes. He's almost done though. That man loves to cook.' Nina aimed that at Alexa. 'It's where Benny gets his talent.'

'In that case, I'm looking forward to dinner.' Alexa turned to Benjamin. 'Should I hang this up, or can I drape it over a chair?'

'Oh, I've got it.'

He took the coat, went to his bedroom and hung it on a hanger from his own cupboard. It was the least he could do, considering the coat had been collateral damage in their make-out session, when he'd tossed it on the floor. He wouldn't have bothered doing anything with her coat otherwise.

His mother would have scolded him, but only after he'd already set the guest's coat down somewhere innocuous. It was the approach he took with most of his clothing, as evidenced by the tornado that had gone off in his room. His parents refused to go in there. Since he helped with the household expenses, they had a *you're an adult, you deserve your privacy* policy. Except he didn't think they meant privacy in the form of someone—including, on particularly bad days, him—being unable to find anything inside the room.

He took another look at things, winced. It would be better if Alexa—

'Is this your room?'

He turned quickly, blocking the doorway with his body. She was a little further down the passage, so she hadn't seen anything. Yet. He would keep it that way.

'Er…no. I mean, yes.' He closed the door behind him. 'It's where I…do things.'

'Things?'

'Sleep.'

'Hmm.'

'Dress.'

'Okay.' She narrowed her eyes. 'Why don't you want me to see it?'

It was obviously too much to hope that she would be polite and ignore his reluctance. But no, not Alexa. She was too straightforward, too unapologetic to allow something like politeness to get in the way of information she wanted.

'It's untidy.'

She waved a hand. 'So was mine the other day.'

'*That* was untidy?' He rolled his eyes. 'Honestly, I have no idea what that word means with some people. My mother says exactly the same thing and the place is spotless.' He paused. 'I'm willing to bet she told you our place is untidy right now. And I know for a fact she spent the entire day supervising our cleaner.'

'I wouldn't take that bet.' She lifted her nose in the air before she grinned. 'Because she just did.'

He chuckled, but stopped when she took a step forward. 'I'm not like you or my mother.'

'What does that mean?'

'When I say something's untidy, I mean it.'

'Well, so do I. I have certain standards, same as in the restaurant. If I say it's untidy, it doesn't suit those standards.' Her gaze sharpened. 'I've never been to yours. Are you saying you keep a sloppy house?'

'Of course not,' he said, offended. 'I have high standards, too.' But he winced. 'That doesn't necessarily translate to my room.'

'So what you're saying is you live in a pigsty.'

'I would not say that.'

'Let me see it, then.' She folded her arms, baiting him. Damn her.

'I'd rather not. Did my mother send you here?' he asked without waiting to hear her reply. 'I was barely gone for a minute.'

'No. I asked to use the bathroom. What with this situation happening…' She gestured to her stomach.

'You *told* her?'

'That I needed to go to the bathroom because I'm pregnant?' She pulled a face. 'Of course not. Why would I?'

'Oh.' He winced. 'I'm sorry. That was an overreaction.'

She rolled her eyes. 'The bathroom?'

'That one.' He pointed to the room across the hallway.

'Thank you,' Alexa said, and walked into it.

Benjamin stood there for a beat, feeling foolish as his heart rate went back to normal. He shook his head. He needed to put this lie behind him. It was making him skittish. But when he went back to the living room to do just that, his mother was sitting with her hands interlocked over her stomach. Her eyes were closed, and to someone who didn't know her, it would seem as if she was napping. To someone who did know her...

'Mom,' he said, lowering himself in front of her. 'Why didn't you tell me you weren't feeling well?'

She opened her eyes, the tight lines of pain in the creases around them confirming his suspicion. 'I'm fine. Stop fussing.'

'Do we have to do this every time? It's been decades.'

'Exactly. Decades and I still have to tell you I'm fine.'

'But you're not fine. You're in pain.'

'Just a little, from the excitement of the day.'

'Mom...' He trailed off, sighed. 'I wish you'd told me. We could have cancelled. You could have got some rest and not put so much pressure on yourself.'

'And miss the chance to meet Alexa?'

'Mom, Alexa's not—' He broke off. Mostly because he couldn't tell her the truth when she was like this. 'Alexa's not going anywhere,' he finished lamely. 'I'd have brought her the moment you felt better.'

'Would you have?' his mother asked, her eyes tired but sharp. 'I didn't even know about her until yesterday. You never tell us about your dating life. I assumed she's your first proper girlfriend, but I don't even know if that's true.'

'It's because—'

'I had to force you to bring her here,' she interrupted him. Her eyes were flashing now, pain mingled in with the anger. 'And she's pregnant, Benny. *Pregnant*. You hid that from us.'

'What? Oh, no, Mom. She's not—'

'Your bedroom isn't that far away, Benjamin.'

She'd heard them. Damn it. Why hadn't he thought about that?

'We can talk about it when you feel better. Let me help you to bed now.'

'No.' Nina straightened, though he could see she was doing her best not to wince. 'I want to have dinner with you and get to know that woman who's going to be in our lives from now on.'

'She's not...'

He broke off, his mind spinning with how to tell her the truth. Through it, he heard the memory of Alexa's voice asking him why he hadn't told his mother when she'd first overheard him. He should have. But he was caught by that excitement on her face, and he couldn't bear to disappoint her.

He was as much to blame for the situation they were in as Alexa was, he realised. At least this situation. And now, his mother was in pain because of him. Because of his lies.

He exhaled. 'Mom, Alexa's baby... It's not mine.'

She was intruding. She'd known it the moment she'd seen Benjamin crouching in front of his mother. When she'd heard them talk, the conversation so personal she'd had to rest a hand on her chest because her heart felt as if it was breaking, she told herself to walk away. Except she couldn't. She was too riveted by this tender side of a man she'd once called a demon.

She'd felt that tenderness during their kiss. It was what had turned the moment from a purely physical one into something emotional. So she shouldn't have been surprised that he had the capacity to be tender. But seeing it up close and personal, especially after *feeling* it up close and personal? It felt as if someone had walked into her body, gathered her emotions together and tossed them in the air like confetti at a wedding.

She was scrambling to get them back together again when his mother had told him she knew about the baby. Then he confessed it wasn't his, and said nothing about their fake relationship. She'd given him a moment to continue, to tell his mother *why* the baby wasn't his. He hadn't. He merely watched his mother gasp, lift a hand to her mouth, his face crumbling.

So Alexa threw the emotions she had just collected to the ground, and stomped over them to help Benjamin.

'Ben,' she said softly. He looked at her, his eyes ravaged with sadness. 'Let me.'

'We need to—'

'No, *I* need to.' She sent him one look to tell him to shut up, then looked at his mother. 'Benjamin isn't the father of my baby. He's just a decent man who…is decent.' She offered him a smile before sitting on the sofa opposite Nina.

'Mrs Foster… Aunty Nina… I found out I was pregnant pretty quickly. After about two weeks. Benjamin and I hadn't started dating yet, and, well… I got myself into a situation.'

She was keeping as far to the truth as possible. The fertility treatments meant she had found out she was pregnant early. When she had, she'd refused to come in to monitor the pregnancy as her specialist had advised. She wanted to have a normal pregnancy as far as possible. Since it had started out in an unusual way, monitoring things had overwhelmed her.

She also hadn't been fake dating Benjamin then.

'I didn't want to tell him when he asked me out because he seemed like a good guy. For once, I wanted a good guy in my life. I didn't tell him for the longest time. It was wrong, and selfish, and it hurt both you and him. For that, I will never forgive myself.'

She swallowed when her eyes began to prickle. Pressed a hand to her stomach because she felt alone in this deeply personal and strangely true tale she was telling Benjamin's mother. It comforted her, which sent another wave of prickling over her eyes, and she took her time before she continued.

'He hasn't known I'm pregnant very long. I think he was still deciding what to do when you found out about me. It put him in an impossible situation. He didn't want you to be disappointed, but bringing me here tonight makes it seem like he wants me and the baby, and he isn't there yet. He didn't tell you about me because he didn't want that, for either of us,' she said with a lift of her hand.

There was a long silence. Alexa didn't know if someone was waiting for her to speak, or if she was waiting for someone to speak. Eventually, Nina broke the silence.

'Knowing all this, you're still here?'

'It's an impossible situation,' she said with a small smile. 'But it's our normal. So...*normally*... I thought meeting his mother was important.'

There was another long silence. This time, Benjamin broke it.

'I'm sorry, Mom. It was never my intention to...to disappoint you.'

His mother heaved out a sigh. 'You haven't disappointed me. In fact, your behaviour with Alexa... I'd like to think *I* raised you to be someone who doesn't judge people by actions you don't agree with.'

'If it were really you,' Benjamin said slyly, 'you wouldn't judge me for my recent actions.'

Alexa bit her lip, but stopped trying to hide her smile when Nina laughed.

'You're too charming for your own good, boy.'

'I've always thought so, too,' Alexa agreed.

'Thank you,' Benjamin replied with a grin.

Nina gave them an amused look. Then she sobered. 'My son clearly cares about you, Alexa. That's enough for me.'

Alexa nodded, pressure she didn't realise was there releasing inside her. 'Thank you.'

Nina shook her head. 'I'm actually rooting for this to work out. Because at this pace, that baby of yours might be my only chance at a grandchild.'

They didn't have time to reply, as a tall man with a shock of grey hair walked into the room.

'Benjie, boy.' In the man's grin, Alexa saw Benjamin.

'Hi, Dad.'

Benjamin's father looked at their faces, frowned. 'What did I miss?'

CHAPTER EIGHT

'THIS ISN'T MY PLACE,' Alexa said, as if only now noticing he hadn't taken her back to her flat. Which was surprising, as they hadn't spoken since they'd left his house, so she hadn't been distracted. In fact, she'd been staring out of the window the entire time.

'No, it's not.'

He didn't say anything else as he drove along the gravel road that led into the quarry. Handy, because if he had, he wouldn't have heard her small gasp when he parked. He couldn't deny that part of why he'd brought her was the wow factor. The quarry was spectacular at night; on a summer's night, even more so. There was no cool breeze to chill them, no dew glazing the grass that stretched out in front of the car park. The sky was clear, the full moon illuminating things enough that he didn't have to get out his phone's torch to guide them to the water.

And really, it was the water that was the star of the quarry. It was nestled in the hollow of the rocks, stretching out in inky darkness. The moon was reflected in it, the stars, too, and it made him wonder if perhaps this was all a little too romantic. But he wanted quiet, and the quarry was quiet. He went to the back of his car, and got out the camping chairs he kept there.

'You prepared for this?' she asked when she got out of the car. 'Were you intending on bringing me here?'

'No.' He carried the chairs to his usual spot beneath the tree at the edge of the water. When he heard her behind him he said, 'I keep these in my car.'

'For this reason?'

'Exactly.'

'You bring ladies out here a lot, then?' She gave him a sly look as she lowered herself into the chair. Then she frowned. 'You'd better be prepared to help me out of this chair. It's low, and being pregnant means I have zero control over my balance.'

'So what you're saying is that I could leave you here and you'd have to stay in the chair for ever?'

'Yes,' she replied, voice dry as a badly made cake. 'That's exactly what I'm saying.'

'Good to know.' He paused. 'Better watch your attitude.'

'You know what? I don't even need your help. The grass looks pretty soft. I can tilt to the side, break my fall with my hand, and figure it out from there.'

'The grass is lower than the chair.'

'I said I'd figure it out.'

He couldn't help his laugh, though he tried to be respectful and kept it quick and low—until she joined in, which he hadn't expected. It was strange to be laughing with her, but he suspected they were relieving the tension of the night. There'd been an undercurrent during the entire meal. He didn't blame his mother for being reserved—both Alexa's news and her pain had probably occupied her mind and her body—but it meant that he'd overcompensated. The result was a strained meal where everyone pretended nothing was wrong and it was…draining.

When they stopped laughing, they lapsed into an easy silence; another surprise. But honestly, he was grateful for it. It gave him a moment to gather his thoughts, prepare his words.

'Thank you.'

'For what?'

'What you had to do with my mom. You made a difficult situation easier.'

She sighed. 'I lied.'

'Did you?'

She frowned. 'You mean, besides the fact that I kept our fake relationship going?'

'Yes, actually.'

It took some time for her to understand.

'Oh, you want to know if the stuff I said about the father of the baby's true.'

He did. But now that she said it, he felt as if he was asking too much. Maybe if he was honest with her, too...

'Look, I know I said the lies had to end. But...' He trailed off, sighed. 'At some point tonight I realised it worked for me to be in a fake relationship, too. It made my mother happy. Maybe I knew it would and that's why I let her think we were together in the first place.' It was something he'd have to think about. 'Your pregnancy complicated things, and I got scared. But your explanation made sense. Hell, it somehow made both of us look good.'

She looked at the water. 'I wouldn't say that.'

'I would.' He let it sit for a moment. 'I realised tonight the only people whose opinions I care about are my parents. So, we can keep this going for as long as we both want to.'

'You're not afraid of disappointing your mother when it ends?'

He heaved out a breath. 'I can't see an outcome that won't hurt her. I'd rather she think I tried and it didn't work out than know I lied to her.'

'Sneaky,' she commented.

'You're one to talk.'

She laughed. 'Touché.' There was a beat. 'Thank you.'

'This isn't only for you.'

For once, he believed it. He wasn't doing this only to help her. It helped him and his family, too. It might have been strained at dinner this evening, but there'd also been light. That light had been because of Alexa. Because of what she represented to his parents.

A future that didn't only involve taking care of them.

He'd sacrifice his reputation for his parents' peace of mind.

'I know,' she said softly. 'Still. Thank you.' Silence danced between them for a few minutes. 'To answer your earlier question, I don't know what kind of guy got me pregnant.'

His brain took a moment to shift gears. 'You don't know…if he's a good guy?'

'I don't know who he is.'

'Oh.'

Sure. That was fine. She was allowed her sexual freedom. If she didn't know who she'd slept with, that was her business. Except…

No, no exceptions. He wouldn't be a judgemental jerk.

'I was waiting,' she said into the silence, 'for some kind of bigoted statement about my sex life.'

'I wouldn't dare.'

She laughed lightly. 'You were basically biting your tongue.'

'It isn't my business.'

'No, it's not.' Her laughter faded. 'Which makes why I'm telling you I was artificially inseminated by donor sperm puzzling.'

'You were artificially inseminated?' he repeated dumbly.

'Yep.' She unclasped the hands that had been locked around her knee. 'I wanted to have a baby and the available men were… Well, I suppose there were none. Whom I trusted anyway.'

'You have no male friends?'

'I don't have any…' She broke off. 'I don't have that many friends. Besides, could you imagine me asking a friend to be the father of my child?' She shuddered. 'That would be asking for trouble. Involvement. People don't tend to keep their word, so the promise that they would never encroach on the way I raised a child would be gone pretty quickly, I bet. Especially if the baby looked like the friend.'

He thought about it. 'Alternatively, you could have gone through this *with* someone. You wouldn't have to make decisions alone. You'd have support.'

'Spoken like a man who's had support his entire life.'

'Is that a criticism?'

'Not a criticism. An observation.'

'In return, then, I observe that you don't trust people.'

'An accurate observation. Trusting people isn't worth a damn.'

He tried to formulate an answer, but found himself at a loss for words. Not emotion though. He felt sorry that she'd lived a life that encouraged her to think this way. There was some rage, too, because it seemed completely unfair that he'd had parents who'd loved him and taught him the value of leaning on family and she hadn't. Or maybe it wasn't so much rage as it was guilt, because he had something she didn't.

'Don't feel sorry for me.'

'I'm not.'

'Your mother wouldn't like you lying to me.'

His face twisted. 'Are you really using my mother to make me feel guilty about this?'

'Yes. I am a smart woman who uses the tools at her disposal.'

He chuckled softly. 'Can't argue with that.'

'Finally, you learn.'

She settled back in the chair, resting her hands on her belly. It had the same protective tint as the way she'd rubbed her stomach that night in her flat. Now he knew she'd done it because she was pregnant. What he didn't know was why *he'd* done it. Why, when they'd kissed, he'd grazed her stomach and felt a rush of protectiveness he didn't know existed inside him. Need had joined so quickly and intensely that he'd had to pull back from their kiss to deal with it. To try and deny it, as he'd done the first time he'd felt that need.

'I don't feel sorry,' he said slowly, 'I feel sad.'

She didn't answer, tilting her head from side to side.

'What?' he asked.

'I'm trying to figure out whether sad is worse.'

'And?'

She looked over, eyes shining with emotion he couldn't read but knew meant something. 'It isn't.'

Without thinking about it, he reached out a hand. She stared at it, at him, looked down, then slowly took his hand. He wanted to stand up and shout for joy. He wanted to thank her for letting him in. He wanted to pull her into his arms and kiss her. Sate the heat the contact sent through his body. Instead, he squeezed and let the quiet of the evening settle over them.

It surprised him by settling the twisting of his stomach, too. He was used to the twisting, since it came whenever his mother was in pain.

When he was young, he had thought he could do something about it. His mother would be in bed, curled up to favour whichever side of her was aching more, and he'd bring her tea. Make her food. Offer to run a bath for her, or cuddle her until she felt better. She'd never accept, and she'd apologise afterwards. She'd tell him the version of her who was in pain wasn't really *her*.

Throughout her illness, she'd tried to separate the person who was in pain and the one who wasn't. Which he understood. Her illness had been relatively unknown in South Africa when she'd been diagnosed, and even the dialogue with her doctors had separated those identities. But he knew, even as a kid, that the same mother who couldn't move some days was the mother who would spend hours reading to him. Or taking him to some exciting place he wanted to see. Or answering all his questions with patience and honesty. As he grew older, he realised his mother had separated who she was because she saw her body as her enemy during her flare-ups. It was separate for her; it was separate *from* her. It was betraying her.

He'd wanted to help her because he wanted her to remember he loved all of her, even if she couldn't do it herself. It was a big burden for a kid to undertake, even though he hadn't completely understood it. And it had evolved as he got older. Now, he tried to nudge instead of directly say. He tried to support instead of fix. It was navigating a minefield—a stubborn minefield—but since there weren't any explosions, at least not yet, Benjamin thought he was doing pretty okay. As long as he was there, he would keep doing okay.

'Is your mom going to be all right?'

He frowned, trying to remember if he'd spoken out loud and the question had been provoked. He was sure he hadn't, which meant Alexa was simply curious. He sighed in relief.

'Yeah, she'll be fine.'

'Is she unwell?'

He took a breath. 'She has something called fibromyalgia. It's a—'

'I know what it is.' At his surprised look, she rolled her eyes. 'People are more open about chronic illnesses these days.'

'But… I mean, it's not something you just know.'

'I didn't,' she agreed. 'Until I went to look it up after seeing an acquaintance talk about it online.'

He kept his mouth shut because if he didn't he was sure he'd make inelegant grunts she'd make fun of.

'It sounds tough,' she said softly. 'Living your life in pain the whole time. I can't imagine.' There was a short pause. 'I *can* imagine how hard it must have been for you.'

He gave her a sharp look, dropping her hand in the process. She didn't seem fazed, only folding her hands over her stomach again.

'What do you mean?' he asked.

'Well, you're the kind of person who agrees to be in a fake relationship with his mortal enemy because you were feeling protective. At least, I guess that was how you were feeling? Maybe it was indignant at how Lee dared to act towards me. I can't tell with you.' She shrugged. 'Regardless, you're someone who does things when other people seem vulnerable. I'm guessing you see your mother's pain as her being vulnerable, which makes you want to do something. Except you can't, because it's *her* pain.'

It was remarkably astute. Uncomfortably astute. Which was why he said, 'No.'

The corners of her lips twitched. 'Hmm…'

'It's been fine for me.'

'Okay.'

'She's the one in pain.'

'Sure.'

'Is it hard for me to see her that way? Sure. But is it worse for me? No.'

'That's not what I said though. I know it's worse for her. Of course it is.' She paused. 'I might be off base here, what with having a messed-up family situation myself, but I don't think it would be easy for me to see someone I care about in pain.'

'It's…not.'

'I don't doubt it.' There was a long pause as the words washed over them. 'It's not an excuse for you not to pick up after yourself though. How do you even find anything in your room? It looks like the aftermath of a police search.'

As soon as the surprise faded—though he should have known she'd look—he started laughing. 'It's organised chaos.'

'Rubbish!'

'It's not rubbish.'

'You're telling me you know where every T-shirt is placed? Every shirt? Pants?'

'Exactly.'

'So if I hid something in there you'd find it?'

'Did you hide something in my room?'

She gave him a sly look. 'Maybe.'

'Alexa,' he nearly growled.

'What?' She blinked at him innocently. 'You said it's organised chaos. I'd just like to prove, once and for all, on behalf of everyone who's been sceptical about organised chaos, that that's nonsense.'

'You're trying to trap me on behalf of an entire group of people?'

'Sometimes your actions have to be bigger than yourself.'

He shook his head, but even his disbelief couldn't overshadow his amusement. Then he thought of something.

'How did you know I'd say organised chaos though?'

'Please. I've spent years trying to avoid interacting with you. It hasn't worked—' she sent him an accusatory look '—but at least I got to know who you are.'

He sighed. 'What did you hide in my room?'

'A handkerchief.'

'You carry a handkerchief?'

'Yes.' She sniffed. 'It's for the essential oils I carry in my purse, too. In case I have an overbearing bout of nausea.'

'Efficient.'

'Thanks.'

'Can you at least tell me what the handkerchief looks like?'

'Pink. Like my dress.'

'That should make it easier to find.'

'It'll be a breeze. You know where everything is, re-member?'

She patted his hand, winked at his glare, and he turned away before he could smile again.

He couldn't say whether it was the teasing that soothed him, but the anxiety in his body had stopped humming. Except it couldn't be the teasing. She'd done plenty of that before, though it had lost its snarkiness at some point over the last few days.

As he thought about it, he realised it was that she understood. His position in his family had always made him feel alone, and finally he didn't feel that way any more.

He let it wash over him. Didn't even question that Alexa had been the one to make him feel that way—or what it meant. Still, he couldn't let her get the upper hand.

'So,' he said casually, 'are we going to talk about that kiss?'

'What kiss?'

He snorted. 'There's no way you don't—'

'What kiss, Benjamin?'

At her tone, he looked over. Saw her determination. It made him laugh, which turned the determination into a glare. Satisfied that he'd won, he stood and offered a hand to help her up.

CHAPTER NINE

ALEXA WALKED INTO the restaurant and saw him immediately.

'You've got to be kidding me,' she muttered, pausing.

It had been a few days since she and Benjamin had had *that* moment. It wasn't a defined moment. She couldn't say—oh, this thing happened and things have changed. Besides the kisses. And the fact that she thought he might be nice, despite the whole stealing-her-chef thing. Or how kind he was with his parents; how eager he was to please them. All she knew for sure was that at some point at the quarry, things had shifted. She needed time to sort through it, and she had other things to do first.

Such as secure her chef before she went on maternity leave.

There was time. She was days away from entering her second trimester, so she had about six months. That was what she told herself logically. In reality, she was freaking out. Hiring a new chef was a nightmare. She knew because she'd done so months before and it had all gone to hell anyway. So she needed time to find the right person, make sure they worked well with the rest of her team. Train them to work for Infinity, with her and with Kenya. She had to be there to observe and make sure everything would go smoothly when she was away.

She only had six months to do so.

No wonder she had indigestion.

That could have been her pregnancy, too, but she had a feeling being stressed about the new chef didn't help. Or being at odds with Kenya, who'd stubbornly refused to talk about anything other than work in the last week. Usually, Kenya was a champagne bottle, shaken and uncorked and overflowing with personal anecdotes. Now she was a bottle of wine; one that was aging and still and not overflowing with anything.

It was hard for Alexa to believe she missed all of Kenya's energy and her much too personal stories about her life. But she did. And now she had to deal with realising she missed the connection of it, too, and think about how to fix it, and about why Kenya was really so mad at her. She did *not* need to face Benjamin and his kissable lips today.

She marched over to the table.

'You're stealing my appointments with Cherise now, too?'

He looked up, smiled at her, and did it all so slowly that it felt as though someone had pushed a button for that to happen. Her heart did a little skip at that face; her mind recognised that his surprise, his pleasure at seeing her were genuine.

'Hey!' He stood. 'You have an appointment with Cherise, too?'

'Too?' She looked at the table. There were only two seats. 'How can we both have an appointment with her?'

He shrugged. 'She called me the day before yesterday to ask me if I could meet her here.' He gestured at the restaurant. It was perfectly nice with black and white décor, some greenery courtesy of plants, and the faint smell of fish because of its position near the water of the V&A Waterfront. 'Said it would be a nice neutral space.'

Alexa huffed out a breath. 'Yeah, because that's what I told her. After I called her the day before yesterday to ask for this meeting.'

He blinked. 'You called Cherise after we spent the night together?'

'I'm not sure I'd describe dinner with your family as us spending the night together, but yes, I did.' She straightened her spine. 'You said we should continue with our plans as usual.'

'Yeah, but I didn't expect—'

He frowned. Shoved his hands into his pockets. Suddenly she noticed that he was wearing a shirt. She'd seen him in one before, but now he looked...different. His shoulders were broad, chest defined, the material clinging to all of it. She half expected him to move and tear through a perfectly good piece of clothing.

Why was a part of her cheering for that to happen?

'I guess she wanted to speak with both of us at the same time.'

'I did,' Cherise said from beside them. Alexa nearly jumped out of her skin.

'How long have you been there?'

'Just arrived,' Cherise replied. 'Sorry to spring this on you.' She narrowed her eyes. 'Although I was sure I wouldn't actually be able to do that, since you two are dating.'

There was a beat as Alexa realised she was going to have to pretend again. Fortunately, Benjamin spoke before she could say anything.

'We keep our personal and professional lives separate.' He smiled, oozing charm. Alexa nearly slipped on the puddle of it before she realised this was what he did. He charmed people. But *not* her. Especially not if she continued ignoring the fact that they'd kissed. 'Thought it for the best, considering we're in the same business.'

'I imagine that must help. Or make things more complicated, if you're meeting up like this.'

'It doesn't happen as often as you'd think,' Alexa answered Cherise. Cherise gave her a rueful smile.

'I thought it might be easier to discuss this together.' She paused. 'In hindsight, I suppose I was using your relationship to make things easier for myself. I wouldn't have to have two meetings about possibly the same thing. I'm blurring things for you,' she added with a frown.

'Don't worry about it,' Benjamin said smoothly. 'We're mature enough to handle it.'

He sent Alexa a look as if to say *I'm mature enough.* It took all of Alexa's willpower not to roll her eyes at him, or stick out her tongue. Or do anything really that would undermine her maturity. She could be mature.

'Should we get someone to add a chair to this table?' Alexa asked coolly. Maturely. She gestured to a waiter. 'I booked a two-seater.'

'This is the table I booked, actually,' Benjamin said, also gesturing to the waiter. When he looked at Alexa, she pulled a face. *This is you being mature?*

'Oh, I booked a table for three,' Cherise interjected. 'I just saw you two here and came directly to speak to you. I'll have the waiter take us.'

Soon they were sitting together and ordering drinks.

'So,' Cherise started, 'I know whatever either of you wanted to say to me today probably isn't going to work out because the other crashed the lunch.'

She and Benjamin exchanged a look. They hadn't *crashed* the lunch. Cherise had invited Benjamin to an appointment Alexa and she had agreed on. If anything, Cherise had done the crashing. By proxy.

Acid pushed up in Alexa's chest. She'd done a lot of research to find Cherise. Her first step had been to call her old mentor at the restaurant she'd worked at after the Institute. He'd recommended two people, one of whom was studying at the same institute she'd studied at—Cherise—the other of whom was still working for him, but was looking for something more, more urgently than what he could offer.

It had taken her a while to find out that Cherise wasn't

studying at the Institute as a newbie who wanted to learn everything she could. No, Cherise had worked under the best chefs, her old mentor included, for almost a decade, and had decided to formalise her knowledge by getting an official qualification. She was interested in something new, which, after speaking with some of the people Cherise had worked with, including the instructors they had in common, Alexa was eager to offer.

Except now it seemed Cherise wasn't going to be that good a match after all.

'I thought I'd say some things to both of you instead,' Cherise said. 'One: I would be happy to work with either of you. I'm looking for something different to what I've done in the past, which tended to lean towards more traditional fine dining. Nothing wrong with it,' she added quickly, 'but I'd like to do something more creative than cauliflower purée. I'm eager to explore that creativity, and I believe your restaurants, both younger, trendier places, would give me the space to do that.'

Alexa rubbed the burning in her chest thoughtfully. It wasn't subsiding, though her doubts about Cherise were. Perhaps that was enough for now.

'Two: I have no idea which one of you I'd like to work for.' Cherise gave them a small smile. 'I've dined at both your restaurants. Both of them were amazing experiences, and each of your spaces I respond to. Yours is more traditional, with the wood and the partitions between each side of the restaurant,' she said to Benjamin, 'but there's something about it that makes me nostalgic. Yet I love how modern Infinity is,' Cherise continued, speaking to Alexa now. 'It's sleek, and so not where I'd expect to be served fine dining.'

'Thank you…?'

Cherise laughed. 'It's a compliment,' she assured Alexa. 'You've brought a younger crowd in by modernising your place, and I respect someone who can instil respect for good food in a generation that fast food was basically designed for.'

'Well, then, thank you,' Alexa said more firmly.

'The conclusion I've come to is that it will depend on who I get along with the best. The only way I can know that is to spend more time with you both.'

'Of course,' Alexa said. 'You can come to the restaurant any time you'd like. I can show you around, have you speak with some of my staff. I'm sure Benjamin would allow that, too.'

'Sure.'

'And I'd love that. But I was thinking of something a little different.'

'What?'

She wrinkled her nose. 'School.'

'Why do I feel like we were being interviewed?' Benjamin asked minutes after Cherise had left the restaurant.

'Not were,' Alexa corrected. 'Are. We now have to take a three-day course at the Institute. Which I don't mind per se, it's just…' Her voice faded and she let out a huge sigh.

'Everything okay?'

'Fine.'

But she dropped her head onto a hand she'd rested on the table.

If his instincts hadn't already been tingling from that sigh, this would have done them in. In fact, it felt as though an alarm was going off in his head. It dimmed the sound of the inner voice warning him not to get involved. Things were already almost impracticably complicated between them; he didn't need to further complicate that by getting involved with her issues.

Except she looked so fragile, sitting there with her hand on her head. It was so different to how she usually seemed—abrasive, bull-headed, *strong*—that he had to fight harder than he would have liked not to ask. And then he found himself fighting against *that* because he did want to ask. Hell, he even wanted to make it better. Which was exactly how things usually went wrong. People would take advantage of his tendency to take over. After he'd had a 'friend' do it recently, he'd learnt his lesson.

He eyed Alexa.

'You okay?' he asked anyway, because he was a fool who hadn't learnt a thing.

'I've already said I'm fine,' she said, but there was no heat in the words. If she were feeling herself, there definitely would have been heat in the words.

'It's just that—' he tried not to show his surprise that she'd continued '—this is turning out to be a lot harder than I thought it would be. Everything is,' she said in an uncharacteristically small voice as she lifted her head. 'I wanted to get Cherise to work for me so I could go on maternity leave without worrying I was ruining my restaurant by having a baby. Leaving it vulnerable in some way. Maybe even to you and Lee. Now I have to do this course with you.' She looked up at him. Her eyes were gleaming, but sharp. 'No offence.'

He wondered if he should dignify that with a response.

'Why can't anything be simple?' she whispered now. 'Why can't I have a family that doesn't suck? Why couldn't my chef have stayed on so that I wouldn't have this stress during my pregnancy? Why couldn't…?'

She exhaled. Waved a hand.

'I'm fine.'

'Clearly.'

She gave him a dark look. He preferred it to the sadness.

'I can't help you with—'

'Any of it,' she interrupted. 'You can't help me with any of it. But I appreciate the effort.'

'I wasn't going to say that.'

'Oh, I know,' she said, straightening now. She took a deep sip of water, but kept her gaze on him. 'I know what you were going to say, Benjamin. It was going to be about what you could help me with. You might even have been considering stepping out of this race with Cherise because things would be easier for me then.'

'I wasn't—'

She cut him off with a single raised eyebrow. And because, of course, he *was*.

'Where would it leave you, Benjamin?' she asked softly. 'You'd have to look for another chef. You'd have to answer to my brother. You're clearly letting your personal feelings override how you feel professionally.'

'There are no personal feelings.'

She looked at him strangely. The confusion cleared in seconds.

'Oh, no, I don't mean *for* me. Of course not.' There was a beat. 'I meant you're letting your desire to fix things for people cloud your professional opinion. Which should be that you should do that three-day course and fight to have her work for you.'

She grabbed her purse, threw some notes onto the table.

'That's what I'll be doing.'

Then she was gone.

He sat, bemused, until the waiter came to the table, saw the money Alexa had left, and asked if he wanted the bill. He said yes, stuffed her notes in his wallet, and paid with his card. Then he walked. Not to his car, where he probably should have gone. He had work to do.

But his thoughts demanded that he pay them heed, and he couldn't do that when he was driving, or working. So he walked. Away from the bustle of the Waterfront, where tourists shopped and locals ate. Down, past the docks, until he was simply walking along the edge of the Waterfront, waves splashing against the rocks beyond the railing.

The conversation he'd had with Alexa…

Well, he couldn't exactly call it a conversation. More a monologue, with the occasional pauses. He couldn't be upset with her though; she was right. There'd been a moment, and not a brief one, where he'd thought about giving up the fight for Cherise.

A lot about that bothered him. The first was, simply, that it was stupid. He'd spent a long time trying to find her. Speaking with his contacts at restaurants she'd worked in and at the Institute. Making sure she had the skills a chef in his kitchen would need.

He'd started out as the head chef, back when Lee had reached out to him years ago. Though that was tainted now with the knowledge that Lee had done it to get back at Alexa, Benjamin could still recognise his luck. Because Lee had been the one to help him make the transition once he'd discovered his passion went beyond the kitchen.

Since Lee had multiple businesses, he couldn't invest much time in the restaurant. So when Benjamin had decided to switch gears and spoken to Lee about his desire to branch out, Lee had offered to train him. For two years, they'd done just that. This was the first year he'd taken on the responsibility fully, and he wanted to make Lee proud. Hell, he wanted to make himself proud. Giving away his chance because he wanted to help out a woman who didn't need his help was definitely stupid.

The second thing that bothered him about wanting to was that she'd seen through him. She had the uncanny ability to do so, which she'd displayed at lunch today and at the quarry the other night. He could blame the ability on the fact that she didn't seem to want his help. Despite what he'd first thought about her, Alexa wasn't using him. If she was, she would have said it by now. She was disturbingly honest like that.

Which was why he couldn't be dishonest with himself when it came to her. She didn't see through him because she didn't want his help. Well, not only because of that. It was also because she knew him, could see him, and he didn't like it.

He had a persona to maintain. An important one. The moment his parents realised he felt responsible for looking after them, they'd stop him from doing so. The moment his mother saw that he'd seen another future for himself because of the fake relationship with Alexa, she'd do anything she could for him to have it.

But he couldn't have it. It wasn't compatible with living at home, helping his father around the house, spending time with his mother. If Alexa saw through him, she might see the things he didn't want anyone knowing, too. What if she mentioned it to his mother? To his father? And just because she wasn't using him now didn't mean she never would. Look at what his friends had done. His cousins.

They pretended to spend time with him, be his friend, but they only wanted things. Money, free food, help with an event. It was predictable in its consistency. As predictable as his ability to fall for it. Because they needed him.

He had reasons to stay away from Alexa. To not give in to the pull he felt between them. Good reasons. Professional *and* personal reasons. He only had one reason to see her: he had to get Cherise to work for him.

One more reason, a voice in his head reminded him. He almost groaned.

Yes, he had one more reason to see her. He was also supposed to be in a relationship with her.

CHAPTER TEN

A FORTNIGHT LATER Alexa arrived at the Institute early, ready to get the first day of the course over with. Perhaps not a winning attitude, but the best one she could muster under the circumstances. She'd been to the doctor the day before for her thirteen-week appointment. Apparently, she'd been blessed with twins.

It did not seem like a blessing at that moment.

She'd known it was a possibility, of course. She'd read many articles about fertility treatments; her doctor had pretty much repeated the information to her verbatim. But she hadn't once considered that *she'd* have twins. Twins weren't for someone who needed to find a chef for her business so it wouldn't fail or be vulnerable to attacks by a sibling or for someone who didn't know how to raise one child, let alone two. *Two!* What had she done to deserve this?

Well, a voice in her brain said, quite reasonably, *you're at odds with your family. You're pretending to date a man and lying to the people you care about. Your only friend isn't talking to you because of the lie, and you refuse to tell her the truth. You also haven't told her you're pregnant—with twins—and you've pushed away anyone who could possibly come to care about you.*

It was a long list of her flaws. Surprisingly long, considering her own head had provided them. Although that the list was there at all wasn't a surprise. She wasn't perfect. The fact that she was prickly, bull-headed, and stubborn wasn't news. But since those characteristics had helped her survive her family and build her business, she could see the good in them, too.

So maybe twins were her punishment for her irreverence.

Not that her children were a punishment. Of course not.

'Sorry,' she murmured to them. 'I'm just surprised. And worried. What if I'm not a good mother to you? There are two of you now, so I'll be screwing up twice as much.'

She let out a huge breath, and sipped the herbal tea she'd bought before she'd left for the Institute. The warmth of it gave her some much-needed comfort. The rap on her window did not—nor did seeing who it was.

She opened the window. 'I'll be sending you my hospital bills.'

Benjamin gave her a half-smile, almost as if he expected her to give him a hard time. Almost as if he liked it. 'For what?'

'My heart attack.'

She grabbed her things, closed the window, and got out of the car. He hadn't moved far away, so when she turned, she found herself in his bubble. His musky scent didn't make her nauseous, as she'd expected it to, since it was in the window of her morning illness time. Maybe because her other body parts had woken up and decided to respond to it.

When she'd read that pregnancy would make her more… sensitive, she'd laughed. She hadn't been sensitive to anyone in such a long time. She couldn't even remember who the last person she'd been sensitive to was. And yet what she was feeling now was anything but amusement. She was incredibly aware of the smell of him. Incredibly aware of his body only centimetres from hers.

He looked delicious in his black T-shirt and jeans; his standard outfit in the kitchen, even when they'd been studying. Again, she noticed his shoulders, his chest. His body was muscular and strong and she wondered what it would be like if he scooped her into his arms. Would she feel light, even now, pregnant with twins? Would she be annoyed that he'd dare do it?

Or would she be amused, attracted? A playful combination of both that would have her inching forward to kiss him…?

'Oh,' she said, and leaned back against the car.

'Are you okay?' he asked, moving even closer.

'Yeah. You're just…um…awfully close.'

He looked down, seemingly only noticing it now. His lips curved into a smile that had her heart racing. Not because it was sexy and sly. Of course not. It was because she knew what that slyness meant.

'Are you having a tough time because I'm close to you, Alexa?'

Oh, no. He was speaking in a low voice that was even more seductive than the smile.

'No.' She cleared her throat when the word came out huskily. 'I'm having a hard time because I'm pregnant. I need air and space and…stuff,' she finished lamely.

It was a pity. He'd believed her until she'd said that. Now he was smirking, which was quite annoying. But it gave her an idea.

'It's probably good that I'm close to you though. I'm so dizzy.'

She braced herself, then rested her head on his chest. The bracing didn't help. Not when his arms automatically went around her, holding her tighter against him. His heart thudded against her cheek, her own heart echoing. She closed her eyes as she realised her mistake.

'It's okay,' he said softly. 'I've got you.'

The words had a lump growing in her throat. She looked up, defiantly, she thought, because she didn't need him to *have* her. But she completely melted at his expression. It was soft and concerned and protective. Then he ran the back of his finger over her cheek, his gaze slipping to her lips, and she was melting, all right, but for the wrong reasons.

'I should…sit down.'

'Yeah,' he said shakily, stepping away.

He'd been as affected as she had.

She wrapped her hands around her cup. How was she still holding it? How hadn't she dumped it all over Benjamin? She began to walk over the strip of stones that separated the car park and the grass. They settled on the bench under a large tree metres away, and she sighed at the view of the vineyard. Bright green and dark green with the brown of the sand stretching out in front of them. At the very end of the vineyard rose a mountain; tall and solid, it enclosed the area and made everything seem private. With the quiet of the early morning settling over them, Alexa realised she hadn't come early to get the day over with as much as she'd come for this.

She could remember the days she'd done the same thing when she'd been studying. She'd still been living at home, paying her parents for the pleasure with the little she earned working part-time as a kitchen hand. She couldn't wait to escape to this beautiful place every weekday. Away from the attention her parents had lavished on her about her goals in life. Goals that weren't aligned with the ones they'd had for her life, which was why they had kept pushing.

Pushing and pushing, until she had been sure she would fall over from the stress of it.

'Is it better now?'

'Hmm?' She looked over at him. Blinked. 'Oh, the dizziness? Yes. Tons.'

He smiled, but apparently knew better than to comment. 'What distracted you just now?'

'I used to love coming here early. It's so beautiful, and

peaceful.' She exhaled, forcing out the bad memories that came with the good ones.

'It really is something,' he agreed. Except he was looking at her. Intensely.

She cleared her throat. 'Is…um…is this why you're here so early?'

'You know what they say. Early bird gets the best view.'

'And maybe the station third from the front.' She laughed at his expression. 'We all know that one's the best.'

'Not true. Station seven is.'

'Station seven's left stove plate can't simmer.'

He laughed. 'How do you know this place so well?'

'You mean, how is it that you can't fool me?' She gave him an amused look. 'I pay attention.'

'Yeah,' he said softly. 'You do.'

Somehow, she didn't think he was referring to the stove. She sipped her tea instead of asking him, and nearly spat it out again when he said, 'You've grown.'

Swallowing it back down proved challenging.

'What do you mean?'

'Your stomach is bigger,' he said quickly. Which, of course, she'd known, but it was worth asking the question for that look of panic on his face. She hid her smile with another sip of tea.

'Yes. This happens when you're expecting.'

'It's only been two weeks. Is it supposed to grow so quickly?'

She laughed lightly. 'I hope so. But my doctor is happy with everything. I saw her yesterday. I guess growing fast is what happens when you're expecting two.'

Maybe a part of her had known he would react this way. Multiple blinks, mouth opening and closing, every muscle she could see frozen. He was in shock, and it felt like a vindication of her own reaction. It even made her want to laugh at her own reaction, which was probably as comical as his. No—most likely more. She was the one carrying the twins.

'Two? As in twins?'

She merely raised her brows in answer.

'Of course it's twins. Two are twins.' He stood, began to pace. 'You're sure?'

Though she hadn't quite anticipated *this* reaction, she nodded, eager to see where it would go.

'Man. Twins? *Twins.*' His long legs easily strode back and forth over the distance in front of the bench. 'I can't believe you're having two.'

'I couldn't either,' she said slowly, 'and I'll actually be the one giving birth to them. Raising them.'

It took him a few moments, but he seemed to understand the implication. He stopped, gave her a sheepish smile.

'Sorry. I guess for a moment there I was…' He broke off, confusion crossing his face. 'I don't know what I was doing.'

'Maybe you imagined what it would be like if we really were dating,' she offered. 'Think about it. You started dating a woman who was pregnant, something you didn't sign up for, but you're too good a guy to let that keep you from developing a relationship with her. So, hey, maybe you can be a father to one kid if you liked one another enough. But two?' She gave a slight shake of the head. 'That would freak anyone out.'

'Even you?'

She laughed. It sounded a little deranged even to her own ears. Not that that kept her from answering.

'I always wanted a family. A good one, I mean. I realised about a year ago that I could only create that for myself. I couldn't rely on my own family for that.' She stared at that green in the distance, letting herself speak. She needed to say it out loud. 'I thought someday I'd have another. I'd teach them to cherish one another. To be each other's best friend, not competition. Not like my relationship with Lee. They would be different, how I dreamt siblings would be—always there for each other, so they would always know love.'

She rested her hands on her stomach. On the two lives growing there.

'But I would have time between them. Two right away? It's scary. What if I'm not cut out for this?'

She exhaled sharply; shook her head sharply. Now wasn't the time to have a breakdown. She'd only found out about the twins the day before, and clearly she needed to process. But she wouldn't do it now, in front of him. Well, *more* in front of him than she already had done. She wouldn't say anything about her fear of her restaurant failing. Or failing the people who relied on her there. Less because she felt it—although she did—and more because she knew he'd feel sorry for her. Based on his expression now, he already did. And her pregnancy didn't even involve him.

She inhaled now. Offered him a smile. 'But no, I'm not freaking out.'

He smiled back, because she was vulnerability wrapped up in fire and he wanted to burn himself so badly. He couldn't help it. The combination of her traits—traits that were polar opposites in everyone but her, that made her who she was— was so appealing. Fascinating. Intriguing.

Even as he thought it, he shook his head. How could he find her appealing? Fascinating? Intriguing? He'd just thought—seconds ago—that she was vulnerable. Vulnerability meant she would need someone. It put her in the perfect position to use someone. And that someone couldn't be him.

Mainly because something inside him, *everything* inside him, wanted it to be him.

He'd been trained for this, hadn't he? He'd spent years

managing his mother's vulnerabilities. Not that they needed
to be managed, he thought with a frown. His mother's pain
wasn't a problem he needed to solve; he knew that. It was
just… He'd had to manage his reaction to it. He had to be
the person she needed during her bad times, which meant
he couldn't take over and demand she do what he wanted
her to, no matter how strong the urge. He had to support
her without overwhelming her. It was the hardest thing he'd
ever done. But he'd done it. He was good at it. Maybe that
was why he was so attracted to Alexa—he could be good
at managing himself with her, too.

'Good thing,' he replied, unwilling, or maybe unable,
to dive into the mess of his thoughts. 'If you were freaking
out about it, I wouldn't be able to reassure you.'

She gave him a bland look. He chuckled.

'There's nothing wrong with accepting reassurance.'

'But I don't need to,' she said, voice full of emotion,
though she was desperately trying to control it, 'because
I'm not freaking out.'

'A logical reaction to your news.'

'Hmm.'

'Not freaking out. Who would freak out, finding out
they were going to have two children when they were expecting one?' He sat down beside her. 'I'm going to be honest with you: you don't have to worry about being a bad
mother. There's no way.'

He wanted to reach out and take her hand, but it felt too
intimate. Then he did it anyway, because his gut told him
to and he wasn't going to think about where that gut feeling was coming from.

'It's okay to feel jolted by this. I think anyone would. But
your reaction now doesn't mean you'll be a bad mother.'

'I didn't think…' She broke off. Looked at him. 'I did.'

He smiled. 'I know. But you're strong-minded. Kind
when it counts. Resilient. You'll get through having two.'

'You sound sure about that.'

'I am. You've built a restaurant from the ground up, Alexa. It's successful because of you. Surely raising two kids can't be much harder.'

He winked at her, and she smiled despite the emotion running wild over her face. Then it disappeared.

'What did I say?'

'Nothing. You were doing a perfectly adequate job of comforting me.'

He chuckled. 'As long as it was adequate.'

'Thank you.'

She squeezed his hand. Then, without warning, she leaned forward and kissed him. It was over before he could react, the only evidence it had happened the tingling at his lips.

She stood. 'You can't see that I'm pregnant, can you? I mean, I know *you* can, but as someone who didn't know?'

He opened his mouth. Closed it. Lowered his eyes because what else could he do? He tried to focus on her question. What had she asked him? Oh, yes, her clothes.

She was wearing… He didn't quite know what. It was a brightly coloured piece of material that was draped over her front from left to right. It did wonders for her cleavage, and he had to wrench his gaze away to answer her question. The material hung loosely over her stomach, and, paired with her tights and trainers, made her look both chic and comfortable. And not pregnant.

'You can't tell. It's loose enough that if I didn't know you were pregnant, I'd think…'

He broke off, but it was too late.

'You'd think what?'

He shook his head.

'You'd better say it, Foster.'

He shook his head again, this time more vehemently.

'You're saying that if people didn't know I was pregnant they'd think I was putting on weight?'

'I did *not* say that.'

'Only because you thought better of it.'

But her chest was shaking, and soon, sound joined.

'You think this is funny?' he asked.

'*You're* funny.'

'Wow. Thanks.'

She shrugged. Patted him on the shoulder. 'I appreciate that you wanted to preserve my feelings. But honestly, I don't care what people think of my body. As long as I feel good and everything works like it's supposed to, weight isn't important to me.'

He opened his mouth, then closed it when he realised he had nothing to add to that. It was a healthy way to think of the body, and, because he knew how prevalent weight-watching was in their culture, very enlightened.

'Yeah,' he said. 'You don't have to worry about being a mother, Alexa. You'll do fine.'

Her surprised look made the compliment well worth it.

CHAPTER ELEVEN

HE'D BEEN COOKING his entire life. It started because he wanted to be exactly like his father when he was younger. It continued because he wanted to make his parents' lives easier after his mother's diagnosis. She couldn't work at his father's business for periods of time, and during those periods his father had been overwhelmed at work. At least until he realised a temp could solve his problems. In any case, Benjamin had taken the opportunity before his father had realised that to make himself useful in the kitchen at home.

He hadn't known much at that point, and dinner had often been some form of a sandwich. Then he'd moved on to pasta, which had seemed doable for a boy under ten. He began to study his father more seriously, helping with the harder tasks. By the time he was a teenager, he could fry a steak with the best of them. Soon after, he was adding sauces and presenting meals he saw on the cooking shows he'd come to love. When he had to decide what he wanted to do with his life, it seemed natural to go into professional cooking.

Except he didn't get into culinary school the first year. Or the second, or third. Competition was steep, and he had nothing to give him an edge. He spent the years he wasn't cooking getting a degree in financial management, thinking he could at least help his father out if he couldn't have his dream. When he graduated, he'd pretty much given up on the Institute. Until his parents sat him down and told him he deserved to give it one more try if it truly was what he wanted to do with his life.

He spent the two years after that in kitchens of different restaurants, wherever would have him. Sometimes he got work as a kitchen assistant; sometimes he washed the dishes. But he always, always tried to learn from those in charge. And eventually, the fourth time he applied, he got into the Institute.

And not once in all that time, and during all those experiences, had he thought baking was for him.

Today proved that.

'I didn't realise the course was going to be about decorating,' he said casually.

Cherise was beside him, putting buttercream into several separate bowls so she could colour them for her rainbow cake.

'Yeah,' she said, 'I thought it would be fun. And, since it's the Institute's only short course, it worked.' She looked at him. 'Are you having trouble?'

'Not at all.'

He'd already coloured his buttercream, which he knew would be the easiest part of his day. He hadn't done anything more than that because it would have entailed showing his weaknesses, and he preferred not to parade those if he could help it.

Cherise smiled. 'This isn't a test to see whether you can decorate a cake. I'm aware you probably don't need those skills at the restaurant.'

He took a beat, then realised it was best to be honest. 'It's not that I don't need the skills. It's that I don't have them, no matter how hard I try.'

Her smile widened. 'Well, then, today should be fun for you.'

'Not sure that's the word I'd use.'

She laughed and her focus went back to her cake. He sighed and did the same with his. But not before he sneaked a look at Alexa, who stood on the other side of Cherise. She was already on the second layer of her cake, and looked as comfortable with the task as she did with any other. It was part of the problem he'd had with her when they were studying together. Nothing seemed to faze her. No task, no matter how ridiculous, pulled the rug out from under her.

Back then, he hadn't appreciated how easily she found everything. It had simply seemed unfair that she would have skill with everything in the kitchen. Now, at least, he could admire that skill. Except he saw that Cherise was admiring it, too.

It frustrated him, almost as much as it had in the past— except now feelings were creeping in.

He tried to tell himself he was just a sucker who couldn't resist someone who needed his help. It was clear Alexa did, even if she didn't think so. And he could easily be like her brother, using his vulnerabilities, his desires, to get what she wanted.

A voice in his head told him he had it all wrong. He didn't listen, instead focusing on getting his cake decorated as best he could. It took much more concentration and precision than he would have liked, but when he was done, he was proud of what he'd created.

'Nice job,' Cherise commented.

'Thanks.' He wiped his forehead with an arm. 'It was hard work.'

She laughed. 'Worth it though, don't you think, Alexa?'

Alexa peered past Cherise, appraising his cake before looking at him. 'It looks good.'

That's it. That's all she said. There was no judgement, no praise. Just an honest statement and yet somehow, it made him mad. He was sure she'd decorated her cake with a fraction of the effort he had put into his own. And now she had the cheek to tell him his looked good?

He wasn't being logical. A part of him recognised it. But he leaned into the irrationality of his thoughts, letting it fuel him for the rest of the day. He worked through lunch, though he knew it was silly, considering he was there to get to know Cherise. As far as he could tell, though, it seemed as if Cherise was more interested in chatting with him during their working sessions. Alexa was oddly quiet, though when he glanced out of the window during lunch, he saw her and Cherise laughing about something.

He gritted his teeth, did what he had to do, and at the earliest moment he could he walked out of the doors. Seconds later, footsteps followed him.

'Hey,' Alexa said. 'Wait up.'

He kept walking.

'Benjamin,' she said, her voice exasperated. 'I'm pregnant. There are two people growing inside me. Please don't make me run after you.'

That forced him to slow down, but he didn't stop. He was afraid of what would happen if he stopped. He was well aware he was in a mood. He also knew his mood was tied up in her, in both good and bad ways, except he couldn't discern between the two at the moment. It didn't bode well for their conversation. So when she caught up with him, he decided to stay quiet.

'Cherise wanted to know what's wrong with you.' Alexa rubbed her stomach. 'She asked me like she expected me to know. But I didn't know, and I had to pretend to, because we're together and when you're in a mood, apparently, I need to be able to explain that.'

'What did you say?' he couldn't help but ask.

'That you're competitive. And a perfectionist. When you put the two together, it can be a damning combination.'

'So you bad-mouthed me.'

'Not entirely,' she said easily, ignoring his bad temper. 'I also said it makes you a hell of an entrepreneur. You want to give your patrons the best. It makes you serious, disagreeable perhaps, but it also makes you one of the best people she could work for.'

He took several moments to reply. Even then, he could only manage a, 'Why?'

'Because it's true.' She shrugged. 'Because I don't blame you for a being a good chef and leader.'

He narrowed his eyes. 'Sounds like you're implying something.'

'Why would I?' she asked sarcastically. 'It's not like I gave you a compliment, spoke highly and fairly about you to a potential employee, and you're choosing to focus on the negative in all that.'

All fair points and, consistent with his mood, that annoyed him. He bit down on his tongue. After a few seconds, she sighed.

'Look, I get that you're in competition mode, or whatever, but I'm not going to keep defending you for acting boorish. If you want Cherise to get to know you, you should show her who you are. Unless, of course, you *are* boorish, and the man who was kind to me this morning and this entire time actually doesn't exist.'

She sounded tired, defeated, and his heart turned. But he couldn't tell her that he was going through something. How could he? He didn't understand it himself. It had to do with her, and with him not trusting himself around her, and that sounded like…like admitting that he was still the same fool who had let the people in his past take advantage of him.

'Yeah, I thought I might have been fooling myself,' she said softly. She closed her eyes before he could see any emotion. When she opened them again, they were unreadable. 'Cherise asked if we'd be interested in having a drink with her after work. I said yes, but now I'm not so sure.'

She turned on her heel. It took him a beat before he could move after her.

'You're not going to go?'

'No, I'm going.' She didn't stop walking when he fell into step beside her. 'I'm just not speaking for you. If you want to go, you can tell her yourself.'

It took him all of the way back to Cherise to decide that he would be going, too. In the mood he was in, heaven had better help him.

'You're not drinking?'

'Oh. Um…no.' Alexa had prepared for this in the car. But there was something about actually being asked about her pregnancy, even indirectly, that made her freeze up. Probably the fact that she had to lie. 'I'm driving.'

'One drink wouldn't hurt,' Cherise said kindly.

There was nothing Alexa wanted less than kindness at that moment.

'She's a lightweight,' Benjamin cut in. 'One drink and she's about as tipsy as I am after four. So, to answer your question—one drink *would* hurt.'

If she went by Benjamin's tone, it wasn't kindness that inspired his words. But it wasn't malice either, and he was saving her from having to think about a more intricate lie. She gave him a half-smile in thanks, but looked away before she could see whether he smiled back. He was acting weird, and she didn't want to be hurt by whatever mood he was in.

Because you're already hurt.

No, she told the inner voice. She wasn't hurt by Benjamin's attitude. So what if he was acting like the old Benjamin? The one who was reluctant and competitive and reminded her more of her brother than of the person she was beginning to think of as more than an acquaintance?

If anything, the problem was that she had begun to think of him in a friendly manner. He wasn't her friend— she wouldn't make that mistake—but she'd confided in him and kissed him. No wonder she was feeling a little out of sorts now that he was acting like someone she hadn't confided in or kissed. She should have anticipated it, and she hadn't, and that was partly why she was feeling this way.

Benjamin had always been so competitive in class. She hadn't known him before, so she'd assumed he was just a competitive person. Working with her brother, stealing her head chef... Those things seemed to prove it. Then he'd pretended to be her boyfriend in front of Lee. She'd seen him with his mother, he'd offered to give her Cherise... Those things didn't seem like a person who was inherently competitive, but simply someone who liked competition.

There was nothing wrong with that. Hell, she was even willing to be in the competition with him. But that was before today had happened. Before she'd seen him watching her as she worked and she could all but feel the frustration radiating off him. He glanced at her so many times that she knew he was comparing. It was common sense as much as it was experience; she'd spent her entire childhood knowing what that comparison looked like. Lee had done it to her. And she had no desire, none, to be a basis of comparison again.

That was what this empty feeling in her chest was. Annoyance that Benjamin saw her as someone to beat. Someone to be better than. She didn't think better or worse had anything to do with Cherise's choice; it would be the person Cherise got along with best. Except it was clear Benjamin didn't see it that way. So she was annoyed. Maybe a little disappointed. But that was it.

'He's right,' she said with a quick smile. 'I've never been able to hold my alcohol well.'

'Fortunately we don't have that in common,' Cherise said, lifting the glass the bartender set in front of her. She downed it, hissing as she slammed the glass back on the counter. 'I can drink with the best of them.' She grinned. 'I probably shouldn't tell potential employers that.'

'Why not?' Benjamin asked. 'It's not likely we wouldn't find out.'

'I don't intend on drinking on the job. Or coming in hungover.'

'The longer you spend working with us, the higher the possibility of a fun night out. Or some kind of event.' Benjamin shrugged. 'We would have found out during the second or third drinking game of the night.'

'You play drinking games with your staff?'

Benjamin raised his glass and tilted it to her. 'We're not of the belief that there should be all work and no play.'

'That happens at Infinity, too, Alexa?'

'Oh, no,' Alexa said with a shake of her head. 'I let my employees have their fun on their own time. Making sure they have that time is more of a priority to me.'

'What about team morale?' Benjamin asked her.

'Created through good pay cheques and a healthy working environment.' She waited a beat. 'In the Rough should try it.'

'Ooh,' Cherise said with a smile. 'Harsh.'

'And probably undeserved.' Alexa smiled back, but didn't look at Benjamin.

'Probably?' he said.

She directed the smile at him, but it wasn't genuine. Nor was the teasing tone of his voice.

'You guys are really cute together,' Cherise said. 'You've never thought about one big business?'

'Oh, no,' she said at the same time Benjamin chuckled with a shake of his head.

'Why not?' Cherise asked. 'You're both skilled. Can you imagine what you could create together?'

'You're only saying this because we're both so wonderful and you'd rather not choose,' Alexa teased, trying to ease the tension that was settling in her stomach. 'If we joined forces you would be our second in command, and you're drunk on the prospect of such power.'

'Well, you're not wrong.'

They laughed. The tension unfurled. Then there was a tap on the microphone. They turned to a small stage at the opposite end of the room as a tall woman with tattoos up and down her arms cleared her throat.

'Thank you all for coming to Wild Acorn tonight.'

There were cheers from who Alexa assumed were regulars. They sat at a table in the front, all still fairly formally dressed as though they'd come straight from work. She could see that happening. The bar was down a quiet road in Somerset West near the Institute, and they'd followed Cherise to get there. There was no way they would have found it by themselves, and yet it seemed popular.

'As most of you know, tonight is karaoke night—' she paused for another round of cheers '—and for those of you who don't, I thought I'd go over the rules.'

'There are rules for karaoke?' Alexa said under her breath.

'One,' the lady continued, seemingly answering Alexa, 'you have to take this seriously. No making anyone uncomfortable with a bad rendition of some famous ballad.' There was a beat. 'Just kidding! The only rule is that you have fun. Sing from the heart, dance if you will, and the best performer tonight has their tab taken care of.'

'Nice prize,' Benjamin commented. He looked at Cherise. 'Did you bring us here thinking you could make us sing?'

His smile faded when she answered, 'Hoping to.' She looked from Benjamin to Alexa. 'Who's going to go first?'

CHAPTER TWELVE

'I FEEL LIKE I shouldn't be watching this.' He was about to reply, but Cherise's voiced cracked on a high note and he winced instead. Alexa looked at him with a wrinkled nose. 'Yeah, we definitely shouldn't be watching this.'

'It's a bar. Where are we going to go?'

'You're saying we're trapped.' She took a long sip from her drink, studying Cherise as she executed some dance moves. 'I didn't think we would see how Cherise responds in a disaster at such an early stage.'

'And she responds—' he waited for Cherise to finish moonwalking '—poorly, apparently.'

Alexa gave a laugh. It wasn't the first time she'd done it that evening, but it sounded like her first genuine one. He couldn't be critical of it, of her, when he knew he was the reason she wasn't enjoying herself. And he felt terrible because of it.

With each sip of alcohol, he'd gained clarity. By the end of his second glass, he'd realised he was conflating his insecurities about trusting himself with his insecurities about trusting Alexa. He didn't know if she was fooling him; he didn't know if he could trust his gut when it told him she wasn't. His third glass told him he had been a jerk today, trying to figure it out. He started ordering water instead of alcohol, and was now wondering what the best way was to apologise.

'Look, Alexa—'

'Your turn!' she exclaimed, cutting him off.

He narrowed his eyes. 'I didn't say I was going to go up there.'

'You didn't say you weren't either.' She lifted a shoulder. 'I'm not the one asking you to go on stage.'

She tilted her head, gesturing to Cherise, who was eagerly waving at them.

'That wave could be for you, too.'

'It could,' she acknowledged, 'but since you're volunteering...'

'I'm not—'

In a movement quicker than he could have defended himself against, she stuck a hand underneath his arm and poked his armpit. Hard. The result was both surprise and amusement—he'd always been ticklish there. It was also a hand which popped into the sky, making it seem as though he were volunteering.

'Clever.' He stood, walked until he was so close to her he could smell the mint on her breath from her virgin mojito. 'But I'm clever, too.'

She tilted her head up, her eyes cool. 'Not everything is a competition.'

'No, it's not.' He lowered slightly, bringing their faces close. 'This isn't me competing. It's getting revenge.'

'Revenge?'

'You're going to do this with me.'

She smiled. It was mocking and unconcerned and—though he had no idea how or why—incredibly sexy.

'Oh, no, Benjamin, I will not be doing this with you.'

'Except—' he lifted a hand and tucked a stray curl behind her ear '—you are. Otherwise this would seem like a seduction to anyone looking.'

She pressed up on her toes, bringing their faces closer. 'Isn't it?'

'No.' It was though. And somehow he was being seduced, too. 'It's a request to do a duet.'

'I'm not doing a duet.'

'Not even for your fake boyfriend?'

Her lips parted. He brushed a thumb over it. When hot air touched his skin, he inhaled sharply. Then exhaled, because it felt as though he'd inhaled a copious amount of desire for her, too. His brain scrambled trying to remember what he'd intended when he stood up. To make it seem as if he was asking her to join him? To touch her and remind himself that she was the person she seemed to be, independent and not manipulative and certainly not who his fears made her out to be?

She took his hand, pulled it away from her face. 'This isn't going to happen.' The statement was ambiguous enough that it made him wonder what she was talking about until she clarified. 'I'm not making a fool of myself up there.'

He swallowed. Right. Of course she was talking about the singing and not...whatever had just happened.

'It'll be fun.'

'How?'

'We'll sing together. We'll both sing poorly together, I mean.'

'Yet another reason not to do it.'

'We're not auditioning for a singing competition,' he said, frustrated now. 'We're only singing.'

'No, I meant that if you sing badly, I refuse to sing with you.' She stood, emptying her glass as she did. 'I will not let my perfect soprano be tarnished by you.'

He couldn't even argue with that since he'd said he sang poorly. Then he realised she was moving to the stage, and he blinked. Why had she been arguing with him if she intended on singing? Was he really that awful that she didn't want to be on stage with him?

Yes, probably, he thought, sitting back down and offering Cherise a weak smile when she joined him. He'd been terrible to Alexa all day—save for that morning. But that morning had felt as though they were in a bubble, and once things had got real, the bubble had popped and he…

He'd fallen hard to the ground while Alexa somehow stayed afloat, looking down at him in pity. Disappointment. Could he even blame her?

'I thought you were going to go up with her.'

'Me, too.'

'Your seduction didn't work?' Cherise gave him a sly grin. He smiled back weakly.

'Apparently not. I'm going to have to work on it.'

'Probably,' she said, bringing her beer to her lips. 'She doesn't seem like the type of person to fall for the usual stuff. She's tougher, but that kind of makes it mean more, in my opinion.'

He thought about it as he turned to the stage, watching as Alexa waited for the music to play. A couple of guys in the front were eyeing her in appreciation, and he had the absurd urge to get up and shield her from their view. But that made no sense, the desire less so, and instead he kept looking at Alexa.

She looked comfortable there, her clothing still strange, still chic. She'd tied her hair up again, but it was higher than it had been in the morning, piled onto the top of her head as if she'd put it there and forgotten about it. The waves refused to be tamed that way, though, and they fell over her forehead, created the shortest and strangest fringe he'd ever seen. It was also the cutest. Hell, she was cute. And sexy, and enticing, and he was pretty sure he had a problem.

Then she started to sing and he stopped thinking about that altogether.

Her voice was smooth and clear. Perfectly pitched on the higher notes; soulfully deep on the lower notes. She swayed in time to the beat, slowly, smiling when the lyrics were saucy or snarky.

'You've got to be kidding me,' Cherise said somewhere halfway into the song. 'She sings like it's what she does for a living.'

He agreed, but he was too enamoured to respond. He couldn't take his eyes off her, his ears thanked him profusely, and his mind was incredibly glad he hadn't spoiled this with his own voice, which was comparable to a cat's on a good day. When she was done, the entire room exploded with applause. Everyone was looking at her in appreciation now. She smiled brightly, happily, and he couldn't quite believe she was the same woman who could skin him and lay the spoils on the floor as she walked over them.

Damn if that brightness, that happiness didn't draw him in as much as her sharp wit.

'Stop looking at me like that,' Alexa said as soon as Cherise got into the taxi she'd called. Cherise was having her brother use her spare key to pick up her car, since she wasn't in any condition to drive. 'It's unnerving.'

'I just… I can't believe you've been hiding that voice away.'

'I wasn't hiding it away.' She hoped to heaven her skin wasn't glowing at the compliment the way her stupid heart was. 'It's never come up. Why would I bring it up?'

'Because it sounded like *that*?' He gestured with a thumb to the bar behind them. 'I'm still trying to figure out how you managed to do that.'

'Easy. I opened my mouth, and instead of speaking, I sang.'

'Like an angel.' She laughed. 'I'm not even mad you're being snarky,' he said, his voice filled with wonder. 'You should be singing.'

'Do you know,' she said after a moment, 'I'm really good at maths? I scored in the top five per cent of the province in my final year of school. I had a couple of bursaries to study maths that were generous.'

She didn't mention that her parents had applied for all those bursaries. They'd been so disappointed when she'd chosen not to take any of them that they hadn't even cared that she'd chosen business management instead. Well, they had cared. If they hadn't, she would have gone to culinary school from the beginning.

'Congratulations?' Benjamin's voice interrupted her thoughts.

She laughed. 'My point is that just because I'm good at something doesn't mean I want to do it for a living. I love what I do. I love the challenge of running a restaurant. I love working with my chefs to make efficient meals that are delicious and new and...' She broke off, feeling heat spread over her cheeks. 'Anyway. I won't be leaving to sing any time soon.'

'A pity,' he said with a small smile. 'But I suppose, since you're good at running a business, too, the world isn't completely missing out on your talents.'

Somehow, it didn't feel like a compliment.

'I should get going. The ride back home is long.'

'Yeah.'

But he didn't let her pass him, and, since he was standing in front of her, she kind of needed him to.

'Benjamin—'

'Is there anything you aren't good at?'

And there it was.

There isn't one thing you're bad at. Nothing. You do everything well. It's annoying.

Exhausting, too, she'd wanted to tell her brother. She wouldn't call it lucky that she was good at the things her parents thought she should be good at. It was half luck, half hard work, and all exhaustion. Her parents had come to expect her to be good at everything, so she didn't think she could fail. If she did, they would care for her even less than they already did. As a kid, she couldn't bear the thought of it.

That was the one thing she wasn't good at: accepting that her family wasn't what she wanted them to be. She tried and tried to make her parents proud, but nothing she did would ever be enough. She had tried with Lee, too, because he was the only one who would understand how their parents' pressure could become unbearable. But he'd had no interest. For every outreached hand was a slap in the form of a record she'd set that he'd broken, or a mark of hers that he'd beaten. When he'd bought the building out from under her she'd finally decided to stop reaching out her hand, and hoped it would mean no more slapping.

Except it still came. And apparently through proxies now, too.

'I should really get home.'

She moved past him but he caught her wrist. She looked at him.

'You're not going to answer?'

'What would you like me to say?' She was proud of the stiffness in her voice. It meant the thickness in her throat hadn't tainted her speaking. 'Yes, I'm good at everything. Except making rational decisions, like when I pretended you were my boyfriend. If I hadn't, we wouldn't be in this position. I wouldn't be in this position.'

He frowned, and let go of her arm. 'I'm sorry. I didn't mean to…' He exhaled. 'I'm sorry,' he said again.

'Okay.' She swallowed. 'Now can I leave?'

CHAPTER THIRTEEN

HE WANTED TO say sorry. For acting like a jerk the day before; for making those assumptions the night before. He arrived at the Institute early in the hope of finding a moment to talk with her again before the course started. No such luck. Which wasn't a problem—until the start of the class came and both Alexa and Cherise weren't there. Cherise rushed in ten minutes late, looking like hell.

'Sorry,' she muttered. 'My car broke down on the way. And I probably drank too much last night, made a fool of myself, and I promise you it won't happen again.'

'Sorry to hear about the car,' he said. 'About last night... You don't have to apologise. You're not working for us yet.'

'But I would like to, and I seem to have handed you reasons not to hire me.'

He smiled. 'It's nice to know you actually want this.'

'I really do.' She smiled, but it faded almost immediately. 'Although I think I spoilt my chances with Alexa. I'm pretty sure I'm the reason she's sick.'

'She's sick?'

'Yeah.' She gave him a strange look. 'She didn't tell you?'

'No.' When he realised why she was so surprised, he cleared his throat. 'We're supposed to have a date after this today. I think maybe she didn't want to tell me in case I cancelled.'

'Oh, that's so sweet,' Cherise said. 'You guys are cute.'

'Thanks.'

They fell into silence as the instructor began to guide them in a brand-new decorating nightmare. He couldn't really focus. He was too busy thinking about Alexa. He stumbled his way through the class, but that was pretty usual for him. He did notice that Cherise's hangover, and the rough morning she'd had, hadn't affected her concentration. She did the work perfectly, patiently, without one mistake. Which told him she wouldn't bring personal problems into the workplace. He was almost thankful for the night they'd had before.

She seemed forgiving of his lack of decorating skills, and by the end of it he knew their one-on-one time had done wonders for their professional working relationship. He even suspected that he might have had an edge over Alexa. It made him feel guilty. Not that he had any reason to feel guilty. He hadn't orchestrated her sickness, had he? He hadn't done anything so that he could spend time with Cherise while Alexa stayed home, sick, probably unable to breathe, her nose blocked, chest phlegmy…

He grunted, got into his car, and started it. Then he grunted again, because he already knew where he was going to, even before he started driving to the pharmacy. When he got there, he started grabbing things that usually helped him when he was feeling under the weather. He walked past an aisle, paused, looked down it. Saw a bunch of pregnancy and maternity things. Vitamins, baby bottles. He looked at the things in his hands. She probably couldn't use any of this, being pregnant. He went back to the pharmacist, and got fewer things. Bought ingredients to make some good chicken soup. Some fresh bread, too.

None of that made it easier when he was finally in front of her door. He felt as though he was intruding on her space. She obviously didn't want him to know she was sick, or she would have told him. Now he was pitching up at her door, assuming that she wanted to see him? Especially after how he'd treated her the day before?

He took a deep breath and was brutally honest with himself. He'd told himself guilt was the reason he was there. Maybe it was, but not only because he got to spend time with Cherise when Alexa couldn't. No, it was redemption. For how he had treated her the day before. To ease his conscience, or to make it up to her, he didn't know. Either way, he was there, and he was going to make sure she knew he wasn't all bad.

He knocked on the door. Again when he heard nothing inside. A long while later, he heard some shuffling. Then the door opened. He almost dropped everything in his hands.

'You're, um…you're…' He cleared his throat. He couldn't…point out what the problem was without telling her that he had looked at her chest. But not pointing it out meant he studiously had to avoid looking down. He gritted his teeth, then thought it might look intimidating and offered her a smile. 'You're okay,' he finished lamely.

She folded her arms. Doing so should have covered the flesh spilling out of the top of the loose nightgown she wore. Instead, because of the sheer generosity of her breasts, the movement pushed them together instead.

'What are you doing here?'

'I heard you're sick.'

'Yes.'

He frowned. 'I was sorry to hear that.'

'Thank you.'

He gestured to the bags in his hands. 'Do you think I could come in?'

'Why?'

'I…' Was he really this bad at showing he cared about something? 'I thought I'd make you some soup.'

She studied him, expression unreadable, though there were dark rings around her eyes. Seconds later, as if she knew he'd seen it, she sagged against the doorframe. 'It's a bad bout of nausea. I thought because things weren't so bad in my first trimester—' She shrugged. 'Apparently my babies hate me.'

'They don't hate you,' he said automatically.

'I appreciate that.' She exhaled slowly. 'You can come in. But you can't cook anything. I'm pretty sure I'd throw up if you did.' She cast a look at him. 'That's not a reflection on your cooking or anything.'

'Thanks,' he said dryly.

He followed her inside, closing the door behind him. He wasn't sure what to do now that his grand plan wouldn't work. Plus, seeing her like this was a distraction. She'd gone back to the sofa, curled up and closed her eyes, as if he weren't in her space. And he shouldn't have been.

There wasn't much he could do about morning sickness. With a cold or flu he could ply her with medication, encourage her to sleep. But constant nausea? Enough that she couldn't come in to work? What was he supposed to do about that?

Since she wasn't looking, he asked the internet that question. Then he wandered into her kitchen, set down the things he'd bought, and looked in her cupboards. They were meticulously packed. He couldn't see what order they were in, but they were definitely in order. Same with the fridge. He tried not to disturb anything as he looked for what the internet suggested. Minutes later, he walked into the kitchen, set the tea on the coffee table and crouched down in front of her.

'Alexa?' She opened one eye. Somehow, she managed a glare with it. He resisted his smile. 'Have you eaten anything today?'

'Some toast this morning.'

'This morning?'

'I haven't really had the energy for much.'

'Okay.' He frowned. 'Well, the internet said something bland would do you good.'

'Sounds amazing.'

He chuckled softly. 'How about some brown rice? Plain avocado? Or toast with peanut butter and banana? Broth?'

Her other eye opened. 'Sounds like you're trying to get nutrients into me.'

'They said it would be best if what you ate had nutrients in it.'

'They?'

He scratched the back of his head when his skin began to prickle with heat. 'The internet.'

'You went on the internet for this?'

'Did any of what I offered sound appealing to you?' he asked instead of answering.

'The toast,' she replied after a moment. 'It's not the most appealing, but it's the easiest option, which we'll both be grateful for if I end up throwing it up.'

He appreciated her logic, but he would actually feel better if he could put some more effort into whatever he made her. To assuage the guilt, he told himself. For redemption, he added. Not because he cared enough to put more effort into it.

'On it. Also, I made you some ginger tea.'

'Did the internet tell you to do that?' She was teasing him, giving him a small smile to show it.

He offered her a hand. 'If you want me to help you sit up, you won't get the answer to that.'

'It would almost be worth it.'

But she took his hand and he helped her up. Her colour didn't look good, but that made sense since she was nauseous and hadn't eaten since the morning. He handed her the tea. Her fingers brushed his as she did, and for some bizarre reason a shiver went through him. Bizarre, because things were weird with them, and she was sick, and the only reason he was in her flat was because he felt guilty. He shouldn't feel attraction in this moment—or whatever it was that caused that shiver. It also had nothing to do with her cleavage, impressive and visible as it was. It was simply her, and how much she intrigued and confused him.

He exhaled, leaving her to the tea as he went to make her toast. It was quick work. When he handed it to her, he thought he'd head back to the kitchen, start making a broth even though she didn't seem to want it. But she said, 'Wait.'

He turned. 'Yeah?'

'You didn't make yourself anything?'

His mouth curved. 'Did I make myself some peanut butter and banana toast as well? No. Surprisingly.'

'No need to be smug about your ability to eat something other than this.' But her eyes were warm. 'Thank you.'

'You don't have to thank me.'

'Why not?'

She tore a small piece off the toast and put it into her mouth, looking at him expectantly.

'Oh…er… It wasn't a big deal.'

She chewed and finished. Swallowed. 'It is to me.'

There was a brief moment where they stared at one another before he realised he'd better look away if he wanted to keep his sanity. Although deep down he knew it wasn't his sanity he was worried about.

'Will you sit down?' she asked, looking down now, too.

'Do you want me to?'

'I wouldn't have asked if I didn't want you to.'

'Good point.' He smiled at the dry tone. 'I'll just grab myself something to drink.'

'Yeah, of course. Anything in the fridge is yours.'

He went to the kitchen, got himself a sparkling water, and went back to the lounge. It didn't even occur to him to dawdle, or delay long enough that she would be done with her meal. The opposite, in fact. He wanted to sit with her, talk to her, and he didn't know what it meant.

Or he did, but he preferred not to think about it.

When he got back, he saw her toast looked the same as it had when he left.

'Feel sick?'

'Not at the moment. I'm waiting to see how my stomach's going to react to it.' She took a slice of banana off the toast and ate it. 'It seems cruel to me that someone who enjoys food as much as I do can't eat it.'

'But it hasn't been like this your entire pregnancy, you said?'

'No, it hasn't. I have been nauseous, but it's been pretty consistently in the mornings before work and the evenings after. I thought I was lucky.' She groaned. 'Turns out my body was lulling me into a false sense of security.'

'How has today been different?'

'You mean apart from the waves of nausea all day?' She tore off another piece of toast, but didn't eat it. Instead, she patted the seat next to her. He didn't even hesitate. Just obeyed. 'I've been throwing up more, though that seems consistent with being nauseous more, doesn't it? I've also been a little dizzier, but that could be because I haven't been eating.'

'You should have been.'

'I know,' she agreed, easily enough that he knew she wasn't feeling herself. 'But it seemed like a lot of energy to go to the kitchen and get something to eat when I could lie here.'

He studied her. Took a long drink of his water to make sure he really wanted to say what he thought he wanted to say. Sighed.

'Look, you can argue with me when you have energy for it later, okay?'

Her eyebrows rose. 'A promising start to a conversation.'

'It's concern.' He paused. 'You have to look after yourself, Alexa. That's how you're looking after your babies right now. By looking after yourself.'

Her hand went to her belly, before she brought it back to the toast. She put a piece in her mouth, then opened her palm as if to agree with him. Something in the gesture made her seem so vulnerable, he wanted to pull her into his arms and comfort her. Hell, there was a part of him that wanted to do that regardless of the vulnerability.

He settled for edging closer to her.

She deserved to have people to care about her. She deserved that she care about herself, which he thought she might struggle with. He had no proof, and he wouldn't dare ask, since he was already pushing his luck with their current conversation. But something about Alexa made him think that she put others ahead of herself. Even with her pregnancy. She was trying so hard to make things with Cherise work. Not for herself, he thought, but for her restaurant.

Part of that was because Lee had taught her she couldn't let her guard down. And yes, when he'd offered Victor Fourie that job, he'd shown her that, too. Now she was terrified of going on leave because she thought it would put all she'd worked for in jeopardy.

Someone who'd grown up as she had would hate that idea. They'd hate that it might result in failure, too. He couldn't imagine how much that would mess with someone's mind. He could, however, see that he'd contributed to her fears. That his question the night before, about her being good at everything, would add to that pressure. Which would explain how tense she'd got.

He would apologise for it. Not now. Now he had a different mission.

'You're going to have to take care of yourself when they're here, too,' he said quietly. 'It's the most important thing, your health. Not only because they need you to be healthy to take care of them.'

'What else is there?'

'Your happiness. It's going to be important to them.

They'll want to see you living your life as you would have even if they weren't there. That means taking care of yourself, making sure you're as important in your life as they are.'

'You speak as if you know.'

'I...do.'

It felt a little like a betrayal, admitting that. But if he had to betray his mother—just a little—to make Alexa see she was as important as her children, then so be it. Hell, he reckoned his mother might even agree. She'd called him two days after that dinner with Alexa and told him she liked his new girlfriend.

'The baby situation is complicated,' Nina had said, 'but I can see why you couldn't move on without giving things with her a try. She's refreshing.'

'You're good at it,' Alexa said, piercing through the haze of memories.

'What?'

'Caring for people.'

The words hit him in the gut. 'I've had a lot of practice.'

'With your mom? Inference,' she said when he looked at her.

'I wouldn't say I took care of her.'

'I didn't say that you did. Only that you cared for her.'

He almost laughed at how she'd caught him out. He didn't because it wasn't funny.

'She needed a lot of support with the fibromyalgia.'

'Support can sometimes mean caring for them.'

'That's not what happened with my mom,' he said tersely.

'It was a compliment, Benjamin.' Her expression was a combination of bewilderment, kindness, and...hurt? Had he hurt her? But then she clarified. 'Speaking as someone who didn't have it all that much in her life, it's certainly a compliment.'

'I'm sorry.' He stared at the bottle in his hand. 'I seem to be apologising a lot to you these days.'

She shrugged. 'It's because I rub you up the wrong way. What?' she asked with a little laugh. 'You don't think I noticed? It's kind of hard not to.'

'To be fair, I think the reverse applies, too, and yet you don't seem to apologise nearly as often as I do.'

'I'm more irreverent.' She gave him a half-smile. 'I'm definitely less in touch with my emotions. I find them—' she wrinkled her nose '—inconvenient.'

He laughed, and some of the tension in his stomach dissipated. 'I'm not much more in touch with my emotions. They're inconvenient as hell, and it's easier to ignore them.'

'The apologies tell me you don't do the easier thing,' she pointed out. 'You might not be able to deal with them very well, but you feel them. It's more than I can say for myself.'

'And why's that?'

She heaved out a sigh. 'I don't know. No, no, I do,' she interrupted herself. 'Honestly, it's just... I guess ignoring them is what I'm used to. If I had felt every little thing when I was a kid, I wouldn't function nearly as well as I do today.'

She began to eat again, slowly, and he waited until she was done to ask the questions tumbling into his head. When she was done, she set down the remaining toast on the table. Then she moved closer to him. His heart thudded, but she didn't do anything else. Not one more thing, even though his body felt as if it was bracing for impact.

'Do you want to talk about it?' he asked hoarsely.

'I don't think so.' Her expression was uncertain when she met his eyes. 'Is that okay?'

'Of course. We don't have to talk about anything you don't want to.'

'I will, someday. It seems like a lot of effort to think about it now.'

She rested her head on his shoulder. He froze—but not

for long. Slowly, so he wouldn't spook her, he lifted his arm. She immediately snuggled into his chest.

It was a good thing he was sitting, or the way his knees had gone weak would have taken him to the ground.

'Tell me what your day was like?' she asked. 'Was Cherise as hungover as she should have been after last night?'

Somehow, he managed to laugh. But as he told her about his day, it felt more natural, them sitting like this, talking. He was honest about how things had gone with Cherise, and she didn't seem upset about it. She asked him questions, laughed at his description of how terribly he'd done. He kept talking when she shifted onto her side, curling into much the same position he'd found her in. Except now she was curled into his side, then lying with her head on his lap. When she faltered he lowered his voice but kept talking, since it seemed to soothe her.

She was fast asleep shortly after, but he didn't get up as he should have. He stroked her hair, which was messy and somehow beautiful. He brushed her skin, bronze and smooth. He sat there, her warmth comforting something inside him. Much too long later, he took the dishes to the kitchen and began making her something to eat for when she got up. When he was done with that, he let himself out, but not without one last look in her direction.

She looked so peaceful, lying under the blanket he'd covered her with. His heart did something in his chest. Lurched, turned over, filled—he wasn't sure of the description. He only knew that seeing her, speaking her with her, caring for her…

It had changed him. Something had changed between them, too. He wondered if she would acknowledge it. He wondered if he would.

CHAPTER FOURTEEN

SHE WAS FEELING better the next day. She hadn't thrown up the toast Benjamin made her, and she'd slept through the entire night. It didn't seem normal to feel better when the day before she'd basically been knocked out. She supposed that was pregnancy. Or she hoped it was. If it wasn't, everyone in class, including her, was going to get more than they'd bargained for.

She had a nice long shower, got dressed, and went to the kitchen. Everything was in its place; it was as if Benjamin hadn't been there. And maybe he hadn't been. It seemed consistent with the state she'd been in the day before. Maybe she'd conjured him up, and he hadn't been sweet and patient and caring. He hadn't made her laugh, held her, stayed with her until she'd fallen asleep.

Except when she opened her fridge she found a glass container with clear broth in it and a sticky note—she had no idea where he'd found one.

In case you're feeling up to it. B.

B. B was definitely Benjamin. She couldn't deny that he'd been there any more. Him leaving food for her meant she hadn't imagined he was sweet and patient and caring either. And if that was true, she had to believe that he'd made her laugh, held her, stayed with her as she'd fallen asleep. And he'd cooked. For her.

She took a long, deep breath as she removed the broth from the fridge and heated it up. But it didn't help, and she spent the entire time eating the flavourful liquid quietly sobbing. She was certain it was pregnancy hormones. Mostly. She supposed that was the problem.

But when was the last time someone in her life had checked on her when she was ill? When was the last time she'd let someone in her life do that?

Kenya would have, if Alexa let her. She had, once upon a time. When Kenya had started working at Infinity, something had clicked between them and they'd got along well. But Alexa had confined that relationship to the restaurant. She'd thought it best, easier, better for the restaurant. Now, after the entire Benjamin debacle, Alexa wondered if it was simply better for *her*. If she didn't go out with Kenya, she wouldn't risk getting hurt. Except by doing that, she'd hurt Kenya. And that, by some cruel twist of fate, had hurt her, too.

She thought about it the entire drive to the Institute. Once she got there, she made sure there wasn't a trace of her crying on her face. She had a feeling Benjamin would pounce on it if he saw it. Which turned out to be a fruitless concern anyway, since he wasn't there.

'He must have what you had,' Cherise said with a knowing look. Alexa murmured in agreement. She had no choice but to. She'd told Cherise she had a twenty-four-hour bug, which seemed like a half-truth. But she knew that what she had wasn't contagious. She also knew Benjamin well enough that she could piece together what had happened.

When he'd told her about his day the night before, he'd been excited, but restrained. That restraint had come through most strongly when he was relaying the more fun parts of the day, as if he'd felt bad. The fact that he wasn't here told her he did feel bad. It made her think the reason he was at her place last night had been because he'd felt bad, too.

She set it aside as she spent the day with Cherise. At one

point, her prospective chef pointed out something Alexa was doing poorly. Alexa thanked Cherise, adjusted, and realised that, while it had helped in some ways, it hadn't in others. So she coached Cherise through doing it her way, and Cherise was pleased with the ending.

'Maybe we can put it together and come up with a technique that could give us the best of both worlds.'

'Yeah, that would be great,' Cherise said with a bright smile.

She smiled back, and wondered if Benjamin had felt the same glow of appreciation at connecting with Cherise. Her heart skipped at the thought. Not at its content, but that she'd thought it at all. That she'd thought about him at all. It was dangerous; more so because the thoughts were accompanied by a soft, squishy feeling in her chest that she had no name for but made her feel warm and safe.

But how could she feel safe when even feeling that told her she was in danger? It was a conundrum, one she made no effort to clarify, even when she told herself to. She set it aside again, tried to focus on the day with Cherise. She felt worn at the end of it, her legs aching and her back, too, although it was much too early for her to be feeling that way. Then again, those were normal, non-pregnancy feelings after a long day. Today had seemed long, despite the fact that it was shorter than most days for her. Maybe being pregnant meant the length of what was long would change.

It didn't bode well for all she had to do before she went on maternity leave. Or should she even go on leave at all? She'd thought it would be a good idea to get to know her babies, but now it felt as if she was leaving her first baby, her restaurant, exposed. It was her responsibility to make sure it wasn't exposed. The fact that she hadn't meant that she'd…failed.

She drove home with that troubling thought racing in her mind. When she stopped, though, she didn't find herself at her home, but at In the Rough. It was the first time she'd been there since Lee had bought the building. She'd refused to go, on principle, despite her parents calling her stubborn. But the day that she'd wanted to show them her building, and they'd told Lee about it, had changed things for her. Their disappointment no longer hurt as much as it had. Or maybe it did hurt, but it didn't cripple her any more.

She still tried with them: a phone call every couple of weeks, a dinner once a month, telling them important news. But the truth was that she didn't want them in her life as much any more. Especially when they insisted on having Lee be part of the package.

Slowly, she climbed out of the car, staring up at the sign as she did. Black lettering flickered at her against the brick façade, courtesy of a faint white light outlining the letters. The front of the restaurant itself was all glass, allowing her to see the patrons laughing and enjoying themselves.

She took a breath and walked into the restaurant. She took in the dark wooden feel of the place, noted the red-haired barperson. It was a strange experience, seeing the place done, compared to the last time she'd been there. More so comparing it to the vision of what she'd had for the space. She'd executed the idea almost identically at Infinity, but she'd had to make adjustments because it didn't fit as well in her current space as it would have there.

The disappointment of it washed over her, and she took another breath, deeper this time, before she walked to the bar.

'Do you know where I can find Benjamin?'

The woman quirked her brow. 'Who are you?'

'Oh. I'm…er…'

She didn't know what Benjamin had told his people. Of course, she knew what Lee knew, but that didn't mean he'd announced it to his entire staff. If he hadn't, she didn't want to complicate things by telling his employee she was his girlfriend. But she also didn't want him to know she was there. He'd likely pull a runner, pretend he was really sick, and she couldn't tell him he was being a jerk.

'Is he here?'

'He might be.' She tilted her head. 'You look familiar.'

'I don't think so.'

'No, you do.' The woman came closer, limping slightly as she did. 'Have you been here before?'

'Definitely not.' She tried to cover it up when she realised how that sounded. 'I mean, I haven't had the chance.'

'You're missing out.'

She took a look at the full restaurant. It was barely six in the evening and already the vibe was jovial. The patrons were pretty much as she had imagined when she'd thought about the space. Benjamin had clearly turned it into *the* place though, since it was just about bouncing with energy.

She turned back to the barperson. 'Apparently so.'

'I think, considering it's you and considering you're my main competition, that's almost a compliment.'

She was rolling her eyes before she was even facing him fully.

'Hi.'

'Hi.'

She wasn't prepared for the way he leaned in to her, or the kiss he brushed on her cheek. It wasn't a sensual greeting in theory, but the heat of it seared through her body.

'You're feeling better?'

'Much.' She started to brush her hair off her forehead, but stopped. The movement would make her look nervous. She was already feeling it; she didn't have to look it. 'Thanks for leaving me that broth.'

'Was it good?'

'You know it was,' she said with a half-smile. 'Stop looking for compliments.'

'You gave me one now, I think,' he replied with a half-smile of his own. 'But I won't push you to see if you have any more.'

'Good. You might not like what you find.'

'Mia, could you have a whiskey and—' He looked at her expectantly.

'Oh. Water.'

'And a water sent to my office, please?'

'Sure.'

Mia waved them off, but not before Alexa saw the questioning look in her eyes. Alexa couldn't blame her. A random woman comes to the bar, asking about the boss without giving any reason, and moments later the boss appears and whisks said woman into his office? It looked dodgy, even to her, and *she* was the random woman.

'Please, sit,' Benjamin said when they walked into the small space of his office.

'Thanks.'

She took the seat opposite him. The space was confined, making it big enough only for his desk, two chairs, and a cabinet.

'If you get a smaller desk, have some floating shelves installed, you could create more space for yourself.'

'Why would I want to?' he asked dryly. 'I have everything I need.'

'You're right.'

Purposefully, she swung her handbag to her lap. It knocked a pile of books off his desk. She gave him a look, then bent to pick the books up and set them back where they were.

'Why would you need more space?'

'Fine, you've proved your point.'

He was chuckling when a young man, probably early twenties, knocked on the door and set their drinks in front of them.

'Anything else?' he asked, after Benjamin thanked him.

'We're good for now,' Benjamin replied, looking at her to confirm. She nodded. 'I'll call the kitchen if I need anything else.' He waited until the man left. 'You would have had a smaller desk and floating shelves, wouldn't you?'

'Yeah. I was going to do the shelves on that wall.' She pointed at one wall. 'Put the desk here.' She pointed at the opposite wall. 'I probably would have got some fancy desk, with three sections that were stacked on top of one another, so I could have options to stand and have plenty of space.' She shrugged. 'I didn't need to in the end, because my current office is huge.'

'Rub it in, won't you?' But his eyes were serious. 'You really wanted this, didn't you?'

'I was going to buy it,' she said in answer. 'I had plans for it.' She picked up her water and took a sip to quench her suddenly dry throat. 'It taught me to act first, dream later. An important lesson.'

There was a long silence. She resisted the urge to fidget during it.

'He just bought this from under you?' Benjamin asked.

'Yes.'

'Knowing you wanted it?'

'Yes.'

Another pause.

'Then he offered the space to me.'

'He's smart.'

Seconds passed.

'He was using me.'

'Weren't you using him, too?'

'I don't feel like it's the same.'

'Probably not,' she conceded. 'Don't look so sad.' Sadness wasn't quite the emotion in his expression, but she went with it because it also wasn't *not* sadness. 'It turned out well in the end.'

'Yeah, but it's still…' He offered her a small smile. 'It's

hard to wrap my head around. The man who gave me a chance did so by robbing you of something. I considered Lee to be a friend, and now I'm wondering whether I was a fool to do so.'

She thought about it. Sighed.

'This wasn't what I thought I'd be doing here, but okay.' She set her glass down. 'The Lee you know is the Lee you know. You've known him for years. You've worked with him. Have likely been through a lot with him. The way he's treated me doesn't change that.'

'It does though,' he said softly. 'He has the capacity to be cruel and—'

'Only with me,' she interrupted. 'It's part of why my parents could never understand why I had such a problem with him. They couldn't believe he was the person I was claiming he was, even though they created the environment that forced us to compete.'

'Forced…compete?' He leaned forward. 'What do you mean?'

She couldn't answer him. It would rip off the bandage that she had put over the wounds of her childhood. She'd spent her entire adult life trying to put, to keep, that bandage in place. She wouldn't remove it now because this man was asking her to.

'You, um… You don't look sick.'

He blinked. Seemingly acknowledged she didn't want to talk about it because he didn't press. Instead he leaned back in his chair.

'I am.' He gave a very fake cough.

She rolled her eyes, but smiled. 'You're obviously not. You didn't have to do that.'

'I didn't do anything.'

'Benjamin.'

He frowned. 'Fine. But I was only making sure the playing field was level.'

'Were you?' She bit her lip as she sat back. 'Was that what last night was, too? You were making sure things were level as you spent the night with me?'

'It wasn't quite spending the night,' he protested, colour lighting his cheeks.

'Of course not.' She didn't bother hiding her smile. 'But it was guilt, wasn't it? You felt guilty about getting a day with Cherise, and you came to look after me so you could tell yourself that you tried to make things better.'

'It wasn't exactly like that.'

She lifted her brows, waiting for him to tell her what it was like. He sighed impatiently.

'Maybe there was some guilt. But it was more because I wanted to apologise for being a brute the day before yesterday.'

'What was today, then?' she asked. 'Surely you made up for it last night? More than, even. You didn't have to do it.'

'It was fair.'

'It was stupid.'

'Can you just…?' He stopped, lowering his voice when the words came out loudly. 'Can you just say thank you?'

'No,' she said after a moment. 'I'm not going to thank you for feeling sorry for me.'

She stood, knocking over the books with her handbag again, this time unintentionally. With a sigh, she lowered to pick them up. Then found that she was stuck.

'Oh.'

'Oh.' He stood now, too. 'Oh, what?'

She tried with all her might to push up, but her balance was shot. It only ended up pushing her forward. She put a hand out in time to keep from knocking her head.

'Lex, are you okay? Are you in labour?'

'Of course I'm not in labour.' She scowled. 'I'm thirteen weeks pregnant. Of course I'm not in labour.'

'Okay.' He crouched down in front of her. 'Why are you not getting up, then?'

'Because—' she gritted her teeth '—I can't.'

'You can't get up?'

'Seems you need your core to stand up. Who knew?'

She could almost feel him laughing at her. She chose to ignore it. Largely because she really couldn't get up and the floor was surprisingly terrible to be on.

'Are you going to help me?'

'Yeah.' But she heard the click of a camera. Her head shot up.

'What did you do?'

'Nothing,' he said innocently, taking her under the arms and lifting her gently.

'Benjamin, if you took a photo of me struggling to get up, I swear I'll make you regret it.'

'Which is exactly why I need the photo. For protection.'

'Why do you need protection?'

'You're a voracious opponent.'

'Am I an opponent?' she asked lightly, though she didn't feel light. It had nothing to do with him taking a picture of her or getting stuck on the floor.

'I didn't mean it that way.'

'How did you mean it?'

'You're a sparring partner,' he said, shoving his hands into his jeans pockets. They were close enough that she could reach out and pull them out if she wanted to. 'We argue and debate. It's what we do.'

'Yeah, but all of that started because you saw me as an opponent *in that way*.' She lifted her head because, although it smarted, he was taller than her, and the lack of distance between them meant she had to. 'Something about me in class made you think of me as competition.'

'You were the best, Alexa.' He shrugged. 'People don't

compete against someone in the middle. They do so with the person at the top. And you were.'

Or they compete with the only person who's there, she thought, remembering all the years her parents had encouraged her and Lee to be better than those around them. Their words weren't only for her and Lee; *they* competed with those around them, too. Even with one another. It seemed to invigorate their marriage though, rather than cause the relationship to crumble. Sometimes Alexa wondered whether she was their child, since she was the only one in the family who hadn't been invigorated by competition. She was the odd one out. Lee had simply been following their parents' example.

It didn't make it right though. At least not for her.

'I should… I should go.'

'Alexa,' he said, reaching for her hand. She stilled when he threaded their fingers together. Let herself go to him when he pulled her in. 'I didn't mean to upset you.'

'I know.'

'But you're upset.'

She sighed. 'It's not you. Well, not you alone.' When he only looked at her, the heat of his hand pulsing into her body, landing at her heart, she sighed again. 'I spent my entire life being the person Lee had to beat. Not because I was the best, or at the top, but because I was there. My parents told us to be the best. We got rewarded with love or gifts if we were.' She closed her eyes. 'I don't… I don't want to live my entire life like that. That's why I cut Lee out of it. That's why I barely speak to my parents.'

She dropped her head. It found a soft landing, and she realised he'd moved closer so she could lean against his chest. As it had the night before, it comforted her.

'This entire thing with Cherise is a nightmare for me,' she whispered. 'I just want it to be over. And before you say it—no, it won't be if you step back.'

'It will.'

She looked up at him. 'No, it won't. If you don't fight fairly, I'll know. More significantly, Lee will know. And he'll stop at nothing to convince Cherise to work for In the Rough, which will put me right back in the position I was in in the first place.'

She lifted a free hand and set it on his chest. Curled her fingers.

'You'll know, too. You'll know that you sacrificed this for me. I don't want that.' She beat her fist lightly against his chest. 'I want you to think of what's best for you. Fighting for this is what's best for you,' she clarified when he frowned.

His hand lifted, curled over her fist. 'I thought you didn't want us to compete.'

'I don't. But I'm not naïve enough to believe I won't encounter competition in my life. In my business. Just...' She sighed. 'Just make it a good one so we can all move forward without this haunting us.'

For some reason, she slid an arm around his waist, rested her head against his chest again. Her other hand remained in his as if they were about to dance.

'I'll be fine without you helping me, Ben. I promise.'

CHAPTER FIFTEEN

HE WANTED TO believe her. He really did. But how many times had his mother said she was fine, only for him to find her curled up in pain somewhere? He was tired of the people he cared about hurting. And damn it, he cared about Alexa. No matter how much he tried to use guilt, or logic, or whatever other reason he'd used in the last weeks as an excuse to see her and spend time with her. He cared about her. He wanted her to be okay. Whether that meant her health, or her restaurant.

He needed her to be okay.

The urgency of it was partly from an unknown source, partly from that caring. Hell, it was partly because she was standing in his arms, looking up at him with reassurance in her eyes. Her stomach was pressed into his, and the rounding of it—not much, but enough—sent a rush of protectiveness through him.

Feeling the rest of her body against his wasn't as harmless.

She wore another loose top, but it clung to her breasts if nothing else, as if as amazed by them as he was. He hadn't been as fascinated by this part of the body since he was a teenager discovering his sexuality. His conclusion then had been that their biological function was as important as their appearance. He'd clearly been desperate to separate himself from his physical feelings then, which was most likely a form of protection. If he wasn't into romantic relationships, he would still be able to help at home.

His opinion had somewhat changed over the years. Probably because he'd learnt how to balance things better. If he prioritised, he could enjoy his physical feelings, too. He didn't have to shun them.

Thank goodness, or he might not have appreciated Alexa's breasts in that moment. And appreciating it caused his breath to go from simply oxygenating his body to giving her a signal something had changed. Her eyes fluttered up; something on his face had them clouding with desire. Most likely his own desire, his more rapid breathing.

He could appreciate more than Alexa's breasts though. Those eyes, clouded as they were, made him feel as though he were sitting in front of a fire on a rainy day. When they sparred, her gaze handed him a glass of whiskey, warming him from the inside, too. Her lips parted, and he couldn't resist dipping his head—until he realised what he was about to do.

'I'd like to kiss you,' he whispered.

'Okay,' she whispered back. 'Do it.'

'I was asking.'

'Your hand has been pressed into the small of my back for the better part of five minutes. Seconds ago was the first time you used it to pull me in closer. Now you want to ask?'

'I did?' He had no recollection of it. 'I'm sorry. I should have—'

He broke off when she put a finger over his lips. 'You weren't doing it on purpose. I understood that. It was part of the reason I didn't knee you in the groin.'

He laughed. 'If I ever do anything that makes you uncomfortable on purpose, please feel free to do just that.'

'I didn't need your permission.' Her mouth curved up. 'But thank you, I suppose. Now, shall we get back to that kissing thing?'

He kissed her then, glad she wasn't playing games when his need seemed to consume him. He moaned in relief when their lips touched and he felt the softness of her. Their essences tangled, their souls embraced, and he would never get over the enormity of it—from just a kiss.

Her tongue slipped between his lips, and he opened for her as desire pulsed inside him. She tasted sweet—or was that the promise of her? The idea of what they could share if they ever allowed this feeling to become more than a stolen moment. It didn't matter. All that did was his heart thumping harder against his breastbone, almost as though it were hard work; almost as though there were water in his chest and his heart was thumping despite it.

If that meant he would drown, he didn't mind. He would be drowning in her. In that scent of lemon and mint that came from he had no idea where. But it radiated off her skin, from her lips, and he'd never been a lemon and mint man until now.

His fingers stroked the skin of her arms, aware of how lucky they were to touch her. He memorised the smoothness; the bump near her right elbow where something must have bitten her; the indentations below her left shoulder where she must have got her vaccinations. She shivered when he skimmed her collarbone, when his index fingers stroked her neck. He stored the knowledge away for the future, when he could seduce her more thoroughly, when his desk and his employees weren't in the way.

That didn't stop him from giving it his best effort now.

He cupped her face, angling her into a position that would deepen their kiss. He was rewarded with her hands clinging to his waist, before they drifted up and fisted his shirt. Then they were exploring his skin, flesh to flesh somehow. He didn't know how she'd managed to slip her hands under his clothing, but he was grateful for it. Even if it did mean he'd never be able to let another person touch him this way. He couldn't; not when she was claiming him. Not when he wanted to remember her touching him. To remember how his blood seemed to follow along beneath her strokes, pulsing with need and desire, showing him what it meant to be alive. To live.

How had he not known it before?

'You're very impressive,' she said, pulling back. Her cheeks were flushed, there was a dazed half-smile on her face, and her voice was hoarse. She was the most beguiling she'd ever been. 'I don't suppose you became this way in the last few weeks?'

'I'm not sure what you mean.'

'These muscles.' She scraped her nails lightly over his skin. There was no way it would mark him, but they might as well have with the little sparks going off everywhere she touched. 'They weren't always there.'

'No,' he said slowly. 'I don't think they were when I was born. But I was an impressive toddler.' He laughed when she pinched him. 'Hey, I was using your words.'

'And being obnoxious about it.'

'I didn't want you to think I'd changed.'

Her own laugh was softer than his. Perhaps even thoughtful. 'No, I don't think you have. Even though I seem to be hoping you had. That somehow you'd become this man I'm attracted to and maybe even like in the last few weeks.' She brought her hands out from under his shirt, straightening the material as she did. 'That was what I was implying with the muscles, by the way. I know they didn't suddenly appear. I think I only just noticed them.'

Just like I only just noticed you.

She didn't have to say it. Everything she'd already said implied it. But he wanted to tell her she was wrong. He had changed. He could no longer see Lee without thinking about how Lee had used him. More importantly, what Lee had done to her. He didn't think competing with Alexa was fun any more; didn't see it as harmless. With her, he let himself be himself. He showed her that he cared for her, despite his better judgement. He let himself take care

of her, was honest with her. She hadn't used those vulnerabilities against him either.

Sure, he hadn't entirely opened up to her about how he
felt about his family—but then, neither had she. They were
still checking one another out, tentatively testing whether
they could trust the other. He thought they were there now.
And he wanted to open up to her, wanted to know more
about her.

'Do you want to go out with me?' he asked, desperate
to do just that. 'Tonight, I mean. Do you want to go out?'

Her lips twitched; light danced in her eyes. 'Are you sure
you're feeling well enough?'

'I've made a surprising recovery.'

'Must have been the same twenty-four-hour bug I had.'

'Not quite the same,' he said with a small laugh.

'Hmm. That would be slightly puzzling.'

'Only slightly.'

'Maybe you've had an elixir.'

'I have.'

He moved closer, nuzzled her neck. She angled, giving
him better access.

'What are you implying?'

'You're magical.'

She laughed. Patted his chest. 'That, I know.'

'I don't doubt it.' He nipped at her lips. Then, when it felt
good, kissed her again, lingering. 'Is that a yes?'

'What was the question?' she asked, voice breathy.

He chuckled. 'Can I take you somewhere?'

'I would love that.'

'I know you like kissing me—' *she hoped* '—but taking
me to Lovers Lane seems like overkill.'

Benjamin laughed as he pulled into a parking space at
the edge of the road. All the parking spaces on Lovers Lane
were at the edge of the road. Alexa wasn't a fan of it since

the road was on a cliff, which meant the edge was more dangerous than most edges. But she wasn't going to protest when Benjamin had brought her to this—admittedly—romantic place.

She also wasn't going to move.

Except to eat this broth he'd made her.

But she'd do it very, *very* slowly.

'I wanted to bring you somewhere with a nice view.'

'The quarry was nice. It didn't have such a blatant name. It was safe, too.'

'I've already taken you there.'

It was sweet enough that she leaned forward so she could see the view past his head. It looked much like the night sky itself: dark, save for the lights twinkling back at her. Those lights weren't stars, but the city of Cape Town, and they weren't demure and subtle, but brash and bright. They stretched up until the base of Table Mountain, leaving the landmark to loom over them in darkness. If the lights spoke of the city's vibrancy, its life, then the mountain anchored it. Reminded her that people had families here, careers. Generations had become stronger, less broken, more whole.

'It is pretty nice,' she said on an exhale.

He smiled.

She didn't want to be caught in it, though it was too late to be coy. She'd already given up something of herself when she'd kissed him earlier. Or had he taken it? No, she thought. The permission she'd given him meant that she'd given it willingly. It made her uncomfortable to think she had, so she was trying to blame him.

Uncomfortable didn't feel like the right word though. It was more…like she was going into a battle for the survival of the universe and she had nothing but a sword. Perhaps not even that. Uncomfortable? Sure. Dangerous? Stupid? Completely and utterly irrational? Definitely.

She took a breath and reached into the brown bag for the broth.

'Thanks for swinging by my place to get this.'

'I could have made you a fresh batch.'

'Your kitchen was busy.' She opened the container and sighed at the aroma. 'Besides, I didn't want my first In the Rough meal to be broth.'

She closed her eyes at the first taste of it. It had been hours since she'd eaten, and because she was at the Institute, she'd settled for one slice of toast and a banana. She'd blamed it on her bug when Cherise had asked. She'd also stared longingly at the steak Cherise was eating. But there'd be plenty of steak in the future. For now, she had broth. Warm, delicious broth that wouldn't turn her stomach against her.

Was pregnancy simplifying her appetite? She hoped not.

'Technically it is your first meal from In the Rough,' he said.

'This doesn't count. It doesn't come from the restaurant.'

'Just its manager. Its once-upon-a-time head chef.'

'I forgot about that,' she said, sipping the soup. 'Did you tell me why you decided you didn't want to be head chef any more?'

'Probably not.' He paused. 'I'm happy to share. If you are.'

She frowned. 'What do you mean? I... Oh,' she said when he gestured to the brown bag that still had his food in it. 'Sorry. I got distracted.'

'Yes, I got that.' He was smiling when she handed him his food. He went to open it, but stopped himself. Opened a window instead. Looked at her. 'The smell probably wouldn't be good if you're nauseous.'

'No,' she murmured, touched. 'Thank you.'

'No problem.'

He opened her window, too, and only then dug into his

food. It was lasagne, and her mind salivated over it if not her stomach. She'd steered away from rich food the last three months, with good reason, but she missed the taste of pasta and red meat and bacon. Sighing a little, she took another spoonful of broth.

'I wanted a change,' he said between bites. 'And I thought I was capable of more than being in a kitchen. The idea of running the restaurant intrigued me.'

'Did it live up to your expectations?'

'It did.' His mouth lifted on one side. 'I think I lived up to its expectations, too.'

'If that's your way of giving yourself a compliment, you didn't have to. I could have told you that you were doing a good job.'

'But would you have?'

'Maybe. After some coercing.'

'Of what kind?' His voice had dropped seductively. He leaned closer, but she pulled back. 'What's wrong?'

'I can't kiss you when you're eating that.'

'Oh.' He frowned down at the food, as if it had betrayed him. As if he couldn't believe that it had. 'I wasn't thinking.'

'You were, but not with...' She broke off with a demure smile. 'I'm not going to be crass.' She patted his cheek. 'But yes, that would have been appropriate coercion.'

'Seems a little cruel to remind me when I can't do it.'

'I can be a little cruel sometimes.'

With a small smile that seemed to say *I know*—which pleased her more than offended her—he asked, 'Why did you stop being head chef?'

'I never was. Well,' she reconsidered, 'a lot of my responsibilities blurred the lines with the position, but I knew that I wanted to have other input than in the kitchen to make Infinity the best it could be. I also wanted the business to run independently of me. Or I guess I wanted to run independently of the business.'

'So you could have a life.'

'And maybe babies.'

'You thought about babies then?'

'I suppose I did, though it wasn't "oh, I should do this to have babies".' She set the spoon against the rim of the container. 'I knew I didn't want my life to look like my parents'. Mostly business,' she clarified when she realised he wouldn't know. 'They work a lot, enjoy it, barely spend time at home. I wanted to have more than that. I wanted to have a family. I forgot about it while I tried to get Infinity up and running. Then after an employee brought her kid to work, it hit me: I wanted a home life, too. With babies.'

'That's why your place is so homey.'

'You still sound surprised.'

'Not surprised—jealous. I would love to be so intentional about…everything.' He closed the container his food was in. 'I spent a lot of my time not doing what I wanted to do. When I got to do it, I realised it wasn't really what I wanted to do.'

'But you're there now, aren't you?' she asked. 'You like running the restaurant.'

'Yeah.'

'Great. So you got there in your professional life. Just figure out how to get there in your personal life.'

'Easier said than done.'

'Of course. But you're the only one who can do it.' She closed the container her own food was in and put it in the brown bag. Did the same for his when he handed it to her. 'You can live your life doing the easy thing and going with the flow. It'll take you where you need to be, but maybe there'll be more pit stops. Maybe it'll make you feel as if you should have done more. But—' she dragged the word out '—taking the harder route and doing things intentionally will help you feel proud. Things might still take a long time, but you'll appreciate the journey more.'

She shook her head, rolled her eyes. 'I know I sound silly.'

'You don't. It's…harder, with my mom.'

'How?'

'She needs me,' he said simply. 'If I'm not around, she'll push too hard. My father would be alone to help her with it. It's how our family is.'

'Would you move out if she didn't need you?'

'I… Yeah, maybe.' His lips pursed, then parted to let an exhale through. 'Probably. I'm over thirty,' he said with a quick laugh. 'I shouldn't be living with my parents any more.'

'That's why you're taking me to Lovers Lane instead of home. Not that you should take me home.' She closed her eyes. 'I didn't mean it that way.'

'I know. But maybe that's what you get for being a little cruel.'

He laughed when she punched him lightly in the shoulder. They sat in companionable silence until he said, 'It's cool. The way you've crafted your life. Not everyone can do that.'

She leaned back against the seat. 'I have my parents to thank for that, I guess. For all their faults, they were very clear about having a plan. It was a set plan for them— school, university, work—and they weren't thrilled that mine looked a little different. But I did have one. They just didn't see it.'

She'd faltered at the end, so she shouldn't have been surprised at the hand Benjamin reached out and took hers with. Not even the way he lifted her hand to kiss it should have surprised her. Maybe it was the warmth that spread through her body because of his actions that did. The way it settled in her chest, soothing the holes in her heart her parents had created with their rigidity.

'I'm sure they're proud of you.'

'Maybe.' She reclined the seat with her free hand. Settled both their hands on her stomach. 'I guess they are now. Though they would most likely prefer me to be a business mogul like Lee is. One successful business pales in comparison to that.'

'Which is what he intended,' Benjamin said softly. When she lifted her gaze to him, the edge of his mouth lifted. 'You've told me a lot. I can piece together the rest.'

'So it seems.' She ran the index finger of the hand that wasn't tangled with his over his skin. 'Lee's ambitious. Smart. I like to think those things were the primary motivations.'

'But you know they're not.'

She couldn't admit it out loud, so she hedged. 'Our parents taught us to be the best. I took that to mean people outside of our family. Lee took it to mean…me.' She swallowed. 'But it gave us both motivation, thinking that. If I'm part of it, it's only because of that.'

He tugged at her hand. Frowning, she looked at him. His face was serious, but other than that, she couldn't read his emotion.

'What?' she asked.

'Why are you protecting him?'

'I'm not…' She broke off at his look. 'I'm his sister. His older sister. That's what I'm supposed to do.'

'By that logic, he should be looking up to you, his older sister. Not competing with you so much you've lost your ability to trust people who care about you.'

The shock had her pulling her hand out of his, grabbing a hold of her stomach with both hands. She wasn't sure whether she thought she was protecting herself, or her children. Didn't know why she thought she had to do either.

'Lex—'

'No, give me a moment.' Purposefully, she leaned back against the chair, relaxed her body. She smoothed her clothing, took a couple of deep breaths, let her mind settle. When she was ready, or as ready as she would ever be, she nodded.

'You're right. I realise this. Which is why I've chosen not to have him in my life.'

'I'm sorry. I shouldn't have said that.'

'Stop apologising, Ben,' she said softly. 'You keep doing it.'

'Because I keep messing up.'

'Being honest, caring… That's not messing up.' She bit the inside of her lip at his expression. Tried to fix it. 'Don't get me wrong, it's very inconvenient. Especially when you're trying to avoid your issues. Don't you dare apologise!' she said when he opened his mouth.

He gave her a wry grin and she laughed.

'It's like a disease with you.'

'I can't help it.'

'Sure you can. Just stop doing it.'

'I've been doing it my entire life.'

'Why?'

He didn't reply immediately, his expression contorted in confusion. 'I don't actually know.' He tried to hide the panic that answer brought by giving her a smile. She wondered if he knew how horribly he was failing.

'Okay, we're going to play a game.'

'A game?'

'It's a distraction, Foster.'

'In that case, tell me,' Benjamin said with a smile. It was more genuine now.

'Well, I'm going to try to get you to apologise to me, and you're going to resist.'

'What are you going to do?'

'Nothing specific,' she replied nonchalantly. 'You know that game where, when you're on a road trip, you pick a colour and have to count the number of cars in that colour?'

'Yeah…'

'That's how it's going to be. When the opportunity arises.' She brought a finger under her nose, pretending to stifle a sneeze. 'Oh, my sinuses are acting up.'

'Should I close the windows?'

'Just a little.' She pretended to stop another sneeze. 'Do you have tissues or something here?'

'Yeah, I do,' he said, just as she knew he would.

He reached for the pack of tissues in his door, reached out to give it to her. She held out a hand, but moved it slightly when he tried to drop the tissues into it. The pack fell between the seats.

'Oh. Sorry about that. I thought...' He broke off when he saw her shaking her head. When he saw the smile on her face, too. 'You planned that?'

'Yes. And you failed. Terribly. In the first minute of the game.'

'But that wasn't fair!'

'All's fair in love and war.' When there was an awkward silence, she wrinkled her nose. 'This is war, in case you were wondering.'

'I wasn't.'

But, if she was being honest with herself, she was.

CHAPTER SIXTEEN

WHAT WAS THE SAYING? *Going to hell in a handbasket?* If so, that was exactly what was happening. The handbasket was filled with delicious food courtesy of Cherise, but the tying of the bow, the giving? That was all Lee.

'You invited your sister?' Benjamin hissed the moment he saw Alexa walk into the hotel ballroom.

Okay, not the moment he saw Alexa. The moment he saw Alexa he stopped, his brain stopped, and he was pretty sure his heart stopped. She looked…amazing. It was too inadequate a word, but he clung to it. The gown she wore was somewhere between coral and peach, the colour of it magnificent against the bronze of her skin. It was a halter-neck dress that clung to her chest, ending just below her breasts in a cinch, before flowing down over the rest of her. The material was pleated, and when she moved, it moved with her. When she was still, those pleats created the illusion of space. All for the benefit of hiding the bump he knew was growing by the day.

The reason he knew it was because he'd found a reason, every day since they'd been to Lovers Lane, to see her. He didn't once go to her restaurant—he worried that would be invading her personal space—but he visited her flat under the guise of bringing more food. He asked her to go out for tea under the pretence of picking her brains about something. It had been a week and a half of this, where he was clearly making up reasons to see her, but she never once called him out on it.

He told himself that if she'd wanted to, she would have.

She wasn't the kind of person not to. The fact that she wasn't saying anything told him she wanted to see him, too. As did the small, private smile she smiled every time she saw him.

The days she invited him in were the ones he liked best. Her flat was fast becoming his favourite place, in no small part because they could be whoever they wanted to be there. Turned out, they wanted to be friends. The kissing that happened quite frequently—and sometimes progressed to other things, but never far enough to undermine their friendship—was merely a bonus. But things were so easy between them when they were there. He told her about how he'd grown up trying to help his parents; she told him how she'd grown up trying to make hers proud. They comforted one another, teased one another, and, yes, kissed and touched, and it was all magnificent.

And it was going to end.

'I didn't invite her,' Lee said slowly. 'She wouldn't have come if she'd known the invitation was from me.'

Benjamin resisted grabbing the man at the front of his collar. 'What did you do?' he said through his teeth.

'Used the grapevine.' Lee smirked. 'It still works.'

It took Benjamin a long time to remember what he was like when he wasn't so damn angry. Not that anger was such a bad thing. It gave him a clarity he hadn't had before. Sure, some of that clarity was also because of his conversations with Alexa, but it was clarity nevertheless. And he knew exactly what he had to do.

'I quit.'

'What?'

'Resign, effective immediately.'

'You can't do that,' Lee spluttered. 'Your contract says you have to give me at least a month's notice.'

'Then you have it.'

'What the hell?' Lee's expression was stormy. 'This is

because of my sister, isn't it? She poached you.' He shook his head in disbelief. 'You let her? You let her because you're sleeping with her?'

'Lee,' he warned.

Lee took a breath, clearly trying to get hold of his emotions. 'You can't do this, man. We've been working together for years. I gave you a chance. You can't walk out on me.'

'I'm grateful for what you did for me.' And he meant it. But the weight that had lifted from his shoulders the moment he'd quit told him he'd needed to. 'Truly, I am. You're an incredible businessman. I've learnt a lot from you. I have no doubt I could have learnt more.'

'Then why are you leaving?'

'Because you used me to beat your sister.' Saying it out loud made Benjamin feel in control. As if finally, after all those people had used him, he'd regained what they'd taken from him. His pride, perhaps. Or perhaps it was that he was no longer scared of saying it. 'And you're malicious. To your own sister, who's done nothing but love you.'

'Is that what she told you?' Lee scoffed. 'She must be really good in…'

He broke off when Benjamin, quick as lightning, took his arm. 'I'm warning you about what you say next.'

Lee's chest heaved. 'Okay. I'm sorry.'

He let go. 'I appreciate that.'

'You're serious about this?'

'Deadly.' He straightened his tie. 'I respect who you are in business, but not as a man. I can't, knowing how you've treated the woman I… I love.'

He'd hesitated in speech, just as he had with his feelings. But he could see they'd been there long before the last month. The moment he'd seen her in that class, he'd tumbled. Knocked his head in the process, it seemed, because he went back to being a kid and tried to compete with her so she would notice him.

But she'd never allowed him close enough to see that she had noticed him; not in the way he'd intended. He'd reminded her of her brother, the man, he suspected, had hurt her most. She seemed to have some kind of resignation about who her parents were, but not with Lee. With Lee, she'd tried, and he'd brushed her away. When she let Benjamin in the last few weeks, he could see how much it hurt her—and how much he had hurt her, simply by acting like a teenage fool.

Now what he had seen, what she'd allowed him to see, convinced him that if he hadn't been a fool, he would have had these feelings aeons ago. She might not have iced him out, and he might have seen who she really was. That was who he was in love with. The woman who wasn't even a little cruel. Who was passionate and driven and who cared about people.

It was the biggest honour of his life that she'd chosen to open up to him. She'd let him see her vulnerable, and he hoped with all his might he'd done enough to show her she could be vulnerable with him. He knew she struggled with it, and if he had to be patient he would be, simply because she was worth it.

If he had to spend his entire lifetime proving that she could trust him, he would. Because he loved her. And she deserved it.

He had to tell her.

'Benjamin!'

The exclamation came from a short distance away. When he turned towards it, he saw Cherise.

'Thanks so much for coming,' she said, stopping in front of him. 'I thought I should show you what I can do, too, since I hope we can work together.'

It was what he'd wanted to hear most, once upon a time. Now, what he wanted to hear most was Alexa's voice, saying anything, really, but mostly talking about them sharing a future together. He turned, barely thinking about the fact that Cherise was there, waiting for an answer.

He didn't think about it at all when he saw Lee follow Alexa out of the ballroom.

The moment she saw him walking towards her she knew.

It was silly of her to think that she could walk into an event being catered by Cherise to get another opportunity to speak with her. To perhaps even see her in action. Alexa had found out about the charity event through an acquaintance, thought it would be harmless and beneficial, considering she hadn't heard from Cherise for over a week. When she saw Lee, it all fell into place: she hadn't heard from Cherise for a reason, she'd been set up, and she shouldn't have come.

She didn't give the gorgeous ballroom and its glistening lights and formal guests any more thought. She walked out, down the brick steps, past the fountain. She was on the small stretch of grass between the fountain and the car park when Lee caught up with her.

'Leaving so soon?'

She stopped. Closed her eyes. Turned to face him. 'Sorry I didn't stay for the *gotcha*. That's what you wanted to say, isn't it?'

'No one forced you to be here,' Lee said calmly. 'Although I'm surprised you didn't accompany Ben.' He pretended to think about it. 'Is it that he didn't tell you about this, or that you really are trying to keep your personal and professional lives separate?'

He hadn't told her, though she didn't need to tell Lee that. Nor did she have to figure out why Benjamin hadn't said anything. He was protecting her, or maybe himself, and though she understood it—he was so used to protecting the people in his life—it bothered her on a deep level. But that wasn't important now.

'Look, Lee, I don't want to stick around for the gloating, okay?'

'Not even your own?'

'What are you talking about?'

'Oh, you're going to pretend you didn't ask him to do it. That seems like an odd position, all things considered.'

'Tell me, or let me go,' she said sharply.

'Your boyfriend quit.'

'He what?'

His brows rose. 'Nice acting, Sis. Didn't know you had it in you.'

'He quit? Why?' She narrowed her eyes. 'What the hell did you do?'

'Absolutely nothing.' Though she could barely see it, she knew he was biting the inside of his lip. He used to do it when they were younger, on the side. 'He told me it's because of the way I've been treating you.'

She caught the swear word before it left her lips. Mentally, though, she let the curses fly. The idiot! It was fine if he kept things from her because he thought he was protecting her—okay, not fine, understandable—but this? This was stupid. This was his entire future. It was his life. And he was doing it for her! It seemed much too much for people who'd been close for less than two weeks. This felt more like a gesture; something someone did before proclaiming their love or something.

A thin thread of panic wove between the synapses in her brain. It threatened to overcome her, and for a second she thought she would fall over. But that would hurt her babies, and she had to be strong. She couldn't let them suffer for things she was responsible for.

She looked at her brother. Realised she needed to sort this out if she wanted to keep that promise to her kids.

'If I talk to him, convince him to go back to you, would you leave me alone?' She could already see, before he even said it, that he was going to make some stupid remark. 'I'm being serious. If I get Ben to go back to In the Rough, I don't want to see or hear from you again. Unless there's a family function, which, fortunately, doesn't happen often. But outside of that. No surprises. No manipulation. Nothing.'

'You really want that?'

He'd taken the stance of a victim, his voice hurt and surprised, as if he had no contribution to why she wanted this. It made her snap.

'What I want is to have a brother who doesn't make me feel as if I have to walk carefully everywhere I go in case he pulls the rug out from under me. I want to have a brother who doesn't *enjoy* pulling the rug out from under me. Who, when I fall, asks me why I'm on the ground. Who gets upset when I refuse his help.'

She'd never spent enough time with Lee to learn how his expressions revealed his emotions. Or maybe it was that the only expressions he wore around her were variations of smugness or satisfaction or a combination of the two. So she couldn't tell how he felt now, because none of that came through in his expression.

'I thought… This is what we do, Lex. We compete with one another. We make one another better.'

'What? That's what you think this is? No—*how* do you think that is what this is?' Her voice was high with disbelief. She didn't try to temper it. 'You competed with me, Lee. I *congratulated* you for beating my records, or scoring higher than me.'

'You were conceding.'

'Conceding…'

Now she recognised the look on Lee's face: bewilderment. He genuinely didn't understand why she was so upset. She nearly laughed. He was the least self-aware person she knew.

'I wasn't conceding. I was sincerely wishing you well because I was happy for you. At first. I could see competing with me made you happy and gave you purpose and I wanted you to have that.' She took a steadying breath. 'But you didn't want me to be happy. If you did, you would have supported me the way I supported you. You would have taken the hand I held out every time I asked you to go to a movie with me, or watch a show, or do whatever stupid things brothers and sisters do together. But you said no. Instead you tried to beat me at things that didn't even matter.'

She folded her arms, suddenly cold.

'And you tried to beat me at things that did matter, too.' She blinked when that made her want to cry. 'You bought the building I spent months trying to find. Months,' she said with a shake of her head. 'I did research into who I was buying the building from, into the neighbourhood, into how much it would cost to renovate, how long it would take. Then you swooped in and stole it. Just stole it.' She lifted a hand, dropped it. 'The only thing you knew about it was that I wanted it.'

'I... I didn't realise.'

'You didn't realise that you'd destroyed my dream?' she asked. 'Of both that restaurant and ever having a normal relationship with you?'

He didn't reply, though he ran his hand over his hair a few times, lips moving without sound. He looked at her, and if she wasn't so numb by the conversation, she would have been touched by the vulnerability she saw there.

But she was numb. She had to be. If she wasn't, the reminder of all the times she'd wanted to forge a relationship with her brother would have consumed her. The hope she'd once had was enmeshed in those memories. She'd desperately wanted to shield herself against her parents, had known that if Lee was behind the shield with her she could be stronger. *They* would be stronger together. Except

Lee chose to wield their parents' weapons against her, too, even when she'd surrendered.

She wasn't surrendering any more. It might have seemed as if she was by offering Lee Benjamin, but she knew she wasn't. She was lifting her shield, protecting herself once more. Because the only way she could truly do that against her brother was by coming to a truce with him. Which meant he needed to make the decision, too.

She could smell the faint smoke of guilt at using Benjamin as a pawn, but maybe he would understand. He might even be grateful that he wouldn't have to protect her any more.

'You don't, um…' Lee cleared his throat. 'You don't have to get Benjamin to work for me.'

She just studied him.

'I'll leave you alone. I didn't realise…' Now he shook his head. 'I'll leave you alone. I promise.'

She almost ran a hand over her stomach before she remembered Lee didn't know about her pregnancy. She settled for clasping her hands over the bag she'd brought with her.

'Thank you.'

Neither of them moved. But there was a movement behind Lee. Alexa's eyes automatically shifted to it, before she realised it was Benjamin. Her body wanted to sag against something, let it hold up her weight as she prepared for another conversation that would leave her raw. It was so different to how her body had responded to Benjamin in the last weeks. With relief, excitement, attraction, desire. She'd felt safer than at any other time in her life.

This interaction with Lee seemed to prove how much safety was an illusion.

CHAPTER SEVENTEEN

'ARE YOU OKAY?'

It was the first thing that came into his mind when he reached her, but he immediately realised it was a stupid question. Of course she wasn't okay. He could see it in her stance, in her eyes, in the brittle tone of her voice when she lied and told him she was. She looked broken, tired, and he hated the person who'd put that look on her face.

He turned to Lee. 'Leave.'

Lee looked at Alexa, then back at him. Uncharacteristically withdrawn, he nodded. After one last glance at Alexa, a parting of the lips that made it seem as though he wanted to say something, he turned around and walked away. Benjamin waited until he was out of sight, then turned.

'Come on, let's find somewhere to sit down.'

She didn't fight him on it, and his worry kicked up another notch. But he kept it inside long enough to find a bench. The restaurant was in a vineyard, much like most prestigious restaurants in Cape Town. But instead of looking out onto the vineyard, the restaurant looked out over the stretch of property on the opposite side of it. It was mostly grass and a long deck that went out into a pond. The pond was still, though Benjamin saw the occasional disturbance of water and the rings that resulted from that disturbance. He watched it for a long time, waiting for Alexa to recover from whatever had happened with Lee.

When he thought she might have, he asked, 'Did that go okay?'

'He agreed to leave me alone, so I guess so.'

'That's what you wanted?'

'I asked for it.'

But she didn't say it was what she wanted, and he had a feeling it wasn't. He wasn't sure if she knew that though, or if she needed to figure it out. He wasn't sure about his position in this either: Should he prod? Give her space? Point her in the right direction? None of the options seemed right. He didn't speak, crippled by the indecision.

'Did you quit your job?' she said into the silence.

'He told you?'

'Accused me,' she corrected. 'Apparently I've been using you to get to him.'

'Sounds diabolical.'

'You can't say I didn't warn you.' She opened her palms on her lap, looking at them, not him. He should have taken it as sign, prepared himself. Because he didn't, he was completely taken aback by her next words. 'I hope you didn't do this because of me.'

'No. Of course not.'

'You didn't quit because of me?'

'No.'

'Then why did you?'

'I…couldn't work with him any more. He got you here because he wanted to…' He broke off at her look. 'Fine, maybe it had something to do with you. But it wasn't *because* of you.'

She threaded her fingers together. 'You're going to regret it.' Her voice was neutral. 'You're going to blame me when you regret it.'

'I won't.'

'You will. Unless you can tell me you're leaving because of more than just me.'

'I…want to do my own thing.'

'Liar.'

'I'm not lying,' he snapped. Took a breath. 'I shouldn't have said that. It was—' he relaxed his jaw '—uncalled for.'

'It was, especially since it's the truth.'

'It's not fair,' he replied, barely retaining control over his anger. 'It was never fair of you to expect me to work with a man I don't respect any more.'

'You shouldn't have let the way he treated me affect your working relationship.'

'He used me to get to you.' He stood now. Walked away, trying to keep that control. Came back when it didn't help him have more of it. 'Do you know how many people have used me in my life? Too many,' he answered for her. 'It was worse that he did it to get to you. It was worse that he was still so terrible to you. How can you ask me to ignore it?'

'Because of this!' she exclaimed, shifting to the edge of the bench. 'You quit your job. The one you love, at the restaurant you built. Don't you see that? Don't you see you're going to lose everything you've worked for all because of me?' She dropped her head. 'One day you'll think I used you for this, too. I almost did.' Her voice was barely above a whisper. 'I told him that if I got you to work for him again, he had to leave me alone.'

He took the time he needed to work through that.

'Because you care,' he said, crouching down so he could see her face. 'You know what the restaurant means to me.'

'Maybe. Maybe I did it because it meant getting what I want.'

Her eyes, defiant, met his.

'You're saying this to hurt me,' he said, realising it. 'You're pushing me away.'

'Yes,' she whispered. 'You deserve more than me. You deserve someone who can care as much as you do. Selflessly. I… I can't.'

He froze. Slowly, he rose. He rubbed a hand over his face. 'Why not?'

'Can't you see?' She was sitting up, spine straight. It looked so out of place against the curved back of the bench. 'You're selfless. You protect the people you care about at all costs. Even if you're lying to them.'

He could hardly deny it when that was exactly what he'd done that day.

'I've been alone most of my life. I'm used to thinking about myself. More importantly—' she took a deep breath '—I can't trust someone who won't tell me the truth. And I can't keep worrying that I'm keeping you from doing what you want to do. But if I don't, you'll keep putting yourself last.'

'It's not... I'm not...' He exhaled. 'Why don't we talk about you being unable to accept when people try to care for you?'

She bit her lip. 'Okay. What about it would you like to discuss?'

It took him a moment to get over his surprise.

'Why?'

'Why can't I accept people caring for me?' she asked. He nodded. A short moment later, she continued. 'Because it goes away. In some shape or form, I'll discover I can't trust them. It goes away, Ben.' There was a quick inhale of air. When he moved to her, she held out a hand to stop him. Sniffed. 'No, I'm okay.' But two tears streamed down each of her cheeks. She wiped at them quickly. 'I don't want to go through that.'

'It doesn't just go away.' He went to sit next to her, as far away as the bench allowed so she had her space. 'I can't care one day and stop caring the other.'

'But you can *think* you care one day and realise you don't the other.'

'Has this happened to you?'

'No. I wouldn't let it.'

'You mean you haven't let anyone close enough to allow it to happen.'

She inclined her head in acknowledgement.

'That's not healthy.'

'It's safe.'

'Safe isn't going to give you happiness.'

'Are you speaking from experience?' she asked blandly. 'You're staying at home so you can be safe, so you can protect your mother and help your father. So you don't have to face your real feelings about your family.'

He stared at her. 'There are no feelings.'

'So you're happy?' she prodded. 'You're safe and happy, the ultimate juxtaposition, according to you?'

He stood again. 'This isn't fair.'

'It is, but you don't like it.' She stood now, too. 'Which is fine. You don't have to like it.'

'You're using this as an excuse to push me away.'

'I don't need an excuse. I've told you every reason we can't continue this.' She gestured between them.

'You're really that scared of trusting someone?' he asked. 'Is being alone better than taking a chance?'

She folded her arms, the line of her mouth flat. 'Yes. I've spent my life learning that lesson. I won't let anyone hurt me the way my family has.'

'Even if it means pushing away someone who—' he swallowed. Said it anyway. Because he was a fool '—loves you?'

She blinked. Again, and again, until her lashes were fluttering like the wings of a butterfly. He tried to give her a moment to process. He couldn't.

'I haven't once let you down, Alexa. I've been there for you since this entire thing with Lee started. I lied, yes, but I thought…' He shook his head. 'I wasn't doing it to hurt you. The very opposite, in fact.' He took a step closer. 'Trust me. Trust me because I love you, and I'll try to do better because I love you. Trust me because I've shown you that you can.'

She was shaking her head before he had finished speaking. 'You need to care about yourself, too, in order to love, Ben. I don't think you do.'

With that, she walked away.

It had not been a good week. Someone had forgotten to order the seafood for the restaurant on Monday. It meant that Alexa had to remove all relevant dishes from the menu, make thousands of apologies, and offer substitutes. Then, on Wednesday, someone had forgotten about the staff meeting, come in late, and the event that was being hosted that evening had a few hiccups because the meeting hadn't proceeded.

Everyone made mistakes. She tried to remember that on Friday evening, when she was dead on her feet and contemplating disciplinary action. It complicated things that she'd been the someone who'd forgotten and needed to be punished. Maybe she would get her staff to give her a roasting. Making fun of her would hopefully rebuild the morale that seemed to be lacking, too.

'Hey.' Kenya appeared in her doorway, leaning against the frame of it as though she'd always been there. She was holding two bottles of beer. 'I thought you could use one?'

'Thanks, but I can't drink it.'

Kenya's brow quirked. 'Since when are you this strict about alcohol on a Friday night?'

She couldn't be bothered to keep it a secret any more. She was almost sixteen weeks pregnant with twins, her body was becoming fuller by the day, her plan to have the restaurant secured before her maternity leave had imploded, and she was tired of keeping it all to herself. At least before, she'd had Benjamin to confide in. That was no longer an option. She tried not to listen to the crack of her heart at that thought.

'Since I got pregnant.'

'You're pregnant?' Kenya stepped inside the office, slammed the door, and then put both beers on Alexa's desk. 'Who do I have to kill?'

'Why are you killing someone?' Alexa asked with a laugh.

'Because they knocked you up! Unless…' She eyed Alexa suspiciously 'Did you want to be knocked up?'

'Yes.'

'Oh.' Kenya frowned. 'You trapped them.'

She chuckled again. 'I didn't trap anyone. I went to a sperm bank because your family made me remember how much I wanted my own. How soon I wanted it, too.' She shrugged and let out a small smile. 'Anyway, that's why I've been dressing like this. Trying to hide the bump.'

'I was wondering.' Kenya dropped into the chair on the visitor's side of Alexa's desk. She drank her beer. 'Honestly, I thought you were going through a boho chic period.'

'Seriously?'

'I didn't want to limit you with my expectations of who you are.' Kenya smiled, but it lacked its fire. Alexa found out why a couple of seconds later. 'Why didn't you tell me you were doing this? I could have come with you. Supported you. From what I know about the process, it isn't easy.'

'No, it isn't. And honestly? I could have used the support.' Her heart ached at the acknowledgement. 'But I'm an idiot.' She offered Kenya a small smile. 'I thought that if I let you in, you'd hurt me. I've got so used to doing things on my own, I thought I could do this.'

She wasn't talking about conceiving her children any more, and they both knew it.

'Why would you think that?' Kenya's voice was soft, and a little judgemental. Alexa smiled.

'It's what I'm used to,' she said. 'My family is messed up. And every time I thought something was going right, it was really...not.'

She should have explained it better, but it occurred to her that she hadn't told Kenya anything of her personal life. She knew that Kenya had three older brothers, seven nieces, one nephew and a daughter, and that motherhood had pushed her to finally get the therapy she thought she needed. Alexa knew all of that, but she hadn't told Kenya one thing about her family.

'It's a long story, and I should have told you more of it sooner,' she said softly.

Kenya didn't blink. 'You should have, yes.'

'I'm sorry. For all of it.'

'Good.' Kenya didn't look away as she drank from her beer. 'So, should we thank the pregnancy for this stupendous week, or the family?'

'Neither. Or maybe the family? I don't know.' It was the perfect opportunity to make things right with Kenya. Or at least to start to. 'I think it's mostly because of the fake boyfriend.'

'Explain.'

So she did. She told Kenya about her terrible brother, who'd inspired her to pretend her rival was her boyfriend. How Benjamin had gone along with it, even after he'd found out she was pregnant. She told Kenya about the twins—to which she got a colourful reply—and about how things had snowballed, but in a nice way, with Benjamin. And then how it had all melted, leaving her feeling as though she was drowning.

She ended on an apology, because she'd been a bad friend and a worse boss. She couldn't secure the restaurant before she was on maternity leave. She could probably still try, but time was running out and—

'Firstly,' Kenya interrupted, 'you've been a pretty terrible friend. There's no way you're worse as a boss.'

'Wow. Thanks.'

'Secondly,' Kenya continued with a grin, 'we haven't had a head chef for almost four months now. I know you've been picking up a lot of the slack, but that's because you didn't trust us—' she gave Alexa a look '—to help you with it. You don't have to kill yourself to find a replacement chef before you go on leave. If you do, great, and we'll help train them. If you don't, we'll survive.'

Kenya leaned forward and rested a hand on Alexa's.

'Babe, you've built a damn good team. You've also earned our loyalty. That includes helping out when things get rough.' She squeezed. 'It includes taking care of things while you have your babies. We could probably help you get ready for the babies, too.'

'Oh, that's not—' She cut herself off. 'Thank you,' she said instead. 'That means a lot.'

'Yeah, well, it should.' Kenya softened her words with a smile. 'You mean a lot to us.'

'And you mean a lot to me.'

Kenya blinked. Then took the last swig of her beer. 'Thanks. Now, let's go tell the people out there you're having two babies.'

'Oh. Oh, yeah. Okay.'

'It's been a rough week for all of us. This would help. But only if you want to do it.'

She thought about it for a long time. Then she nodded and stood up. 'Let's go.'

The reaction was more than she could have ever anticipated or expected. A stunned silence followed her words, but after that someone began to cheer. People came forward to congratulate her, offering her words of encouragement and advice, asking how they could help.

Alexa swallowed down her emotion many times in the next hour, her eyes prickling at the support she had no idea she'd already had. When she caught Kenya's eye later, she got a wink and a knowing look in return. It made the tears she was holding back run down her cheeks, and she was immediately handed tissues from three different directions. She laughed, waved off concern, pressed the tissue to her eyes. And in that moment she realised two things:

One, she'd spent so many years afraid of opening up and trusting people. Yet despite that, she'd found the very family she'd hoped for her entire life. And they trusted her, for whatever reason. Apparently, she'd earned it. Maybe it was time that she allowed herself to see they'd earned her trust, too.

Number two was more complicated. Because the entire time she'd experienced this emotional, overwhelming thing, she'd felt as though she were missing a limb. She didn't let herself think of it until she was alone that night in her flat. When she did, she didn't like that Benjamin had wedged himself so deeply in her mind that she couldn't go through her day without thinking about him. That she couldn't have important experiences without wanting him there. Without having him there.

She settled on the sofa, but it smelled like him, so she moved. It didn't make sense—he hadn't been there in over a week and her sofas were regularly cleaned.

Except it *did* make sense. She just didn't want to face it.

At some point during the night as she tossed and turned, she realised she already had. She knew exactly what the problem was: Benjamin hadn't wedged himself in her mind; he'd wedged himself into her heart.

CHAPTER EIGHTEEN

HE'D NEVER THOUGHT his dream job would become a nightmare. But it was. Working in a place he loved but had given up for—his darkest moments in the last week had made him think—nothing. He only had himself to blame. Alexa hadn't asked him to do this, neither had Lee. He'd done it because he'd thought he was being principled.

He *was* being principled. He couldn't work for a man like Lee. Someone whose cruelty would one day be turned on Benjamin or their staff. Benjamin would have left then anyway, so he'd just hurried along the inevitable by handing in his notice.

But principles didn't pay the bills, or help the mind when dreams were dashed. The euphoria he'd felt after saying he was leaving was well and truly gone. Now he only thought of his responsibilities, of what his parents would say when he finally told them what he'd done, and how Alexa had walked away from his proclamation of love.

A knock brought him out of his thoughts.

It was Saturday night after the restaurant had already closed and most of his staff had gone home. Lee's appearance in his doorway was perplexing for more than that reason though. The very fact that he was there after a week of radio silence was troubling. So was the fact that he'd knocked, which he never had, in all the years they'd worked together, done.

'Can I come in?'

Benjamin opened a hand, gesturing to the chair opposite him. He tried not to think about how Alexa had filled it almost three weeks before. Or anything else they'd done in the office.

'I'm surprised to see you here,' Benjamin said.

'I should have come earlier.'

'Should you have?'

Lee smiled at the casual comment. Or maybe not smiled, but Benjamin didn't think there was a description for Lee simply showing his teeth.

'Yes. We should have had a meeting to discuss the implications of your resignation and the transition plans. Have you told the staff yet?'

'No.'

'Great. We'll—'

'Lee,' Benjamin interjected. 'Did you really come here this time on a Saturday night to talk business?'

'No,' he said after a moment. He leaned forward, rested his arms on his knees. 'I'm here to apologise.'

'Apologise?'

'For setting this in motion.' Now he clasped his hands. 'I always knew you were ambitious, and that In the Rough wasn't where you'd end up. But… I sped it up, by acting like a complete jerk to Alexa. And to you. I'm sorry.'

Benjamin sat back and let his mind figure out what was happening and what he should say next. 'I appreciate that. I'm more concerned about whether you're extending that apology to Alexa.'

'No.' Lee looked down. 'She doesn't want to see me. I want to respect that.'

'I bet she'd want to see you if you're intending on apologising.'

'You think?'

'You spent your life torturing her. I think an apology would be a nice change of pace.'

Lee winced, but he straightened and ran a hand over

his face. 'I don't know how I didn't see how much I was hurting her.'

'We all have blind spots when it comes to family.'

It was one of the little nuggets of wisdom his brain had come up with at three or so in the morning some time in the past week.

'Yeah, but hurting her?' He shook his head. 'That's more than a blind spot. It's…' His voice faded, and for a while after, he didn't speak. 'It's not what a brother should do to his sister.'

'Agreed.'

Lee nodded. Got up. 'I don't have anything else to say right now.'

'You could talk about the transition.'

He laughed a little. 'That was me hedging so I wouldn't have to apologise.'

Benjamin chuckled, too. 'I've been there.'

Lee walked to the door but, before he left, turned back. 'We do have to talk about the transition.'

'I know.'

'Maybe we could talk about you buying this place from me.'

'What?'

'It's lost its appeal, now that I know what it did to Alexa.' He angled his head. 'This seems like a good way to restore balance.'

'You should sell it to her, then.'

'Are you kidding me? Her place is much more popular than this. It would be a downgrade.'

With a quick wink, Lee was gone.

He hadn't left things any worse than the way he'd found them. Not even his offer to sell the place to Benjamin had made much of an impact. Perhaps because Benjamin already knew the answer: he wanted In the Rough. He wanted to run the business himself, and do things the way he'd learnt to do them. He had no doubt he would make mistakes, but that was part of the package. He was very much looking forward to making mistakes, in fact.

So yeah, he'd been lying to himself when he said he didn't know why he'd decided to leave. He'd done that because he wanted something else. But he'd also done it because he was standing up to Lee—because he was standing up for Alexa. It smarted that she didn't want him to do that. It hurt that he'd offered and she'd rejected him. She couldn't see that he wanted to do this, that he needed to, so that he could make up for...

He paused. He didn't have to make up for anything. He'd already apologised to Alexa for what he'd done to her before he'd known her. He'd tried his best to show her none of that would happen again. Why had his brain automatically gone there, then? To make up for something, as if he were in the wrong?

Because he'd taken responsibility for her life in some ways, he realised. He thought he could make the hurt she'd been through better by protecting her. But she was right: the way he'd protected her was all wrong. He had done what he thought was best, knowing that she wouldn't appreciate it.

Did he always do that with her? With anyone? With his...with his mother?

Yes. He did. It was so clear to him that he could have been staring at its physical form right in front of him. But he didn't want to look at it by himself. He wanted to talk to Alexa. He wanted to share it with her; share everything with her. Because she was his friend, and because he loved her.

He was halfway to her place when he wondered whether it was a good idea. It was the middle of the night on a Saturday. Not to mention the fact that she clearly didn't consider him her friend. She certainly didn't love him. It took the rest of the journey there for him to realise he didn't do a good enough job of fighting for her. She might not love him, but he was sure she cared about him, and maybe they could still be friends. He'd take her friendship if he could have nothing else of her.

Then she opened her front door in her pyjamas. A cotton nightgown that dipped in the valley of her full breasts and caressed her growing stomach. He felt a lot of things in that moment. Protectiveness. Desire. Tenderness. Love. None of it inspired him to think of friendship, and he knew he'd made a mistake.

'I shouldn't have come.'

'You realised this because I opened the door?'

'Yes, actually. What were you thinking, coming to the door like this?'

'Excuse me?'

'You're wearing lingerie.'

'This is not lingerie,' she scoffed. 'It's an old cotton nightgown. My oldest, in fact, because it's the most stretched and none of the others fit me.' She frowned. 'You're one to talk.'

He looked down at his T-shirt and jeans. 'I'm perfectly respectable.'

'Except I can see your biceps and your chest muscles.'

'You can't see my chest muscles.'

'Your T-shirt is tight. I can imagine them.'

'You think I'm dressed inappropriately because of your *imagination*?'

She folded her arms. 'Isn't that what you were doing?'

'I… Well, no. Your breasts are right there.'

She looked down, as if seeing them for the first time. 'Oh. I guess this is not only stretchy around my waist.' She shrugged. 'It's not like you haven't seen this much of them before.'

He closed his eyes and prayed for patience. And maybe a douse of cold water. Maybe an ice bucket, because then he

could stuff his heart that was beating with love and amusement for her in it, too.

'Do you want to come in?' she asked when he opened
his eyes.

'Yes. No. Yes?' He honestly didn't know. 'I have stuff
to say.'

'You don't know where you want to say them?'

'I...think I might get distracted inside.'

'Why?' She leaned against the frame. 'Never mind. It
doesn't matter.' Folded her arms. 'Say the stuff.'

'You were right,' he blurted out, because he was avoiding her chest and her eyes and because it was bubbling up
inside. 'I take responsibility when I don't have to. But I've
been doing it my whole life. With my mom, I mean. She
needed me, so I don't know if I didn't have to—'

'You didn't,' she interrupted. 'You chose to. Because
she's your mother and you love her, and the way that you
show you care is by helping. Doing. Protecting.'

He frowned. Her lips curved.

'Maybe I have some stuff to say, too. But please, continue.'

'Very gracious of you.' He cleared his throat. Tried to
remember where he was. 'I blamed myself. For her being
sick. I had no reason to. She never made me feel that way.
But in my kid brain I thought that if I hadn't been there,
hadn't been born, she wouldn't have got sick and—'

She'd moved forward, so when he stopped because of
the pain, because he needed to, she took his hands. Slowly,
she put them on the base of her waist. Cupped his face.

'Just look at me,' she said. 'Look at me and tell me what
you need to say.'

She must have woven a spell on him because he said, 'I
don't know why I blamed myself. Maybe because my father said we could make things easier for her. If we could

make it easier, we could make it harder. Maybe I already had made it harder. Maybe I was the cause of it?'

'Oh, Ben,' she whispered, lowering her hands to his chest. 'She got sick when you were too young to understand it. Of course your father telling you to help her made you think you needed to because you contributed to it.'

'"Maybe", not "of course",' he replied, though he appreciated the understanding. 'But it happened. The responsibility of caring for her was heavy, but I got stronger. Too strong. I carried it even when she didn't want me to. She might not have wanted me to carry it at all.' He shrugged. 'I did the same with you.'

She sucked in her cheeks, releasing it before her mouth fully became a pout.

'Remember earlier, when I said I have some things to say, too?'

'You mean a few minutes ago? Yeah.'

She'd begun to walk her fingers up his chest. At his comment, she paused to pinch him.

'Okay, okay,' he said with a small laugh. 'No more wise-guy comments.'

'Good, because I need to be serious for a moment.' She took a breath. 'You need to learn how to balance it. Caring for someone, and protecting them so blindly that you do silly, unnecessary things.'

'I know. Lex—'

'Shh,' she said, putting a finger on his lips. 'I'm not done yet.'

He nodded for her to continue.

'I need to learn how to not push you away because I'm scared.' She knitted her brows. 'It might be easier for me because I'm tired of doing it. Protecting myself... It's so much work. It takes so much energy to keep up the shield and to be careful.' She leaned her head against his chest. 'And I'm tired of doing that and of being pregnant.' She lifted her head. 'Do you know how tiring it is to be pregnant? I still have five months to go. I can't do it all.'

He bit his lip to keep from laughing.

'Yeah, okay, laugh at the pregnant lady.'

'I'm not laughing at you,' he said, catching her hand and pressing it to his lips. 'I'm happy. It sounds like you're telling me you want me to do the protecting for you.'

'Did you hear nothing of what I just said?'

'Yeah, but I'm still me. I'm still going to want to protect you. But I'm going to try,' he said sincerely. 'It's not healthy. I know that. I know the situation at home with my family isn't healthy, too. It's…it's safe.'

'For them,' she said gently. 'For you, it's familiar. But it's hard. And every time you see your mother in pain, you'll think it's because of you.'

'I can't snap my fingers and have it disappear.'

'I know that. I'm not asking you to. But I am telling you to be intentional. If you want to be happy, you need to move away from safe. You need to stop taking responsibility for people and things that don't need you to do that for them. Or that, quite simply, aren't your responsibility.' She ran her hands up and down his arms. 'Your mother's illness isn't your fault. Nor is my pregnancy. Or my problems.'

He inhaled, then exhaled. Again, when the first time he did made him feel lighter. He hadn't realised until that night how much he'd blamed himself for a range of things. This conversation made him think that he'd gone along with Alexa's plan because he'd blamed himself in some way for how Lee had treated her. He wanted to make up for it, though he couldn't possibly do that when he wasn't the cause of the treatment.

He saw it now. And, as he told Alexa, it wouldn't immediately go away. Especially not with his mother, where things were more complicated. But he promised her he'd try, so he would.

'Does this mean you're not pushing me away any more?'

'What do you think?'

He smiled when she bumped her belly lightly against him, reminding him of how close they were.

'I need you to say it.'

She rolled her eyes. 'You're annoying.'

'But you love me.'

She hesitated, but her eyes were fierce and sure when she nodded. 'I do.'

Who knew such simple words could set off such intense emotion in him?

'I love you, too,' he said softly.

'I know. You've loved me from the day you first saw me.'

'An exaggeration, I think.'

'I could see it in the way you looked at me. You were such a sucker.'

They were still debating when she led him into her flat. Smiling, he closed the door.

EPILOGUE

Four years later

'DO YOU KNOW what's worse than having twin toddlers?'

Benjamin didn't look over, too busy trying to get Tori, his daughter, off her brother. 'Tori, come on. You know you're bigger than Tavier.'

'Don't you dare get off your brother because you feel sorry for him,' Alexa said, kneeling on the sofa and looking over its back at them. 'He needs to learn.'

'You're encouraging this?' Benjamin asked.

'He loves it.'

Tavier gave a giggle just then. Benjamin threw up his hands. 'Honestly. I was trying to help you.'

Tavier grinned, and pulled his sister's hair. She responded by sitting on him. All things considered, they were playing fair.

'You haven't answered my question.'

He went to join her on the sofa. 'I'm too tired to pretend to remember what you asked.'

'What's worse than having twin toddlers?'

'Is this a riddle?'

He pulled her against him. Because she'd been kneeling, she had no way of resisting. Not that she would have resisted, he knew. Their marriage was a lot of debating, teasing—she was still talking about how he'd never found her handkerchief in his room—but none of it had to do with touching.

'It's not a riddle,' she said.

'A puzzle, then?'

'Same thing.'

'I don't think so.'

'Ben,' she said, taking his face in her hands. She did it whenever she was being serious with him. After four years together, two of them in marriage, it had happened all of four times. So he knew she was serious.

'What's worse than twin toddlers?' he repeated. 'I'm not sure. Our restaurants failing.'

'Our restaurants aren't failing.'

Of course they weren't, but he'd needed to say it because he needed to get over that fear. It was still there, though he'd been running In the Rough for three years now. It was still competing with Infinity, but somehow that competition didn't matter, since they were both doing what they loved. They both seemed to be good at it, too.

Of course they weren't failing.

'I give up.'

'So easily.'

'Baby.'

'Fine. What's worse than twin toddlers…is another baby.'

He blinked. 'I'm not sure I follow.'

'I'm pregnant, dummy.'

'You're…' He trailed off. Looked at the twins. 'But they're only three.'

'They'll be four when the baby gets here.'

'You're sure?'

'I'm pretty good at maths,' she said, rolling her eyes.

Now he rolled his. 'No. I meant, are you sure you're pregnant?'

'Doctor's results came back this morning.'

Because he had no words, he drew her in, holding her so damn tightly. Their lives together had been tough. Their family situations weren't easy. His father had passed away round about the same time he'd got the restaurant, but his mother had refused to live with him and Alexa. She'd found herself an assisted care facility, visited them occasionally, and Benjamin had had a tough time accepting that. Alexa had, a year after Lee had promised not to contact her, agreed to see him. It had taken them a lot of work to get to where they were now: Lee's monthly visits.

But all of that had been okay because they'd had one another. Their family, their kids... It was a life he'd never imagined. It was better than anything Alexa had imagined, she'd told him one night after the twins were born and they were staring at them.

'I can't believe they're yours.'

'Ours,' Alexa had replied, gripping his hand. 'You were here through everything, and you know you love them as much as I do. They're ours.'

She'd changed his life. And now she was doing it again.

'You're the best thing that ever happened to me,' he whispered.

'Wait until we're outnumbered before you say that.'

But she was smiling when he pulled away.

'We're having another baby,' he said.

'We are.' She leaned forward and kissed him. 'I love you.'

'I love you.'

A vase crashed as the twins rolled against the table. He and Alexa both jumped up, but the vase had been on the kitchen table, and the twins had knocked the coffee table, which had then knocked the vase to the ground in the kitchen, away from them. Their children were unharmed. The vase? Not so much. Tori and Tavier stared at them with wide eyes.

'I guess this means they love us, too,' Alexa said when they each had a twin in their arms.

'What a life.'

'What a life,' she repeated, and kissed him again.

* * * * *

RULES IN DECEIT

NICHOLE SEVERN

To my Bat Signal group, this book never would've gotten finished – twice – without you.

Chapter One

"You're not dead." Rage and relief urged Elizabeth Dawson to push away from the conference room table and tackle her former partner to the floor, but she held her control.

"It's good to see you, too, Sprinkles." Braxton Levitt's rich, seductive voice skittered under her skin. The sound of his handpicked nickname for her on his lips— as if they were still friends—tightened the muscles down her spine. That gray gaze pinned her against the back of her chair. A rare occasion. His eyes were normally green, depending on what he wore. She pushed the useless fact to the back of her mind as he planted his elbows on the massive wood table, leaning forward. Thick muscle and tendons flexed beneath his thin T-shirt, and goose bumps prickled down her arms. After all this time, did he honestly think he could walk back into her life after what he'd done?

"Don't call me that." No matter how many times she'd imagined this moment—of confronting him after all these months—there'd always been a small part of grief lodged in her chest. Her fingers curled into the center of her palms beneath the table. She had to stay in control. He wasn't the man she thought he'd been. Her heartbeat pounded loud behind her ears. Something alive—full of fury—clawed its way up her throat, but she couldn't touch him. Not in any way that counted. He'd made damn sure of that when she'd been pulled into countless interrogations after his disappearance. He cost her a career she'd spent a decade building. Now, no one but Blackhawk Security would hire her. Too much of a risk. Elizabeth mirrored his movements, clasping her hands in front of her on top of the table. "You paid my boss for my time, so get on with it. What do you want, Braxton?"

Despite the federal charges stacked against him, Braxton leaned back in his chair as he ran one hand through his dark shoulder-length hair, completely at ease. No longer was he the clean-cut, out-of-shape intelligence analyst she'd known back at the NSA. He'd changed, now something more primal, as though he'd seen things he couldn't possibly forget. New, bulky muscle stretched against the seams in his clothing. Physically different, yet the same man reflected underneath the confidence in his eyes, in his heart-stopping, manipulative smile. Under all those changes, he was still the man who'd walked out on her.

"I missed you." Stubble ran along his jawline, a little fuller than she remembered, deepening the permanent laugh lines around his mouth. She'd once missed the effects of that smile, the gut-clenching delirium he brought to the surface from no more than the upward tilt of his lips. The trust. Scary what that smile could hide.

"Is that why you're here?" she asked. "Because you missed me?"

The blue ball cap pulled low over his head failed to hide the bottom of a scar cut through his left eyebrow he'd gotten during a fight as a teenager. He studied the dark, rainy view of the Chugach mountain range through the floor-to-ceiling windows as if her words hadn't registered then recentered on her. He tapped his fingers against the gleaming conference room table as he sat back in his chair. "No." His shoulders rose on a deep inhale. "Dalton Meyer is dead. Someone tied your old NSA supervisor to a chair and tortured him so they could hijack Oversight and find you. I'm here to make sure that doesn't happen."

Elizabeth's blood iced. "That's not possible."

The facial-recognition program she'd been contracted to build for the NSA had the highest level of security ever coded. She'd designed the system to run autonomously. No human interference. Not even the director of the NSA had access. Its job was to strictly surveil the American population to identify threats to national security using security cameras, traffic cameras, email scanning. Law enforcement, FBI, CIA— they all relied on those feeds. If they'd gone off-line or been hijacked as Braxton suggested…the possibilities were endless.

The threats were endless.

Elizabeth released the breath she'd been holding. There was only one other person in the world who had the ability to override Oversight's programming. And he sat across the table from her. "How did you find me?"

"The fact I'm sitting here says a simple name change isn't working for you, Sprinkles," he said. "If I was able to find you in less than twenty-four hours, how long do you think it'll take someone who's hijacked your program and is gunning for you?"

"Stop calling me that. We're not friends anymore." Her jaw tightened. She followed passing movement outside the conference room through the blinds. Blackhawk Security provided home security, protection and investigative services and handled military contracts. She'd left the NSA behind, left that life behind. She'd moved on. Whatever this was, whatever Braxton wanted from her... No. Protecting her clients was her life now. Sullivan Bishop, Blackhawk Security's founder and CEO, and the rest of the team had taken a chance on her. Trained her without questions about her past. She wasn't about to blow it based on some wild theory the man who'd turned on her had cooked up to come back into her life. If someone had tortured her former project supervisor and was using her own program to hunt her, she had an entire team she could count on now. Former SEALs, Rangers, con men, a profiler. She didn't need him.

"Is that all you thought we were? Friends?" Braxton studied her, staring up at her from below thick, dark eyebrows. "I remember that night, Liz. Hard to believe I was that easy to forget."

"I haven't forgotten anything." She fought against the urge to swipe her hand across her lower abdomen. She'd waited four long months for this moment. Time to get it over with. Time to move on from him. "Since you've brought up that night, you should know I've been trying to find you for a few weeks now to tell you I'm pregnant."

Braxton sat forward in his chair, staring at her from across the table. "H-how?"

Really? That was the question he wanted her to answer? "You want me to explain to you how a woman gets pregnant? Okay. You see, when a woman thinks she's in love with her best friend she's trusted for years—"

"That's not what I meant." He exhaled hard. "We were careful. We used protection."

"Yes, well, obviously that didn't work." The pressure of his full attention tightened her insides. Liquid fire burned through her. She swallowed hard against the sensation. He wasn't supposed to affect her like this. Her crush had ended the night he'd left her to pick up the pieces of his mess. He exuded confidence with his subtle movements. The haze clouding her head dissipated, and she forced everything inside her to go cold as she stood. Digging for her phone, she swiped her thumb across the screen and set the timer. "Now, if you came here for my help, you're out of luck. I don't work for the NSA anymore. So I hope you've got your money's worth. This meeting is over. I'll give you a ten-minute head start before I call the FBI."

"You're being hunted, and you just told me you're pregnant with my baby." Braxton pushed away from the table. Three distinct lines deepened at the bridge of his nose. A day's worth of dark stubble that matched his hair shifted over his strong jaw. "I'm not going anywhere."

"I bet all the girls fall for that line. And, to be fair, I tried to tell you before now, but I couldn't find you." Elizabeth reached for the large oak door. Her instincts screamed for her to put as much space between them as she could. Her muscles had tensed so hard she ached. What did he expect her to do? Take him at his word that he was here to protect her? That he didn't need something from her? Not happening. She flashed her phone's screen at him. "Nine minutes. You're wasting time, Braxton."

He moved fast. Faster than she thought possible. His rough hands pressed into the door, hiking her blood pressure higher as he caged her in the circle of his massive arms. The faint scent of soap and his own masculine scent filled the air, urging her to breathe him in deeper. Two years as coworkers. He'd recruited her for the NSA, helped her land the contract of her career. Taken her to his bed.

"I'm the only one who can protect you, Liz. You know that," he said.

Fury built behind her sternum. A deadly wrath that couldn't be contained anymore.

"How would I know that?" Only the pounding of her heart working overtime filled her ears as she leveled her chin with the floor. She'd been naive to think anything could work between them. Elizabeth fisted her hands at her sides to control the trembling raking through her. She'd trusted him to the end. Denied the allegations the NSA had thrown at her in those interrogations after he vanished.

Braxton Levitt had an entire arsenal of body language, stories and personalities to force his marks into believing he was who he claimed. That was all she was to him. All she had been to him. A mark. "Everything I knew about you turned out to be a lie."

He straightened but kept her caged against the door. "I never lied to you."

"Really? Up until four months ago, I thought we knew everything about each other. You recruited me for the NSA to build Oversight, became the only person I could trust, then took me to your bed, and that same night, you disappeared." The last word hissed from her mouth. She lowered her voice in case the doors weren't soundproofed. "Now you're here, asking me to trust you with my life?" Elizabeth stepped into him, his clean scent surrounding her. It took everything she had— every last reserve of energy—to keep her control in place. "I don't know a damn thing about you, Braxton. I don't think I ever did. Now, let me go before I find a reason to reach for my gun."

His expression fell as he stepped back, taking his body heat with him. "I would never hurt you."

Her heart jolted in her chest from the sincerity in his voice. She studied him with a new mind-set. No emotion. No ties back to the past. Not as a spurned one-night stand but as an operative of Blackhawk Security. The creases around his mouth and the hollow circles under his eyes revealed the exhaustion he'd been dealing with since his disappearance. Worry lines, perhaps? A man on the run certainly became paranoid once stepping back into the spotlight. Every federal organization in the country had searched high and low for him since his disappearance. How had he managed to stay under the radar all this time? Whom had he relied on for help?

Not her. She locked her back teeth together. Didn't matter. This was the last time they'd be in the same room together. He'd slide back under the radar, and she'd go back to doing what she did best: protecting herself—and their baby. She wasn't heartless. She'd just taught herself how to use her heart less. Elizabeth's short black hair slid out from behind her ears as she wrenched the door open. "You already have."

A deep rumble reached her ears, claiming her attention a split second before Braxton shoved her into the hallway, and an eight-foot solid oak door rocketed into her.

Braxton Levitt slammed face-first into the nearest wall. Heat tunneled through his clothing as glass rained down around him. Emergency lighting cast the entire floor into shades of red as alarms kept rhythm with his pulse. He shifted his weight into his hands, flexing his jaw against the pain spreading through his ribs. Something wet slid down his cheek. He swiped at it as a gust of cold Alaskan air and rain rushed through what used to be an entire wall of windows. Blood.

"Liz!" Squinting through the rising smoke, he shoved to his feet. He blinked as a wave of dizziness tipped him into a fern still standing beside the one unhinged door. Yells punctured through the ringing in his ears. The sprinkler system fought to drench the sporadic fires clinging to the walls and the remains of the conference table. He stumbled through what was left of the massive door frame. "You better be alive."

Pain seared through his rib cage. His temples throbbed in rhythm to the alarms. She had to be alive. If he lost her again… No. He couldn't go there. Couldn't think like that. A dull ringing filled his ears. Then a moan. *Her* moan. Braxton's insides burned with an energy he'd learned to contain. A pair of familiar black boots registered in his peripheral vision. "Liz."

Air stalled in his lungs. Not because he'd nearly died in the timed explosion but because for thirty horrible, mind-numbing seconds, he'd lost her all over again. The hollowness of four months and ten days' separation from her vanished as he hauled an oak door and a few other pieces of debris off her with a guttural groan.

Brushing her hair out of her face, he lifted her into him, and the rest of the world fell away. Lean muscle flexed beneath her black leggings and leather jacket as her hand moved to her lower abdomen. Flames crackled around them, sirens already echoing off the surrounding buildings in the street below, but he didn't give a damn. His body's response to Liz had always been off the charts. She'd been the only woman who could make him lose control. Still was. Black smudges highlighted the sharp edges of her cheekbones and jawline. The steady thump at the base of her throat relieved the pressure in his chest, but that relief didn't last long. The bastard who'd hijacked Oversight had set a bomb—for Liz. He was sure of it. That rumbling sound right before the explosion? Had to have been a cell phone on vibrate. A detonator. He should've known the SOB hunting her would've tried to get to her at work. The more casualties, the better chance he had of getting away with murder. More time, more evidence to sift through. Braxton fought the rage spreading rampant beneath his sternum. "Come on, baby, open your eyes. Can you hear me?"

"For once in your life, call me by my actual name." A cough ripped up her throat. She jerked in his arms. Once. Twice. Brown eyes, as dark as chocolate, focused on him. "You do remember what it is, don't you?"

A smile fought for release. He'd missed her fire. Her attitude. Missed her. They'd been a great team back in Fort Meade. Saving the country one line of code at a time. Back before he'd destroyed everything between them to keep her safe. The smile disappeared. None of that mattered now. Keeping her alive—that was all that mattered.

"We've got to go." They had to get out of here before whoever had set that bomb realized he hadn't killed his target. Her lavender-scented shampoo invigorated his senses as she wrapped both arms around him, raising goose bumps on the back of his neck. It'd been a long time since he'd breathed her in. He tightened his hold around her waist. Get her to safety. Find the man using her own program to kill her. Maybe convince her he wasn't the man she believed.

"Liz!" Blackhawk Security's founder and CEO, Sullivan Bishop, shielded his face from the flames as he ran toward them. Braxton had done his homework. He knew the former SEAL had a woman of his own—a JAG Corps prosecutor—but the use of one of his nicknames for her still grated on Braxton's nerves. Liz didn't let anyone give her a nickname. The two had obviously gotten close since she'd relocated to Anchorage, and his gut tightened in response. One of the other operatives followed close on Sullivan's heels. Blackhawk's disgraced NYPD officer, Vincent Kalani, studied the scene, ready for battle. "You all right?"

"I'm fine." Liz wrenched out of Braxton's grasp, struggling to her feet on her own, all contact between them severed. She brushed debris from her clothing and huffed a piece of hair out of her face. From the outside, it was such an innocent movement, but Braxton understood her tells. He always had. Despite her hard exterior, she'd been rattled. And with good reason. Someone had tried to kill her. But she refused to allow anyone to see vulnerability, especially those she worked with. "But I think it's safe to say our conference room is not. Was anybody hurt in the explosion?"

"No fatalities. From what we can tell, most suffered only minor burns and scrapes from the blast." The forensics expert—Vincent—checked a gash on his forearm, swiping the blood away against his long-sleeve shirt. The muscled, tattooed Hawaiian ran a hand through his shoulder-length brown hair. "Was anyone else in the conference room with you?"

Liz shook her head. "No. Just the two of us."

"Good. As much as I'd like to scour through debris for evidence of who attacked us, let's get to the street. Then you tell me who the hell detonated a bomb in my building." Sullivan turned down the long hallway leading past several now-empty offices, a med clinic and the elevators and stairwell.

"Whoever it was targeted Liz," Braxton said.

Liz rounded into his vision. "There's no evidence proving that bomb was meant for me."

Sullivan twisted around, lips thin, hands ready to tear into the person responsible. "You used to work for the NSA, right? Sold classified intel and disappeared?" The CEO closed the distance between them, expression hard, calculating. "How do I know it wasn't you who set a bomb in my conference room? Some sick game to get Elizabeth back in your life."

"I'd kill any one of you before I let something happen to her. Is that a good enough answer for you?" Braxton straightened, surveying Vincent's position in case the ex-cop made a move, then centered on Sullivan again. "The only thing that matters is this guy is going to keep gunning for her. I'm not going to let that happen."

"Let's move out." Sullivan didn't take his attention off Braxton. "I don't trust you, Levitt." Veins pulsed under the skin of the CEO's arms as he pointed a dirt-smudged finger at him. "If anything happens to her, I will find you, understand?"

"I get that a lot." Despite the threat, Braxton didn't take offense. Liz had an entire team watching her back. He couldn't fault the former Navy SEAL for protecting a member in his unit.

Vincent rounded behind him and Liz to take up the rear with silent obedience.

The sirens grew louder. First responders had arrived on the scene.

But Braxton didn't move. The bomber hadn't attacked Blackhawk Security. Not directly. The bastard had had only one target in mind, and he was staring right at her. The bomb was just the beginning. Whoever had set it would try again as soon as they realized Liz had survived. And what better way to ensure a target had been killed than enter the building as an EMT or firefighter for confirmation? Braxton lowered his voice, instincts prickling. There was more at stake now. They had a baby to consider. He shifted closer to her, pain radiating at the base of his skull as they made their way down the hallway, and lowered his voice to prevent the security cameras from picking up their conversation. "Listen to me, Liz. We can't go to the street."

"Wow, you do remember my name." Liz moved to follow her colleagues.

He threaded his fingers around her arm and pulled her to a stop, holding her against him. The small fires burning around them had nothing on her body heat tunneling through his clothing right then. He covered his mouth and nose in the crook of his arm. "The garage. The only way in is with a key card, right? One exit? He'll expect us down on the street with the others. Not exiting the garage."

"What are you talking about?" She wrenched away from him as though his touch had burned her, his fingertips tingling from the friction against her jacket. Those dark brown eyes locked on him. One second. Two. Wisps of her uneven exhales tickled the oversensitized skin along his neck as she turned on him. "You're insane if you think I'm going anywhere with you."

Damn her stubbornness. One day it was going to get her killed. And then where would he be? He couldn't find the bastard hunting her down without her. No matter how many times he'd tried to keep his distance, every road, every move to stay off the Feds' radar had led him to Anchorage...to her. He didn't care that her program might've already recognized him and reported his location to the NSA. He wasn't going to leave her unprotected again.

The floor rumbled underneath his feet. The explosion had most likely damaged the building's structure. They didn't have a whole lot of time.

"We need to get moving." Vincent stepped toward them as Blackhawk Security's CEO disappeared into a cloud of smoke toward the stairwell. Close enough for Braxton to reach out and touch him.

He didn't want to have to do this, but the hard determination in Liz's gaze said he didn't have any other choice. "All right. If you're not going to come with me willingly—" Braxton spun, wrapping his grip around the Sig Sauer in Vincent's shoulder holster, and twisted the weapon out of the cop's reach. With one hard swing of the butt of the gun to the operative's head, Vincent went down. Hard. Braxton hefted the gun up, attention leveled on the shocked woman in front of him.

Liz lunged for the unconscious operative. "What the hell are you doing?"

"I'm kidnapping you. Once the bomber realizes you're not dead, we lose the upper hand." He pointed to her jacket with the barrel of the gun. "Toss your sidearm. Please."

"Do you honestly expect me to leave him here?"

Digging beneath the leather, she tossed her handgun to the floor.

"Of course not. Rescue is already on the way." He kicked the weapon out of her reach and motioned her to her feet. "Head for the garage."

"You should shoot me now, because I'm sure as hell going to shoot you when I get the chance." She rose slowly, expression controlled, voice dropping into dangerous territory. Her almond-shaped eyes narrowed on him. Exhaustion—maybe a bit of pain from the blast—broke through her movements as she stepped around the unconscious forensics expert at her feet.

"Wouldn't expect anything less from you." The muscles in Braxton's arms and neck tensed. In the thousands of times he'd imagined this moment, this wasn't how he'd expected their reunion to turn out. But there was a killer on the loose, and he wasn't about to lose her again. Not Liz. And not their baby. She shifted in front of him. Every second she stayed out in the open notched his blood pressure higher. "I'm trying to save your life, damn it. Trust me."

"Stop asking me to trust you." Liz headed for the stairwell, fire reflecting in her dark gaze. "I'm still trying to get over the last time you betrayed me."

Chapter Two

A wall of cold slammed into Elizabeth as they hit the parking garage. Only a handful of Blackhawk Security vehicles waited in their assigned spaces. There was no mysterious bomber waiting to ambush them as Braxton had suggested upstairs, but the illusion of safety never settled.

Could have had something to do with the fact the man she'd thought she'd loved all those months ago—the man whose child she carried—had a gun pressed against her spine. Smoke still registered on the air, the flashing of emergency lights bouncing off the cement walls from the street. There were only two ways out of the garage, and a bomb had taken out one of them. The other was the gate leading to the street, but she didn't reach for the key card all operatives were required to carry. And she wouldn't. Not until she had some answers. Scanning the SUVs, Elizabeth stopped dead in her tracks. "What's the plan now?"

"Now we get out of here." Braxton pressed his hand into the small of her back, bringing her into his side as he moved them toward one of the SUVs. His natural scent wrapped around her, but she didn't find comfort there like she used to. "Don't suppose you brought a set of car keys?"

"Must've left them in the jacket that doesn't smell like smoke." Pain washed through her. She glanced down at the gun aimed into her rib cage then quickly back to their surroundings as they closed in on the nearest SUV. Safety still on. Interesting. Sweat dripped down her spine as rain struck the cement at the edges of the asphalt. Him coming back here, the explosion... Her pulse throbbed at the base of her skull. This was insane. That bomb could've been meant for any operative on the team. For all she knew, it could've been meant for him. So why come back? Blackhawk Security wasn't in the habit of filling in the authorities on their clients, but her boss should've made an exception for Braxton Levitt. The NSA wouldn't stop looking for him. He'd never be a free man as long as treason charges were on the table. "What makes you think whoever set that bomb is targeting me?"

"Someone tortured your project supervisor and hijacked Oversight." He kept his attention on the prize ahead, occasionally studying their surroundings as they moved. Ten feet until they reached the nearest SUV. His expression tightened beneath the shadows cast from the baseball cap. "Call it instinct."

"Tell me you're joking." Elizabeth ripped away from his touch and shoved him away. He wouldn't use the gun on her. This entire kidnapping was a charade. "That's not enough evidence to insert yourself back into my life. You left, Braxton. You lost the right to pretend you care about anybody other than yourself."

The green-gray eyes she'd been trying to forget for the last four months locked on her, those mountainous shoulders deflating beneath his heavy brown jacket. "Liz—"

The stairwell door slammed closed behind them. Braxton twisted back over his shoulder, hefting the gun up and over toward the imagined threat. He stepped in front of her as though he intended to protect her from harm. But he wasn't a protector. No matter how many times he claimed he'd come back to keep her safe.

Thrusting her knee into the back of his, Elizabeth pushed him forward. The gun dropped to the pavement, metal on asphalt loud in her ears as he fought to balance. Lunging for it, she barely wrapped her fingers around the grip before he pulled her upright, his grip on her wrist cutting off circulation. Damn, he moved fast.

His breath fanned across the sensitive skin along her collarbones. Warmth spread from her neck up into her cheeks as he held her close, his mouth mere centimeters from hers. A mouth meant for spilling lies. "I'm not here to hurt you, Liz. I would never hurt you."

Did she really have to remind him there were more ways to hurt her than the physical? He'd destroyed her career, gotten her pregnant and disappeared. It wasn't until Sullivan Bishop and the Blackhawk Security team had offered her a place as their network security analyst three months ago that she'd started pulling the shattered pieces of her life back together. Without them, who knew where she would be right now.

"Let me go." She fought to free herself, but Braxton only held her tighter. Once upon a time, she would've enjoyed that strong grip around her. Her insides instantly clenched. Now, the only thought running through her head centered on getting as far from him as possible. "What do you want from me?"

Her hand shook around the warm steel of the gun. She couldn't let him get inside her head.

"I want you alive, for starters." He pressed her against him, his fingertips leaving impressions in the small of her back. He studied her from forehead to chin. "If that means I have to knock you unconscious and throw you over my shoulder, I will."

Air rushed from her lungs. The sincerity in his gaze, in his voice… He meant it. A short burst from one of the police sirens tensed the muscles down her spine but brought her back into the moment. "You actually believe someone is trying to kill me?"

"I have the proof." Braxton released his hold on her wrist but let her keep the gun. Offering her a hand, he gave her the space to make the choice for herself. "All you have to do is trust me."

"You make it sound so easy." Every cell in her body urged her to take his hand. The sharp angles to his jaw, the heavy five o'clock shadow, the slight bend in his nose where he'd broken it playing football one summer, even the thin slice of scar across his palm where he'd slipped on ice in elementary school… It was all so familiar. Comforting. But she didn't know this man. The Braxton she'd known never would've deserted her in the first place. She forced her attention to his eyes.

"If I agree to go with you, you will answer every question I have."

"I give you my word." His voice dropped an octave. Sensual, compelling.

Her chest tightened on a deep inhale. She loosened her grip around the gun, the tingling sensation in her fingers subsiding as she leveled her chin with the asphalt. Handing over Vincent's stolen Sig Sauer, Elizabeth drew back when his fingers closed on top of hers. In an almost militaristic manner, he cleared the loaded round, dropped the magazine, slammed it back into place and chambered another. No. Whoever stood in front of her wasn't *her* Braxton. This man was hardened, muscled. Dangerous. She exhaled against the nausea churning inside. "And when this is over, you'll crawl back to the rock you've been hiding under for the last four months. Are we clear?"

The lines etched between his dark eyebrows deepened. He dropped the gun to his side, so casual she'd believe he'd handled a firearm all his life. Which wasn't the case. "Do you remember what I said to you that first day we met?"

The words forced their way forward from the back of her mind. Her throat tightened around the memory of her first day of working for the NSA, the day she'd met him. She swiped her tongue across her dry lips. "I sat down at the desk next to yours with my ice cream from the cafeteria, and you made fun of my choice of topping." Rainbow-colored sprinkles. The nickname he'd called her ever since. A smile pulled at one edge of her mouth. "Then you said, 'One thing you need to understand here, Sprinkles. This place will eat you alive. Stick with me, and no matter what happens, you can count on me to get you out of it.'" A hint of smoke coming off his clothing singed deep into her lungs as she focused on him. "And I believed you."

"Do you still believe me?" he asked.

Yes. No. Her stomach flipped. If someone was trying to kill her, she wouldn't stand around here all day waiting for it to happen. "I don't know what to believe."

Movement registered in her peripheral vision at the automatic gate. A firefighter. He'd presumably been assigned to check the rest of the building for signs of structural damage and flames. Dressed in full protective equipment, including face shield, he stopped just outside the gate and tried to pull it up manually. Wouldn't work. That gate didn't open for anybody unless they worked in the building. He'd have to get the fire code from her boss, Sullivan Bishop. Stiffness drained from the muscles around her spine a split second before the gate lifted on its own. "Everything okay down here?"

Braxton turned, maneuvering the gun behind his back. Out of sight.

"We're fine. How'd you get in? That gate is supposed to be sealed." Warning bells rang loud in her head. That wasn't right. Nobody could access that gate—not even emergency personnel—without a Blackhawk Security operative key card or individualized code. She dropped her voice as the firefighter advanced. Too fast. Alone. "Braxton…"

The firefighter lifted a handgun and took aim. At her.

A strong hand pushed her to the ground as a bullet

ripped past her ear. The garage turned on its axis. Braxton took position in front of her as he returned fire. Pain shot up through her knees, loose asphalt ripping holes in her leggings, but Elizabeth didn't hesitate. Digging in her jacket pocket, she wrapped her hand around the keys to her company SUV near the shooter and hit the panic button.

Headlights flashed; the alarm blared. It'd only distract the shooter for a few seconds, but that was all she needed. The gunfire died. She shoved to her feet and sprinted for Elliot Dunham's SUV. Blackhawk Security's private investigator usually left his keys in the front seat, and she silently prayed he hadn't changed up his routine. "Come on!"

Footsteps echoed close behind her as bullets two and three barely missed their mark. Chunks of cement nicked at her exposed skin, and she raised her arms to protect her face. Wouldn't do a damn bit of good against a bullet, but instinct and adrenaline drove her now. She rounded the tail end of Elliot's SUV and wrenched the door open. No keys. She dived inside, ripping the visor down. The keys dropped into her lap.

Braxton took cover behind the hood, squeezing off another shot. Then a third.

"Get in!" Elizabeth pulled the driver's side door closed and started the engine. Shoving the SUV into Drive, she paused as the shooter positioned himself directly in front of them.

Hiking himself into the back seat, Braxton tapped on her shoulder. "Liz, go!"

The firefighter raised his gun, taking aim. One second. Two. And fired.

She froze as the bulletproof glass held against the shot. Then unfroze as rage coursed through her. The shooter had come for *her*, targeted *her*. Lifting her foot from the brake, she slammed on the accelerator and steered directly into the shooter. The growl of the engine drowned the pounding of her heartbeat in her ears. Pressure built in her lungs. "Hang on back there."

Her leather seat protested against his grip on the headrest. "Liz…"

The shooter pulled the trigger two more times, each bullet caught in the windshield, a split second before he launched himself out of the way of the vehicle.

Elizabeth spun the steering wheel toward the still-open security gate. Bouncing in her seat as they catapulted over the gate's tracks, she fishtailed out of the garage. Blackhawk Security grew distant in the rear-view mirror. Two familiar faces stepped into the middle of the road behind them, but she didn't have time to stop and explain everything to her team. Braxton had been telling the truth.

Someone was targeting her, but she wasn't the only one she had to worry about now. She lifted her gaze to the rearview mirror, to the father of her unborn baby. "Fine. You can take me to whatever safe house you've set up until we figure out who you think is trying to kill me. But to be clear, it's not because I trust you." Elizabeth took a deep breath, her ribs aching from the explosion in the conference room, then forced her attention back to the road. "It's because you got me pregnant."

"I STILL CAN'T believe it." Braxton couldn't think. Couldn't breathe. Someone had tried to kill the woman he vowed to protect, but it was more than that. Adrenaline drained from his veins in small increments, but not enough to clear his head.

Wow. Liz was pregnant. And he was the father. She'd told him before the explosion, but he hadn't been able to process that until now. It'd been kind of hard to think when the bullets were flying. Reaction—that was what he was good at. But…he was going to be a father. A smile threatened to overwhelm his features, pure joy exploding through him.

"Someone just tried to kill us. Twice. Can we please focus on that?" The weight of her attention pinned him against his seat from the rearview mirror. "I think we have bigger problems to talk about."

"I think the fact you're pregnant is pretty big." He swayed with the SUV as she wound through neighborhoods, around strip malls and into the edges of the city. Days of staying off the grid, months of grueling physical training, years of working for the NSA…none of it had prepared him for this. A baby. He compressed the safety button on the stolen gun and set it beside him on the seat. They were going to have a baby. "Might as well not have used protection at all."

"Yeah, apparently, latex wasn't strong enough for your swimmers." A hint of a smile played across her mouth, the first softening of her guard since he set sights on her in the conference room. "If you're thinking about asking me whether or not I'm sure the baby is yours, I'll save you the time. Yes, Braxton, she's yours.

No, Braxton, I haven't been with anybody else since the night you took me to bed then disappeared without a word. And, yes, I'm keeping the baby. I plan to raise her on my own without help. Any other questions?"

"It's a girl?" He ran his palms over the baseball cap and interlaced his fingers at the crown of his head. He turned away from her, surveying the curve of the street but not really seeing where they were. The muscles across his back strained under the self-induced pressure. He didn't know what else to say, what to think. They were having a girl?

"I found out the sex a couple days ago." The vulnerability in her voice compelled him to face her again, but she'd turned her gaze back to the road. Snow and ice kicked up along the SUV. She rolled her lips between her teeth. "This wasn't how I wanted you to find out. I tried to find you, but four months is a long time waiting for you to come back. Figured you'd moved on and I could do the same. When I got tired of the NSA interrogating me about your whereabouts, I changed my name in every federal database I could hack and relocated."

He'd known about her search effort but ultimately decided to stay away. It'd been the hardest decision of his life and the only way to keep her safe. Until four days ago when he'd learned about Dalton Meyer's murder and that Oversight's feeds had been hacked. Until he'd uncovered the program's surveillance logs. Someone had put her in their crosshairs.

Intense pressure built behind his sternum as she took a sharp left. The city came into focus for the first time since Braxton had gotten in the vehicle. A familiar line

of bare trees surrounding Fairview Lions Park cut off
his air. A good foot of snow covered the all-too-familiar
horseshoe pit and most of the green and purple playground where he'd spent countless nights as a kid after
his father had lost the house to the bank. Right there,
under the small rock wall. He forced his attention back
to the rearview mirror as a group of homeless made
their way down the street, back to her, his anchor. No
point in studying the weathered faces as they passed.
His old man had most likely died from his addictions
a long time ago. Wasn't important. The past was dead,
and he sure as hell would make sure it stayed that way.
"Did you also figure moving here was enough to keep
me from finding you?"

"I'd accepted you weren't coming back." Liz cocked
her head. "In retrospect, I guess Anchorage had been
on my mind since you told me you'd never step foot
in this city again. It'd worked until an hour ago." She
glanced at him—almost too fast for him to catch it—
then back to the road. "You never told me how you
managed to find me."

"You're predictable. I knew you'd never change your
first name." Not after what she'd told him about her
mother and the long line of Elizabeths in her family.
"As for your new last name, I remembered your favorite TV show growing up. Wasn't hard to sift through
the short list of Elizabeth Dawsons and track you down
from there."

Nothing would've stopped him from finding her.

"I'll keep that in mind next time." Her knuckles
tightened over the steering wheel. There wouldn't be a

next time. Not if he had anything to say about it. She turned the SUV east, leaving the park and memories he'd worked hard to bury behind. "So are you going to tell me where this safe house of yours is or are we going to drive around all night?"

"Make one more loop around the neighborhood." Braxton studied the cars behind them. They hadn't been followed. Whoever had taken shots at them in the parking garage probably hadn't been able to make it past the wall of police officers and emergency personnel surrounding the building. At least, not in a hurry. On top of that, her team had seen them race from the scene. His pulse hammered at the base of his skull, and he wiped at the dried patches of blood along his forehead. He should've known the bastard would come at her at Blackhawk Security. As far as he'd been able to tell over the last few days, that was where she'd spent most of her time. Day and night. Protecting her clients just as she'd protected millions of lives during her contract work for the NSA. And now with a baby. "Have you told your team?"

"No. Not yet." Her shoulders rose on an audible inhale. Hesitation tightened the cords running down her neck. She made another turn, seemingly refusing to look back at him. "I was thinking of telling Sullivan about the baby today, but then someone blew up the conference room and it sort of slipped to the back of my mind."

A laugh escaped from his control. She always did have a way of downplaying stressful situations with sarcasm. "Understandable."

"I work in network security now." Liz ran a hand through her hair and levered her elbow against the driver's side door. "My clients come to me to assess their firewalls, encrypt the information on their servers, basically make their networks unhackable. I analyze shell corporations and perform background checks for everyone on my team. I can't think of a single person who would want me dead."

"All I know is someone tried to kill you back there." He wouldn't discount the possibility the threat was tied to Blackhawk Security. They had to consider all the angles. Past, present, someone invested in the outcome of the firm's military and private contracts. The list of suspects with the kind of knowledge and training that shooter had to have was endless, but military training was a definite. He needed access to her client files. "And I'm not going to let them succeed."

"Do you think this could be linked to my contract with the NSA?" Her voice wavered. To someone who hadn't memorized every inflection, every emotion, it would've gone unnoticed. But not to him. He knew her inside and out, down to a cellular level. Even with filtered moonlight coming through the SUV's tinted windows, he noted the color draining from her face. Hell. The nightmares. How could he have forgotten about her damn nightmares? Her throat worked to swallow. "Maybe a family member or someone who'd gotten a look at the files?"

Her fear slid through him, and his body reacted automatically. Ready for battle to protect what was his. One breath. Two. "You still have nightmares."

Not a question. He was there during Oversight's trial run. He'd witnessed how it'd affected her.

"Assuming the person who shot at us in the garage is the same person who hacked those feeds, which might not be the case, you should be able to use my backdoor access to narrow down a location." Him? Liz twisted the steering wheel to the right a little too hard. He fell back against the seat and reached out for his gun before it fell to the floor. Okay, so she didn't want to talk about what kept her up at night, but he couldn't find this bastard on his own. He needed her to run the program. "The only problem is the access opens a two-way door. The second you lock on to a location, he has yours."

"Don't you mean he'd have *our* location?" he asked.

"No, Braxton." She set her jaw, chancing a quick glance into the rearview mirror. "I told you the day I terminated my consulting contract with the NSA. I'll never touch that program again. If you want to trace those feeds, you're doing it alone."

Braxton didn't answer.

"Turn right at the next street. Third building from the end of the road." The apartment he'd leased under a fake name off one of those online sites where home owners rented out their homes wasn't much. Two bedrooms, two bathrooms. But it would get the job done while he was back in Anchorage. However long that would be. He studied Liz as she pulled the SUV to the curb then shouldered his way out of the vehicle behind her. She stepped onto the pavement, hand supporting her head where shrapnel had cut into her during the explosion. A groan worked up her throat, and his blood pressure spiked. He stepped into her, her rough exhale skimming across his neck as rain pounded onto his shoulders. "You okay?"

"It's nothing." She dropped her hand and stepped away. Her right hand shook slightly. She tried to hide it by curling her fingers into her palms, but she couldn't hide from him.

She was scared. Rightfully so, but he'd die before he let anything happen to her. Or their baby. "I'm not going to let that bastard lay a finger on you. I promise."

Silence settled between them. Tight, thick and full of distance.

"I only agreed to your help because someone was shooting at us, and I didn't want to die." Liz shook her head. "So I don't need your promises. I need you to keep me alive until I figure out who wants me dead."

Chapter Three

Elizabeth hefted the SUV's gate above her head and lifted the black duffel bag standard for all Blackhawk Security operatives from the dark interior. Mostly supplies. A couple changes of clothes, ammunition, food storage, emergency flares. The basics of her new profession. Never knew what kind of weather or client would come calling. Although they'd borrowed Elliot's SUV, and the clothes weren't going to fit her. "If you're not going to trace Oversight's feeds on your own, fill me in on your plan."

They'd wound a lot of circles through neighborhoods, parks and strip malls, finally ending up at what looked like an apartment complex. The shooter hadn't followed them. She would've spotted him through the maze of routes they'd taken. The SOB who'd taken a shot at her was most likely licking his wounds and devising another way to kill her. If Braxton had been telling the truth about the shooter's target. She paused at the thought. She took care of network security for a start-up security company. Wasn't exactly the kind of job that would land her in a killer's crosshairs. But if this had anything to do with her work for the NSA...

No. It couldn't. She'd left that life behind months ago. Besides, those files were classified. It'd take someone with much higher security clearance than the director of the NSA to access them. That'd been part of the deal. She'd signed dozens of nondisclosure agreements about the program's trial run, and the federal government would hide Oversight's existence at all costs.

"First, I want your forensics guy to analyze those bullets in the windshield." Braxton leaned against the back quarter panel mere inches from her, arms crossed across that broad chest of his. The weight of his attention pressurized the air in her lungs. He watched her carefully, as though he couldn't miss a single moment. "Maybe we'll get lucky with an ID on the unsub trying to kill you, and—"

"And you go back into hiding." That was the deal. She'd agreed to his protection, and as soon as they had a viable lead on that shooter, he'd go back to whatever rock he been hiding under for the last four months and let her move on with her life. Alone. Storm clouds shifted overhead as the last remnants of rain pelted against her leather jacket, but the crisp, cleansing atmospheric scent did nothing to clear her head. Unzipping the duffel, she reached in, wrapped her shaking hand around her teammate's backup weapon, and loaded a fresh magazine. Full.

"Right," he said.

Setting the bag back in the trunk, she faced Braxton with her emotions in check and her guard in place. He might be the father of her unborn baby, but that didn't mean she had to trust him. Elizabeth lifted her gaze to his. "You think going back to Blackhawk Security to hand over the bullets is a good idea? I seem to remember half of the penthouse floor is missing, and we almost died in the garage."

Braxton moved in close, too close, his clean, masculine scent mixing with the aroma of rain. The combination urged her to lean into him, to forget how much she'd missed him. She'd told herself—hell, told him—she'd moved on, but her body had yet to grasp the idea. "I told you I won't let him touch you. You have my word."

"And I told you your word doesn't mean a damn thing to me." She fought back a quiver. Tightness ran down her neck and back. After countless hours—months—of trying to find him, here he stood less than a foot away. In the flesh. Tightening her grip around the duffel bag, she scrambled for purchase as the past threatened to drag her under. No. She'd been down this path once before. She'd trusted him, and it cost her everything. "We should ditch the vehicle and get inside. If the shooter is the same person who hijacked Oversight's feeds, he'll be able to track us to this area and try to shoot me again."

Ten minutes later, they'd abandoned the SUV, sans bullets in the windshield, and hiked back to the apartment on foot. Braxton led her up two flights of stairs and toward an apartment in the back of the third building, his clothing barely concealing the muscle he'd put on since the last time she'd seen him. And not just in his upper body. His legs flexed beneath denim, powerful and strong. Inserting a key in the lock, he turned the doorknob and shouldered the door open. "Wait here a minute."

He didn't wait for her answer as he disappeared inside.

A breeze shook the trees below, and she stepped to the railing. No shooters waiting in the trees. No bomb ticking off nearby. She smoothed her hand over her lower abdomen as a rush of nausea churned in her stomach. Who would want her dead? And why now?

"Surveillance is clean." Braxton filled the door frame just inside her peripheral vision. "The place isn't much, but it gets the job done. We've got power, water, gas, and I had groceries delivered yesterday."

She followed him inside, the skin along her collarbones prickling with the onslaught of a draft coming from the vents above. "Hiding your how-to-be-a-good-spy magazines before I came inside?"

"No, I keep those locked up all the time." Braxton's laugh replaced the cold-induced goose pimples along her arms with heat, but she couldn't afford to give it much notice. Find out who was trying to kill her and why, then move on with her life. That was it.

He'd been right about the apartment. It wasn't much, but it'd work for what they needed. Large windows took up most of the east wall, providing a jaw-dropping view of the mountains. A large sectional had been positioned in the corner of the living room, only photos of wildlife and scenic Alaska hanging on the white walls. Two bedrooms, two bathrooms from the looks of it. Simple.

Bare. But the setup of surveillance equipment across the dining room table said secure. It suited him. Her, too.

"You can take the back bedroom if you want to clean up. There's a bathroom attached to that one, so we don't have to share." Braxton maneuvered behind her, and she straightened a bit more. "I'll have some food for us by the time you're done."

"Good idea. Give me a few minutes." She checked her wristwatch. Nine at night. They weren't going to get much done at this hour. The investigation would have to start in the morning. Another rush of nausea gripped her tight, and she fought to breathe through her nose to counter it. Didn't work. The target of a shooter, re-united with the man she thought she'd never see again, and suffering from morning sickness all at the same time. Great.

"Take your time." He headed toward the kitchen, tossing his baseball cap onto the counter. His dark hair skimmed his shoulders, and, hell, she'd be lying if she didn't admit the look worked for him.

Elizabeth forced one foot in front of the other. Space. She needed space. Away from him. The lighttan-colored walls passed in a blur as she escaped to the nearest bedroom. She wasn't sure if this was the room he'd meant for her to take, but at the moment, she didn't care. Tossing her duffel onto the floor, she exhaled hard and ran a hand through her hair.

It'd been four months since she'd made the worst mistake of her life by climbing under the sheets with Braxton. That should've been long enough to get control of her physical reactions. Damn it. This wasn't the plan. She'd accepted there would be a bottomless hole in her heart where she'd shove everything she felt for Braxton Levitt in order to raise their daughter on her own. But he'd come back. To protect her. Still, while she might have to stay within physical proximity of him, she wouldn't let him hurt her again. Keeping her emotional distance would have to do. That, and a securely locked bedroom door. "Just a few days, baby girl. We've got this."

The bedroom came into focus. Single queen-size bed, nightstand, dresser with some papers settled on top, same type of photography on the walls as she'd noticed in the living room. And a cardboard box full of phones stashed in the corner. She fished out a phone from the middle of pile and studied the room again. Groceries delivered, a box of phones, surveillance setup. How long had Braxton planned on staying here?

She swiped her thumb across the screen and dialed Vincent Kalani's number from memory. She'd left her phone with the SUV about a mile west of here. Anyone who tried pinging it for a location would only find disappointment. Blackhawk Security training 101. The other line rang three times. Then four. "Come on, Vincent. Pick up the phone." Another ring. If he hadn't made it out of the building alive, she'd never forgive herself for leaving the forensics expert in the middle of a crime scene. "Pick up the damn—"

"Kalani." Vincent's usually smooth voice sounded rough, damaged.

"You're alive." Relief flooded through her. She exhaled hard, closing her eyes with a hand on her forehead. Turning her back to the door, she ignored the burn in her lower lash line. Hormones. Crying came too easy these days. "I was beginning to worry I'd be stuck with your vengeful ghost for the rest of my life."

"No thanks to your new bodyguard there." Muffled static reached through his end of the line. "What number are you calling from?"

"A burner I picked up out of a box full of phones. Consider this my new number for the time being." She chewed on the end of her thumbnail. They shouldn't have left him behind. She could've fought Braxton harder, could've done *something*. "Tell me you're okay."

"I'm good," Vincent said. "Confirm you're safe and give me permission to punch your ex in the face the next time I see him."

"I'm safe. For now. And permission granted." She dropped her hand and rolled her shoulders back. Pain shot through the right side of her rib cage, and she doubled over with a rough exhale. "But you'll have to get in line."

"Liz?" Vincent asked. "You okay?"

"Fine for someone who took an eight-foot oak door to the right side." She breathed through the pain. "Listen, whoever set that bomb tried to finish the job in the garage. I pulled three slugs out of Elliot's windshield, but I'm not sure how to hand them off to you without putting myself back in the open."

"Stay put," Vincent said. "I'll have Anchorage PD's crime scene unit check it out. Maybe we'll get lucky on a stray casing. If that doesn't work, we'll set something up to get me those slugs. You should know, as of right now the Sovereign Army is taking credit for the bombing."

"The privacy activists? Explosives aren't usually their forte." Headlines had taken over national news with the group's intent to sell and publish congressmen and women's browsing histories and darkest secrets, but setting a bomb at a security company? Although if the extremist group discovered she'd helped the federal government create a surveillance system to spy on them for the past year, who knew how far they'd escalate. Still, something about that didn't sit well. A knock at the door pushed her pulse higher. Braxton. She nodded, even though Vincent couldn't possibly see it, and turned as the bedroom door cracked open. "Thanks for the intel. Call me if you find anything else."

She ended the call, nervous energy skittering up her spine.

Green-gray eyes locked on her and, suddenly, the last four months disappeared to the back of her mind. Braxton made his way inside, a white box in one hand and a steaming bowl of something intoxicating in the other. "Your team?"

"Yeah. Hope you don't mind I borrowed one of your phones to make the call." She tossed the burner onto the bed, crossing her arms over her midsection. Grinding her teeth, she fought against the pain ripping through her side. "Looks like Sovereign Army took credit for the bombing. Vincent's sending Anchorage PD to analyze the scene in the garage. He'll call back if he finds something. He's very much looking forward to punching you in the face when he sees you again."

"Fair enough." A smile curled at one edge of his mouth, and his all-too-familiar pull hooked into her. Damn it. When would he stop affecting her like this? Braxton closed the space between them, coming within mere inches of her. Her breath caught in her throat as he maneuvered around her to set the bowl on the nightstand. Straightening, he backed away slowly, that mesmerizing gaze steady on her. "So now that there's nothing more we can do tonight, take off your shirt."

EXPERTS SAID TIME healed old wounds, but what the hell did they know? Braxton popped open the first aid kit beside him on the bed. How many times had he called her over the last month from this very same safe house only to hang up when she answered? Two? Five? Maybe more. She wouldn't have spoken to him if he'd opened his mouth. That was clear now. More than likely, she would've demanded a trace on the call the second she'd realized who was on the other line and sent any resource available his way. His disappearance obviously hadn't torn her apart as much as it had him. But, hell, he deserved it. Even if leaving had been to protect her.

"Excuse me?" Liz cradled her rib cage. Her features contorted but smoothed almost instantly. As though she'd caught herself in a moment of weakness.

Stubborn woman. On a scale from one to ten, he pegged her pain around a seven. Yet she hadn't said a word. He'd noticed the way she favored that side, the small flinches in her expression. She'd been lucky to survive that explosion. If it weren't for the very same oak door that'd possibly cracked her ribs protecting her from most of the shrapnel, she might not be standing here. The ache under his sternum, the one connected with the woman standing mere feet away, refused to subside as he studied the fast tick of her pulse at the base of her throat. "The only way for me to see if your ribs are broken is you taking off your shirt."

"I'm fine. I'm sure it's a rib out of place. It'll either pop back when it's ready, or this girl will kick it back where it belongs in the next few months." She stared up at the ceiling, her fingers prodding into her side. Small lines creased her expression, and his gut clenched. In her next breath, she took back control. "Besides, I'm pretty sure you're just looking for a way back under my shirt. Which isn't going to happen."

A laugh rumbled from deep in his chest. Exhaustion played a wicked game across her expression, but she'd keep going until they identified the unsub responsible for that bomb. That'd been one of the reasons he'd recommended her to Dalton Meyer for the Oversight project at the NSA two years ago. He'd studied her work programming drones for the small start-up company in Washington, DC, and admired her determination to get the job done. Nothing had changed in that respect. But sacrificing her health in the name of the investigation wouldn't get them anywhere. "Can you blame a guy for trying?"

Her burst of laughter filled the room but cut off in her next breath. She doubled over, hiking her hand into her side.

"All right, enough stalling." Braxton tossed the first

aid kit onto the bed and propelled himself to his feet. "I'm taking a look at your ribs whether you like it or not."

"Why?" Liz straightened slowly, pain evident on her features. "Unless you got your medical degree while you were in hiding?"

"Not exactly, but you learn a few things when you're on your own and the government has plastered your face on the front page of the FBI's website." He feathered his fingertips under her shirt and lifted the black silk. Her sharp gasp quickened his pulse, and a rush of satisfaction shot through him. He'd always been able to change her breathing patterns with one touch. Nice to know some things hadn't changed. Smooth skin slid against the rough calluses on his hand. And wasn't that the perfect metaphor for their relationship—rough versus smooth. Bruises had already started darkening around her bottom rib on the right side. He studied her expression in his peripheral vision as he pressed his thumb into the bone. "It's no way to live, though. Strange cities, fake names, avoiding human interaction." Avoiding her. "Gets old real fast."

"Well, now it looks like we have something in common." She hissed as he prodded the third rib from the bottom. "Now I'm being hunted like an animal. Only this predator isn't the federal government and has tried to blow me up and shoot me in the same day."

He locked his jaw to cool the anger churning in his gut. If he hadn't left, none of this would've happened.

"Nothing feels broken." Braxton dropped his hand. Every cell in his body screamed for him to erase the worry lines from her expression, but he couldn't move.

He studied the vulnerability playing across her face. What he wouldn't give to help her forget the nightmare of the last couple hours. "I'll get you a heating pad for the soreness and ice for the inflammation. Should be good as new in a couple days."

A weak smile played across her mouth. "Thanks."

He turned away from her and headed toward the door. If he didn't, the unquenched desire that'd burrowed itself beneath his skin and crackled along his veins when he touched her would take control. Her life—their baby's life—had been put at risk because of him. Anything more between them would only make it that much harder to walk away. That'd been the deal. She agreed to his protection. He'd go back into hiding. Fighting to keep his focus trained, Braxton forced one foot in front of the other.

"Why'd you come back?" she asked. "Why now?"

He froze, his hands curling into fists at his side. Ten seconds. That was all he needed to clear his head, but she couldn't even give him that. "Liz—"

"I'd finally worked out what I would say to our baby the day she asked about her father, but then you walked right into Blackhawk Security. Have to admit—" she fitted her shirt back into place out of the corner of his eye "—I never saw it coming."

Braxton turned. No point in lying. He'd never been able to stay away from her for more than a few days at a time. Even now, he was caught in the undeniable gravitational pull of hers, and he wouldn't be able to fight it much longer. "I always planned on coming back."

"Did you ever think you never should've left in the

first place?" Her expression shifted from genuine curiosity to outright fury. The small muscles along her jaw flexed. Liz took a step back as he approached then brushed right past him. As though his revelation ignited that anger she desperately fought to control. "Maybe then we wouldn't be in this mess."

He wrapped his hand around hers and pulled her into him. Lean muscle flexed along her arm, and he imagined all too easily exploring every inch of the strength under her clothing. Every mole. Every scar. The soft curve of her lower abdominals where their baby thrived. He brushed his thumb over the back of her hand and loosened his grip. Desire surged through him, a mere taste of the chaos capable of rendering him completely useless when she was around. Damn what she thought of him, damn the investigation or the reason he'd stayed away from her for the last sixteen weeks. She had to know the truth. She deserved to know.

Liz stared up at him with that gorgeous fire in her expression—almost daring him to make his next move—but didn't wrench out of his hold.

He forced the words to the tip of his tongue, but no sound left his mouth. Licking his lips, he dropped his hand from hers. No. Now wasn't the time. Because he couldn't lose her again. Every decision he'd made over his career had a price, but he'd never expected her to pay for any of it. And she would once she learned the truth.

"You're right. I never should've left, and I'll spend the rest of my life making it up to you and our baby if that's what you want." He framed her hips between both hands, his thumbs grazing her lower belly. Braxton stepped into her, relishing in the slight widening of her eyes, of her exhale rushing against the skin along his neck. "Starting now."

Reaching past her, he skimmed his hand over the top of the dresser and grabbed the yellow envelope resting on top. He slid it between them and handed it to her. Everything that'd happened today at Blackhawk Security—the bomb, the shooter in the garage—had to do with what was in the envelope. "You asked me why I came back. Why now? This is why."

She took the envelope from him, the furrow between her dark eyebrows deepening. She slid her fingers inside the envelope and pulled out the short stack of surveillance photos he'd collected from Oversight's servers. Photos of her. Confusion deepened the lines across her forehead. "What is this?"

She blinked as realization hit her hard.

He wanted to reach for her. To comfort her. But didn't.

The envelope protested in her hand. Liz shook her head and took a step back. She shuffled through the stack of photos, one after the other. But studying photos wouldn't make the truth any less real. Someone had been hunting her for months. "Wh-how did you get these?"

"I programmed an alert into Oversight's code to notify me when you were the subject before I left the agency." If he hadn't, she—and their baby—wouldn't be standing here right now. "I started getting alerts six days ago. Right after I read about Dalton Meyer's murder and discovered Oversight's feeds were hijacked."

"So many photos. Outside the office, getting into my car." Her voice barely registered. Too soft. Too full of fear. The muscles down his spine responded. She swallowed hard, eyes wide. "This one is from a traffic camera as I drove home." Liz ran a hand through her hair as her mouth parted. "Someone's been watching me? For how long?"

"No, someone has been stalking you." He picked out one particular photo from the back and handed it to her. A photo of her leaving her own home. Whoever had been watching her knew where she lived. "And I'm here to find out why."

Chapter Four

"I don't think the Sovereign Army took these pictures." Elizabeth dropped the photos in her hand to her side. She'd been followed for weeks—maybe months. She'd had no idea, but she couldn't let the fear spreading at the back of her mind take control. What else had her stalker uncovered? Her head spun. Nausea festered. *Focus.* She forced herself to breathe deep. She'd started a new life here, loved her job, was having a baby. Nobody would take that from her. Not some extremist group. Not Braxton. And not whoever had tried to blow her up three hours ago.

She headed for the door. Braxton was a former analyst. Analysts ran secure networks. All she needed was a computer. She trusted her team—trusted Vincent—with her life, but she had to see the Sovereign Army taking credit for planting that bomb at Blackhawk Security herself. The shooter in the garage, the photos Braxton uncovered. Neither of those were part of the group's MO. "An extremist group bent on protecting Americans' privacy wouldn't run illegal surveillance on their target."

"They didn't seem so concerned about protecting privacy when they threatened to leak officials' browsing histories to the public." Braxton cut her off, his mountainous shoulders blocking her view of the door. "I watch the news, too. These guys have been known to do what it takes to get their message across, violently if forced. The best shot we have to uncovering who's coming after you is Oversight's backdoor access."

The breath she'd been holding rushed from her lungs as the past threatened to overrun the present. She fought back the memories, but how could she when all she thought about when she closed her eyes was the last time she'd accessed that code?

"I told you I can't do that." Her voice rose with each word. He should understand that better than anyone. He'd been there. He'd watched how Oversight's trial run had affected her. No. He didn't get to decide how they handled the threat on her life. He'd lost that right the night he'd walked out on her all those months ago. "This is what we're going to do. First, you're going to get out of my way, so I can review the bomb squad's findings for myself. Second, we're going to arrange to get Vincent the slugs we pulled from the windshield. If he gets a hit on ballistics, you get to keep your end of the deal, and we pretend this whole thing never happened. Go our separate ways."

"I'll keep my end of the deal—" Braxton closed in on her "—but if he doesn't come up with our suspect, I expect you to keep yours."

"Agreed." Silence settled between them. It wasn't an empty silence. It was full of anger, of something else

Elizabeth didn't want to identify. "You're pushing me out of the investigation by trying to keep me behind a computer. Why?"

"You know why." Veins fought to burst from beneath his skin. He'd have an embolism if he didn't take a breath. Her guard softened at the concern etched into his features.

"I'm pregnant, Braxton. Not an invalid. I protect my clients, whether it's from behind a desk or strapped in Kevlar, and I'm damn good at my job." Elizabeth shook her head, a disbelieving laugh escaping from between her lips. She tried to swallow around her dry throat. "Just because you're the father of this baby, doesn't give you the right to dictate how I live my…"

Dizziness muddled her vision. She reached out to balance herself, fisting her hand in his T-shirt. She pulled him into her, knees weak. "Whew. If I pass out, don't let it fool you. I'm still going to win this argument when I wake up."

"Liz?" Concern sharpened his voice.

She fought to steady her heart rate. A dull ringing filled her ears as he wrapped his arms around her and led her to the edge of the bed. His clean, masculine scent surrounded her, and she breathed in as much as she could to clear her head. Didn't work. She closed her eyes as the back of her knees hit the mattress. "This conversation is not over."

"Tell me what the hell is happening, or I'm taking you to the hospital right now," he said.

"My blood sugar is low." She'd had it under control the last few days. But running for her life must've forced her body to use up her last meal sooner than she'd expected. She opened her eyes, still clinging to the valleys and ridges of muscle carved into his chest. Nope. Couldn't think about that right now. Food. She needed food. "The baby makes me hypoglycemic. As soon as I eat, I'll be fine."

"Here." Braxton unraveled her fingers from his shirt but refused to let go of her hand completely as he reached for the bowl on the nightstand. Which actually helped anchor her. Steam still escaped from the glossy red ceramic, and the scent of something spicy and warm filled her as she breathed it in. "This should help."

"What is it?" she said.

"Turkey and vegetable soup." He wiped his palms down his jeans. The mattress dipped with his added weight beside her, and she struggled not to lean into him with everything she had. "The protein should bring your glucose back up in a few minutes. I made more if you need it."

"You made this?" Elizabeth heaved a spoonful into her mouth. Vegetables perfectly cooked, ground turkey flavored with spices. No. Not possible. The Braxton she'd known had survived on a diet of cheap cafeteria food and fast food restaurants. Although, studying the lean muscle across his torso, the new bulges in his arms and thighs, he'd obviously made some changes. Living off junk food didn't carve muscle like that. Her mouth watered for more than the soup in that moment, and she fought to concentrate on not dumping the entire bowl in her lap. The pounding of her heart behind her ears faded. "And look at that, not a gummy worm in sight."

Resting his elbows on his knees, he laughed. "Nope. The only sweets you're going to find in this apartment are chocolate ice cream and rainbow-colored sprinkles."

Elizabeth froze, another spoonful of soup halfway to her mouth. "I still can't believe you remember my favorites."

"How could I forget?" His green-gray gaze, grayer now, centered on her. A smile thinned his mouth, and her grip on the bowl weakened. Damn that smile. Damn the soup. Damn the fact he'd saved her life—twice— in the past three hours. "You kept a pint of ice cream in the freezer at the office and a container of rainbow sprinkles hidden in your desk." Braxton straightened. "I still remember the look on one of the other analysts' face when you screamed at him for five minutes for ignoring the 'do not touch' sign on your ice cream. Bad day for that guy."

"Yeah, well, not all women are made of sugar and spice and everything nice. Some are made of ice cream, rainbow sprinkles and a whole lot of swear words." Elizabeth took another bite, talking around a mouthful of soup, then pointed at him with her spoon. "He was an analyst. He was trained to read between the lines, but he flat out ignored my note. He deserved it. Don't touch my ice cream."

Braxton raised his hands in surrender. "I won't. Not after that."

She couldn't help but laugh. Then caught herself. The man in front of her had done something far worse than ignore a note taped to her ice cream in the office freezer. For the past four months, he'd been the epitome of an uncaring, coldhearted, manipulative jerk who'd taken her to bed then run. But now Braxton refused to fit inside the box she'd created for him in her mind. Elizabeth cleared her throat, more to free her head of his clean scent than anything else, and motioned to him with the empty bowl. "Thanks for the soup. I'm feeling better."

"Anything for you." The sincerity in his voice, the way his hand brushed over her knee closest to him, spiked her flight instinct. Taking the bowl from her, he stood and headed for the door. She couldn't stop the flood of warmth rushing through her. And not just from the soup.

No, no, no. She'd been down this road before. She'd trusted him, relied on him when she'd needed someone the most. He'd been the man who would've done anything to protect her, the man who'd had her back when the NSA sought to destroy her career after Oversight's first real-world test run. But the man in front of her wasn't him. Maybe never had been. And falling for him had left her pregnant and alone.

Wouldn't happen again.

Braxton stopped short of the hallway, as though the weight of her attention cemented his feet in place. His dark hair brushed across his shoulder blades as he rested his head back. "You haven't asked me why I left."

The warmth drained from her system. No. She hadn't.

He turned. The scar cut through his eyebrow shifted as he centered his attention on her. The world threatened to pull out from under her feet when he looked at her like that, like she was the only woman in the world for him.

She glanced over the surveillance photos she'd dropped onto the floor—a dozen Elizabeths staring up at her—but didn't really see the details. "I've spent countless hours obsessing over that question, determined to find out the answer, imagining the moment you'd come back into my life. To be clear, none of it involved a bomb under a conference room table or being shot at in the parking garage."

Locking her attention on Braxton, she tightened her grip on the edge of the mattress. Did he realize how much he'd hurt her? How many nights she'd cried over him leaving? Probably not. Stay in control. Survive the investigation. Move on with her life. That was all she had to do. Elizabeth notched her chin parallel with the floor. "But after finding out I was pregnant a few weeks ago, I decided in the end, I don't care."

All that mattered was that he had, and that he would leave again.

That was the deal.

"I'm sorry. I never meant…" The corners of his mouth turned down, those brilliant eyes filled with… guilt? Braxton shifted his weight between his feet, knuckles white around the bowl in his hand. "I never meant for any of this."

"Fortunately for you, you're not responsible for the man trying to kill me or we'd be having a very different conversation." It was nearly ten at night now. Exhaustion pulled at her muscles, but Elizabeth shoved to her feet. No dizziness. No ringing in her ears. His soup had done its job, and she was about to make sure this baby didn't lower her blood sugar for a few more hours. "Now, take me to the ice cream."

LIZ WAS WRONG. He was responsible. He'd left her unprotected.

Lavender filled his lungs as she maneuvered past him toward the kitchen. His heart rate kicked up a notch. Even after all this time, she affected him in ways he couldn't explain, in ways no other woman had. Only her. "I knew you wouldn't be able to resist."

"Which begs the question, why have it on hand at all?" Liz turned toward him, cocking her head to one side as she shifted her weight against the opposite counter. Still reading between the lines. Back facing the wide expanse of windows and the mesmerizing view, she crossed her arms beneath her chest. Clouds clung to the peaks of the Chugach mountain range, rain hitting the glass in rhythmic intervals, but he only had attention for her. "Unless you knew I'd come back here with you."

There'd been no other option when he'd discovered Oversight's feeds had been hijacked to hunt her down. Not for him. He didn't trust anyone but himself to keep her safe. Braxton wrenched open the freezer door and excavated her favorite brand of chocolate ice cream. "I'm damn good at my job, too."

"True," she said.

"I'm almost afraid you would go with anyone who offered you ice cream and sprinkles, though." He grabbed a bowl and a spoon then scooped two huge servings of ice cream and handed it to her. Holding up one finger, he spun the spice turntable around, pulled rainbow-colored sprinkles from the first tier and offered it to her. "Almost forgot the secret ingredient."

Her fingertips overlapped his for a moment, and something resembling an electric shock shot up his arm. A rush of color climbed up her neck, and he fought the urge to close the small bit of distance between them in the tight galley kitchen. Nice to know he wasn't the only one affected by their proximity.

"You seem to forget the more I weigh, the harder I am to kidnap, so ice cream is essentially saving my life in the long run." Liz dumped an unhealthy amount sprinkles onto her ice cream.

"Good point." A laugh reverberated through him. Although he'd kill anyone who tried. Nobody came after her and survived. The pregnancy only made his protective side stronger. "But I only have enough for the next couple of days, so take it easy."

"If you think we're going to be here for a couple days, I'll eat it all tonight, and you won't be able to stop me." Liz spooned a heavy bite into her mouth. She closed her eyes, a moan working up her throat. His gut tightened at the sound, all too eager to bring up memories of their one night together. The stress that'd been etched into her features since the moment she'd set sight on him in that damn conference room melted with one spoonful of her favorite dessert.

"Wouldn't dream of it." Anything to make her happy. Even if that included going back into hiding after the investigation ended. His gaze shifted to her lower abdominals, where their daughter barely made herself known in the soft curve there. Even if it meant never meeting his daughter. He would leave to protect them, to make them happy.

Liz opened her eyes, the chocolate brown surrounding her pupils darker than a few minutes ago. The effect raised the hairs on the back of his neck, his entire body on high alert. Because of her. Her rough exhale skimmed across his neck in the small space. "I never thanked you."

"What for?" The edge of the granite countertop cut into his backside, keeping him in the moment. Rain pounded against the windows, a ripple of thunder shaking the framed photos on the walls. He flexed his fingers into the center of his palms. Reminded him of far too many unprotected nights as a kid under that damn fake rock wall in the park when the shelter was full, something he hadn't thought about in years. Until he'd uncovered Liz's new name and address. Of all the places she could've run, she'd chosen Anchorage. To get away from him.

"I wouldn't be standing here if it weren't for you. We wouldn't be standing here." Liz slid her hand over her belly then set her ice cream, only half eaten, on the counter. The sound of stainless steel on ceramic grated in his ears but didn't distract him enough to take his eyes off her. Nothing could. "You saved our lives."

"Which time are you referring to? The bomb, the shootout in the garage or with the bowl of ice cream?" He notched his chin toward her and crossed his boots at the ankles. "I'm losing count."

"All three. Maybe more for the explosion and the shooter than the food, but it certainly helped me from going into hypoglycemic shock." Her brilliant smile rocketed his heart rate into dangerous territory before it disappeared. Gripping the edge of the counter on either side of her waist, Liz locked her gravity-inducing gaze on his, and he felt a pull. "Maybe we can come at this a different way. Forget about the Sovereign Army as a whole for a minute. The shooter in the garage was alone. It was a single-man assault. Looking for one shooter in the group would narrow down our suspect list." She picked up her spoon and bit down against the steel. "Only problem is, if he is a member, I doubt anyone in the Sovereign Army would roll on him."

They'd already been through this.

"I swore I'd keep you alive." Braxton closed the distance between them, her sharp inhale audible as he reached around her for the discarded bowl. Turning his head slightly, he leveled his attention on her right shoulder. Smooth, flawless skin stood out against the black lace of her cap sleeve, and he wanted nothing more than to taste her again, to see if his memory of her was as good as the real thing. He raised his eyes to meet hers. "And I will do anything to keep that promise."

"Protection is not the same thing as controlling someone's life." She swiped her tongue across her lips, pulling his attention to her mouth and the small purple sprinkle stuck to her bottom lip. "If I was meant to be controlled, I would've come with a remote."

"People don't wake up wanting to be victims." His voice came out too rough, too deep. "They don't ask for bad things to happen. They don't ask for pain they have to live with for the rest of their lives. Every day things destroy someone's life. Attacks like today happen. It doesn't matter how strong they are—anyone can get hurt, but I sure as hell won't let it be you and our baby. Understand?"

Sliding one hand along his face, Liz stared at him. Her mouth parted as though the words were on the tip of her tongue. "Braxton—"

His name on her lips was all it took. In one swift move, he threaded his fingers at the nape of her neck and set his forehead against hers. She tried to escape, but the counter kept her caged against him. Damn, he'd missed her. Missed her scent, the way she fit against him perfectly, her sarcasm, the feel of her skin. Electricity lightninged through him as he slid his body in line with hers, her front pressed against him, her hands reaching for his at the back of her neck. Her fingernails bit into the backs of his hands. Hell, no. His memory hadn't done her justice. She breathed against him, her mouth mere centimeters from his. Dropping his hands to her hips, he lifted her onto the counter and centered himself between her thighs. Her fingers fisted in his hair, locking him against her. Right where he needed to be.

What had he been thinking, leaving her behind? He could've told her the truth. Could've asked her to come with him. He moved his fingers back up to her hair, where her erratic pulse beat against the palm of his hand. He did that to her. He changed her breathing patterns. He expanded her pupils so only a thin ring of brown remained. Braxton swallowed hard. Damn it, no. It wouldn't have been fair to expect her to pick up her life and disappear off the radar. Her life was at risk because of him. Because he'd gotten involved with her in the first place. And there was no telling how far that shooter would go to get to her again. Ten minutes ago, nothing would've stopped him from closing that short distance to her mouth, but he couldn't now. He wouldn't put her in danger again.

Spearmint and lavender exploded across his senses, and he reached between them, swiping his thumb across her lip. The sprinkle fell to the kitchen floor, out of sight. He forced himself to cool things down. "You had a purple sprinkle stuck to your mouth."

Liz planted a hand against his chest, his heart fighting for freedom to reach her, and pushed him back. She cleared her throat, the pink in her cheeks and down her neck fading. "It's getting late. I've had a hell of a day. I'm going to go to bed. We can talk about our next step after we've both gotten some rest."

His backside hit the opposite counter. He'd never been more thankful for the granite than in that moment as cold tunneled through his clothing. He nodded and swiped a hand down his face. Lightning streaked through the front windows as the rest of the world came back into focus. "Yeah. Good idea."

She slipped off the counter. Her gaze glittered at him. "Good night, Braxton."

"Good night." Braxton gripped the edge of the counter hard as she headed into the guest bedroom and closed the door behind her. The lock clicked into place, and he nodded as he stared at the tile. Hell, what was he trying to prove? That he still wanted her? No question about it—he'd never stopped wanting her. Never would. But if he'd learned anything over the last four months, it'd been that emotional ties could and would be used against him. Didn't matter what precautions he took or how long he stayed under the radar. Two attempts on her life in the span of an hour was enough for him. There wouldn't be a third.

Chapter Five

She was supposed to be smarter than this. Stronger.

Muted sunlight filtered around the edges of the thick blackout curtains. They had work to do, but Elizabeth didn't move from the bed. The instant she left this room, reality would set in. Braxton, the shooter, the fact she would most definitely be raising this baby on her own in a few short months. A few more minutes of ignorance. That was all she needed.

Hiking her forearm over her face, she fought to purge the heated moments between her and Braxton from her memory, but her efforts were in vain. The raw desire in his gaze had burned straight through her, marked her. And damn it, she'd almost given in to him. Almost wanted him to kiss her, to make her forget about the fact she'd become a target. A low groan ripped from her throat as she threw the blankets off and hauled herself to her feet. Ice worked through her veins as she padded barefoot across the cold hardwood floor, hand over her lower abdominals. "We're in trouble, baby girl. And I have no idea how to get us out of it."

She'd survived Braxton leaving once. She wasn't so sure she could do it again.

Get ready and come up with a plan. That was all she had to think about right now. Elizabeth froze, arched over her duffel bag, and cocked her head toward the door. Was that…? No. It couldn't be. Straightening, she headed for the bedroom door and opened it slowly, careful to avoid the creak in the floorboard right outside the guest room. The low *plunk* of guitar strings filtered down the hallway, and she set her head against the door for support, just listening. How long had it been since she'd heard him play? A year? More? The muffled sound of strings from down the hall made it hard to recognize the song but pulled her toward the end all the same.

Before she understood exactly when she'd made the decision to push open his cracked bedroom door, there he was. Her insides constricted at the wide expanse of ridges and valleys of muscle flexing across his back as he played, his hair brought back in a loose ponytail to keep it out of his way. Despite the release and contraction of muscles in his broad shoulders, he looked completely at ease, relaxed. And hell if that didn't vault her heart into her throat.

"Did I wake you?" His voice barely registered over the low chord of music, only one side of his features visible from her position at the door.

"No, I can blame that on your daughter at all hours of the night." She shifted her weight into the door frame and crossed her arms. He kept playing, kept pulling at some part of her she thought she'd buried for good when he'd left. The same part that had protected her against wondering where he'd gone, who he'd been with, if he'd ever had feelings for her. "I wasn't sure you'd kept it. When I searched your apartment after…" Elizabeth dropped her attention to his discarded shirt at the edge of the bed and centered her focus. No point in rehashing the past. Wouldn't change anything. "Everything was still there."

Except the guitar she'd bought for him for his birthday last year, the one he held now. That alone had clued her in that something hadn't happened to him. He'd left.

"You are the only person who's ever given me a birthday present. Did I ever tell you that? We never had a lot of money growing up, but after my dad lost his job, then the house, we had nothing. My mom tried. Collected aluminum can tops for me—one for every year—and strung them on a necklace my dad had given her when they were dating. But this…" Braxton paused, sliding his fingers up the guitar's neck, across the engraving she'd had done in the guitar shop. *Everything is better with sprinkles.* They were supposed to be best friends forever. Her fingernails dug into her arm, keeping her in the moment. He finally locked those brilliant green eyes on her as he rocked forward on the edge of the mattress, and a rush of heat flooded through her. "Do you remember the chords I taught you?"

A burst of laughter escaped from between her lips as she shook her head. He'd spent hours trying to teach her to play. Didn't work. She was the least musically inclined person in existence. "Not a single one."

Braxton shifted on the mattress, making room at

the end. With a single nod, he beckoned her forward. "Come here."

Her lungs seized, but the rest of her body refused to follow her brain's orders to fight. They needed to come up with another plan to identify the man trying to kill her. Not mess around on his guitar. Still, she put one foot in front of the other until the backs of her knees hit the mattress, and she sat down beside him. Warmth flooded down her left side as his arm brushed against hers.

Braxton set the instrument across her lap, one hand wrapped around the neck, the other sliding between her arm and her rib cage. A shiver chased down her spine despite the fact she was burning up inside. Goose bumps pimpled down her arms as he set his mouth close to her ear. And the world disintegrated from in front of her, leaving only the two of them and his guitar. He fit his fingers over hers, the calluses rough against her, as she settled against him. Flashing her that gut-wrenching smile, he studied her face from forehead to chin as he forced her fingers to move with his. "You got it."

"It sounds like I'm skinning a cat." His laugh reverberated down her side, and Elizabeth tightened her grip on the guitar. She stilled, heart threatening to beat out of her chest, as she turned her head toward him. She rolled her lips between her teeth. His gaze shot to her mouth as the thick ring of green around his pupils disappeared.

One breath. Two.

"You're doing great." He strengthened his hold on her, almost pressing her into him as he had the night before. He felt so good right now. Her head begged her to run, to not go down this path again, but her body had taken control the second she'd walked into that conference room. After the explosion, the shooter in the garage, she needed this. Needed him.

The shrill ring of her burner phone from the other room brought her back to reality.

She blinked, shook her head. Shifting forward, away from him, she cleared her throat and ran a hand through her hair. Wow. What the hell had she been thinking? Elizabeth shoved to her feet. "That's Vincent. I gave him the number in case he made progress in the investigation."

Setting the guitar up against the wall, Braxton reached for his discarded long-sleeve shirt. "Better answer it then."

She nodded, escaping down the hallway. The problem was she hadn't been thinking. That'd always been the problem when he was around. She shook off the rush of comfort that'd settled into her bones and hurried to answer the phone. "Vincent, hey—"

"Elizabeth Bosch," an unfamiliar voice said. "Or should I call you Elizabeth Dawson now? Remind me, which one of you created Oversight and single-handedly destroyed over a thousand people's lives with one press of a button?"

Her blood froze in her veins. She hit the speaker feature on the screen and dropped the phone away from her ear. Hitting the home button, she raced to record the call and took a deep breath to steady her nerves. "How did you get this number?"

"You're not the only one who can run a trace. I've

got my sources, too." Static reached through the line, making it hard to identify any kind of background noise. But the man from the garage—maybe the same one who tried blowing her up—was a professional. If that same man was on the other side of the line, he'd thought this through, made contingencies. There wouldn't be any mistakes on his end. "I almost had you back at Blackhawk Security. I would have, too, if it hadn't been for your new bodyguard. Have to admit, I hadn't accounted for him."

Confirmation. They were dealing with a professional.

A tingling sensation climbed up her spine, and she turned.

Braxton stood in the doorway, rage and violence carved into his features.

"You set the bomb in the conference room. You knew I had a meeting in there and timed it just right." She needed confirmation, needed to know they were looking for a single suspect in a numberless group of possibilities. She tipped the phone's microphone closer to her mouth and forced herself to focus on the caller, the man who had tried twice now to kill her. "Well, not perfectly. I was halfway out the door when you triggered the explosion. So you had to make sure your target wouldn't get away. That's why you came after me in the garage."

"I'm not going to let you get away with what you've done." Heavy breathing interrupted the static through the line.

Elizabeth swallowed around the dryness in her throat. "What do you want from me?"

"I want you at Town Square Park in one hour. Alone," he said.

Glancing up at Braxton, she licked her lips. The man she'd known—the man she'd loved—had disappeared in the span of a few seconds. All from an unknown voice on the other line. Tension tightened the muscles down her spine as she considered the situation. "And if I don't show?"

"I know who you've been spending your nights with, Elizabeth. I know why your grocery bill has nearly doubled the past few months, why you visit the park so often after work." Another flicker of static from the other line, then muffled words. Then the undeniable sound of a bullet loading into a gun chamber. "Would you really want him caught up in the middle of this?"

No. No, no, no, no. Elizabeth straightened a bit despite the urge to collapse back on to the bed nearly consuming her. "He has nothing to do with any of this."

"One hour," the shooter said. "I'll be waiting."

The call ended.

She stared at the phone. Either she walked straight into what was undoubtedly a trap or she risked losing the only family her daughter might have left once Braxton disappeared.

"Who have you been spending your nights with, Liz?" She almost didn't recognize Braxton's voice. Too distant. Too dangerous. Her stomach flipped at the sight of the violence still burned into his expression, in the tightness of all those new muscles. "Who was he talking about?"

"Okay. I was going to tell you earlier, but the timing

never seemed right." She tossed the phone onto the bed. Braxton wouldn't hurt her. Never her. But the thought of telling him the truth dried her mouth. A wave of nausea threatened to unbalance her, but whether it was from the possibility of revealing what she'd been doing in her spare time or morning sickness, she had no idea. Elizabeth straightened. He deserved to know. No matter how hard the truth would be to get out or how much he'd hate her afterward. "Since I moved to Anchorage, I've been looking after your father."

HIS LUNGS PROTESTED as though he'd been hit in the chest with a two-by-four. She what? "That man literally put us out on the street when I was a kid to support his habit, and you've been visiting him? Bringing him food?"

"He's not the man you remember, Braxton. The drugs…" Liz took a step closer, but where her proximity usually relieved the pressure coursing through him, it now made it stronger. She seemed to realize her effect on him and froze, that full bottom lip dropping open. "Sometimes he recognizes me, asks about you, asks about the baby. Most of the time I'm the only person keeping him alive."

Was that supposed to make him feel better? She'd never met his father when they'd worked together at Fort Meade. Which meant she'd come to Anchorage and tracked the old man down. She'd spent night after night making sure he had a roof over his head when the addict hadn't even had the guts to do the same for his own flesh and blood. "And now whoever is coming after you is using him as leverage."

"I'm sorry," she said. "I didn't know the shooter was watching me—"

"Why?" His head spun. His vision was a blur, a haze of everything but the woman in front of him. A woman who'd betrayed his deepest secret. The old man he'd called Dad for years had never chosen his family over the poison he could buy on the street. Never even bothered to show up to his mother's funeral after she'd caught a cold and died from pneumonia lying in a cardboard box. Because of his father. Because of what he did to their family. Braxton had grown up without the support he'd needed at the time, and he'd vowed never to fall back into that old man's manipulations again. The SOB was selfish. Only looking for a way to score. "I told you about what that man put me and my mother through, what happened to her. Why would you look for him? Why would you try to help him?"

"You weren't here, Braxton. You left." Her lips thinned as she rolled them between her teeth. "And this baby deserves a family."

His blood pressure spiked. Of course she deserved a family. Every baby did. Someone to sing to her at night, to kiss her in the morning, to help her count her fingers and toes. "You don't need him. I can give her that. I'm her father."

"For how long?" she asked.

"What?" What the hell did that mean? She'd told him he was the father.

"How long are you going to be around?" Liz pulled back her shoulders. The oversize T-shirt and baggy sweatpants did nothing to hide her mouthwatering curves underneath as she interlaced her fingers under her lower abdominals. "The NSA interrogated me after your disappearance. They claimed you sold classified intel to an anonymous third party. They're not going to stop looking for you until they've got you in cuffs. So how long are you going to stick around before you choose to go back into hiding?"

He didn't have an answer. The idea of being a distant father—having practically grown up with a shell of one himself—was too much. He couldn't do that to his daughter. And no way would he do that to Liz. Anxiety wound itself through his gut. But serving a possible life sentence behind bars for treason wouldn't do them a damn bit of good, either.

"As much as you might hate that man, he's still your father. He has a lot to answer for, but right now, he needs our help. And I'm going to give it to him." She nodded, her expression resigned, as she strode past him toward the bedroom door. "Now if you'll excuse me, I need to find a hammer to smash this phone to pieces before it gives up anything else today."

He couldn't fight the smile pulling at his mouth as he envisioned her with a hammer in one hand and her burner phone in the other. The shooter shouldn't have been able to get a lock on that number so easily. Braxton had checked that phone personally, along with the others in his stash. No spyware. They were new numbers, too. Which meant her Blackhawk Security teammate Vincent Kalani, the only person to reach Liz at that number, could've been compromised and not even know it. Or if he did… What had he read in the ex-cop's file? Something about taking bribes. The forensics expert had some explaining to do. He called back over his shoulder but didn't follow Liz from the room. "Check under the kitchen sink."

Hell, he couldn't face her yet. Disbelief still coursed through him as he studied the personal belongings she'd left in plain sight from her duffel bag. She'd been taking care of his father these last few months. Every night. And now his old man was being used as leverage against her, and Braxton was expected to risk Liz's life for a man who'd done nothing but disappoint him for years. The meeting was a trap. If he lost her...

No. It wouldn't happen. Without her, there would be no one else. And that wasn't an option. He'd already lost too many people in his life. He wasn't about to lose her, too.

Heavy thumps echoed down the hall, and he worked to shove his own selfish need to keep her in his life to the back of his mind. Sounded like Liz had found the hammer. He spun toward the door to survey the damage but froze as the edge of a photo stuffed into her duffel bag claimed his attention. Not a photo. A black-and-white sonogram. Checking back over his shoulder as another round of hammering reached his ears, he closed in on the bag. His hand shook as he reached for the single piece of thin, glossy paper. Liz's name, the date of the sonogram, the doctor's office and the measurements in centimeters stood out in white lettering around the edge of the dark background. But there, right in the center of the cone-shaped ultrasound, was a baby.

His baby. Sixteen weeks old.

Her perfectly shaped head, her knees drawn up almost to her nose. Braxton couldn't make out much else, but he didn't have to. She was perfect. Sliding his thumb over where he thought her right ear might be, he exhaled hard at a block of letters he hadn't seen before. His heart dropped.

Baby Karina.

Liz had named their daughter after his mother.

He rubbed his free hand over his face and turned toward the door. Five steps. That was all it took before she came into sight. He couldn't breathe—couldn't think—as he closed in on her. Catching her wrist before she swung the hammer down into the debris of what used to be a cell phone, he twisted her into him.

Her eyes widened. "Braxton, what—"

He crushed his mouth against hers. Fire burned through him, raising the hairs on the back of his neck. Sliding one hand around her back, he fought to bring her closer, make her a permanent part of himself. The scent of lavender worked through him, filled him as her pulse beat hard in her wrist beneath his fingertips. Forget the explosion. Forget the shooter. Forget the charges he'd face once the NSA realized he'd stayed in the country. Braxton only had attention for this moment. Only had Liz.

And she kissed him back.

Her grip loosened around the hammer and it fell, barely missing her bare feet. He released his grip on her wrist then held his breath as she planted her palms against his chest. But not to shove him away. Her lips, soft and silky, pressed into his. He licked the edge of her bottom lip then drew it between his teeth.

A gasp escaped her control, and his blood pressure skyrocketed. He thrust his tongue into her mouth, every cell in his body determined to make her his. He set the sonogram on the counter behind her then threaded his fingers into her hair at the base of her skull in a tight grip. Exploring, memorizing, claiming, he consumed her as a dehydrated man consumed water. Damn, she tasted good. How had he been able to live without her all this time? How had he been able to walk away?

Desire blazed inside him as he kicked the hammer out of the way and maneuvered her toward the same countertop he'd caged her against last night. He felt too rough for her, too punishing, but he couldn't stop. Not until he'd claimed every inch or she told him to back off. She tasted too good, and he'd become addicted to that taste a long time ago. What he wouldn't give to kiss her senseless every morning.

The calluses on his fingertips caught against smooth skin along her midsection.

Hell.

Braxton pulled away then set his forehead against hers. His lungs fought to catch up with his racing pulse. As much as he wanted to strip her bare and help her forget the past two days, he couldn't…they couldn't. They'd run out of time. "The meeting."

He couldn't say much else. Not when she was still pressed against him, when her touch seared him down to his core.

"Right. Shooter. Trap." Her short exhales beat against

the underside of his jaw, those brown eyes swirling with confused desire. She blinked then dropped her hands away from him. "I need to change out of my sweats. My shoulder holster doesn't exactly work with this shirt."

"You look good in anything you put on." A laugh rumbled from deep in his chest. His fingertips grazed over the bare column of her throat before he put a good amount of space between them. He had to. Otherwise, they might never leave the safe house. Notching her chin higher, he forced her to meet his gaze. "I won't let him touch you, Sprinkles."

She nodded. "I know."

"Good." He needed her to believe him. "Then let's catch us a bomber."

Chapter Six

When he'd kissed her, she'd lost all restraint.

One second, she'd been working out her frustration at putting an innocent man in danger, at not being able to hold up her emotional guard against Braxton, on the burner phone, and the next his mouth had been on hers. Her heart had thundered so hard, blood pouring through her ears, she'd felt as though she'd been underwater. Couldn't breathe. Couldn't hear. But she hadn't been able to pull away.

Pushing the memory back—a memory she'd never let go—Elizabeth cracked her knuckles as she walked east down the sidewalk toward the Alaska Center for the Performing Arts. She stuffed her shaking hands into her now empty coat pockets and hunkered deeper into the faux-fur folds as a blast of frigid air fought to chase the heat from her skin. They'd handed off the bullets from the SUV's windshield to Vincent as soon as they'd arrived, but she doubted he'd be able to glean anything useful. Whoever had tried to kill her had been planning this from the beginning. He wouldn't slip up unless he meant to slip up. She scanned the rooftops of the surrounding buildings. And the chances of that seemed slight. "No sign of our target yet."

Anchorage's snow-covered Town Center stretched a half acre in front of her. Blue and white Christmas lights had yet to be removed from the branches of pines decorating the grounds, even though the holiday season had ended three weeks ago. Her boots fought for purchase on the icy sidewalk. Or was it the possibility she might be centered in a shooter's crosshairs unbalancing her? Cloud cover made it hard to see into the shadows, and the hairs on the back of her neck stood on end.

"He'll show. You're too good of an opportunity to pass up." Braxton's voice in her ear settled the rush of nervous energy shooting down her spine. Well, that, and the fact he'd taken position thirty yards to her right in case he had to get to her fast. Mostly settled her nerves. There was still the issue of a possible ambush, and the conversation they would have to have after this little operation was over. About him leaving again. The open line between their earpieces crackled as the wind kicked up. A haze of snow danced in front of her. "Remember, I've got a giant bowl of ice cream and rainbow sprinkles waiting for you when this is over. So you better make it out of this alive."

"You always know exactly what to say." Studying the park for a second time, she fought the urge to look in Braxton's direction. The caller had told her to come alone. He should've tried convincing her bodyguard. She slowed her progress as she approached a single snow-covered bench in the middle of the park. With January temperatures dropping by the minute, most visitors had gone inside to warm up. Lower risk of putting innocent bystanders in danger if things went south.

"The cavalry has arrived, and guess what? I brought the big guns." Elliot Dunham's voice penetrated through the stiffness gripping her shoulders and neck, and a smile automatically stretched across her lips. What would they do without Blackhawk Security's con man turned private investigator? Rescued by the CEO and founder of the security firm from an Iraqi prison on fraud charges, the reformed criminal with a genius-level IQ never failed to amuse her. No matter how many times his compulsive sarcasm grated on her nerves, he'd never failed to have her back in the three months they'd worked together. And she'd always have his. "Admit it, Dawson, you missed me."

Gratitude flooded through her. Calling in Blackhawk Security had been her idea, but Braxton had taken point in getting them in place. She buried her mouth in the lining of her coat to hide her response in case the shooter had already arrived and was searching for signs she hadn't come alone. "If by big guns you mean Vincent and Glennon, then yes, I missed you."

"They won't let me touch the sniper rifle without taking a class first." Elliot's lighthearted attitude and the additional backup helped alleviate the nausea building in her stomach. Short exhales said he was still trying to get in position. "Personally, I think they like being the only ones with the heavy-duty weapons."

"Does this guy ever shut up?" Braxton asked.

"No." Vincent Kalani entered the park to her left, head down, barely raising his attention to her before he cut across the open terrain. Hands stuffed into his coat pockets, he moved with lethal grace. The former cop hid his face beneath a mane of wavy dark hair, but the tattoos climbing up his neck stood out. If the shooter had done his research, there was a good chance he'd recognize Blackhawk's forensics expert. "Trust me, we've tried."

"Head in the game, gentlemen." Glennon Chase, the firm's newest recruit and recent wife to their weapons expert, slid into sight at the edge of Elizabeth's peripheral vision. Armed with her own rifle, the former army investigator nodded as Elizabeth took a seat on the bench. Planting her eye against her scope, Glennon shifted out of sight along the rooftop of the building overlooking the park. "I've got movement at the north end of the park."

Elizabeth fought against the urge to look. Instead, she surveyed the area as a whole before redirecting her attention to the man stumbling toward her. Stained jacket, ripped jeans, thick gray hair and beard. Recognition flared, and she pushed off the bench. Wild eyes locked on her as Brolin Levitt reached for her, a prominent limp in his left leg. "Don't shoot. He's not the target." Slowing her approach, she lifted her hands, palms facing him. "Brolin, it's me. Elizabeth. You remember me? I'm friends with your son, Braxton."

Same introduction. Same approach. Every time. Over the past few months, the chances of him recognizing her steered toward sixty-forty. Sixty percent of the time, he didn't remember his own name. He closed in on her faster than she thought possible for a drug-addled old man.

Brolin didn't answer.

"Liz, I've got a bad feeling about this." Braxton's concern echoed through the earpiece, but she didn't pay it any attention. He'd made his feelings for his father perfectly clear, and there wasn't any scenario in which he'd trust the man in front of her. She didn't care. Brolin was innocent in all of this and had obviously been injured.

"I'm wearing Kevlar, I've got a gun and I know how to use it," she said. "I'm only helpless when my nail polish is wet, and even then, I can pull a trigger if I have to."

"While you make valid points, the shooter drew you here using Brolin as leverage. So why let the old man go?" he asked.

"I think I know why." Elizabeth caught a glimpse of two wires coming from the bottom of Brolin's stained old jacket. Her breath caught in her throat. Every cell in her body froze. One second. Two. Too long. "Braxton, your father is wired."

"What?" he asked.

A gunshot echoed off the surrounding buildings.

She spun toward the sound.

Braxton broke away from his position at her left, his ball cap flying off his head as he pumped his arms and legs hard. "Liz, get down!"

Pain splintered across her left arm and she spun, clamping her hand over the graze. She hit the ground hard. Snow and ice worked through her clothing as she scrambled toward Brolin. The shooter had used Brolin and the bomb strapped to his chest as a distraction. Long enough to get her in his sights. Fisting her hands around his jacket, Elizabeth wrenched the old man into her and pushed him forward. Her boots slid against the dusting of snow covering the sidewalks. They had to get moving. They were still out in the open. "Find that damned shooter."

"Got him. Suspect is rabbiting across the roof of the building to the south. There's a car waiting in the alley between buildings. Alaska license plate echo, uniform, sierra, six, eight, seven." Vincent's calm did nothing to ease the adrenaline surging through her veins. "Can't get a clean shot. Glennon?"

Braxton wrapped his hand around her arm and hauled her and Brolin their feet. He shoved them ahead of him as a black GMC pulled up to the curb fifty feet away.

The front passenger window lowered, revealing Elliot Dunham's dumbass smirk. "This never would've happened if they let me have a sniper rifle."

"Now's not the time, Elliot!" They reached the SUV. Elizabeth wrenched the passenger side door open and threw Brolin inside. No time for hellos. There was a shooter on the loose. "Meet your new assignment. His name is Brolin Levitt. He dies, you die. Understand?"

Elliot's deep gray eyes widened. "Is that a bomb?"

"I'm pretty sure it's fake, but you might want to take a look at it just in case." She slammed the door closed, not waiting for an answer.

"I've got a shot." The familiar sound of Glennon

loading a round into the rifle's chamber echoed in Elizabeth's earpiece as Braxton forced her to take cover behind a park bench. The SUV fishtailed away from the curb, shooting down the street. Brolin was safe. "I'm taking it."

The thunderclap of another bullet leaving the barrel of a rifle thudded through her. She held her breath as Braxton wrapped her in a tight hold against his chest. Waited. Silence settled around her. Her pulse throbbed at the base of her throat, the pain in her arm pulling at her attention. The second shot hadn't been meant for her, but a rush of relief escaped from her lungs all the same. Sirens filtered through the pulsing in her head.

"I missed him." Glennon hauled her rifle off the edge of the rooftop above and disappeared from sight. "If anybody tells my husband I missed that shot, you're dead."

"How are you going to kill us when you can't even hit your target?" The growl of the SUV's engine filtered through Elliot's earpiece. Good. Brolin would be safe as long as he stuck with Blackhawk's private investigator. Although getting him to stay might be a challenge, but she was sure Elliot would figure something out.

"I'm starting with you, Elliot," Glennon said.

Squealing tires reached her ears as Elizabeth caught sight of a high-class Mercedes sedan fishtailing out of the alley across the street. The windows were too tinted for her to make an identification, but her instincts said that was their shooter. She dug her nails into Braxton's jacket. "He's getting away."

"No, he's not." Braxton wrapped his hand around

hers, tugging her after him. "You remember that license plate number?"

"Yes." Puffs of her breath crystallized in front of her, freezing air reaching down to the bullet graze on her arm through the new hole in her jacket. The pain slid to the back of her mind as she forced her legs to work harder.

"Good." Braxton pulled her around the south corner of the park, toward another Blackhawk Security SUV. "Get in."

HE WASN'T GOING to let Liz become a victim from circumstances he'd created. If he hadn't tried to keep her in the dark in the first place, she wouldn't be in this situation. And if that bullet hadn't only grazed her arm, he'd have had to live with that the rest of his life. The idea pushed his foot against the accelerator harder. Everyone was created by a defining event. Something that changed them just enough. A loss, a trauma, the end of a relationship. Liz would be his. Always his. "You okay?"

"I'm fine. Focus on the road." She clamped a hand over the wound in her arm, swaying as he forced the SUV around a tight turn. Downtown Anchorage blurred in his peripheral vision as they closed in on the Mercedes's bumper. A minivan pulled out in front of them, and he swerved. She grabbed onto the handle above her head with one hand and the dashboard with the other with a groan of pain. "If I ever need a skilled getaway driver, you are not the person I'm going to call."

Uneven roads lifted them out of their seats. The

shooter barreled through a construction zone ahead of them, taking a sharp right.

Liz tapped her earpiece with bloody fingertips. "Vincent, we need Anchorage PD to set up a roadblock. We can't let this guy get away."

"Copy that," Vincent said.

"Hang on." Braxton made the turn, the SUV's fender barely missing a car pulling out of an underground parking garage. Checking back over his shoulder, he shook his head. "Don't people know how to drive anymore?"

Liz swiped her hand across her face, attention out the windshield. "For crying out loud, it's not this psychopath who's going to kill me. It's your driving."

Those words hit him like a hammer fall. Braxton sobered, knuckles tight around the steering wheel as they cleared downtown, and sped up the ramp onto south Seward Highway. If the bastard thought he'd be able to lose them by disappearing into the trail entrances along the coast, he was wrong. Braxton had had to know them better than anyone else in this city in order to survive on his own. "I'm not going to let anything happen to you."

"You guys realize your coms are still online, right?" Elliot's voice in his head was not what he needed right now. "This seems like a private moment."

"All you need to worry about is keeping Brolin alive, Elliot. Leave the rest to me." Liz shot a quick look in his direction. While putting his old man under Blackhawk Security protection hadn't climbed its way to the top of Braxton's priority list, the drug addict could at least do some good to identify the shooter who'd taken him. "Vincent, we've turned south onto Seward Highway, and this guy isn't showing any signs of stopping. Where are we at with Anchorage PD?"

"There's a pileup downtown, thanks to your driver there." Vincent's disappointment echoed through the earpiece. "And any other available units are closing in on the park due to a wave of calls about shots fired. I'm having the chief send as many as he can your way, but that could be up to an hour."

Braxton picked the device out of his ear and tossed it into the back seat, eyes on the prize ahead. He maneuvered around a fifty-two-foot semitruck, losing sight of the Mercedes for three seconds. Four. Cloud cover made it that much harder to keep their target straight, but he soon had a lock on the shooter again. The bastard wasn't going to get away. Not when they were so close to ending this nightmare. Desperation clawed up his throat. He'd vowed to protect the woman in the seat beside him. He couldn't let her down now. "Guess we're on our own."

"You want to be the one to catch him." Her voice worked to ease the tangle of tension coiling tight at the base of his skull. The Mercedes swerved to maneuver around a group of three cars ahead, but she'd always been able to consume his attention with a single look. A word. "Why?"

The engine growled in protest as he pushed the SUV harder, trying to close the distance between them and the shooter. He had no idea what they were going to do after that, but he'd always been good on his feet. The sun would start going down in the next hour. They'd lose him altogether if they didn't end this.

"You know why. I told you I'd protect you, and I meant it. Catching this guy is the only way to do that." He locked his jaw against the lie, the muscles along his neck and shoulders straining. Chancing a quick glance at her, he read the questions carved into her expression.

"No, that's not it. It's something more than that." The weight of her attention pinned him to the back of the leather seat. She'd never been an analyst, but she could make a damn good career out of reading people. How the hell did he think he could keep secrets from her? "What aren't you telling me?"

The Mercedes disappeared in the midst of four cars ahead of them.

Braxton sat forward in his seat as he sped around a small sedan. Narrowing his gaze, he studied car after car as he backed his foot off the accelerator. "He's gone."

"What?" She turned her attention back to the road then twisted in her seat to inspect the cars behind them. "That's not possible. There aren't any exit ramps in this section of the highway."

Didn't make the shooter's disappearing act any less real. Braxton checked his rearview mirror as a pair of headlights flared to life behind them. "He didn't get off the highway. Get ready—"

Two gunshots broke the soothing sound of tires against asphalt, but the bullets ricocheted off the glass. Bulletproof windows were a nice touch. Braxton swerved into the next lane, narrowly avoiding another sedan, but the maneuver did nothing to distract the shooter. The hood of the Mercedes closed in fast.

"He's going to try to run us off the road." Panic tinted Liz's words, but he couldn't worry about that right now. Keeping her alive. That was all that mattered. She could panic all she wanted as long as she was alive.

The first hit to the bumper thrust them forward. The steering wheel jerked in his hand, but Braxton kept a tight hold. Civilian cars slowly backed off as another collision to their bumper forced them onto the highway's shoulder. The grooves cut into the shoulder to keep drivers awake drowned out another gunshot to the back of the SUV. He fought to keep the SUV on the road, but slowing down, pulling over even, would put Liz directly in the shooter's sights. Not an option. Time to end this, but with the Turnagain Arm waterway on one side and nothing but thick wilderness on the other, he only had a small window to make this work. "Hang on to something."

Her hand shot to the handlebar above her head just before Braxton slammed on the brakes. Tires screeched in his ears, the smell of burned rubber filling the interior of the SUV as momentum thrust them forward in their seats. The Mercedes's headlights disappeared behind the bottom of the back window. His lungs seized half a second before the shooter rammed into the back of their vehicle. The third collision forced the SUV to one side despite how hard Braxton pulled the wheel in the opposite direction.

Tires caught on the road. The world went hazy as the vehicle wrenched to one side then flipped. Every instinct he owned urged him to reach out for Liz. He loosened his grip on the steering wheel, fighting against gravity to touch her, but the highway rushed up to meet the windshield too fast. The terrorizing fear etched into her features vanished as the roof crumpled under the impact. His head snapped forward, glass breaking all around them. Metal protested against asphalt in his ears, but all he could focus on was Liz's scream.

The SUV swung up again, depleting his brain of oxygen, then slammed into the ground. The seat belt cut into his shoulder and across his chest.

Then there was stillness as the vehicle righted itself.

His head throbbed in rhythm to his racing heartbeat. A dull ringing filled his ears, but not loud enough to block out the screech of tires nearby. He blinked against the onslaught of chaos surrounding the SUV, vision hazy, tongue thick in his mouth. "Liz."

No answer.

Braxton strained to look at her. "Liz, baby, can you hear me?"

Footsteps heightened the headache spreading from the crown of his head. Something wet—blood—trickled down the side of his face. He'd hit his head against the driver's side window during the roll. Shadows crossed his vision on Liz's side of the vehicle. Wait, no. Just one. The outline of a man closed in on the SUV.

Black ski mask. Pressed suit. Gun in his hand. Every muscle in his body tensed. Not a civilian.

"Come on, Sprinkles, wake up." The seat belt kept Braxton secured in the seat. He fought to reach for his gun that'd fallen from his shoulder holster. He couldn't move his arms, stomach rocketing into his throat. He leveraged his heels into the floorboards but couldn't move otherwise. "Elizabeth!"

The shooter reached in through the broken passenger side window—too close to Liz—and unlocked the door. Raising the gun in his hand toward Braxton, he wrenched the door open then reached for Liz's seat belt. The SOB wasn't going to take her. Not happening. Dark eyes centered on him. "Well, that went easier than I imagined."

Braxton didn't recognize the voice, the posture, the suit. No accent. Nothing to lead him to an identity of the man taking the most important thing in his life from him.

"I'm going to kill you, you bastard." Braxton ordered his body to move, to reach for his gun, to do anything. No response. A feral scream ripped from his throat. Blood and sweat stung his eyes. He couldn't lose her. Not yet. Not when she'd just come back into his life. "I'm going to hunt you down, and I'm going to end you."

The shooter laughed, dark, merciless, as he compressed the button to Liz's seat belt, wrapped his grip around her delicate wrist and hefted her over one shoulder. All the while keeping the gun aimed on Braxton. "Good luck with that."

Chapter Seven

Pain. Dizziness. A hard pulsing behind her ears that she could only describe as the beginning of her own death.

She felt as though she'd been weighed down by lead. Elizabeth struggled to open her eyes, blinking back the heaviness in her brain. Blackness consumed the edges of her vision. She narrowed in on the movement of patterns in front of her. Blackness and…pinstripes? The subtle lines shifted, and she realized the unbalanced sensation charging through her wasn't dizziness, but movement. The intense pressure in her midsection meant someone had flipped her over their shoulder and was carrying her. She used her remaining strength to raise her head. Tendrils of hair blocked her peripheral vision, but there, straight behind her, was the remains of her destroyed SUV. Sullivan wasn't going to be too happy about another of Blackhawk Security's vehicles being totaled, but she couldn't afford to care. Not with a shooter on their tail. Wait. Confusion gripped her in a tight vise as she sank back against the man carrying her. "Braxton?"

"Not exactly." That voice. She recognized that voice from somewhere.

A whiff of expensive cologne tickled her nose and worked deep into her lungs. No. Not Braxton. He didn't wear cologne. Which meant... Recognition clicked into place. The air rushed from her lungs. The shooter. He'd called her on the burner phone. He'd—

A thread of anxiety unraveled inside her, tangling up with anger, resentment and fear. The edge of her shoulder holster dug into her armpit, but with one look, she discovered she'd been relieved of her weapon. Black asphalt passed beneath her. *Think, think, think.* Rolling her hands into fists, Elizabeth focused all of her attention on the small of the shooter's back and sank her elbow hard in the curve of his spine as hard as she could.

His grip around the back of her knees disappeared, and she toppled backward. The highway rushed up to meet her faster than she expected, and she hit the ground. Loose rocks cut into the side of her head, but she rolled in an effort to get to her feet. Stinging pain spread across the other side of her skull as the shooter fisted a chunk of her hair in his hand and hauled her to her feet.

Six-foot-plus frame, lean, preferred a Windsor knot and a nice suit over Kevlar. It wasn't much to go on, but it was a start. Elizabeth wrapped her grip around his wrist as he wrenched her into him. The black ski mask hid his mouth as he spoke, but those dark eyes would always stick in her memory. Cold. Calculating. Dangerous. "You're going to pay for that, but first, you're going to help me."

"You've tried to kill me three times and put an inno-cent man's life in danger." Her voice remained steady despite the earthquake exploding inside her. "There's no way I'd do anything to help you."

"We'll see about that." Pulling his weapon, the shooter wrenched her into his side and aimed for the totaled SUV. For Braxton still in the driver's seat. "You should've known changing your last name wouldn't stop me from finding you, Elizabeth. Not when I have Oversight at my disposal." He pressed his mouth against her ear, and a shiver threatened to overrun her. "How about now? Should I pull this trigger, or are you going to get in the damn car?"

Bystanders' screams and panic infiltrated through the pounding of her pulse in her ears. Car doors slammed; tires peeled against the road. Others raised their phones to get the scene on video or capture a photo but didn't move to interfere. She couldn't breathe. Couldn't think.

Braxton's life or her own certain death.

"Liz, run!" His voice punctured through the sensory overload wrapping itself in a tight fist inside. Braxton struggled to free himself from the crumpled SUV, pull-ing against the seat belt. The sound of liquid hitting the road claimed her attention. She scanned the wreckage until sunlight reflected off a pool of gas beneath the SUV. Any second now the vehicle could catch fire, and Braxton would be gone.

"If you kill him now, you lose your leverage. I'll never help you." Her heart turned over in her chest, her stomach squeezing tight. No. She wasn't going to leave him. He wouldn't leave her. With the shooter's forearm braced against her collarbones, there was only one thing she could do.

"True, but you've made yourself a new life here. Gotten to know quite a few people." His laugh rumbled between her shoulder blades. "I have an entire list of leverage, Elizabeth. And I'm not above ticking them off one at a time until you do as I ask. Elliot Dunham, Vincent Kalani, Sullivan Bishop. And your friend Kate? Hasn't she lost enough?" He moved his finger over the trigger, cocking his head away from her neck. "But today, I think I'll start with your bodyguard there."

She locked her attention on Braxton. "Come find me when this is over."

"Good girl." The shooter dropped his weapon to his side. "Now get in the car."

"No." She took advantage. Inhaling deeply, Elizabeth dropped to her haunches. She rocked back on her heels and sprang back up, shoving her shoulder into his midsection to knock him off balance. He hit the ground, the gun sliding across the asphalt. They both followed its track. One second, two, and then Elizabeth lunged. The shooter recovered almost instantly. Any physical fight could cost her everything, but she wasn't going to let him hurt anyone else. Not when she could end this now. Her best option was that gun. She wrapped her fingers around the barrel as a shoe stomped on her wrist. Bone crunched, and a scream worked up her throat.

"Elizabeth!" Braxton's yell barely registered over the high-pitched ringing in her ears.

The shooter bent down to claim the weapon from her. "You're not going to win, Elizabeth. I've been waiting for this moment for too long. You're going to help me. Even if I have to kill everyone you've ever cared about to force your compliance."

She hadn't been trained in combat like Blackhawk's weapons expert Anthony Harris, hadn't been trained to fight like a SEAL as Sullivan had. Hell, even Glennon could take down a room full of men on her own if pushed. But Elizabeth wouldn't give up. Her life wasn't the only one that mattered anymore. She was this baby's mother, and she would do everything in her power to keep her safe.

"Go to hell." Elizabeth tossed the gun into her opposite hand and swung up as hard as she could. Metal met flesh and bone of the shooter's left zygomatic, and he stumbled back. The pressure released off her broken wrist, but as long as adrenaline pumped through her veins, she could deal with the pain. She pushed to her feet and pumped her legs hard. Get to Braxton. Bright green eyes widened as she raised the gun. "Move!"

Braxton raised his arms over his head and faced toward the broken driver's side window.

She pulled the trigger, and the lock of his seat belt exploded. "You're welcome."

A strong hand wrenched the gun from her hand, another latching around her throat. Air pressurized in her lungs as the shooter backed her up against the SUV then aimed the gun at her temple. "Move from the vehicle and I kill her now, Levitt."

She couldn't see Braxton, couldn't hear him over the drowning sensation threatening to pull her under, but she didn't have to. He'd promised to protect her, to fight for her, and if there was one thing she couldn't fault him for, it was that he kept his promises.

"Let her go. You and I will end this right now." Fury battered Braxton's words. The SUV door slammed closed, reverberating through her. Then footsteps. Braxton strode into her peripheral vision, hands tense at his sides. Ready for a fight. "You're not going to kill her. You need her. Otherwise you would've already done it."

Calm exhales puffed the ski mask out over the shooter's mouth. Black eyes studied Braxton as a single tear slipped from Elizabeth's left eye. He'd cut off her oxygen. She'd either pass out in a few seconds or die right here. And he knew it. He was buying his time, showing he had control. The shooter lowered the gun from her temple then aimed at Braxton. "Then I'll guess I'll have to put a bullet in you."

He pulled the trigger.

Braxton spun as the bullet made contact and fell to the ground.

The scream didn't make it out as the shooter tightened his hold around her throat. Pulling her into him, he leveled that dark gaze with hers. Sirens and flashing lights closed in on the scene. "One down, Elizabeth. How many more people are you willing to watch die before you give in?"

Her vision blurred, her body growing heavy.

He didn't wait for an answer, wrenching her forward when all she wanted to do was fight back, when all she wanted to do was get to Braxton. But fighting back put her baby at risk.

She fought to stay upright as blackness closed in at

the edges of her vision. Faster than she thought possible, the shooter had shoved her into the trunk of his Mercedes. The engine growled to life as darkness consumed her.

"CALL AN AMBULANCE!" Unfamiliar voices pulled him out of blackness.

Braxton shot up straight with a gasp in his throat, gravel and glass cutting into his palms. The ache in his chest burned through him, and he clamped a hand over the brand-new hole in his T-shirt and Kevlar. A groan escaped as he pushed to his feet and stumbled through the circle of civilians surrounding him. "Where is she?"

He scanned the scene as Anchorage PD and a dark SUV identical to Liz's rolled onto the scene. Vincent Kalani stepped out onto the pavement, and everything inside Braxton froze. While he'd been the one to initially put Liz in the crosshairs by leaving, the call to her burner cell had sealed the deal. None of this—the bullet graze, the crash, her kidnapping—would've happened if she hadn't picked up that call. There was only one number she'd dialed on that phone. Only one way the shooter could've gotten through to her.

Braxton closed in on the forensics expert fast. Rage pushed through him as he fisted his hands in Vincent's cargo jacket and hauled him back against the SUV. "Where is she? You're the only one who called that burner. You're the only one—"

A right hook to the face knocked Braxton off balance. Vincent straightened to his full six-foot-four frame. Violence etched deep lines into the forensic expert's expression. "The next time you come at me, you better be sure to finish the job. Understand?"

A group of Anchorage PD officers stood ready to draw their weapons around him.

"He took her. That bastard took her." Braxton ignored the pulse at the left side of his face, a combination of sweat and blood sticking to his scalp. His heart threatened to explode out of his chest. Every minute he'd been unconscious had been another minute she'd gotten farther away. Damn it. One breath, two... Reason returned in small increments as he forced his blood pressure under control. "He contacted her through her burner phone. You're the only one who had that number."

"I would never put Elizabeth in danger. I trust her with my life, and she trusts me with hers. You see, that's what a team does, Levitt. We trust each other. We risk our lives for each other." Strain tightened the cords running down Vincent's neck as he stepped closer. Thick, dark eyebrows drew together. He extracted his phone from his jacket pocket, swiping his thumb across the screen. Handing the phone off, Vincent nodded. "Take it. If we're going to find her, you've got to trust me."

Braxton took the phone, his attention immediately drawn to the blinking red dot speeding south along a map of Seward Highway. His hand tightened around the device, the back hot to the touch. Elizabeth. "You're tracking her."

"I'm tracking her earpiece. You've got a range of ten miles. I'll take care of things here." Vincent extracted the tiny device from his ear then tossed him a set of keys, pain from the bullet flooding through Braxton as he caught them midair. Setting the earpiece in Braxton's palm, the forensics expert nodded. "Go. Get my teammate back."

Braxton pumped his legs hard and inserted the earpiece as he wrenched open Vincent's SUV door. The engine growled to life as he shoved the vehicle into Drive and jammed his foot into the accelerator. "I'm coming for you, baby, hang on."

No answer.

Seward Highway stretched out in front of him, 125 miles of majestic scenery, trailheads and a hell of a lot of places to take care of a hostage. A groan fought its way up his throat. No. Whoever this guy was, he needed Liz. Otherwise she'd already be dead. Braxton pushed the SUV harder. The shooter would keep her secluded, away from the touristy cabins along the highway. "He's not going to kill her yet."

He glanced down at the phone. Still in range. It'd be another few minutes before he caught up to the Mercedes. Every cell in his body couldn't stand to be apart from her for another second longer, but he couldn't force the SUV faster. His fingers drummed hard against the steering wheel. If her kidnapper hurt her, he'd spend the rest of his life hunting the SOB down. "Come on, come on."

"Braxton?" Her strained voice spread through him like a wildfire.

"Liz." He swallowed hard against the tightening in his throat. She was alive. "Baby, are you hurt?"

"My wrist…" A hard *thunk* registered through the

earpiece. Then another. She hissed. "I think it's broken, but I'm okay. He put me in the trunk. Took the burner phone and my gun. I'm trying to kick out the taillight to see where we are."

"I'm coming for you." He glanced down at the phone's screen. The red dot blinked strong. A few more miles. That was all it'd take to have her back in his arms. He hadn't given much thought to his future. All that'd mattered when he'd come back to Anchorage was keeping her alive then moving on with his life if she decided he needed to leave. But now? There was no life without Elizabeth. And he wasn't going to lose her or their baby now. Brolin might've raised him, but Liz and baby Karina were his family now. And nobody threatened his family. He gritted his teeth, fighting against the rising pressure behind his sternum. "Save your energy. I'm tracking your earpiece. I'm not far behind."

"Braxton," she said. "If I don't make it out of this alive—"

"You will." There was no other option. He was already redlining the RPMs. If he pushed the SUV any harder, the engine would explode. His breath came too fast. His heartbeat shook behind his rib cage. Headlights blinded him from the other side of the highway as he made the last curve. Less than a mile between them. "Just keep talking. Focus on my voice, and we'll get through this. You're not going to be a vic—"

Tendrils of smoke rose from the SUV's engine, the needles in the dashboard falling no matter how hard he pushed the accelerator. Soft ticks from the engine kept rhythm with the headache at the back of his skull as

Braxton jerked at the steering wheel. The vehicle slowed from ninety miles plus per hour to a mere twenty in the span of ten seconds. No, no, no, no, no. "Come on!"

"Braxton? What is it? What's wrong?" Liz's voice dropped into panic.

He pulled the SUV into the shoulder, barely able to see through the thick smoke coming out of the edges of the hood. He wouldn't make it to her—not in time. His feet hit the pavement, and he rounded to the front of the vehicle. After hauling the hood overhead, he braced himself against the white-hot temperatures as he reached for the radiator cap. Pain scalded across his hand, but he got the cap off and looked inside. Empty. Damn it. "Nothing. I'm coming for you."

He tossed the cap on top of the radiator then extracted Vincent's cell phone from the interior of the SUV. He'd trained day in and day out for this. Come hell or high water, he'd get to her. Slamming the driver's side door behind him, he checked his weapon and started running, phone in hand. The shooter might never pull over, but Braxton would never stop looking for her.

"We're slowing down." Rustling filtered through the open line as she shifted inside the trunk. Then stopped. "He's pulling off the highway. I can't tell where we are. I can't see anything."

"That's okay. I know where you are." He confirmed her location on Vincent's phone, air tight in his chest as he tried to keep his voice even. A half mile up ahead, the shooter had pulled into the trailhead for McHugh Trail, a heavily wooded and rocky journey to McHugh Peak. Without snowshoes this time of year, the bastard would have a hard time getting very deep into the wilderness with a hostage, but there were plenty of places to disappear.

Or to hide a body.

Braxton spotted a distant pair of red lights down the highway. Cliffs and trees backed against the highway on one side, Turnagain Arm on the other. Every second he lagged behind, the higher the chance he'd lose them altogether. "Listen to me. I have your location. I'm going to find you. I promised I would protect you, and I will."

A loud thud resembling the slamming of a car door reverberated into his ear.

"He's coming." She lowered her voice to a whisper, a plea on her lips. "Braxton…"

His grip tightened around the phone in his hand. His muscles burned, but he pushed the pain to the back of his mind. "I'm coming, Liz. I'll be there in two minutes. Fight back. Run if you have to. I'll find you."

The high-pitched protest of metal reached his ears. The trunk lid? Muffled static claimed his attention, an all-too-familiar voice growing louder. "You've been holding out on me." Another round of static drowned out Liz's response as though someone was handling a microphone. "Whoever this is, you think you're coming to save her. Well, I've got news for you. You're too late. Elizabeth is mine."

The deafening crunch exploded in his ear.

"Liz?" A quick glance at Vincent's phone said it all: the shooter had destroyed Liz's earpiece. And any chance he had of tracking her location. "Liz!"

Chapter Eight

Her hands shook as the shooter pulled her from the trunk of the Mercedes. He'd found her earpiece almost instantly and crushed it beneath polished shoes. No passing cars. No hikers out as the sun started to lower in the sky.

No one to hear her scream.

Rough hands maneuvered her around the car and toward the trailhead up ahead. Clear skies gave way to a few twinkling stars this far out of the city, but where Elizabeth normally would've taken a few minutes to appreciate the view, now she was being forced deeper into Alaskan wilderness. "You don't have to do this."

She didn't know what else to say as branches from pines scraped across her jacket and the exposed skin of her neck and face. He'd gone out of his way to find her. Tortured her former supervisor, hijacked Oversight's feeds, stalked her for weeks. Something deep in her gut said no matter what she said, he wouldn't listen.

"Walk until I tell you to stop." His voice remained calm, collected. Dangerous.

Her boots scuffed against rocks and downed branches

along the trail. She couldn't see more than five feet in front of her. He hadn't bound her. She'd catch herself if she fell, but she couldn't do much else with her broken wrist. And running into the middle of the wilderness as temperatures dropped for the night in the middle of January would be as lethal as taking a bullet to the head. Braxton had promised he'd find her, but freezing to death out here, where he couldn't track her anymore thanks to the man with the gun pressed into her back, wasn't a chance she was willing to take. Elizabeth checked his position back over her shoulder. "You obviously plan on killing me and leaving me out here for hikers to discover later. Don't I deserve to know why?"

"You don't deserve anything but what's coming to you." He pressed the gun deeper into her back, nearly to her spine despite the padding of her coat.

Freezing air burned her nostrils the higher they climbed up the trail. What did he expect her to do, make it all the way to McHugh Peak with a bullet graze, a head injury and a broken wrist? Her lungs fought against the climb in elevation, her breaths getting shallower with each step. "The Sovereign Army took credit for the bombing at Blackhawk Security, but you've made this personal. This isn't about protecting the American population's privacy, is it? You're using an extremist group as your cover."

She was only guessing, but from his lack of response, Elizabeth bet she had hit the nail on the head harder than she'd estimated. "Somehow you figured out I'd created Oversight for the NSA and changed my name. Then you tracked me down here in Anchorage and started planning my murder." She kept pushing forward. She'd only hiked this particular trail once during one of Sullivan's mandatory wilderness survival trainings, and it was difficult to decipher their location along the trail as shadows crept across the path, but there should be a branch heading off soon. At least a place she could gain the higher ground. She couldn't fight him physically, but she could disorient him long enough to buy herself time to run back toward the trailhead.

Toward Braxton.

"Why go through the trouble?" she asked.

"That's far enough." How the man determined to kill her breathed through the thick ski mask over his face, she had no idea. She chanced another glance behind her. The effect of his pressed suit combined with the mask chased a tremor down her spine. Like Death coming to collect the next soul in his crosshairs. Too bad she'd sold her soul to the father of her unborn child a long time ago.

She stopped in her tracks, about four feet ahead of him. Her pulse beat hard at the base of her throat. The only people who knew about her facial recognition program worked for the NSA or in the Oval Office. Which meant the shooter had either hacked his way into the NSA servers—which was unlikely given she'd set up the latest security—or he'd worked for them. Then again, he'd hijacked Oversight's feeds. Or he had a partner. Her toes tingled, going numb from the dropping temperatures. If he wasn't going to kill her soon, the wilderness would. Elizabeth wiggled her fingers to keep the circulation flowing. She strained to hear footsteps—anything—that indicated someone was coming. A hiker, police. Braxton. The man had a gun aimed at her, and there was nothing Elizabeth could do. "Is this where they're going to find my body?"

Keep him talking. Keep him distracted.

A gloved hand gripped her arm and spun her around, and her breath caught in her throat. Those dark eyes seemed black now with only muted sunlight coming through the trees. His hold on her hurt, bruised. "You're trying to stall, but it won't work. I've been waiting for this day for too long."

Without hesitation, the shooter hauled her off the worn path into shadowed darkness of thick pines and underbrush. Thorns pulled at her jeans and boot laces, but he dragged her along with ease. Dry branches cracked under her boots as they got farther from the trail. Nobody would think to look for her out here. Nobody would find her.

Trees thinned ahead. The muffled sound of passing cars grew louder. He wasn't going to leave her for a hiker—or worse, her team—to find. Elizabeth swallowed hard as they cleared the tree line. The cliff rushed up to meet her before she was ready. Her heel slipped off the edge, her knees buckling as panic spread through her. Loose rocks and dirt cascaded down below onto Seward Highway, but she never saw them land. Too far down. Only the shooter's tight grip on her arm kept her from falling, but she had a feeling that anchor wouldn't last long. Her breath lodged in her chest. She couldn't take her eyes off the black ocean of pavement a few hundred feet below where he intended to let her drown. Gravity pulled at her, but she fought against it.

"Tell me why. You've tried to blow me up, tried to shoot me on more than one occasion now." She didn't dare move, didn't dare face him for fear of taking the wrong step. She wasn't a profiler like Kate, she wasn't trained to read people, but the gunman at her back had certainly made this personal. He wanted her dead, wanted revenge. There was only one reason a man acted so passionately. "There has to be a reason."

"Give me the override password to Oversight's security and I'll make this quick." The slight exhale from behind her barely reached her ears over the sound of passing cars below. Silence settled. His voice became rough, fierce, as her arm tingled from her cut-off circulation. He placed his mouth against her ear. Too close. Intimate. She closed her eyes against the flood of nausea taking hold. "Or I can draw this out until you're begging me to end you."

That was why he hadn't killed her yet. While he might've been able to reroute the feeds, he hadn't been able to get past Oversight's security to operate the program himself. Her insides suddenly felt hollowed out, the rest of her body heavy. Her heartbeat echoed through her. The work she had done for the NSA haunted her every time she closed her eyes at night. She never should've agreed to build that damn program. Never should've let them use it before it was ready. The secrets, the lies, the deaths. Oversight saved lives, but at what cost? Elizabeth licked at dry lips, the dropping temperatures wicking moisture from her mouth. Opening her eyes, she internally braced herself. "It won't do you any good. The password is only the first level to gaining control. You won't be able to hack the second. Not without me."

And not without a retinal scanner.

"Then this is going to be a long night for you." The slightest movement at her back threatened to launch her over the side of the cliff. "You know a person can sustain a three-story fall and live to tell about it. But not much else. You see, your body will be so broken, you'll never be able to do more than blink from your hospital bed until you finally give up on life." He jerked her against him then maneuvered her closer to the edge. "So save us both the time. You have five seconds to give me the password."

The back of her heel slipped off the edge of the cliff, and she held on harder to the man threatening to throw her over the edge. Panic consumed her. Her breath came quick. Her heart rate rocketed into dangerous territory. She didn't want to die. Elizabeth squeezed her eyes tight, fought to keep her balance. One wrong step. That was all it would take and everything would be over. Her stomach pitched as her mind put on a nausea-inducing slideshow of what that meant. She'd never meet her baby girl. Never protect another client. Never take control of the life she wanted.

"Two seconds," he said.

Braxton.

His name slipped between the layers of panic and demanded her attention. Her heart rate dropped, the flush of cold sweats dissipating. She opened her eyes. Fighting to breathe through a rush of dizziness, she shook her head. The shooter wouldn't be able to get past the second level of security. Not without her. So if giving him the password saved her life—saved her baby's life—there wasn't much to think about. "All right!" She licked at dry lips. "The password is 'Inicial Lake,' from my favorite TV show."

His laugh slithered down her spine.

"Your government turned its back on you the same as they did me. Tell me, *Sprinkles*," he said. "How does it feel turning your back on them now?"

"Don't call me that." Something shot down her spine, like an electric shock. Her fingers tightened as fury exploded through her. Elizabeth dug her heels into the dirt and shoved back into his chest. Her momentum knocked him off balance, but his grip still around her arm pulled her down with him. The tree line blurred in her vision as they rolled, locked around one another, in a fight for the gun. A scream worked up her throat as her already broken wrist sandwiched between them, the gun's barrel pointing straight at her forehead. He was stronger, so much stronger, than she was. But she wasn't going to die out here.

She slammed into a nearby pine, bark and dried needles scratching the skin along the back of her neck. A wave of dizziness unbalanced her as she tried to stand. The shooter fought to straighten, the gun missing from his hand.

There. Discarded in a bed of pine needles and leaves, the weapon stood out against the washed-out foliage and ice. Elizabeth lunged, but she wasn't fast enough. A leather-gloved hand wrapped around her ankle, and she hit the ground hard. Clawing at the ground, she fought to reach the gun. Dirt worked under her fingernails, but she didn't care. Without that gun, she was dead.

The shooter pulled her back against him, the weapon farther out of reach than before, and flipped her onto her back. She kicked at him, punched. He was too strong. That same gloved hand wrapped around her throat for a second time and squeezed. She clamped one hand around his wrist as leverage, trying to get oxygen, and reached for his left eye with the other despite her broken wrist.

"Get the hell away from her." Braxton's voice pierced through the darkness. She fought to scream though no sound left her mouth. The few stars above transformed into indistinct balls of light as Braxton raised his own weapon, taking aim. "Or I put a bullet in your head."

"I SAID GET away from her." Braxton widened his stance, pulling his shoulders back to make himself a smaller target. Pure rage filled his lungs, pure fire burning through his veins. Didn't matter the sun had dipped below the trees. He'd rip this SOB apart blind for coming after Liz. Family wasn't who he'd been born with. It was who he'd die for, and he sure as hell was ready to die right here, right now for the mother of his child if that was what fate held for him. But he wouldn't make it easy, either. He motioned the bastard up with the barrel of the gun.

The shooter released his grip around Liz's throat, and she fell back against the dead pine needles and foliage.

Her gasps reached his ears, but Braxton never took his attention off the man standing above her. "You're nothing but a disgraced analyst, Levitt. You might've put on some muscle. Learned some fancy new moves, right? But I've been doing this for years. You can't stop me."

A smile curled at one edge of his mouth. Braxton tossed the gun, his fingers contracting into the center of his palms. Adrenaline dumped into his blood and hiked his pulse higher as he relaxed his stance. "Why don't we find out?"

The shooter took that as his cue, pulling a blade from an ankle holster. Her attacker headed straight for him, that mask still in place.

Braxton met him halfway, the small amount of sun providing enough light for him to make the first strike. The shooter lunged for him blade first. Catching the operative's wrist, he hauled the blade upward and swept the shooter's legs out from under him. They hit the ground hard, the air crushed from his lungs. His elbow made contact with the shooter's sternum, and the knife flipped into the underbrush. Out of the corner of his eye, Liz turned over onto her stomach, struggling to her feet. She searched for something in the grass. Maybe a weapon.

The shooter took advantage of the distraction and wrapped a forearm around Braxton's neck, his back pressed against the bastard's chest, and squeezed. His heartbeat pulsed hard at the base of his throat and grew louder in his ears. He leveraged his fingers between his own neck and his attacker's forearm and took a single deep breath. "Give it up, Levitt. You can't save her. Not this time."

Liz was the one he'd lived for. And he'd fight for her until the end.

A growl resonated through him. Braxton shot his knee directly back into the shooter's face, and the SOB's grip disappeared. He rolled out of range then pushed to his feet, fists up. The shooter closed in on him before he could take his next breath. He blocked the first punch. Blocked the second. But a hard kick to Braxton's sternum sent him sprawling head over heels through the dirt. Dead pine needles and something wet clung to his clothing. He forced himself to his feet as the shooter went for Liz again.

"Braxton!" She threw her hands out behind her as she backed herself toward the tree line, those mesmerizing brown eyes wide and filled with terror.

Braxton closed the distance between them, fisting the shooter's suit in his hand, and shoved a boot to the back of the operative's knee. He followed through with a punch to the face for good measure. His muscles ached, his head pounding hard from the accident. Blood still clung to the side of his face and wouldn't come off with the swipe of the back of his hand. Didn't matter. Getting Liz out of here. Protecting their baby. Ending this sick game. That was all that mattered.

The shooter went down, narrowly missing Braxton's boot to his face as he rolled. A glint of sunlight flashed before the assailant came at him with another blade. Damn it. How many other weapons was the bastard hiding in that suit? They faced off again. Hard exhales and the faint hooting of an owl cut through the groan of dodging the knife. Black eyes locked on him as Braxton sank lower into his stance. "Not just an analyst after all. Where was this fire when you practically begged me to take the intel on Oversight four months ago?"

Braxton straightened a fraction of an inch. Four months ago. The night he'd left his entire future asleep in his bed and walked away. The anonymous transaction had saved Liz's life, but how many others had been destroyed because of his moment of weakness? His attention shot to Liz as she sank to her knees near the tree line, out of hearing range, seemingly out of energy. She couldn't find out the truth. Not yet. Not when they were so close to moving on from the past. Not when the chance of them being a family—a real family—stared back at him through her eyes. "You."

"Me." The shooter rushed forward, knife up. He used the blade as a distraction, hiking a knee into Braxton's rib cage.

Bone crunched under Braxton's fist as he slammed his knuckles into the assailant's face. Once. Twice. A muffled scream escaped from the shooter's mouth underneath the mask as he swung the blade down. Agony washed over Braxton as metal met flesh. Blood dripped onto his shoelaces, the sensation of small taps against the tops of his boots the only indication of how deep the laceration went. He suppressed the scream working up his throat. No telling how fast he was losing blood without being able to take his eyes off the shooter, but the faster his heart beat, the more blood he lost. With a single punch to the shooter's midsection, Braxton used the same distraction technique to reach for the blade. He wrapped his hand around the bastard's wrist and twisted the shooter's arm until the second blade fell to the ground. His opponent dropped to one knee as Braxton forced the arm backward. "You will never lay another finger on her as long as I'm around."

Wide eyes comprehended Braxton's next thought.

"Braxton, no!" Liz's voice fought to penetrate through the haze of violence consuming him. Then her shaking fingers slid over his left shoulder. She tightened her grip on him, her fingernails digging into his flesh, her voice strained. "You can't kill him."

One kick to the sternum. That was all it would take to end this nightmare, to ensure Liz never discovered the truth about the deal he'd made. But…he couldn't do it. Not when she expected him to be the good guy, to take the higher ground. "He's not going to stop."

"He'll pay for what he's done," she said. "The bomb, the shooting in the garage, the shooting in the park and kidnapping me. He's going to spend the rest of his life behind bars. But if you kill him now, you'll be on the run for the rest of your life. And you'll be no better than him."

Braxton let go of the SOB's wrist. The shooter lost his balance, hands desperately seeking something—anything—to grab on to. He came precariously close to toppling over the edge, but Braxton reached out, gripping the bastard's suit jacket, and hauled him away from the edge. He should've felt relief. Should've been able to release the tightness building behind his sternum. But Braxton knew the truth. This wasn't over. Wouldn't be as long as the operative's heart was still beating. "Don't make me regret not killing you."

"He'll never be able to touch me from behind bars. And he's going to have to live with that knowledge until he dies." Liz's grip softened as she raised a gun and took aim. The weapon shook in her hand and, for the first time, Braxton took his attention off the shooter to look at her. Muted sunlight highlighted the sheen of sweat between her brows as she fought to keep her eyes open. She struggled to straighten fully, free hand clutched around her lower abdominals.

"Liz?" Something was wrong. Braxton released his grip on the shooter, panic coursing through every cell in his body as he reached for her. "Liz—"

Her pupils rolled up behind her eyelids as she collapsed. Braxton caught her before she hit the ground, her skin cold and waxy. Pain shredded through his injured arm under the pressure, but he didn't give a damn. Something dark and sticky stained the arm of her coat. Blood. But not enough for her to lose consciousness. Something else was wrong.

A long shadow cast darkness across Liz's features as the shooter straightened. "Looks like my job here is done, after all."

Before Braxton had a chance to stand, the bastard jumped off the edge of the cliff.

Pressure built in his lungs, crystallized puffs forming in front of his lips. What the hell?

Liz. He had to get Liz out of here. Digging his heels into the ground, he tipped her back against his injured arm and used every ounce of strength left to stand. Her thready pulse beat in rhythm to the pounding at the base of his skull. "Hang on, baby. I'm going to get you help."

Pines clawed at him as he ran straight back down the small path he'd used to find her. Another dose of adrenaline flooded through him, but the human body couldn't live off the fight-or-flight response forever. He'd crash soon. But he'd sure as hell get Liz help first. The last remnants of sunset lit the path as he took a sharp left. Rocks and twigs fought to trip him as he descended down to the trailhead. He wasn't going to lose her. Not now. Not ever. He hit the trailhead, nearly sprinting toward the shooter's abandoned Mercedes. The sight of the car alone was enough to push him harder.

He set her down then wrenched the back passenger door open, laying her across the back seat. Framing her jawline between his thumb and first finger, he swept a strand of hair away from her face. "Almost there, Sprinkles. Don't you dare give up now. Fight. Listen to my voice and open your eyes, baby."

No answer.

Braxton climbed from the car, rounding to the driver's side door. And froze, hand on the door handle. The cliff where he'd fought the shooter fifty feet above claimed his attention. He checked the pavement below. That was the same plateau where the shooter had jumped. The hairs on the back of his neck rose on end as he studied the rest of the highway.

So where was the body?

Chapter Nine

"He shouldn't have been able to find me." New name, birth certificate, driver's license, Social Security number, credit cards, established social media accounts. She'd done everything aside from getting plastic surgery. Even with full access to her program, the shooter shouldn't have been able to track her down. At least, not without help. Oversight ran off federal databases, and everything there said she was Elizabeth Dawson. Plain and simple. She'd made sure before terminating her contract with the NSA.

The IV in the top of her hand tugged at her attention, cold fluid working through her veins. Braxton had gotten her to the hospital two days ago, but according to him, the nightmare was far from over. The shooter had jumped off that cliff he'd meant to use as her final resting place, but his body hadn't been recovered. He was still out there. Hunting her. "I changed my name. I relocated."

"Why didn't you tell me?" Sullivan Bishop had taken the seat beside her bed. Protection detail, he'd said. Her boss hadn't taken any of his own cases since taking down one of the most trained stalkers in Anchorage history—his brother. So why was he really here? The former SEAL centered that sea-blue gaze on her, and everything in her heated. Not from attraction—Sullivan had the best damn army prosecutor in the country waiting for him up the road at Joint Base Elmendorf-Richardson—but from embarrassment. "I told you when I hired you, we'd have your back. No matter what, but that comes with conditions, Liz. We're a team. I can't expect my team to function if my operatives are keeping secrets from me."

"I came to Anchorage to start over. I'd left that part of my life behind. I didn't see any reason to fill you in because none of this was supposed to happen." But hadn't she'd always known this day would come? Always looking over her shoulder for those green eyes she hadn't been able to forget. Didn't matter where she'd gone. Braxton would've found her sooner or later. "How is Braxton?"

"The nurses threatened to strap him down if he didn't let them stitch his arm. Knowing what little I do about him, he'll barge through that door any moment to get to you." Sullivan's five o'clock shadow shifted as the small muscles along his jaw flexed. He crossed his arms, massive muscles fighting to free themselves from the signature black T-shirt he always seemed to wear. "He said the shooter jumped off that cliff edge, but neither Vincent nor the crime scene unit have been able to recover a body or any evidence the bastard got up and walked away. Do you trust him?"

Wasn't that the million-dollar question? Elizabeth

pressed the edge of the bedsheet under her fingernail. She had no doubt Braxton would do what it took to protect her. Even if that meant neutralizing the threat after she'd passed out from the cramping in her abdomen. Snapping her gaze to her boss, she pressed her shoulder blades into the pillows behind her. "It's complicated."

"What about the pregnancy? When were you going to tell me about that?" he asked.

Elizabeth swallowed against the bruising around her throat, the rising rhythm of her heartbeat registering on the monitor beside her. The pain she'd experienced on that cliff, the sensation of building pressure... She'd feared the worst as Braxton raced her to the hospital. When the doctor had wheeled in the ultrasound machine, she'd expected for him to tell her the baby was gone. But baby Karina's heart beat strong. Her lower lash line burned as relief still coursed through her. "To be fair, I only told the father three days ago."

"Braxton," he said.

"Yes. What...what happened between us happened before I came to Anchorage, but I only found out about a month ago. I swear I didn't know I was pregnant when you hired me." She focused on a stray thread trying to escape from the white hospital blanket. She licked dry lips as she fought against the memories of Braxton on that cliff, of the shooter's blade cutting through him. He risked his life—yet again—for her. He'd saved her. And she wasn't sure that was something she could ever pay back. Elizabeth moved her hand over the baby. At least, not without letting him back in her life permanently. She forced herself to level her chin with the floor. To prove she could. Her baby wasn't a mistake. She was, however, a surprise Elizabeth hadn't been counting on when she'd taken on her share of clients for the firm. Her work had been the only thing keeping her sane these last few months. But if her withholding information from her boss lost her this job, she wasn't sure what she'd do. Where she'd go. "If you're worried whether or not I'll be able to protect my clients—"

"I'm not." Sullivan leaned back in his chair. "You're one of the best operatives I have. And if you feel you can still do your job while carrying this baby, I trust your judgment to know what you can handle." He ran a hand down his five o'clock shadow, the sound of short whiskers against his fingers louder than she expected. "What I am worried about is the people who blew up my conference room trying to get to you, and what they're going to do next."

"Is that why you're in here and Glennon is standing outside my room?" The Sovereign Army had taken credit for the bomb at Blackhawk Security three days ago, but now she wasn't so sure they were actually responsible. Wasn't sure they were even aware they'd been pulled into the shooter's game. What had he said? A headache pulsed at the base of her skull. The memories had gone fuzzy when she'd lost consciousness.

"I don't know much about your work for the NSA, but I've seen groups like this before, and they're not the kind of people who take government involvement in their lives lightly. For whatever reason, you're their main target." Sullivan sat forward, elbows on his knees, the butt of his favored .40 Smith & Wesson swinging forward from his shoulder holster.

"It's not them." Elizabeth had no doubt in her mind. "The man who shot at me in the parking garage after the explosion was the same one who kidnapped me off Seward Highway. I wouldn't be surprised if he used their cause to throw me off the trail. He's coming after me by himself. It's personal for him."

Elizabeth struggled to sit up without putting pressure on her broken wrist, now in a cast. Her throat tightened. The NSA had run dozens of missions with Oversight after she'd left. Some successes. Some failures. Hundreds of lives had been affected. Every family member, friend and radicalized militant involved could have reason to hunt her down for the program's creation alone. Add losses to that number? There were too many suspects to count. "He's doing this out of revenge."

"Well, that changes things." Sullivan's eyebrows pulled together, deepening three distinct lines in the middle. "Do you know who it is? Did you get a good look at the guy?"

"No. He wore a mask the entire time we were together." Flashes of those dark eyes materialized when she closed her eyes. She shook her head. "But I'm going to find out."

"And we'll be there every step of the way if you need us," Sullivan said. "On one condition."

Her stomach tightened.

Blackhawk Security's CEO shifted forward in his chair, his attention on her. "I want to know who I really hired."

She couldn't keep the truth from him or her team any longer.

"My real name is Elizabeth Bosch. I was born in the smallest town you can imagine in the middle of nowhere, Montana. My parents ran the ski resort there, and that's basically all I can tell you about them." Only the memories of photographs came to mind now. Elizabeth trapped air in her lungs, firming her lips. How long had it been since she'd given up her secret? Four, five months? "They died when I was four. My aunt came to live with me after that, and the minute I graduated high school, I got out of there as fast as I could and haven't looked back."

"And your work with the NSA?" he asked.

"Two years ago, I was working for a start-up company, programming and piloting unmanned drones for their military contracts, when one day…" Elizabeth picked at her chipped nail polish. She was unraveling at the seams, starting with her pathetic chipped, dirt-caked nails. "A man named Dalton Meyer approached me. He said one of his analysts had been keeping an eye on my career and thought I would be the best person for a job they had in mind. The analyst was Braxton. He offered me a contract so I could get the chance to serve my country in a bigger capacity. Turned out, the NSA wanted me to create a facial recognition program called Oversight to identify possible threats across the country. Anything from small-time crime to terrorist plots. And I did. Utilizing surveillance cameras, news coverage, phone cameras, social media, you name it, the program uses that information to predict threats." Her mouth dried. "But I ended up terminating my contract after Oversight's first trial run." She fought to breathe evenly. "Creative differences."

Movement on the other side of the single window to her room raised the hairs on the back of her neck. She didn't have to look at the man trying to force his way past Glennon at the door. Every cell in her body recognized every cell in his. Had since the day she'd met him. Would that ever change?

Door hinges protested loudly. Then he was there. Braxton was there, and she fought back the burn in her eyes from the pure relief rushing through her. "Hey."

"Hey." Goose bumps prickled along her arms. Bruises decorated his face, scratches cutting into his jawline. Proof he'd fought like hell on that cliff. For her. Silence settled between them. Comfortable. Electrically charged.

Sullivan stood and headed toward the door. "I can tell this is going to get awkward real fast, so I'm going to leave, but Liz—" He spun around, pinning her against the hospital bed with that hard sea-blue gaze. "Never withhold intel from your team again. Got it?"

She nodded. "Got it."

"Good. Call if you need something." The former SEAL maneuvered around Braxton without a word then shut the door behind him.

Braxton dropped a black duffel bag and closed the space between them. His bandaged fingers threaded through her hair at the back of her neck then pulled her into him. Right where she belonged. He tilted her head up and kissed her. Slow at first, then with more pressure, harder, as though he thought he'd never get the chance to kiss her again. Which he almost hadn't. If it hadn't been for him… If he hadn't come for her…

A dull ringing filled her ears as she fought to catch up with her shallow breathing. The monitors beeped rapidly a few feet away, and she couldn't help but laugh. Because if she didn't allow herself this small release, she might've shattered completely. Elizabeth pulled back but kept her undamaged hand gripped in his shirt. Meeting those compelling green eyes, she tugged him down onto the bed beside her. "Take me home."

WHEN A PHOENIX rose from the ashes, she was more beautiful and stronger than ever before. And, damn, he couldn't stop stealing glances at Liz as she rested her head against the window. She'd faced death and survived. How many others could say the same?

The stitches in his arm stretched tight beneath the gauze, but he pushed the discomfort aside, attention on the all-too-familiar road. A light dusting of snowflakes fell across the windshield, but it wasn't enough to detract from the intense hollowness setting up residence in his gut. Silent seconds stretched into minutes as Liz closed her eyes.

The baby was okay. Seeing their daughter on the ultrasound, hearing her tiny heartbeat. It was as though a dam had been destroyed and a flood of emotions had washed forward. He'd nearly sank to his knees right there in the middle of the hospital room. And in that moment, he'd allowed himself to imagine things he hadn't before. Meeting his daughter for the first time, celebrating her first birthday, sending her off to kindergarten, walking her down the aisle on her wedding day. The three of them—him, Liz and Karina—together as a real family.

Slush splashed up onto the windshield, bringing him back to the moment. He'd forfeited those fantasies the night he'd walked out on Liz after they'd conceived their baby. Forfeited his right to happiness. His right to ask her for the possibility of a future between them— wouldn't work. Not with the NSA dead set on putting him behind bars for treason. He couldn't ask her to wait, to hope.

Braxton tightened his grip on the steering wheel of another Blackhawk Security SUV, fighting back dark memories of tearing down Seward Highway in pursuit of saving her life in another vehicle exactly like this. He might've forfeited everything that night, but he'd do whatever it took to keep his girls safe. No matter the cost.

Soft snoring filled the interior of the vehicle, and he looked over to see Liz's lips slightly parted, her features slack. As much as he'd been able to research during the last two days of her in the hospital, the first few months of pregnancy were the most exhausting. Keeping up with a growing fetus took a toll he could only imagine. But fending for her life on top of that? Liz deserved to climb under the covers of the nearest bed and never climb out. He could give her that. If only for a few days.

He turned into a long asphalt driveway, and his gut clenched. A gallery of pines lined the property of the forty-year-old, two-story home. Wood-paneled siding and a contemporary design helped the cabin stand out against the others in the area, the nearest a quarter mile away. Typical cabins out here had been designed with winter months in mind, but not this one. The flower boxes still attached under the first-story windows and the long expanse of grass leading to the backyard paid homage to the past best left forgotten, but he didn't know where else to go.

Home sweet home.

The shooter had gotten away. Braxton didn't know how. He only knew that bastard had put Liz in his sights. And Braxton's gut said he wouldn't stop until the job was done. But they would be safe here. Then he'd move them to another safe house. And another. He'd move her around the entire country if it meant keeping her alive until they had a lead on the man hunting her. Braxton turned off the engine, the keys jingling against his leg. Reaching out, he slid his beaten knuckles along her cheekbone and lowered his voice. "We're here."

"Five more minutes." She buried herself deeper in her coat, the one arm still torn from the bullet graze at the park. White gauze lay at the bottom of the hole covering a row of stitches. "Too tired to move."

A laugh escaped through his nose. He dropped the keys into his jacket pocket and shouldered the door open. Rounding to the front of the SUV, he fought the urge to burn the entire cabin to the ground and walk away before she had a chance to step a foot inside. Leave the memories in the ashes. A gust of fresh, chilled breeze cleared his head. Get her inside. Keep her safe. He carefully opened the passenger side door, a smile thinning his mouth as she caught herself tipping out. "I can help with that."

"Haven't you done enough?" She slid her hands up his forearms for balance. Despite the freezing temperatures, he didn't feel the cold. Not with her in his arms. Then again, she'd always made him run hot. Her feet hit the pavement, but Liz didn't make any move to free herself of his hold. "You know, saving my life and all. That one time."

The smile stretching across her face was enough to stop his blood pumping. If it weren't for the thin scratches, the bullet graze at the top of her arm, the broken wrist and the four stitches in her hairline, it would have. But knowing she'd almost died because of him, because he'd left her unprotected all these months, had twisted him into a sick mess. He slid his hand into hers, locking her against him. "Let's get you inside."

She studied the cabin for the first time, it seemed. Took in the wide expanse of windows at the front, the balcony hanging over the covered patio, the line of trees threatening to overtake the roof at any moment. "Another one of your safe houses?"

"No." He took a deep breath, leading her to the sidewalk and toward the front door. He'd told her about his past. Told her about his family, about how Brolin Levitt had lost this same exact cabin to the bank after he decided his addiction was more of a priority than paying the mortgage. Braxton tightened his grip around her hand. It'd taken a lot of negotiation under a fake name with the couple who'd purchased the home after his parents had been foreclosed on, but something inside him hadn't been able to let it go. Now he knew why he'd kept it around for so long. To keep her and their baby safe. "It's the cabin I grew up in."

"You bought it?" She followed him along the sidewalk, past the crack near the front steps where he'd tripped and broken his arm when he was ten. Past the large pile of firewood he'd been chored with stocking most summers before they hit the wooden steps leading to the front door. "Why?"

"For you." Wood protested under their weight as he climbed the nine steps it took to reach the threshold of his childhood. All in all, his family had had happy memories in this place. His parents had bought the cabin right after finding out they were pregnant with their one and only son. Brolin had been manager of a bank then, and Karina had stayed home to raise Braxton. He dug for his keys then inserted the key into the dead bolt and turned. That'd been before Brolin's addiction destroyed everything Braxton had ever known.

A rush of cinnamon-and-apple-scented air slammed into him as he pushed the door open. With Liz's hand still wrapped around his, he led her inside. The crew he'd hired to gut the insides had done a damn fine job. New white tile in the entryway, the perfect color of hardwood flooring off to the left in the living room, peach walls the same exact color as he remembered, only fresher. Windows let in natural light from nearly every angle imaginable, welcoming him home. But Braxton couldn't move. How long had it been since he'd stepped through that door? Twenty years? The house had gone through a lot since then. He'd gone through a lot.

"What do you mean, for me? When did you buy it?" Liz studied the gleaming tile, the sparse furniture, the hallway leading straight back to the renovated kitchen.

"Last year, when I realized I wanted to be more than your friend." When he'd realized he'd fallen in love with the woman who'd sat less than five feet from his cubicle. He didn't dare look at her as he tugged her toward the stairs off to the right and up to three massive bedrooms for her to choose from, two smaller, one master. Beds and bathrooms for each. Braxton slowed down at the top of the stairs but didn't dare drop her hand. Not yet. Not when she was the only thing keeping him anchored in the present. "Have your pick. We're going to be here for a few days."

"Where did you set up your surveillance?" she asked.

"In that one. My old room." He led her to the right, stopping under the door frame as he pushed the door wider. After the renovations, he barely recognized it. No posters from his favorite band, no dartboard, no toys and action figures. Just peach-colored walls, a window with blackout curtains, a king-size bed with new bedding and a desk with his surveillance systems. Braxton leaned his weight into the door frame. "The other bedrooms won't have the glow from the monitors keeping you up."

"I don't mind." Liz dropped his hand. She moved inside, taking in the room, and sat on the edge of the bed. Dropping her coat beside her, she looked completely at ease despite the bruises and scratches marring her perfect skin. Now fully lit from the natural light coming through the window, he noted the dark circles under her eyes, the lack of color in her lips, the slight tremor in her hands. He'd seen her like this before. Only once, after Oversight's real-world test run in which a CIA agent had lost his life. She'd tried not to internalize that guilt, but he'd read it on her face that day, and it'd taken one night of him finally getting the guts to kiss her senseless until she forgot. The same night he'd gotten her pregnant. The same night he'd disappeared. "I want to be able to see him coming."

His gut sank. Damn it. He should've thrown the SOB who'd taken her off the cliff like he'd planned. He could've ended this nightmare. Could've brought her some justice. He pushed off the wall, closing the space between them. Crouching in front of her, he fought the urge to use the same tactics he had the night they'd been together that single time. "Liz—"

"I don't need you to talk." Framing his jawline with her hands, Liz pulled him closer and crushed her mouth against his. A burst of her lavender scent destroyed the wall of care he'd put in place for her. She swept her tongue past his lips, and his knees hit the hardwood. No matter how much muscle he'd put on, no matter how many hours he'd trained, none of it stood against her. Pressing his palms against the small of her back, he took anything he could get from her and more. Then she pulled away. "I need you to stay with me tonight."

Chapter Ten

She didn't want to think about the explosion. Not the shooting in the garage, her kidnapping. The fact she'd very nearly been thrown off a cliff and was still the center of a hit man's plans for revenge. None of it. The only thing Elizabeth focused on now was him. All she wanted in this moment was him. His five o'clock shadow prickled against her palms as she framed his jawline. Seconds passed. A minute?

He backed away from her, those green-gray irises widening as his pupils shrank.

Confusion gripped her hard. "Say something."

"You don't want me to stay with you…not right now." His phone chimed, but Braxton didn't move. He looked over her, her skin burning everywhere his gaze made contact. Raising his hand, he slid his fingertips up her arm and rested his thumb against the hollow at the base of her throat. The tendons along his neck ticked. "I promised to protect you and failed. I should've gotten to you sooner."

"I'm perfectly capable of deciding what I want for myself. I know exactly what I'm asking you to do."

Low-grade pain spread from the bruise around her neck. Elizabeth automatically swallowed against the tightness overtaking her entire body, but instead of flinching, she reached out for him. Fisting her fingers in his long-sleeve T-shirt, she tugged him into her, where he belonged. Tendrils of his hair hid half of his face from her, and she brushed them out of the way with her casted hand, refusing to think of how she'd ended up with the broken wrist in the first place. "I'm alive, Braxton. We survived. And we'll keep surviving as long as we're together. So don't get any bright ideas about pulling away now."

"You should've let me kill him." His voice dropped into dangerous territory, but this had a new edge to it. So sharp it threatened to cut straight through her. The Braxton she remembered vanished as steel hardened his expression. "I could've ended this once and for all."

"Ended this." The words were more for herself than for him. The bullet wound in her arm burned, her muscles wound tight with strain and overuse. But none of that compared to the sinking of her stomach from a combination of the guilt etched into his features and the disappointment consuming her. He blamed himself for the events of the last few days—that was clear—but what he should be worried about was the baby he'd helped conceive. About whether or not he was going to fight to stay in her life. "I know you'd do anything to protect me and this baby, but killing him would've put you back on the NSA's radar. Self-defense or to save me. It wouldn't matter. They would've taken you, and I'd never see you again."

"Wasn't that my end of our deal?" he said.

Silence settled between them as reality closed in. Yes. Back in the garage, before he'd given her a glimpse of how thoughtful he was, how caring, before he'd risked his life to save hers, she'd made him swear to crawl back to the rock he'd been hiding under for the last four months when this was over. Since he'd come back into her life, he'd gone out of his way to prove how much she'd meant to him. The ice cream and sprinkles, the nicknames, the slight lift of his lips when he looked at her, the undeniable physical attraction they shared. Or had it all been an act? A way to force her to accept his protection in order to extinguish his own guilt for leaving? She blinked to clear her head, to build up the wall that'd been in place for so long, and shut down her initial reaction. "You're right. Killing him wouldn't have changed anything."

No response.

She released her grip on his shirt and stepped away from him. She couldn't breathe, couldn't think. Four months ago, he'd taken her to bed, given her everything she'd wanted between them, then disappeared without a word. He was the one who'd tracked her down. He was the one who'd promised to protect her. He was the one who'd kept her alive these last few days. They were having a baby together. But apparently not even the tiny creature in her uterus who'd disrupted absolutely everything could make him want to stay. Damn it, how could she have been so stupid to think this time would be different? The NSA's charges against him hadn't changed. Why would he?

"You should leave when this is over." Elizabeth maneuvered around him toward the attached bathroom. She swiped at the tears in her eyes as the peach walls and surveillance monitors blurred in her peripheral vision.

Cool air rushed against the exposed skin along her arms as she closed the bathroom door behind her. No footsteps on the other side of the door. No knock against the wood. Braxton hadn't followed her. But she wasn't sure if she'd wanted him to. Tapping the crown of her head against the door, Elizabeth steered her attention to the white, brown, tan and teal tile of the soaking tub. What had she been thinking, asking him to stay with her tonight?

That was the problem. She hadn't been thinking. Being the center of a madman's revenge, of nearly dying not once but three times had distorted the single rule she'd set for herself when this whole thing started. Protect herself. Emotionally, physically, mentally. At whatever cost. But for the briefest of moments, he'd slid past her defenses, and she hadn't realized it until right now. For the briefest of moments, she'd let him have control.

Elizabeth forced herself to put one foot in front of the other until she'd reached the tub, and she turned the knob for hot water. To rinse some of the rawness down the drain. She undressed and added a lavender-scented soap beneath the water stream. The same brand she used at home. Wasn't surprising. Seemed Braxton had held on to a lot of things from the past. She studied the rest of the bathroom for the first time. For a while there, it seemed he'd held on to his feelings for her, too, as he'd held on to this house. But now she recognized her own wishful thinking.

He was shutting her out.

And hell, it hurt. She should've been used to that by now. She blinked back the burn in her lower lash line as the truth began to show. Stay in control. Stay strong. Whatever she imagined might happen between them was a fantasy, some twisted desire to have the support system neither of them had had growing up.

She stepped into the bath, flinching from the sting of the water on her fresh cuts, and curled in on herself. Her knees pressed against her cheeks. If the past four days had proven anything, it was that she and Braxton wouldn't work. Not with the NSA's charges over his head. Not with his flight instincts so engraved into his personal arsenal. Not when he tested everything she knew about herself.

She tightened her hold around her shins. The fact she was pregnant, the fact she'd been put in the shooter's crosshairs, was truly as bad as things could get, right? How much more pain did she have to go through before giving up was okay? Elizabeth ran a hand through her hair. No. She wouldn't give up. For the sake of her baby, she had to see this through. Even if her daughter lost a father in the process.

The doorknob clicked a split second before Braxton pushed it open. She lifted her attention toward him but didn't move. Didn't speak. She couldn't. Because the anguish etched across his expression gutted her to the bone. Green-gray eyes locked on her and, suddenly, she was losing the battle against him all over again.

He heel-toed off his boots one at a time then lifted his shirt over his head. The stitches across his arm almost bore resemblance to the bullet graze across hers. He'd been through hell just as much as she had the past three days. She had to remember that. He'd risked his life for her, almost died for her.

Valleys and ridges shifted across his abdomen as he closed the distance between them. Two steps. Three. Her mouth dried as he stared down at her, his dark, fathomless eyes burning straight through her. Climbing into the tub behind her, Braxton sank beneath the water almost fully clothed. Water rushed over the edge of the tub, but she didn't have the energy to care. Traitorous, treacherous need overtook her as he slid callused palms along her shoulders and pulled her back against him. All she wanted was him. Skin against skin, she wanted to feel alive. He wrapped his arms around her and pressed his mouth to her ear. "I've got you, Sprinkles."

A shiver chased down her spine despite the warmth of the water around her and Braxton's heat at her back. The tears came then, so strong she couldn't hold them back anymore. She shook against him, and he only held her tighter. This. This was what she missed about him. Not the promises. Not the offer of ice cream or the nicknames. She'd missed being in his arms, missed knowing she had someone she could count on, if only for a night.

"And I'll never let you go." He swiped her hair out of her face and turned her onto her side. Holding her against him with one arm, he rubbed small circles between her shoulder blades. When the sobs had racked her body and the water dropped in temperature, Braxton lifted her out of the tub. Goose bumps pimpled along her skin as he carefully dried her off with a fresh towel off the rack then led her back into the bedroom without a word.

Droplets of cold water hit her skin from her wet hair as he pulled an oversize shirt and a pair of sweats out of the dresser. He helped her dress, sliding his fingers along the back of her calves and down to her Achilles' heels. Another tremor lightninged through her, one that had nothing to do with the drop in her body temperature. Once she was dressed, Braxton interlaced his fingers with hers, tugging her down onto the bed. Shedding his own clothing, he pulled a pair of sweats from the dresser and shoved his legs into them. His weight on the mattress settled against her, hiking her heart into her throat. The past four days had destroyed her inside and out. And she had nothing left to give. Not to him. Not to the man trying to kill her. Not to her team. "Braxton, I can't—"

"I don't need you to talk." Her own words to him released the anxiety climbing up her throat. He maneuvered under the covers, his heat chasing the chill from her bones, and coiled around her. His fingers encased hers against her collarbones. They hadn't solved anything, but right now, pressed against him, she didn't care. His exhales kept rhythm with hers. "I need you to go to sleep."

Exhaustion pulled her under.

THE SHRILL RING of his burner phone ripped him out of Liz's warm hold.

"What is it?" The grogginess in her voice revealed

she wasn't entirely awake yet, and he smoothed his hand over her shoulder.

"Just my phone. Go back to sleep." Four hours. That was all the peace they'd gotten. Braxton threw the covers off and collected the phone from where he'd left it on the desk with his surveillance equipment. Unknown number. Warning spread through him. He checked the monitors. No movement along the tree lines or around the house. But that didn't mean Liz's stalker hadn't found another way to get to her. Studying the steady, slow rise and fall of her shoulders, he swiped his thumb across the screen then headed for the bedroom door, closing it behind him. If the shooter had somehow gotten ahold of yet another of their burner phone numbers, she didn't need to hear the shooter's voice after what she'd been through. "Talk."

"Hello to you, too, sunshine." Vincent Kalani's voice eased some of the tension climbing up Braxton's spine. He'd handed the operative one of his old preprogrammed burners while Liz had been recovering in the hospital after they discovered cloning tech on Vincent's device, but had pushed the investigation to the bottom of his priorities. New phone. New number. No chance the shooter could listen in on their calls this time. "Guess you didn't get my message."

Memory of his phone chiming earlier—before Liz had walked away from him with tears in her eyes—rushed forward. It hadn't been important then. "Guess not. What do you have?"

"We got a hit on the fingerprints from bullet casings recovered after the shooting at Town Square," Vincent said. "I sent the report to your phone, but looks like you're not checking email right now. Is it safe to assume you two hooked—"

"Say another word and I'll change your name to Veronica Kalani in every federal database I can hack. Which is all of them." Braxton checked over his shoulder. The door to the bedroom was still closed, and he moved farther down the hallway so this conversation wouldn't wake the woman in his bed. What'd happened between them a few short hours ago, her apparent fear of him leaving again, had left him hollowed out. Useless. The dark, raging creature inside him, the one that would do anything to stay with her, even if it put her in more danger, had taken control then. And he'd been lost. Seeing her in the tub, so vulnerable, so lost… It'd broken him. He never wanted to see her that way again. Not Liz. Him leaving had been part of the deal they'd struck before the shooter had tried to take them out in the parking garage. But everything had changed since then. "What does the report say?"

"Can you really change anyone's name?" Vincent asked. "Elliot thinks I don't know he's been stealing my lunch out of the refrigerator here at the office, and I'm currently looking for ways to make him pay."

Braxton took a deep breath, running his hand over his jawline. His normally groomed five o'clock shadow had thickened over the past few days. No time to shave when a shooter had put the woman he'd die to protect in his sights. "As tempting as that sounds, let's go back to the fingerprints."

"Right. Prints match a CIA agent named Justin Valentin," Vincent said. "You heard of him?"

Braxton dropped the phone away from his ear. It wasn't possible. Justin Valentin had been the field operative killed during Oversight's test launch. None of this made sense. Had the NSA identified the wrong corpse? Had Justin survived? The moment Liz heard about the evidence… He didn't know what she'd do. Vincent's voice reached through the haze threatening to suffocate him. Raising the phone to his ear, he pinched the bridge of his nose and closed his eyes. "Are you one hundred percent sure those fingerprints match that name?"

"I ran it twice. Why?" Vincent's confusion reached through the line. "Isn't this good news? You got your man. Liz can put this behind her."

"Not in the least. Did you run a background check after you matched the prints?" If the forensics expert had, they wouldn't be having this conversation. Braxton looked up and froze. Every cell in his body caught fire at the sight of Liz staring back at him from the bedroom door. "I'm going to have to call you back." He lowered the phone again, hitting the end button.

"Vincent found something." Not a question. Liz crossed her arms over her midsection, one of her textbook moves when she slammed her invisible guard into place. Dark circles still haunted her beneath those chocolate-brown eyes, exhaustion evident in her features, but the tears were gone. She'd gotten only a few hours of sleep over the last few days. With the added strain of the baby and the stress of being kidnapped on her body, it was a wonder she was still standing. "Tell me."

"We don't have to do this now." Braxton's bare feet stuck to the cold hardwood floor as he closed in on her. "You can go back to sleep—"

"I'm fine," she said. "Just tell me."

He nodded.

"Vincent recovered bullet casings from the shooting at Town Square. He was able to match the partial fingerprints on them to a CIA agent who died last year." He opened Vincent's email on his phone and handed it to her. "He matched them to Justin Valentin."

"That's not possible." Her exhale swept over his bare neck and chest. Her voice gained strength with each word out of her mouth. "I was there where Dalton Meyer ran the trial run, Braxton. I saw Agent Valentin die on the screen right in front of me. I watched as they lowered his coffin into the ground a week later. Justin Valentin is buried in Rock Creek Cemetery in Washington, DC."

"I was there, too, remember? I know what happened." He remembered every minute. Oversight's first real-world test run would stay ingrained in his memory forever. The program had identified a group of Afghan rebels intent on taking out the US Embassy in Kabul. What the program failed to identify, however, was the CIA agent deeply implanted within the group when the order for neutralization came down from on high. Liz had told them the tech wasn't ready, but her supervisor, Dalton Meyer, hadn't listened, and an American life had been lost on the program's first test run. Liz had never forgiven herself. "Vincent ran the prints twice. Unless you've got another explanation, we need your boss and

whatever connections he has to get a court order to ex-
hume whoever is in that coffin."

"No. The shooter…whoever is doing this is trying to
mess with my head." She thrust the phone back at him,
not bothering to read the ballistics report. Liz ran a hand
through her short hair, and she took a step back. The
past three days had her spiraling and, hell, he couldn't
blame her. But ever since her stalker had tried to kill
her with a bomb, they'd been reacting. The explosion,
the shootout in the garage, her kidnapping. It wouldn't
end until Liz was dead. And that wasn't an option. Not
for him. "He must've known about that mission and
somehow gotten access to those confidential files. Justin Valentin is dead."

"You think Justin's prints were planted." What was
the point of trying to set up a dead man? It didn't make
sense.

"In the last three days, there's only been one man I
know of who's trying to kill me. He's planned this out
for months, if not years." Liz crossed her arms again,
accentuating all the mouthwatering curves under his T-
shirt. "Do you honestly believe he'd be stupid enough
to leave his own fingerprints on those bullet casings
where we could find them?"

Not a chance. They were dealing with a professional.
No way in hell he'd leave evidence behind without reason. "How do you get a dead man's prints on a bullet
casing?"

"That's the million-dollar question," she said.

Braxton checked his phone for the time. "It's too late
to have Sullivan get a court order from a judge. But I'm

not going to wait around for this guy to take another shot at you. We need to trace Oversight's feeds and attack him head-on."

"That's not a plan." She dropped her arms to her side. "That's a death sentence."

Frustration built. "I don't want you to spend the rest of your life looking over your shoulder, Liz. Especially not with our daughter in tow. She deserves better than that."

Liz stepped back as though she'd taken a direct hit, and his stomach dropped. Waves of pinks and greens filtered through the wide expanse of windows, highlighting the sharp angles of her features. Aurora borealis rippled across the night sky, brighter than he'd ever seen it before. "Are you willing to bet your life on that?"

"I know why you won't touch Oversight's code, but running for the rest of your life is no way to live. I know that better than anyone." Braxton stepped into her range. He couldn't think with her so close. But he was tired of thinking. Tired of running.

"Dalton should've listened to me." Liz shook her head. "Oversight wasn't ready. I told him that the day before the scheduled trial run. I told him the programming kept skipping the background checks because of a broken line of code I hadn't been able to find, but he didn't care. A man died because of my mistake. You really want to take that risk?"

"I'll take my chances on you every day for the rest of my life." He countered her retreat, and his body temperature hiked at least two degrees. "Because of all the variables I bet the shooter calculated before making his move on you in that conference room, I know he didn't account for you fighting back."

Chapter Eleven

She'd stick to her end of the deal. Elizabeth would let him protect her until the threat was neutralized, then he could go back into hiding until the NSA forgot his name.

Her gut tightened at the thought, and she squeezed his hand draped across her hip. He'd convinced her to come back to bed, but she couldn't sleep. The sooner they ended this investigation, the sooner she'd have to watch him walk away. Again. But as much as she wanted to drown in fantasies of Braxton helping her raise this baby—of them becoming the family their daughter deserved—he couldn't stay. And the sooner she realized that, the better. For her and their baby. She trusted him enough to keep her alive. That would have to be good enough.

"You're still awake," he said.

She pressed her shoulder blades against his chest. His body heat tunneled through her borrowed sweats. What'd happened on that trail...she couldn't get that dark gaze out of her mind. "I see him when I close my eyes. I can't get him out of my head."

Braxton hiked her against him, dropping his mouth to her shoulder. "You're not responsible for any of this, Liz. This guy might be doing this out of some sick need for revenge, but I know you. You'd never deliberately put anyone in danger."

"Except I did. On the dozens of missions I let the NSA use my program." She turned her heard toward him, only the glow of the surveillance system highlighting one side of her face. "He used the Sovereign Army to take credit for the bomb, but what if this is about Oversight like we originally thought?"

"If this guy is connected to the work you did for the NSA, we'll find out who he is." He traced his fingers down her arm, coaxing goose bumps in his tracks, and placed his mouth at her ear. He slid his hand beneath the hem of her shirt, right over their growing daughter. "But right now, you and this baby have been through hell. You need to sleep."

"I can't sleep." Not when every time she closed her eyes, fear gripped her throat to the point she couldn't breathe. Elizabeth turned into him, framing one side of his jaw with her palm. His beard prickled against her skin. Images of their one night flashed through her mind. He'd been comforting her then, too, right after Oversight had failed its first test run in the field. A CIA agent had lost his life that day, the same man whose fingerprints Vincent had found on those bullet casings. Justin Valentin. And Braxton had been there for her. How many more mistakes had her program made since she'd told the NSA she'd never work for them again?

How many more lives was she responsible for? She didn't want to think about it.

Four months. Such a long time, yet not long enough for her feelings to disappear as fast as he had. She hadn't expected that. That chaotic tangle of emotions should've left by now. But they hadn't. He'd become part of her a long time ago. And there weren't exactly exorcists for this kind of thing. When it came to Braxton Levitt, she had the feeling he'd never leave her system entirely. But maybe that didn't have to be a bad thing. "Where have you been all this time?"

"Everywhere. Cambodia, Taiwan, Russia. I made it a point to stick to nonextradition countries." A shiver rushed down her spine at his touch, and Braxton flashed her that gut-wrenching grin of his. "But that's not what you want to ask me, is it?"

He could read her so well. Too well. Nervous energy exploded through her. All she'd been able to think about when the shooter had held her at the edge of the cliff had been Braxton's name. She didn't have any right to ask. He'd moved on. So had she. New city, new job, new name. She'd fought to leave her old life behind, a life that had included him up until the end. But the question still nagged at her. Clenching her teeth against the oncoming disappointment, Elizabeth studied the shadows lining his collarbones. "What was…" She swallowed around the growing lump in her throat. "What was I to you?"

He set her chin between his thumb and index finger, urging her to look up. The color of his eyes was lost in the blue light of his surveillance system a few feet away, but she read every change in his expression. Because she'd learned how to read him, too. "Everything."

Her breath came too fast. Her heartbeat seemed to shake behind her rib cage. Everything she'd done to this point—refusing to work with him, laying out the rules, putting up her guard—had been to protect herself, but he'd figured out a way around all of that. He'd buried himself beneath her skin and become part of her. Would it always be like this? When the smoke cleared, could this work? When someone wasn't trying to kill her, when the NSA wasn't trying to put him behind bars for the rest of his life.

"Come here." The lines at the edges of his mouth deepened with his smile. Braxton offered her his hand, sliding off the bed when she took it. Rough calluses caught on her skin, but right now, she only had attention for the slow burn of desire swirling in his gaze.

Her bare feet hit the cold hardwood floor, and he tugged her into him. Right where she needed to be. Without letting go of her hand, Braxton turned toward the desk and pulled open the top drawer. He handed her a small glass bottle with a long neck, the weight of his attention crushing the air in her lungs. "Black fingernail polish?"

"You've been through hell the last few days." He closed the short space between them, crowding her until her knees hit the edge of the bed. Collapsing back, she held her breath as Braxton sank to his knees in front of her. He tugged her sweats up around her calves, his touch somehow hot and cold at the same time. Or had her nerve endings started playing tricks on her again? "Let me take care of you."

"You happen to have black fingernail polish on hand?" Of course he did. Just as he'd put her favorite brand of lavender soap in the bathrooms, how he'd stocked the freezer with chocolate ice cream and the drawers with rainbow-colored sprinkles. He'd gone out of his way to ensure her small comforts came first. At first, she'd thought it'd been to manipulate her, to get her to trust him again. But now? Now a familiar feeling climbed up through her insides. The feeling of falling.

"I've got supplies stashed in this house you can't imagine." He feathered his fingertips down the tight muscles in her left calf then applied pressure. Her grip tightened on the edge of the mattress as she tipped her head back against her shoulders. "We could stay here for weeks without stepping outside this bedroom."

Elizabeth leveled her gaze with his. Her leg jerked beneath his hands as he pressed into one of her more sensitive ticklish spots. A laugh burst from her between her lips. "Sorry. I don't normally let people massage my calves. I'm afraid I'll kick them in the face, I'm so ticklish."

"I'll have to remember that." Half a smile stretched his mouth thin, and her stomach shot into her throat. Setting her foot on top of his thigh, he reached for the glass bottle and twisted off the lid. In the glow of his surveillance system, he touched up the tips of her toenails effortlessly. But what couldn't he do? He'd saved her life from a gunman, tracked her down to the edge of that cliff, fought a professional shooter as though

Rules in Deceit

he'd trained to fight all his life, established safe houses to keep them off the grid and learned to cook a turkey and vegetable soup she still couldn't stop tasting at the back of her throat. Blowing on her wet toenails, he sat back on his heels then swung himself up to stand. "Good as new."

Elizabeth couldn't take her attention off him. Something had changed. Some defining moment had altered his life that night he'd disappeared. "The night you left. Something happened, something to make you want to change your appearance, to learn to fight, to handle a gun." Because the man she'd known had never picked up a gun in his life or learned how to throw a punch. He'd been an analyst, glued to his computer screen. "What happened to you?"

His rough exhale reached her ears. The mattress dipped under his weight as he sat beside her, elbows on his knees, the little black bottle of nail polish gripped between his hands. He nodded once. "You happened to me. I couldn't protect you then. That needed to change."

Her lips parted to ask every question running through her mind. Protect her from what? Why hadn't he told her the truth? Did it have something to do with the NSA? But did any of it matter? Not really. This moment, that was all that mattered. "Kiss me."

"Don't start something you can't finish, Sprinkles." He shifted at her side, his dark hair skimming over his shoulders. Braxton moved a strand of hair off her forehead. The past four months living off the federal government's radar had hardened his features, but she still recognized the man beneath the guarded exterior and new muscle. And she wanted him now more than ever. "I have very little control when it comes to you."

"Please. I need this." She rolled her lips between her teeth and bit down. This wasn't an attempt to get him to stay after the investigation ended. It wasn't an attempt to satisfy her own attraction. Pure, unfiltered need coursed through her. The need to be touched, to be cared for, loved, even. If only for a night. Her throat dried. Before she lost him forever. "I need you."

Braxton threaded his fingers through the hair at the back of her neck, pulled her into him and set his mouth over hers. His clean, masculine scent clung to her borrowed clothing, to the sheets, became part of her, and she couldn't get enough. He maneuvered over her, pushing her onto her back, and slid his hand along the outer part of her thigh. He hiked her calf around his hip. Tightening her grip on him, Elizabeth breathed a bit easier despite his added weight. Patience was a virtue, but they didn't have time for that. She cocked her head to one side and opened her mouth wider for him.

Any second now reality would work its way back, but she'd stretch this night to last as long as possible. With a freshly painted set of toenails.

He'd lied to her.

The changes he'd made over the last four months hadn't been about the realization he couldn't protect her. If he'd known being part of her life would end this way, Braxton never would've recruited her for the NSA. But there was no changing the past. As for the future…

Hell, he needed her as much as he needed oxygen in his lungs. And that was a very dangerous thing.

Braxton buried his nose at the crown of her head, lavender and woman fighting to drown the guilt clawing its way through him. He should've ended it on that cliff side, gotten her free of this nightmare. Gotten her free of him. A murder charge would've kept him out of the country for the rest of his life and put a digital target on Liz's back, but at least then she'd be safe. He'd underestimated the shooter, banked on the SOB taking the intel on Oversight and staying the hell out of her life. Braxton had been wrong.

Wouldn't happen again.

Muted sunlight lit the room enough for him to make out the handle of his Glock across the room. He'd shed his shoulder holster and gun before getting in the tub with her, literally let down his guard for her. But it was time to end this. Maneuvering out from beneath Liz's warm body, trying not to wake her, he crossed the room in three steps and reached for his clothing. He'd track Oversight's feeds himself and finish this today. The bastard had tried to hurt his family, and Braxton would make him pay. He'd make sure the guy never touched her or their baby again.

He dressed fast then fastened his shoulder holster into place and collected a backpack of supplies and a secure laptop he'd stashed in the closet. Liz shifted beneath the sheets, a small moan escaping her throat as she rolled onto her side, and Braxton froze. The backpack in his hand worked to cement him in place. As though it knew the repercussions of leaving her in the middle of the night after taking her to bed yet again. But what choice did he have? Whoever'd kidnapped her would try again. And would keep trying until her pulse stopped beating. Braxton forced himself to breathe evenly through the thought. No. He'd end this now. He'd do what he had to, to keep her safe.

He followed the edge of the bed until he stood over her. Planting a kiss on the top of her head, he memorized the way she smelled, engraved the memories of their night together in his mind. Ran his fingers through the ends of her hair one last time. Dropping his voice, he crouched beside her and whispered more to himself than to her. "It'll always be you, Liz."

Braxton pushed to his feet, out of time, and scanned the surveillance monitors on the other side of the room before making his escape downstairs and toward the front door. He tossed his burner phone onto one of the couches in the living room to his right as he reached for the doorknob. He'd start with the fingerprints recovered from the rooftop shooting. Justin Valentin had been buried back in Washington, DC, but there had to be somebody—a family member, an old partner, a friend—who knew of his work for the CIA and had access to his personal belongings. The only other option was that the agent had faked his own death after Oversight's trial run. He gripped the doorknob hard as metal grew warm beneath his hand. Exhaling hard, he squeezed his eyes shut. Focus. Find the shooter. Keep Liz safe. He'd gone off the grid once, he could do it ag—

"I must be horrible in bed if you have to make a quick getaway in the middle of the night every time you sleep with me." Heat shot through him at the sound of her sleep-ragged voice. Soft footsteps padded down the stairs, but Braxton didn't dare turn around. He dropped his hand from the doorknob as Liz stopped short behind him. "But to be fair, I guess it's morning now, isn't it?"

He turned his head toward her. "Liz—"

"Don't worry, Braxton. I'm not mad." Her voice hollowed. "In order to be mad, you'd have to disappoint me in some way, which implies I had expectations. And I didn't. I knew you'd have to leave." She studied him. "But for the record, you don't have a promising future in clandestine work. You're the noisiest dresser on the planet."

"I can end this." The muscles down his spine tensed, ready for battle. "I can make sure he never comes after you again."

"What happened to us ending this together?" Liz circled into his line of sight. Exhaustion played a wicked game in her expression, but she'd never let it control her. She was determined, strong. Stronger than he was. "Brolin might not have been able to describe the man who'd taken him, but we can trace the fingerprints back to where they originated. We'll find him—"

"I'm not going to lose you again!" The words left his mouth harsher than he'd meant. His ears rang as she flinched. He fought to breathe evenly, rage exploding through him. She wasn't the only one who had nightmares because of what happened on that cliff side. "I almost didn't make it in time when he took you. If I'd been one minute later…"

Braxton wouldn't play the what-if game. He shook

his head to dislodge the memories. Reliving the past would only slow him down, consume him, and he'd lose the war before he had a chance to finish it.

"Do you really think I'd let him touch me again?" Liz locked onto his wrist and, faster than he thought possible, twisted his arm up and back. His childhood home blurred as she spun him head over heels. He hit the ground hard, the air crushed from his lungs. The chandelier above the entryway shook in the middle of the blackness closing in around the edges of his vision. He rolled onto his back, a groan escaping. *What had just happened?* She moved over him as pain radiated up his spine. His head throbbed, shoulders ached. Crouching beside him, she brushed his hair out of his face. "I didn't fight back when he put me in the trunk of his car because I want this baby more than anything, Braxton. I don't want to lose her. But don't mistake my decision for compliance. If he comes after me again, I will do what I have to, to survive."

She offered her hand, and he took it. Shoving to his feet, he ran his fingers through his hair to get it out of his face. "Where the hell did you learn to do that?"

"You're not the only one who's changed." Crossing her arms across her midsection, Liz shifted her weight against the mammoth wood banister lining the stairs. The sweats he'd dressed her in hung off her lean frame, but damn if she wasn't the epitome of everything he wanted. Everything he'd die to protect. "Let me guess. You were going to attempt to trace the feeds yourself from a laptop you stashed in your bag. Public place.

Maybe a coffee shop close to the Anchorage police department that offers free Wi-Fi in case shots were fired."

Braxton slipped the backpack from his shoulder and set it on the floor. Rolling one shoulder back, he ignored the pain of landing on his own arm. "It crossed my mind."

"Except it won't work." She put one foot in front of the other, closing in on him slowly. Her mouth parted slightly, giving him flashbacks to the night they spent together, and his gut tightened in response. Liz dropped her voice. "You can try to convince yourself otherwise, but you need me in order to access Oversight."

Amusement hiked his eyebrows a little higher, his head still pounding from her little move that'd landed him on his back. "Wasn't hard to guess your password."

Just as it hadn't been hard for him to uncover her new name. He'd only had to think like her and home in on what she valued most in her life.

"But even you can't fake a retinal scan," she said.

Retinal scan? "I did not know you'd added that level of security."

"Give me the laptop." She stretched out her hand, a weak smile playing across her mouth. "Vincent already forwarded the ballistics report on those bullets from the SUV. They're clean. So the shooter was sending me a message leaving the casings on the rooftop at the park. He wanted me to know this has to do with Justin Valentin. I'll dig into Agent Valentin's background, see if there's a connection there the NSA might've missed."

It was a start, and her plan wouldn't put her in immediate danger unless the shooter was monitoring Justin Valentin's records. Even then, Braxton's network re-routed his IP addresses all over the globe. The shooter would have a hard time nailing down their location for at least a couple of days. Braxton hefted his backpack up, handing it off to her. "And what am I supposed to do in this plan?"

She shouldered the pack and leveled her chin with the floor. Brilliant beams of light stretched through the wall of windows to his left, highlighting the spots of amber in her eyes. "You'll tell me you're going to stay."

His stomach dropped. Stay? That wasn't part of the deal. "It's not that easy—"

"Say those words, and I will do everything I can to make sure the NSA can't touch you." Stepping into him, she framed the side of his face with one hand. "I'll make sure you can come home. We can raise this baby. Together. We can give her a family, and whether or not that includes your father is up to you."

"You don't know what you're asking, Liz." Air stuck in his throat. Curling his hands into fists, he put a few more inches of space between them. He slipped out of her reach, her eyebrows drawing together in confusion. "You need to know the truth before you ask something like that."

A half-hearted smile stretched across her mouth. "What are you talking about?"

"The reason I left four months ago." He stroked one hand down his beard. Hell, it wasn't supposed to be like this. She wasn't supposed to want him to stay, not when they both knew it couldn't last. Braxton dropped his hand to his side. "I'm the one who sold classified intel on Oversight."

Chapter Twelve

He'd…sold the intel on her program. "To the man trying to kill me and our baby?"

"Yes," he said. "The transaction was anonymous. I had no idea what he was going to do with the intel or that he'd come after you…"

His voice faded in her ears. Her knees shook as she stepped back. Despite the size of his childhood home, the entryway wasn't that big. There was only so far she could go and stay within reach of slapping him as hard as she could. "So all those interrogations the NSA put me through…when I told them you weren't the leak, I was committing treason."

Elizabeth ran a hand through her hair, fisting a tight knot between her fingers. No, no, no, no. None of this made sense.

"Everything that is happening is one hundred percent my fault, and you have my word I will never stop trying to make it up to you." He took a step forward, but she countered almost instantly, and he froze, hands raised.

"You make it sound so easy." Think. Focus. No. Fury exploded from behind her sternum, and all rational thought disappeared. Elizabeth dropped the laptop bag and shoved at him with her unbroken hand as her lower lash line burned. "You put my life in danger." Pushing him again, she fought to keep the tears from falling. "You put our baby's life in danger."

The head wound, the bruised ribs, the broken wrist. She could take the physical injuries. But the emotional? She couldn't put a cast on that. Nausea rolled in her stomach. Oh, hell. Not now.

The three notches between his eyebrows deepened as Braxton dropped his hands to his side. He made another attempt to close in on her. "Sprink—"

"Don't call me that." She forced herself to breathe evenly around the bile working up her throat. Around another wave of betrayal. Around the stabbing pain in her chest. How could she have been so stupid? When Braxton had first informed her the feeds had been hijacked, she'd said it was impossible. Because it was. Less than a dozen government officials had clearance to know about the project. Without chalking it up to luck, a civilian wouldn't have been able to uncover her darkest secret. Unless someone handed them the information. She studied Braxton now and, for the first time, saw him for what he really was. "The intel you sold. It was how to hijack Oversight's feeds, wasn't it? Only in order take control of my program, you knew he needed me. That's why you came back. You realized the second you handed over that intel, he'd hunt me down."

"He already knew about the program. Knew exactly what he wanted and how to get it. I don't know how." Braxton nodded. "But when Dalton Meyer was killed, and the feeds were rerouted, I thought him coming after you next was a possibility."

"Why? Why would you do this to me?" She shook her head. "No. Don't answer that. I think I have a pretty good idea." Her hands shook at her sides. Elizabeth dug her toes into the hardwood to keep her balance, but her entire world had been upended. Slinging the bag over her shoulder once again, she maneuvered around him toward the front door. She didn't care she'd left her clothes and boots upstairs. She'd stop for supplies along the way. Reaching for the door, she turned her head enough to put him in her peripheral vision. "When you realize the mistake you've made, don't try to find me. I don't *ever* want to see you again."

Shattering glass ripped her attention to the living room on her right. Then a hard *thunk* of metal against wood. An M84 grenade rolled toward her. Elizabeth caught only a glimpse of it before a wall of muscle crashed into her and pinned her against the floor. The oxygen knocked from her lungs as she covered her ears and closed her eyes. The thump of detonation reverberated through her. The backpack fell from her arm. Before she could take her next inhale, Braxton ripped her and the pack off the floor.

"Come on!" Smoke filled the room, stung her eyes as he led them toward the back of the house. "Cover your face with your shirt and keep your eyes closed. I won't let you go."

Another grenade broke through the window above the kitchen sink as they rushed through, and she didn't have enough hands to cover both ears without losing

Braxton in the smoke. A white flash, an ear-deafening blast. Her ears rang, a high-pitched keen that worked to unbalance her and overwhelm her senses. Her shoulder hit the wall beside her, and she dropped Braxton's hand.

They were under attack. The shooter had found them. Found her.

His rough grip wrapped around her arms and thrust her forward. She jerked to the right into the downstairs office and dared to crack her eyes open. Smoke worked its way under the door, but not enough to sting.

Braxton pushed the black backpack toward her. She held on to it, heart pounding at the back of her head as he unzipped the bag and removed a gun. His lips moved. Nothing but muffled words reached through the ringing in her ears. He checked the gun's magazine, clicked off the safety and chambered a round. The movements were automatic, something he'd obviously worked at over the last few months.

She shook her head, pointing to her ear.

He took her hand then and mouthed, "I've got you."

A third percussion grenade shattered the office window as though the shooter were following them through the house from outside. She reached for Braxton, spinning them both inside the closet, and closed the door a split second before discharge. They had to get out of the house. Breathing ragged, head pounding, Elizabeth pushed out of the closet and went for the hallway.

Braxton's hand on her shoulder stopped her short of passing the large full bathroom on this level. She poked her head around the door frame from the hall. The bay window around the tub provided a perfect view into the spacious backyard.

And of the single masked man waiting for them outside.

Two taps on her shoulder spun her head around.

Braxton signaled them to the ground.

Getting to her hands and knees, she slipped past the bathroom, safeguarded by both walls that constructed the hallway. The garage was straight ahead, less than ten feet away. The backpack weighed her down and there was a chance they'd slip on the hardwood floors, but they didn't have a choice. They had to run for it.

Sliding against the wall, she sat back and closed her eyes, her hand across her lower abdominals. One breath. Two. They were going to make it out of this. She had to believe that. One tap on her arm brought her back into the moment. A combination of guilt and violence swirled in Braxton's gaze. He traced his fingers down one side of her face, and a shiver shook through her.

Elizabeth ripped away and pushed to her feet. No. He should feel guilty. He was responsible for all of this. She pumped her legs fast, panting through her mouth. The strain at the back of her head increased. Her ribs protested, and her legs felt spongy and untrustworthy. Shattering glass and gunfire exploded from every direction the instant she left the cover of the hallway. She covered her head in a vain attempt to keep a bullet from turning her brain into mush and dropped, sliding into the garage door like an MLB player hitting home plate.

She didn't bother looking back for Braxton—he could take care of himself—and ripped the garage door open. She fell down the six concrete stairs into the garage. The door slammed shut on its own a moment later, Braxton crashing down beside her. Gunfire echoed from behind the thick steel as musty air worked its way into her system, but they couldn't stop now.

Braxton took her free hand again, helped her to her feet and pointed to the only window on the far wall of the garage. Wrenching out of his grip, she exhaled hard. It was their only escape. They wouldn't make it to the SUV parked outside. Not without putting themselves at the end of the shooter's barrel. He maneuvered her ahead of him. She climbed up the steel shelving, pulling off the pack in the process. Elizabeth shoved the bag through the window first as a loud bang erupted from inside the house.

The shooter had breached.

She pushed herself backward through the window, hung onto the ledge for a brief moment then dropped to the ground. The ringing in her ears subsided slightly. Thank heaven her pregnancy wasn't farther along. She might've never gotten through the window had the shooter come after her a few weeks from now. She got her bearings and listened for any sign she'd been seen.

Nothing.

Braxton dropped beside her, studying their new surroundings as she had. Without a fence separating the house from the woods, nothing could stop them from disappearing into the wilderness. Sirens echoed in the distance. Even a quarter mile away, one of the neighbors had most likely called police from the sound of the grenades.

The definitive sound of a chambering round swept a chill down her spine.

They weren't alone.

Her attention diverted to her right, toward the shadow at the corner of the garage, and Elizabeth stepped back. How had he found them? Her stomach dropped. "Braxton…"

"Neither of you seem to understand." The shooter followed their every move as her bodyguard shifted in front of her. Dressed in a nicely pressed suit, ski mask included, the shooter obviously wasn't working for mobility, an advantage if things got physical. The ringing stopped in one of her ears, but the percussion grenade had knocked out her balance. She'd fight through it. Because there was no way in hell she'd let him take her again. The man who'd kidnapped her not forty-eight hours ago approached slowly, those black eyes sizing up Braxton from head to toe. Then raised his gun. "Elizabeth is coming with me."

He fired.

"No!" LIZ'S SCREAM pierced through the pain-induced haze clouding his head. Blood slipped through his fingers as Braxton gripped his left thigh. The muscles in his leg strained as he kept himself from screaming. The bullet hadn't come out the back of his leg. Which meant there was a good chance it'd hit bone. Didn't matter. Liz mattered. Keeping her safe mattered. He focused on the feel of her fingernails digging into his shoulder to keep him upright, her mouth at his ear as the shooter closed in on his prey. Her. "Come on. Get up, damn it."

He shoved the pain to the back of his mind. The bastard wouldn't touch her. Not again.

"Get out of here, Liz." He shifted his weight onto his uninjured leg and took position in front of her. His jeans clung to him in spots where blood spread, but it wouldn't be enough to slow him down. This ended now. Right here, right now, this was where Liz's new life started. "And whatever happens, don't come back for me."

He didn't give her a chance to respond as he rushed toward the shooter. The bastard fired another shot, barely missing Braxton, and squeezed the trigger a third time. The bullet skimmed across his chest as Braxton turned to avoid the shot. Snow and ice worked into his boots, distracted him from the pain shooting up his leg. He collided with the shooter and tackled him to the ground. The gun disappeared into a snowdrift, out of sight.

The shooter slammed a knee directly into the right side of Braxton's jaw, but Braxton didn't loosen his grip around the operative's perfectly pressed suit. Braxton pulled his elbow back and slammed a fist into the shooter's face. Once. Twice. He pressed his knee into the shooter's sternum to keep him in place as he hit the shooter again and again. His heart threatened to beat out of his chest as the man beneath the ski mask blocked the next hit. With a kick to center mass, Braxton flew backward, his childhood home nothing but a blur as he landed in three inches of snow.

The shooter hauled himself to his feet, brushing snow from that damn suit. "I told you before, Levitt.

You can't stop me. Elizabeth is going to pay for what she's done. One way or another. And you? You're just in my way."

Pain splintered down his sternum. Braxton bit down harder and shook the ice from his hair as he straightened. Blood dripped into the snow, into his boots. If he could still walk, he could still fight. And hell, he'd fight to the death for Elizabeth Dawson. In fact, there was nothing he wouldn't do for her. He'd already lost her once. He wouldn't lose her again. "Even with a bullet in my leg, you won't get to her."

"In my experience, the strongest always fall the hardest." An audible snap broke through the pounding of Braxton's heart behind his ears, and a glint of sunlight reflected off the switchblade in the shooter's hand. The masked man came directly at him.

Wrapping both hands around the shooter's wrist, Braxton twisted to one side to avoid being gutted right on his own front lawn. He hauled the SOB's wrist down over his knee—hard—and forced the shooter to drop the blade. Swinging himself around, he wrapped his forearm around the bastard's neck and squeezed. He locked his arm in place with his free hand, leveraging the shooter's head against his chest. Gloved hands fought to pry off Braxton's hold. In vain. But a swift hit of the shooter's elbow to his rib cage knocked the air from his lungs. The shooter wrenched free, gripped Braxton's throat and forced him to the ground.

The attacker wrenched Braxton's arm behind his back and applied pressure. Pain unlike anything Braxton had experienced exploded from his shoulder joint. "Look at her, Levitt."

Deep in the snow, his body temperature dropped, froze his muscles, anesthetized the bullet wound in his thigh, but he found the strength to lift his head. There, not twenty feet away, Liz searched through the snow. Presumably for the gun the shooter had dropped. Damn it. Why hadn't she listened to him? She should've run as far and as fast as she could. It would've been the only way to keep her safe. She wouldn't find the Glock. Not in time.

"I'm going to kill her after I get what I need from her, but first, I'm going to make her watch you die." Leaning into Braxton, the shooter intensified the pressure in his shoulder until a bone-crunching pop blacked out his vision. "You should've killed me when you had the chance."

A scream ripped from between his clenched teeth. He couldn't stop it. The operative had dislocated his shoulder and possibly torn one of the ligaments. The scream died to a groan after a few seconds, and Braxton fought to breathe through the tremors and the wave of dizziness rocking through him. He crushed his forehead against chunks of ice and snow beneath him to stay in the moment. "Touch her, and I'll kill you."

"Unfortunately for you, you're not going anywhere." The weight against his back disappeared. Snow crunched beneath footsteps, and Braxton shot his hand out to stop the shooter from reaching her and hauled him back. The man in the suit slammed into the ground, and Braxton pushed to his feet with his uninjured arm.

"You're not very good at listening." He circled around the bastard, his injured leg barely holding him up. A wave of dizziness distorted his vision. He was losing too much blood. His body had started going into shock. Soon he wouldn't be able to think. To breathe. His blood pressure would drop, and he wouldn't be able to stand. His words wheezed from his aching throat. He wrapped his free hand around the operative's throat and pulled the man in the mask against his chest for better grip. "I said you're not going to touch her."

Liz scrambled to her feet, empty-handed. Hair in disarray, her eyes red from the percussion grenade smoke, she only stared at him. Waiting.

Braxton could kill the shooter now. End this. But Liz had too many nightmares as it was. She didn't deserve to live with that for the rest of her life. He should incapacitate the SOB, tie him up and wait for Anchorage PD to arrive. Then extract himself from Liz's life once and for all. It was what she wanted. What he should've done in the first place. Snowflakes fell in a thin veil of white between them.

"Braxton, look out!" Liz's warning came too late.

Pure agony washed over him as a second blade buried deep in his gut. The shooter's gloved hand fell away. Braxton dropped his hold on the shooter's throat and stumbled back as the man in the mask rolled out of reach. Hell, he hadn't seen that coming.

Liz rushed forward from across the yard, eyes wide. Too far away. Snow kicked up around her as he collapsed to his knees. His heart pounded even louder behind his ears. He had to slow his pulse. Braxton swallowed to get rid of the muffled ringing in his ears. The faster his blood pumped, the faster he'd pass out. And that wasn't an option. Cold worked through his jeans. He placed his uninjured arm on the ground to keep from falling over. No. He wasn't going to die. Not until she was safe. He fought to stand but fell back as the muscles in his thigh finally gave out.

The shooter maneuvered into his vision. Headed straight for Liz.

"Liz." A growl reverberated through him as he climbed to his feet. His vision blurred again, only the spotting of red dots in the snow clear enough. He forced one foot in front of the other. Move. He had to get to her. Determination propelled him to his feet. No thought. Only her. His Elizabeth.

Sweat dripped into his eyes, but he had enough focus to keep her in sight. A glint of metal caught his attention at his feet. One of the shooter's blades. Sinking into the snow a second time, he wrapped his hand around the handle then used every last bit of strength he had left to stand. Two steps. Three. Pain and exhaustion drained from his muscles as he caught sight of Liz's wide, fearful gaze. She countered the shooter's steps as he closed in on her but wouldn't be able to outrun him. Not unless Braxton slowed him down.

That was all he had to do. Give her the chance to escape.

Police sirens echoed in the distance. Anchorage PD would take him in, the NSA would send an agent to the station claiming him in the interest of national security and he'd never see Liz again. Probably spend the rest of his days locked away inside some black site the government would deny existed if she ever came looking for him. But she would be safe.

And he could never hurt her again.

Reaching out for the shooter, Braxton clamped his hand on the bastard's shoulder, but he was caught off guard when his opponent spun in his grip. Braxton hiked the blade over his shoulder and thrust down with everything he had left. Only the blade never made contact.

Grip tight around Braxton's wrist, the man in the suit wrenched the knife to one side and forced him to drop it. "Don't worry, Levitt. I'm going to take real good care of her for you."

"No." The rush of adrenaline Braxton had been surviving off drained from his veins as blood pooled in his shirt and jeans. Pain flared up his uninjured arm, but he wouldn't back down. And he'd never give up. Not when it came to Liz.

"Let him go." The chambering of a round into a gun barrel claimed his attention. Over the shooter's shoulder, he spotted Liz as she widened her stance, both hands gripped around the shooter's gun. Chocolate-brown eyes shifted to him as the man in the suit dropped his hold. With hands above his head, the shooter turned toward her, and she followed every move. "I stopped Braxton from killing you the first time. I'm not going to make the same mistake twice."

Braxton stumbled back, hand over the stab wound in his side. Blood dripped onto the snow as sirens grew louder. It was over. The nightmare was over.

"Are you going to kill me in cold blood, too, Elizabeth? Just like you killed Justin Valentin or any number of other operatives with your program?" The SOB didn't give her a chance to answer, lunging straight at her.

"No!" Braxton rocketed to his feet. Darkness closed in around the edges of his vision, but he fought back with everything he had.

Liz pulled the trigger. Once. Twice. The gun never fired. Her mouth dropped open. She stumbled backward toward the tree line, caged by a line of pines, reaching for something to use as a weapon as the shooter closed in. "Braxton!"

There was too much distance between them. He couldn't get to her fast enough.

"That gun doesn't work." Wrapping his arms around her, the man in the suit hauled Liz off her feet and spun her around, her back to his chest. The shooter pulled a smaller gun from his ankle holster and aimed directly at Braxton. "But this one does."

Gunfire exploded in Braxton's ears—then pain—right before darkness closed in.

Chapter Thirteen

"Braxton!" Elizabeth couldn't take her eyes off him, off his lifeless body in the middle of ever-darkening red snow. No. He wasn't dead. It wasn't possible. Because the last words she'd spoken to him had been filled with hatred for what he'd done. She'd told him she never wanted to see him again, that he'd never get to meet his daughter. The shooter tightened his grip around her waist, hauling her into him. She pushed against his hands, but he didn't budge. "Get up! Please, get up."

Her throat burned. Eyes stung. He couldn't be dead.

"Save your energy, Elizabeth." The man in the suit pressed the gun's barrel against her temple. Police sirens drew closer, but the shooter barely seemed fazed. "You're going to need it before I'm through with you."

She clenched her teeth to fight the fresh rush of hot tears. No. Something inside her snapped. Adrenaline flooded through her system. Digging her bare heels into the snow, she wrenched out of the shooter's grip and shoved him back. He wouldn't take her again. He wouldn't win. Braxton couldn't protect her anymore. She had to protect herself. And their daughter.

"I don't want to shoot you, but I will." The shooter stalked toward her, gun still in hand.

"That's funny. I really want to shoot you." Elizabeth stepped back toward the pines to keep space between them, hands fanned out to her side. Pain shot through the back of her foot as she stepped on a medium-size tree branch that'd fallen near the tree line. Cold worked through her borrowed sweats as her attention flickered to Braxton, still unconscious twenty feet away. She'd trained to defend herself and she'd do just that. For him. No time to grieve. Time to survive. She wrapped her grip around the dead branch and swung as hard as she could. The wood reverberated through her hand at contact with the side of the shooter's head.

She didn't wait to see if he'd gotten up and pumped her legs hard. The police must be close. They had to be close.

A growl reached her ears, and she pushed herself harder. Puffs of crystallized air formed in front of her lips as she headed for the thick wilderness behind Braxton's childhood home. Tears froze in their tracks down her cheeks, the dropping temperatures working to slow her down. She was a runner, but exhaustion pulled her down. Barreling footsteps echoed from behind.

"Help!" She screamed as loud as she could, branches cutting the skin across her neck and face as she raced into the woods. It was the only place she could lose him. Her mouth dried, her breathing loud in the silent wilderness. Was that an Anchorage PD cruiser she'd just heard from behind?

The trees started to thin, the light brighter here. She

didn't dare stop. Didn't dare look back. *Keep going. Get to the road. Survive.*

A wall of muscle slammed her into the icy dirt.

"You're faster than I gave you credit for." His lips pressed into her ear, his breath hot against her skin. A tremor raked across her chest, intensifying everything around her. The trees. The roots. He wrapped both gloved hands around one of her ankles and pulled. "You know, in a way, I've always admired you. Your determination. Your creative nature when it came to your work. Who else but you could've created a program like Oversight?"

Elizabeth dug her nails into the frozen ground. All too easily, she imagined her boss, Sullivan Bishop, having to come down to the morgue to identify her and Braxton's bodies. Not going to happen. She had to go back. She'd lost Braxton once. She couldn't do it again. He was a part of her. The good and the deceit. He was hers to protect now. He was the family her daughter deserved.

"You've chosen a really awkward time to hand out compliments." Clamping on to the nearest root, she heaved herself closer to the base of the large pine. The root broke away clean, and he dragged her backward. She couldn't think—couldn't breathe—but kicked at him as hard as she could.

A groan filled the clearing, his grip on her ankle loosening, but she sure as hell wouldn't ask her attacker if he was okay. She clawed across the foliage, jaw locked against the pain tearing through her. A *whooshing* sound reached her ears, and she exhaled hard, frozen tears stinging her cheeks. A car. She'd reached the next road over.

Elizabeth embedded her fingernails into the nearest tree and lifted herself to her feet. Run. No looking back. Just run. She stumbled forward, gaining strength with each step before she was finally able to pick up speed. Every muscle in her body screamed for release.

Another car drove past. Louder. Closer. Breathing became easier, but...slower. Something wet and sticky clung to her borrowed clothing. Sap? Taking refuge behind a large tree, she looked back over her shoulder. No movement. He hadn't followed her? Pain registered as she forced her heartbeat to slow. Not sap. She touched the spreading stain on her right side. Blood. When had that happened? She hadn't even felt an injury. She couldn't think about that right now. Braxton was bleeding out from at least two gunshots and a stab would. She'd run out of time. Deep breath. She could do this. Clamping her hand over her wound, she pushed forward. Couldn't stop. The shooter would catch up any minute. She had to flag down a car and circle back to Braxton—

The ground dropped out from under her feet. The world tilted on its axis as she rolled end over end. Branches and bushes scratched at her skin as blackness closed in at the edges of her vision. Sliding down the last few feet before the road, Elizabeth closed her eyes as the oxygen rushed from her lungs, unsure how long she lay there.

"Liz!" a male voice called.

She recognized that voice. A deep rumbling tore

down the road, growing louder, and she forced her eyes open. "Sullivan?"

"I've got tracks!" Her boss's voice grew fainter, but she couldn't respond. Not without giving away her position to the shooter.

No. This wasn't the end. Not today. Another explosion of pain throttled through her as she flipped onto her side. Her team had come. She wasn't alone. They'd recover Braxton, and— She covered her mouth to prevent the scream in her throat from escaping. Save energy. Keep moving. "Any extra calories you can sacrifice would help a lot right now, baby girl."

Thick trees lining the road made it nearly impossible for her to spot movement. If the shooter had followed her, there were countless points where she could be walking straight into another ambush. She wouldn't be able to see him coming. Elizabeth ran a bloodied hand through her hair. She had to risk it. She had to get to Braxton. Had to get to her team.

Briars and weeds sliced into the bottoms of her feet, but she forced herself to keep moving. Anchorage PD wouldn't have been far behind Sullivan and the rest of the team. Somebody was getting Braxton the help he needed. She had to believe that. The alternative would rip her world apart, and she wasn't sure how much more she could take after what they'd been through the last five days. How much more heartache was she supposed to bear.

Swiping a hand beneath her runny nose, Elizabeth held her breath at the sound of a snapping twig. Her head pounded in rhythm to her racing heartbeat. She froze, only redirecting her gaze toward the tree line. He'd found her. Was hunting her. The weight of someone watching her—stalking her—pressurized the air in her lungs. Her fingertips tingled with the need to find a weapon. A shadow shifted to her left, and every ounce of willpower screamed for her to run. The tree line was the only way back to Braxton. If the shooter stood between her and getting to him…

"There's nowhere you can run, Elizabeth. Nowhere you can hide." That voice. She'd never be able to forget it, and she automatically dug her fingernails into the center of her palms. The shooter stepped from the tree line, gun in hand. The black ski mask shifted as he spoke. "Haven't I already proven how far I'm willing to go?"

"You can't get access to Oversight's programming, can you? Even after I gave you the password when you threatened to throw me over a cliff." Elizabeth straightened. He was right. She couldn't run. She couldn't hide. She'd have to finish this herself. She'd have to go through him. It was the only way to save Braxton. "That's why you haven't killed me yet."

Which meant he wouldn't kill her until she gave him the access.

"Seems you've implemented security measures even I can't get past." The man in the mask held the high ground. Any movement and he'd have the advantage. And the longer they stood here talking, the faster Braxton bled out.

"And you never will." Despite the failed mission that cost Agent Valentin his life, Oversight saved thousands of lives every day by predicting violence and threats.

She'd always be proud of that, and she'd do what she had to, to protect it.

Silence stretched between them for the space of two breaths. Three. Time was slipping away too fast. Every beat of Braxton's heart endangered his life. They were wasting time. Wrapping one hand around his opposite wrist, gun pointed toward his toes, the shooter seemed more businessman than professional hit man. Maybe federal agent. "I'll make you a deal, Elizabeth. You give me what I want, and I guarantee your bodyguard lives."

"There's no way I would ever trust you." She wasn't stupid enough to believe he'd ever keep his end of a deal between them. But if she could get close enough to Braxton—ensure he was alive—she could shut down Oversight on her own and end this nightmare.

"Then the alternative is letting him bleed out, and I put a bullet in you now." The shooter raised the gun with one hand. Taking aim, he scrambled down the hill and closed the short distance between them. He fisted the ski mask with his free hand and tugged it over his head. Familiar dark eyes centered on her. "Do we have a deal?"

"You." Her knees shook as she stumbled back from the man in the suit. Shaking her head, she fought to keep her balance. "That's not possible. They said you were—"

"Dead?" Faster than she expected, the shooter slammed the butt of his gun into the side of her face, and Elizabeth dropped hard. Darkness closed in around the edges of her vision, but in the center, a ghost from the past still stared down at her. "Let's just say it didn't stick."

DEATH HAD TO be earned.

But Braxton wasn't willing to pay the price. Not until he recovered Liz.

A migraine pulsed behind his eyes. Three hundred stitches. Two bullet wounds. One stab wound to the rib cage. Two transfusions of blood. Hell of a way to die. But this wasn't over. Liz was missing. Vincent Kalani and Sullivan Bishop had tracked her path through the woods behind his childhood home to the road. As well as the shooter's. Then they'd simply disappeared. Spots of blood had stained the snow in her tracks. She'd been injured. According to the forensics expert, there'd been clear signs of a struggle, but no evidence of where the bastard had taken her.

He forced his legs over the edge of the hospital bed, and another wave of pain shot through him. Braxton gripped the sheets in his hand. He neutralized the groan working up his throat. Didn't matter how many bullets he'd taken or how much blood he'd lost, he was getting Liz back. And he'd kill anyone who tried to stop him.

The hairs on the back of his neck stood on end. Damn, he wasn't alone, and hadn't realized it until right this second. How much anesthesia had the doc given him?

"Look at you sacrificing yourself for others, Levitt." Elliot Dunham, Blackhawk Security's private investigator, propped his feet up on the edge of the bed and laced his fingers behind his head. "From what Liz told me about you, I didn't think you had it in you."

Hell. Of all the people on Liz's team to send, her boss sent this one. "Aren't you supposed to be babysitting?"

"Ah, yeah. About that…" Elliot planted the chair back onto the gleaming white tile and rested his elbows against his knees. Narrowing his gaze, the former con man cocked his head. "I kind of…lost your dad."

A laugh stretched the stitches down his side. Braxton highly doubted that. His old man had a way of disappearing at exactly the right time with exactly the right amount of cash he'd stolen from people's wallets. "You might want to cancel your credit cards. You're about to learn who Brolin Levitt really is."

Elliot patted his back jeans pockets, then his jacket. "Wow, he's good. Didn't feel a thing. I'm going to have to get him to show me some moves."

"Good luck finding him." He'd probably never see his father again. No loss there. Although Liz might have a hard time with the old man's disappearance. She'd kept tabs on the addict, made sure he had a place to sleep at night, food to eat. One day she'd understand how pointless all of that was. Brolin Levitt was a selfish son of a bitch. She'd be better off not knowing the real coward behind the drugs. Shoving off the bed, Braxton dropped onto the floor and shot his hands out for balance. He'd been brought in through the emergency room doors seven hours ago. Liz could be anywhere by now. If that SOB hadn't gotten to her first.

"If you're going after her, you're going to want to see this." Elliot reached for a file folder on the side table and tossed it onto the bed beside Braxton. "Did a little digging into the background of the CIA agent who was killed during the trial run for Liz's program. Justin Valentin."

"You don't have clearance for that intel." Anticipation flooded through him as Braxton reached for the file. A clean-cut photo of the agent had been paper-clipped in front of a military service record, driving record, residency proof and a whole lot more classified documentation Braxton had never seen before. Specific missions, confidential informants Agent Valentin kept. Even as an analyst, he would've had to get clearance or federal warrants for the paperwork in this file. "Where did you get all this?"

"You don't want to know." Elliot leaned in closer from his position in the chair, dropping his voice to a whisper. "It's blackmail. I have files on everyone I investigate. And some people I don't investigate, but that stays between us. Also, I can see straight through your—"

Braxton closed the file and reached for the opening in the back of the hospital gown. If there was another way to make patients more uncomfortable, he didn't know how it'd be possible. He searched the room. Where the hell were his clothes?

"The hospital staff had a hard time getting all the blood out of your clothes. You know, because there was…a lot. So they were incinerated. Good news, though—" Elliot hauled a duffel bag from beside his chair into his lap "—I brought you some of mine. Should fit. Had to guess your shoe size. Don't tell Vincent, but they're his." The private investigator tossed the bag at him, and Braxton was forced to release his clutch on the gown to catch it. Elliot guarded his eyes, chin to chest. "So Liz built a program for the NSA to spy on civilians, huh? I knew I liked her."

Digging into the duffel bag, Braxton pulled jeans, socks, boots and a long-sleeve shirt from the depths. He dressed fast. Every minute he wasted here, the higher the chance he'd never see her again. Hiking his foot to the edge of the bed, he suppressed a groan as he laced his borrowed boots. Pain was temporary. Losing Liz, that would be forever. "The program was designed to identify terrorists and criminals before crimes actually happened. It worked ninety-nine percent of the time, too. Oversight has saved thousands of lives."

"But the one percent got a CIA agent killed last year," Elliot said.

"That mission tore her apart. Valentin had disguised himself as part of the group he'd infiltrated, and Oversight hadn't been able to tell the difference because of a line of broken code. Liz blames herself for the mistake." Braxton studied the photo of Justin Valentin for the second time and narrowed in on the color of the agent's eyes. Ice blue. Not dark enough for the man in the mask. Justin Valentin wasn't their unsub and had only a wife and two young boys left behind. None of whom he considered a threat as he looked over their financials within the file. The shooter could be anyone, doing this for any reason, as far as Braxton knew. His shoulders deflated, the stitches protesting along his rib cage. They were back at square one.

Hell, all of this could've been prevented if he'd just stayed.

"So does someone else. Whoever is trying to kill her

planted Agent Valentin's fingerprints on those casings from the rooftop shooting." Elliot leaned back in the chair. "They wanted her to know they knew she created Oversight and about the failed trial run."

The fingerprints. They were the only piece of evidence left behind in this investigation. He had to look at that report again. "Give me your phone."

The private investigator tossed him the device, and Braxton wasted no time logging in to his own email for the ballistics report Vincent had forwarded him less than twelve hours ago. Scrolling past the diagrams and countless pages of analysis, he focused on the latent fingerprints recovered from the casings. The shading was too light to have been pulled directly from wherever the prints originated. Elliot was right. They'd been planted on those casings and purposefully left at the scene. Which meant the shooter had pulled them from somewhere else using tape or another adhesive. Something Agent Valentin had to have in his possession and the bastard coming after Liz had gotten ahold of.

"What do you got?" Elliot stood, circling the bed.

"These prints are too light to have been taken directly off the source. They were transferred at least once more onto those casings." Braxton zeroed in on a corner of one print and turned the phone on its side to zoom in on the area. A small, clearly defined arrow interrupted the impression at the edge of the print. He'd seen that exact shape, combined with a circle and two more arrows like it, before. On the Trident—Beretta's logo. "The prints were originally lifted off Justin Valentin's service weapon. A Beretta 92 FS, if I had to guess."

Elliot took the phone, studying the impressions on the screen. "The CIA's favored handgun for their field agents. Very nice. Good catch."

"Whoever wants Liz dead got ahold of a CIA agent's service weapon in the middle of Afghanistan. Can't be a long list." The shooter had made this personal by coming after her. He'd obviously been close to Valentin, blamed her for the agent's death. Why else plant those fingerprints? Why else play this mind game? Braxton rolled back his left shoulder where he'd taken the second bullet during the fight. He exhaled hard against the pain but rolled it back again. "Valentin didn't have a partner?"

"Not according to his records." Elliot reached for the file on the bed, thumbing through the pages. "The last time Justin Valentin was assigned a partner was…" The private investigator scoffed. "A year ago. The agency suspected the partner had sold classified information to the Russians, but the agent died in the line of duty before charges could be brought up. That sucks."

Braxton straightened a bit more, his instincts on high alert. "What's the agent's name?"

"Liam Waters." Elliot looked up from the file. "Why? You know him?"

"No." He'd never heard that name before, but it was the only lead they had, and his gut screamed this would get him closer to Liz. Hell, he should've fought harder. He should've been a step ahead of the shooter who'd taken her, but he'd been so caught up in…her, he hadn't been able to think straight for days. And it'd gotten her kidnapped. Again. Braxton stretched the stitches in his shoulder. He'd tear this entire city to pieces to find her. And kill anyone who got in his way. "How fast can you get access to Waters's files?"

"An hour, tops." The private investigator folded his arms across his chest, file still in hand, and leveraged his weight against the edge of the bed. Gray eyes, darker than Braxton's, narrowed on him. "What are you thinking?"

"Make it thirty minutes." He couldn't wait that much longer. Not when Liz's life was at risk. Braxton pulled the shoulder holster, complete with a smuggled handgun, from the duffel bag, and maneuvered into it slowly. Another round of pain lightninged through his injuries, but he pushed it to the back of his mind. Nothing would stop him from recovering Liz. And if the shooter turned out to be a dead man after all, he'd make damn sure the bastard never got up again. "I want to know if former agent Liam Waters is really dead."

Chapter Fourteen

A dull ache at the base of her skull beat through her in rhythm to her heart rate. Elizabeth cracked her eyes then closed them again against the brightness of a wall of active monitors in front of her. Blurry streaks cleared. The wide bay window had been covered with thick blankets. Blue light from the screens highlighted the three walls and large box near a door in her vision but nothing more. No other details. No telling where the shooter had taken her.

Not the shooter. He had a name. Former CIA agent Liam Waters.

And he blamed her for his partner's death.

"You're awake." Footsteps echoed off the worn hardwood flooring, growing closer. "I was beginning to think I'd hit you too hard."

Flashes of the woods, of Braxton facedown in the snow, crossed her mind, and Elizabeth fought to swallow around the tightness closing in. If Anchorage PD or her team hadn't made it to the scene in time… She pulled against the handcuffs behind her back and two more pairs around her ankles and the legs of the chair.

She wasn't going anywhere. A rush of nausea forced bile into her throat. She licked at dry lips. "How long have I been out?"

"About eight hours." Waters maneuvered into her vision and stood in front of her, gun loose in his grip at one side. Lines furrowed between his thick eyebrows, a head of dark hair wilder than she remembered from his files. Before he'd joined the CIA, Liam Waters had been part of the fleet antiterrorism security team, or FAST, where he'd been partnered with Agent Justin Valentin for a number of years then accused of selling classified intel to a Russian contact. After Oversight had misidentified Valentin for an extremist, she'd hacked into the agent's files. Wanted to know the man her program had killed. Agent Liam Waters had been in those files. As were the charges the CIA planned to bring against Agent Valentin's partner before Waters had been killed in action. Bruising shadows shifted in the light of the monitors as he spoke and, suddenly, he seemed so much…older than she remembered from his files. Worn. Desperate. Not dead after all. "Recognize what's on the monitors?"

Elizabeth shifted her focus to the screens. City names from across the country popped up on the bottom of each monitor as it scrolled from image to image. Cars passed beneath cameras, civilians walked down streets, thin white squares homed in on, processed and identified facial features. The weight of Waters's attention settled on her. "You're the one who hijacked Oversight's feeds."

"And you're the one who killed my partner with it."

Cords looped circles behind Waters's feet. Hundreds of them, all connected to the monitors, disappeared behind the door to her left. Not an exit. Most likely a server room, which meant the only way to escape was behind her. Waters crouched in front of her, his knees popping with the movement, gun still in hand. "Justin Valentin had a family. A wife, two boys. I showed up at his house every morning to pick him up for work for four years, and when their youngest was diagnosed with leukemia and they couldn't pay for the treatments, I did what I had to do to make sure they could. Of course, they'd known what I'd done. There was no hiding the fact I'd started selling intelligence to the Russians from my own partner. He was a good agent, but, as it turned out, a father would do anything to save his son. Justin helped me plan my own death. Because you see, they were my family, too." Waters stood, fanning his grip over the gun's handle. The monitors cast his features into shadow from behind. "Now those boys can't look at me without thinking of their dead father. His wife refuses to see me, won't take my calls. You did that. You took my family from me."

"I'm sorry." She forced herself to breathe evenly. Every moment of that failed trial had been burned into her memory. Braxton running to her cubicle with news of the mission go-ahead from her project supervisor, Dalton Meyer, her trying to shut Oversight down remotely. Nothing had worked. In the end, she'd been restrained by security and sealed in an office while the NSA had taken control of her program. She'd only learned of Oversight's mistake after the fact. And had taken the blame for it all. "I tried to stop them. I told them the program wasn't ready, but Meyer wouldn't listen—"

"You think I did all of this for an apology?" A low, dark laugh rumbled from deep in his chest, and a shiver shot across Elizabeth's shoulders. She interlaced her fingers tighter as he closed the short distance between them, her wrists straining against the handcuffs. He leveraged his weight against the back of the chair with one arm. A combination of spicy aftershave and sweat dived into her lungs. "No, Elizabeth. I brought you here so you can watch your creation burn. Then I'm going to kill you."

Shock rocked through her. Her mouth dried. She searched for something—anything—that would get her out of these cuffs. A paper clip. A nail. Maybe if she vaulted herself backward, the wood chair would break enough for her to get free. She was on her own. No matter how many times he'd been there before, Braxton couldn't save her now. "You can't shut the program down. Oversight made a mistake—*I* made a mistake— but it has saved countless lives over the past year. It's protected this country, stopped terrorists. Just as you have."

"And how many more families will be destroyed— families like Justin's—because of your mistakes?" Waters wrapped gloved hands around the back of the chair and shoved her forward until her knees hit the desk. The former agent gripped the back of her neck tight and thrust her over the keyboard. "You built the security for Oversight. You're going to tear it down."

Elizabeth clenched her teeth against the stiffness in her neck. She pushed back, but Waters was so much stronger. And not handcuffed to a chair. A rush of dizziness distorted her vision. No, no, no, no. Not now. The sinking sensation that accompanied her blood sugar crashing pulled her farther into the chair. She fought to breathe through the disorientation. Didn't work. Nothing but food would combat the crash. Closing her eyes against the sudden brightness of the monitors, she dropped her head. And saw blood. The injury from the woods. Her blood pressure spiked. "My side is bleeding. My blood sugar is crashing. I need to eat. I'm no good to you in shock."

He dropped his grip on her neck and instead replaced it by pointing the gun at her left temple. He pressed so hard the steel cut into her skin, but she wouldn't disable the program. Not when the safety of an entire country had been put on the line. "Surprise me."

She bit her lower lip to distract herself from the crushing weight behind her sternum and the pain in her ribs. Nobody was coming to save her. She had to save herself. But she couldn't even do that if she was cuffed to this damn chair. Her senses had started adjusting to the surrounding darkness. There had to be something in this room she could use as a weapon. "If you want me to shut down the program, you're going to have to uncuff me."

"I've read your file, Elizabeth. I've watched you for months." He centered her in front of the nearest monitor. "I know what you can do with your hands. You tell me the second password, and I'll enter it."

He wanted to do this the hard way? Fine. "I told you before when you were threatening to throw me over a cliff. Even if you enter the password, there isn't only one level of security. Oversight doesn't work like that. I made sure no one person could take control of the system. So unless you have a retinal scanner in this dump, you're not getting into my program."

"Then I have no use for you." His rough exhale hit her collarbones as Waters compressed the gun's safety button off. "Blackmailing your bodyguard to get the intel I needed on Oversight was worth less trouble than you are. I'm done with you."

Blackmail?

"You don't have to do this. Justin wouldn't want this. His wife and those boys wouldn't want this." This wasn't how she'd die. Not after everything she'd been through the last five days. Not after losing the only man she'd ever wanted to spend the rest of her life with, the man who'd never get to meet his daughter. Her eyes burned. From the moment Braxton had shaken her hand at their first meeting to the moment he'd sacrificed himself for her to get away in his own front yard, he'd protected her. He'd stood by her side. He'd given her a glimpse of the family she'd always wanted. Needed.

"Guess we'll never know, will we?" he asked.

Elizabeth licked at her lips one more time. She might've already lost Braxton. She wasn't about to lose their baby. "Please, I'm pregnant."

The gun faltered in Waters's hand. "That's not possible. I've been following you for months. I've read your medical records."

"Then you suck at your job. Otherwise you would've noticed me walking into my doctor's office last week." She scanned the room a second time, locking on a blue-and-white pen on the floor to her right. She could do a lot of damage with a pen, but getting her hands on it was a different skill set entirely. Pressing her toes into the floor, she tipped the chair's front legs back a few centimeters at most. She didn't dare look at Waters's face. Any sudden movement on her part could force him to pull the trigger. But if she could walk out of this unscathed, she'd take the risk. "You hijacked the feeds to an all-seeing program. Review the records again. I'm sure they're updated by now."

"You're lying." Keeping the gun aimed at her head, the former agent rounded into her vision. Bruising darkened the shadows beneath his eyes where she'd clocked him with the handle of his gun on Seward Highway, and a small bit of her hoped it hurt like hell. But then those dark eyes centered on her, and everything inside her went cold. "At this point, Elizabeth, I think you'll say anything to stay alive, but you can't get out of this. You're going to die today."

"No, I'm not." She kicked against the floor, every muscle in her body going rigid as the chair tipped backward. The room blurred a split second before she hit the hardwood. Cracking wood claimed her attention, but not for long. Pain stretched up her crushed arms as she rolled from the debris, her wrists still cuffed. She wrapped her fingers around the pen and pushed the sharp end into the keyhole. Slim chance this would work, but she wouldn't go down without a fight. For Braxton. For her baby.

"Clever." Liam Waters stood over her, gun raised. Slipping his finger over the trigger, he widened his stance. "But, tell me, honestly, how far did you think you could run this time?"

"Who said I'd try to run?" The cuff loosened from around her casted wrist, and Elizabeth shot her foot upward. Connecting with Waters's gun, she sent it flying across the room. The gun discharged, the bullet arching wide, forcing her to cover her head with her arms in an empty attempt to avoid being shot.

With her next breath, Waters straddled her midsection and crushed the oxygen from her lungs. He pinned her against the floor. "Why won't you just die?"

The door behind her slammed open. "Get your damn hands off of her."

BRAXTON FLEW OVER LIZ, tackling the former CIA operative to the floor. Monitors on the desk shook from the quake then toppled face-first around them as he pulled his elbow back. Glass and metal hit the hardwood, but nothing would distract him from finishing the job. Not this time.

"How many times do I have to kill you before it sticks?" Waters slammed an elbow into his face and twisted out of Braxton's reach.

Shooting his hand out, Braxton caught the edge of the shooter's suit jacket, but not enough to pull the bastard back. The sound of tearing fabric drowned the pounding of his pulse behind his ears. Waters went for one of the largest monitors, hauling it over his head.

Every stitch in his body protested as Braxton rolled out of the way and shot to his feet. He grabbed Waters by the arm and whirled him into the nearest wall. Adrenaline sang through his veins, blocking out the pain of his injuries. It wouldn't last long, but he'd sure as hell make the most of it. Shifting his weight back as Waters swung a right hook, Braxton kicked out the operative's knee and followed it up with a punch to the gut. "No one hurts my family and gets away with it."

Waters stared up at him. Blood dripped from the former agent's lip. Swiping it off with the back of his hand, the SOB cracked a smile. Then Waters swung up. Flesh met bone and Braxton spun backward, barely catching a glimpse of Liz as she worked to free herself from three different sets of cuffs. He landed face-first against the floor. Footsteps echoed off the hardwood. "Funny. I was thinking the exact same thing."

Liz's gaze shot up, widened at the sight of Waters closing in, then homed in on the gun against the far wall. Braxton could tell from the determination in her eyes she was going to make a run for it.

Waters lunged as Liz pushed off the floor. He got there first, wrapping his hand around the gun and swinging it wide toward her. Braxton launched to his feet, but not before Liz caught Waters's wrist in one hand and pushed her casted hand up under his jawline. Shoving him back, she wedged the former agent between herself and the wall, but there was nowhere else to go.

"Liz!" Braxton took a step forward then collapsed to one knee. The stitches in his thigh had torn. Blood seeped through his jeans. Damn it.

She let go of the former agent's throat then slammed her cast against the gun, dislodging Waters's hold on the Glock. And hell if that wasn't the sexiest thing he'd ever seen. But Liz wasn't fast enough. With one blow to the face, she went down. She hit the ground hard, a groan filling his ears, and nothing but rage consumed him.

Braxton closed the space between him and Waters in two steps and lunged feet first. His boots connected with the shooter's sternum, and they collapsed to the floor. Air stuck in his lungs, but he barely had time to stand before Waters came around. Braxton stumbled, shooting his hand out toward the dropped gun. The metal slipped against his palm. He tightened his grip and swung the gun around.

But Waters had the bigger card to play.

With a simple white-and-blue pen.

Crouching over Liz, the operative held the pen to her jugular, waiting for Braxton to make his next move. Waters's shoulders rose and fell in rapid succession in rhythm to his strained breathing. If Braxton had to guess, the operative had broken a rib or two, but he hadn't let it slow him down. It'd take more than a few broken bones to finish this. "I've spent the last year waiting for this moment. You're not going to stop me from getting my partner's family the justice they deserve, Levitt."

Blood spread through his T-shirt, soaking the waistband of his jeans, but Braxton pushed the distraction to the back of his mind. Hell, he'd tear every stitch a hundred times if it meant protecting the woman he loved. Screw the pain. Screw the NSA. He'd left Liz behind once. He wouldn't make the same mistake again. He wasn't going anywhere. Not without her. Lifting the gun, he centered the former CIA operative in his sights. Liz had stopped him from killing the bastard once, and it'd been a mistake. "It's over, Waters. Liz is mine. And I don't share."

Swaying, the former agent dropped his chin but only fanned his fingers around the pen. "I should've killed you four months ago when I had the chance."

"Yeah." Braxton held the gun steady, ready for the last round. Liam Waters wasn't leaving this room alive. Killers like him didn't give up easily. The former CIA agent would keep coming after her. And Liz—and their baby—deserved a life better than one on the run. He could give them that. "You should have. But if you make another move, I'll make damn sure you never get back up."

"Let's see who's faster." Waters raised his hand, ready to plunge the pen into Liz's throat as she lay unconscious, and Braxton pulled the trigger. One bullet ripped through the operative's shoulder but didn't bring Waters down. He fired again, the gun kicking back in his hand. The second shot hit center mass. The shooter held his arm up but dropped the pen. Collapsing to the floor, Liam Waters stared at the peeling yellow ceiling, one hand pressed against the wound beneath his sternum.

"I feel like you should've known not to bring a pen

to a gunfight." Braxton approached slowly, heart threatening to break apart his rib cage. He kicked the pen out of Waters's reach as the shooter dived into unconsciousness, head slumping to the side. The operative's chest stilled, one last exhale reaching Braxton's ears.

Liam Waters was dead.

Dropping to his knees, he framed Liz's face with one hand, sliding the pad of his thumb across her bottom lip. "Liz."

Her resulting groan set every cell in his body on fire. She swung her head toward him and cracked her eyelids. Deep brown eyes locked on him, and his world shattered. Hell, they'd survived. Together. The nightmare was over. And they—relief coursed through him—they could get their lives back. They could start their family. If she'd have him. Brushing her hair behind her ear, he studied her for any other injuries. "Can you move?"

"My blood sugar…" Her hands shook as she wrapped them around the back of his neck. "I haven't eaten."

"Here." He set the Glock on the floor then reached into his back pocket and pulled out two granola bars. Unwrapping both, he dumped the broken pieces into his palm and lifted her against him. "It's not much, but I brought something in case you crashed again."

She closed her eyes, chewing methodically, and sank against him. "You really know the way to a woman's heart."

"Just yours." A smile pulled at one corner of his mouth. He held on to her, resting his cheek against the top of her head. A combination of lavender and chocolate overwhelmed his senses, and he breathed in as much as he could. "I got you. You're safe now."

A gunshot exploded in his left ear.

Liz arched against him, mouth open, eyes wide, but her gasp said it all.

She'd been hit.

Tearing her away from him, Braxton spun. He reached for the gun in Waters's hand. The bastard wasn't dead yet, barely keeping himself upright. Braxton wrapped his fingers around the barrel and wrenched it from the SOB's grip, turning the gun on the shooter. Braxton pulled the trigger. One shot. Waters's head snapped back, a bullet between the eyes. The body dropped hard. And the threat was neutralized.

A sharp inhale brought him back into the present. Braxton lunged. On her stomach, sprawled across the hardwood, Liz didn't move. He reached for her, lifted her upper body into his lap. The bullet hadn't come out her chest. The damn thing was still inside her. No. He would not lose her. Not after everything they'd been through.

"It burns." A tear streaked down the side of her face into her hairline. Her throat worked to swallow as blood rushed over his fingers. She fought to speak, licking her lips, her gaze heavier than he'd ever seen before. Streaks of blood coated her tongue. Hell, the bullet had punctured one of her lungs. Her breath shortened. "Braxton…"

"I've got you, Sprinkles. Stay still. I'm not going to lose you again. I'm never leaving you again." The peeling walls blurred in his vision as Braxton hoisted her into his arms and encased her against him. He carried her out of the room as fast as he could. Footsteps echoed up the second level as Vincent and Elliot raced to intercept. He'd had the private investigator inform the rest of the Blackhawk Security team about this property owned under one of Waters's aliases before Braxton had raced from the hospital. He owed them his life. Stairs jostled their descent, and he tightened his hold on her to keep the slug from shifting deeper. The bullet was too close to her spine. He nodded back toward the room upstairs to direct the team to Waters's body, his focus entirely on the woman in his arms. The love of his life. The mother of his child. Neither Vincent nor Elliot bothered examining the crime scene. Instead, they followed Braxton downstairs to the waiting ambulance. "Stay awake, baby. I have more granola bars where these came from. And there might even be some ice cream and rainbow-colored sprinkles left over for you. But you've got to stay awake, okay?"

"There sure as hell…better be." Liz went slack in his arms as she gave in to unconsciousness.

Chapter Fifteen

Searing heat enveloped her scalp as Elizabeth held herself under the shower spray. Her tailbone had been bruised, if not cracked. The laceration in her ribs from the woods was almost too much to bear. Luckily, surgeons had been able to remove the bullet from her back and patch her lung. But, hell, it felt good to be in her own house. She didn't even want to look at the rest of her body. She washed two-day hospital grunge off, the simple idea of soap helping her muscles relax. As did the gun sitting on the small bathroom sink to her right. Cold air rushed against her as she stepped from the shower and tied a towel around herself.

She didn't have to turn around to know Braxton had let himself in. The weight of his attention from the doorway pimpled goose bumps across her back. "How are you feeling?"

"Still hurts to breathe, but I'm alive." Two days. Two days since he'd charged through that door and shot the man determined to destroy her life. Two days since she'd woken up, facedown on a stretcher getting wheeled into surgery with him by her side. He'd promised never to leave her again, but the situation between them hadn't changed. He'd sold classified intel to an enemy combatant, and the NSA would charge him with treason the second they got their hands on him. So what were they supposed to do now? "Thanks to you."

Liam Waters's body had been recovered by Anchorage PD, as had mountains of evidence proving he'd been stalking her for months. He'd been careful, planned every step and stayed ahead of her the entire time, but even knowing the former agent would never come after her again, she couldn't relax.

"You did a damn good job protecting yourself, Sprinkles." Braxton crossed his arms over his torso, all three hundred stitches securely in place again. "Have you slept?"

"No." The memories running through her head wouldn't let her. It'd take time for her to scrub the slate clean. She reached for the gun on the sink.

Braxton struggled to straighten, the pain in his expression evident. She wasn't the only one who'd been through hell over the last week. "Liz—"

"Waters told me why you did it." She fisted the towel tighter. Waters had blackmailed him. She didn't know all the details, but if Braxton had proven anything over the last week, it was that he'd do anything to protect her. And he'd left thinking the former CIA agent would leave her alone after he'd delivered the intel. But killers rarely kept their end of the deals they struck. She'd learned that the hard way. "He threatened to kill me unless you got him the intel on Oversight, right? Why didn't you tell me?"

"Any reason I gave after you found out would look like a desperate attempt to win you back." The vulnerability and sorrow in his voice raised her body's awareness of him to new heights. "I needed you to find out on your own."

Elizabeth gripped the weapon harder, hot tears in her eyes. "And if he'd never told me, you were willing to walk away from us forever? Never meet your daughter?"

"If it kept you alive, yes." The solemn expression etched onto his face penetrated deep into her soul, as though he'd stolen the very oxygen she needed to live. "I told Waters how to access Oversight's feeds, and people died because of it. Because of me. I'll never be able to forgive myself, and I'll understand if you can't, either. But I made you a promise. I'm not leaving you behind. Not again. I'll avoid arrest as long as I can to stay in Anchorage. For you."

The guilt she'd witnessed inside Braxton consumed his irises. The shock of his admission cut her like a blunt blade, rough and painful. Dalton Meyer and Liam Waters had been killed, an entire country had been put at risk, all because Braxton had tried to protect her.

"You gave up classified intel to a former CIA agent then came back to stop him when you realized that he was going to use it to hunt me down." She could barely believe the words coming from her own mouth.

"He threatened to kill you. I may have lost my temper." He stepped forward, slowly closing the space between them. The steam from the shower penetrated through the thick towel wrapped around her. Or was it her heart racing out of control? He glanced at the gun in her hand. "You don't need the gun, Liz. Not for me."

Silence reigned, perfect silence almost too good to be true.

It took three deep inhales before she could look at him again. Liam Waters would've gotten his hands on Oversight's intel one way or another, maybe tortured and killed dozens more people to do it. She knew that now. There was no reasoning with him, no convincing him killing her wouldn't bring his partner back. And she and Braxton had stopped him. The man standing two feet from her had ensured the world had one less killer to worry about.

Her body ached as Elizabeth set the gun back on the sink. The internal torture he'd put himself through showed in his expression, and she reached for him, framing the side of his jaw with her uninjured hand. His warmth burned a hole through the last bricks of the wall she'd created around her heart, desolating everything she'd held against him.

He'd done it all for her.

"The gun's not for you. I just…need it for a little while longer. What you did, it made me feel protected." She swiped her thumb beneath one bright green eye. Careful to avoid the bandages over his left shoulder, she stepped into the comfort of his arms. How could she ever have thought he'd betray her? The past week alone was proof enough. He'd do anything to protect her and their baby. And she'd do anything to keep him in her life. "Made me feel loved."

"You're safe now. It's over." He ran his fingertips

through her hair. The slight tremble against her scalp mimicked the uneven thump of her pulse. Elizabeth caught the struggle to fill his lungs but couldn't force herself to straighten. Not yet. She hadn't felt so content in months, his skin warm, traces of his clean, masculine scent diving deep into her pores. Her nerves settled the longer she counted his heartbeat. "I won't let anyone hurt you ever again."

"I know," she said.

Physical tension drained from him. Only the sound of their combined heartbeats filled her ears, but her fingers tingled with the urge to touch him. Elizabeth slid her hand across his torso, following the peaks and valleys created just for her. The soul-deep craving she'd always had for him erupted as she craned her head up. The emptiness in those irises had vanished, leaving nothing but her reflection in his gaze.

"I was going to stock your freezer for you." Braxton swiped a strand of hair behind her ear, sending liquid pleasure shooting to her core. His laugh vibrated through her. "Then realized you already have three gallons of chocolate ice cream."

"I stopped at the store right after they released me from the hospital." Something stirred in her lower abdominals. If she was honest with herself, she'd already made her decision, but so much had happened between them. He'd sold classified intel to save her life, had gone as far as putting his own life in danger for her, but the sting of his disappearance hadn't lessened. Four months of wondering, of questions, had nearly driven her to the point of insanity. She couldn't go through that again. "I was hoping we might be able to share a bowl tonight. And every night after that."

Disappointment overwhelmed his features, and her heart shattered from the agony consuming him. She'd experienced the same pain when Braxton had vanished and had completely lost herself inside that betrayal. "I can't. Not without dragging you and the baby into the NSA's manhunt for me. I'll stay in Anchorage, but it'll be at a distance."

Stepping back, Elizabeth ran the pad of her thumb over his left cheekbone. He lifted his gaze to her, staring at her as though she was the center of his entire world. Just as he had when they'd first met. She'd never get used to that. "And if I told you the NSA didn't get to decide our future?"

Those mesmerizing green eyes narrowed on her. "What do you mean?"

"Answer the question." Elizabeth pulled back, eager for his response. This was the defining moment, the chance to risk it all. And if he didn't take it? Her insides churned at the thought. But she'd move on. She'd raise this baby alone. She'd tell her daughter the truth. That her father had to stay in hiding to protect them. "Would you stay here with me—with us—and give us another shot if the manhunt was called off?"

"Damn right I would." Braxton threaded his fingers through the hair at the back of her neck, molding her to him. "Making you mine is the only thing I've wanted since you walked into the office all those years ago."

Her cell phone dinged with an incoming message from the other room. Perfect timing. "Good. I called

Dalton Meyer's replacement when I got home from the hospital and told them I would only help restore Oversight's feeds for the NSA if they cleared the charges against you."

Braxton's expression slackened. He tried to pull away, but she secured him against her. No. No more running. No more lies. From now on, they'd be honest with each other. "Liz, you didn't have to do that. I would've figured something out—"

"Yes, I did. You saved my life more times than I can count. It was time to return the favor." She'd vowed never to work for the NSA or touch Oversight's programming again but ensuring Braxton could help raise their daughter, that he could make them a family, was worth it. "As twisted as it sounds, Waters died for the one person who mattered most to him in the world. His partner. I realized when he had that gun to my head, if I had to, I would do the same thing for my partner." Fisting her fingers in his T-shirt, she pushed against him slightly. "I love you. I never stopped loving you, and I want you here. I want you to help me raise this baby. I want to be a family."

"I love you, too." His breath warmed her neck. Pressing himself against her, he smoothed the tip of his nose along the outside cartilage of her ear. A shudder ran across her collarbones and down her spine, and she closed her eyes to heighten her senses. "What do you say we get out of here? You, me, no more secrets, no guns. Just the open ocean and sandy beaches for a few weeks."

After what they'd been through, she needed it. She

spun in his arms, securing the towel around her once again, and wiped steam from the mirror. She'd have to clear the time off with Sullivan and the rest of the team, but she doubted Blackhawk Security needed her for the next month or so. "I'm bringing my gun."

"You say the sexiest things." Braxton slid one hand along her thigh, below the hem of the towel. The rough patches on his fingertips scraped against her skin, but not uncomfortably. He buried his lips in the crook between her neck and shoulder. He planted a kiss against her skin, tracing the edge of her tendon with his lips. She grew painfully aware of the reaction his lips elicited in her lower abdominals. He slid his hand over their baby from behind, lowered his chin onto her shoulder and held her against him. "Marry me."

Interrupting her next inhale, he guided her head toward him and crushed his mouth against hers, urgent, warm. Her vision wavered as she surrendered herself over to him completely. After almost four months of missing his touch, she couldn't think of anything but the towel and his clothes separating them. Their injuries wouldn't allow them to fulfill all of their physical desires, but having him close was more than enough. Pulling away for a moment, her lips growing cold without his, she reveled in the weight lifting from her chest. He was a free man. He was hers. "Deal."

Hints of that gut-wrenching smile pulled at one corner of his mouth, and her pulse rocketed higher. He swept a stray piece of soaked hair off her face then brought her hips into the circle of his arms. "I only have one condition."

"You realize you're the one who proposed to me,

right? I'm supposed to make the conditions." She melted from the warmth radiating from under his clothing. Something exploded inside, seared her from the inside out and destroyed the horror-filled memories of the last week. Her heart thundered with a renewed possibility of finally having the man she'd wanted from the start, of starting their family together, and she smiled against his lips. "But go ahead. Name your price."

"We get on a plane tomorrow," he said. "And you marry me by sunset."

"What are we supposed to do until then?" Elizabeth had meant the question innocently enough, but the desire burning in Braxton's gaze filled her thoughts with plenty of things they might be able to do despite the near-death injuries they'd sustained.

"I have a few ideas." Braxton pulled her closer, her back pressed to his front, and fit her against him. His pulse was slow and steady between her shoulder blades, and she collapsed her head back against his shoulder. "One of them involves getting this towel off you."

She wrapped her hands around the Glock on the counter and dropped it to her side. Safety on. She might need the extra security for a few more weeks, until the nightmares subsided for good, but at least she'd have Braxton at her side to help her forget. Forever. "Good luck with that."

Five months later...

SCREAMING. BLOOD. ICE CHIPS. More screaming. All for the tiny, perfect human in his arms.

"Karina Dawson-Levitt." He couldn't believe it. Braxton cradled his daughter tighter. Mere hours ago, they'd rushed to the hospital, and before he knew it, here she was. Their baby girl opened her mouth wide in a yawn, and his eyes burned. Hell, he'd never been so happy in his life. A laugh rumbled through him. "Welcome to the world, half-pint."

"Hey, I pushed that watermelon out. I get to hold her, too, you know." Liz slid her fingers across his arm, pulling him back toward her on the bed. The damn thing wasn't wide enough for all three of them, but there was no way he was moving from this spot. Liz pressed against him on his right, baby Karina in his arms. His wife rested her head on his shoulder and set her hand over his heart, right where it belonged. A moan filled his ears as she glanced up at him. "She's so perfect, I want to eat her up. Want to count her fingers and toes again?"

"No, let's let her rest. She's got to save her energy so she can keep us up all night." Planting a kiss in Liz's hair, Braxton caught movement through the small window in the hospital room door. They'd held them off as long as they could, but the team had gotten restless. There was no stopping it, but he was determined to stretch out this moment of peace as long as he could. Stroking his fingers over Karina's baby-soft skin, he braced himself against the oncoming chaos. "They're going to break down the door if we keep them waiting any longer."

"You can let them in in a minute. But only because I'm afraid Elliot will start telling the staff he's a doctor to get in here." Liz leveraged her hands into the mattress and straightened, then ran her hands through her hair. "Hell, he probably has the credentials already made just in case."

"You look beautiful." Braxton brushed a stray piece of hair behind her ear, sliding his thumb across her bottom lip. "You grew a human inside your body. What you did was amazing, and you're more beautiful now than ever."

He still couldn't believe she'd married him on that beach, couldn't believe she'd chosen him after he'd failed to keep her safe. With her work for the NSA behind her, Oversight up and running, and the charges dropped against him, he'd spent the last five months making it up to her every way he knew how. And he'd keep trying for the rest of his life. Without her... No. He wouldn't think of a life without her. There was no life without her. She'd been the one to get him through the darkness. Everything he wanted was right here in this room. And he'd fight like hell to keep it that way.

The CIA had taken possession of Liam Waters's body after the fight in his hideout. The bastard would never hurt her again. Only after receiving confirmation his remains had been incinerated had her nightmares finally subsided. She didn't need to sleep with the gun stashed under her pillow at night. She was safe. And the past was officially dead.

She leaned into his palm, kissing the callused skin there with a wide smile. Her breath brushed lightly over his wrist, and every nerve ending in his body went haywire. For her. "You're just saying that so I'll let you eat the cookies the nurses brought me to get my blood sugar back up."

"I love you." Braxton kissed her with everything he had then handed off the tiny human to her mother. He maneuvered off the bed and crossed the room. Spinning back toward her before he opened the door, he pointed at her. "But I'm getting those cookies one way or another."

He wrenched the heavy metal door toward him, and in three breaths her team flooded the room with congratulations. Sullivan Bishop, Elliot Dunham, Vincent Kalani, Anthony Harris and Glennon Chase all closed in on his wife and daughter. The only operative missing was Kate Monroe, but he was sure the profiler would get to meet the newest member of the Blackhawk Security team soon.

Liz's smile brightened despite the grueling process she'd gone through to deliver their baby, and a rush of joy had him cracking his own smile.

That was his wife. His daughter. His life.

Braxton saw the future in that moment.

And, damn, it looked good.

* * * * *

TEMPTED BY THE
HOT HIGHLAND DOC

SCARLET WILSON

To my fab editor Carly Byrne,
for supporting me to write the stories I love – no
matter how crazy!

PROLOGUE

'ABSOLUTELY NO WAY. I'm not doing it.' Kristie Nelson shook her head and folded her arms across her chest.

Louie, her boss, arched one eyebrow at her. 'Do you want to pay your mortgage or not?'

She shifted uncomfortably on her chair. 'I was promised a chance at working with the news team. These puff pieces are driving me nuts, and if you send me in the direction of another quiz show I swear I'll grab that ceremonial sword from behind your head and stick it somewhere nasty.'

Louie let out a hearty laugh. They'd been working together far too long to be anything but straight with each other.

He sighed and leaned his head on one hand. 'Kristie, your last two projects have bombed. You fell out—in a spectacular fashion, I might add—with the producer on the TV series you were scheduled for. I've had to search around for work that might fit with your other obligations.'

She swallowed, her throat instantly dry. Louie knew her well—better than most because she revealed nothing to most people—and, although she didn't tell him so, she did appreciate it.

She stared down at the file he'd handed her. '*A Year in the Life of the Hot Highland Doc*? Really?' Her voice arched upwards, along with her eyebrows. She tried to ignore the involuntary shudder that went down her spine.

She straightened her shoulders. 'Sounds like another puff piece to me.'

Louie looked her in the eye. 'A puff piece that involves filming three days a month on the island—paid travel to and from the island, all expenses covered, and a salary better than any news channel would pay you.'

She shifted uncomfortably in her chair. When he put it like that...

Louie continued. 'These streaming TV channels are the ones with the big budgets these days. They're making all the best new TV shows, and they're not afraid to take chances. Don't you think it might be a good idea to get in there, and make a good impression?'

Her brain was whirring. She knew it all made sense. She knew it was an opportunity. How many people really made it onto the terrestrial TV channels? She didn't even want to admit that she'd subscribed to this streaming service too. Some of the shows were addictive.

Louie shrugged. 'Filming is taking place all around the world. There's a volcanologist in Hawaii. A museum curator in Cairo. A quarterback from an American football team. Someone training for the space station.'

'And I get the Scottish doc?' She held up her file, not even trying to hide the disappointment on her face.

Louie didn't speak and the silence told her everything she needed to know. She'd got what was left. Louie had probably had to campaign hard to even get her this gig.

She flicked through the files sitting on Louie's desk. There was also a vet. A firefighter. A teacher. A policewoman.

If she'd had to rank each of the possibilities, she knew the work with the doc would have been last on her list. The thought of being around a medic all day—possibly being in a hospital environment—made her feel sick.

Six years ago as a media graduate she'd thought she was

going to take the world by storm. But somehow that storm had changed into a long, hard slog with only a few glimmers scattered throughout. Part of her resented this job already. It wasn't exactly her career goal. But what was?

Things had shifted in the last few years. Real life events had left her jaded and knocked her confidence in the world around her. Sometimes she wasn't even sure what it was she was fighting for any more.

'Isn't describing someone as a Hot Highland Doc considered sexist these days?'

Louie shrugged. 'Who cares? That's the title we liked. It should draw viewers in. Who wouldn't want to see a Hot Highland Doc?'

Her brain was still ticking. She wrinkled her nose. 'Geography isn't my strong point. Hold on.' She pulled out her phone and stuck in the name of the island. 'Arran? That's on the southwest coast of Scotland. That's not even in the Highlands.'

Louie laughed. 'Like I said—who cares? At least it is an island. It's the UK, so trade descriptions can't get us on that one.'

Kristie closed her eyes for a second and thought about the pile of bills currently sitting on her dresser. This was money. Money that would be guaranteed for one year. She would be a fool to turn this down.

'Smile. Arran—who knows? You might even like it. You just need to go there three days a month and film as much as you can. You need enough footage for forty-one minutes of screen time.' Louie waved his hand. 'And if it's boring, do something to mix it up.'

This time it was Kristie that raised her eyebrows. 'Mix it up? What exactly does that mean?'

Louis shrugged. 'I mean, make it interesting viewing. If you work on another show that gets cancelled midway, people will start to think you have the kiss of death.' He met her gaze. 'People won't want to work with you.' He left the words hanging.

She gulped. She knew he was right. TV and media were ruthless. One minute you were the belle of the ball, the next you were lucky to pick up the leftovers—just like she was now.

She gave a slow nod of her head then frowned as she compared her file with some of the others. 'This guy? There's no photo.'

'Isn't there?' Louie had moved over to his appointment diary, obviously ready to move onto his next task.

'And how do you even say his name?'

Louie moved back around the desk and leaned over her shoulder. '"Roo-ah-ree", I think.' He winked. 'At least try and get the guy's name right.'

She stared at the scribbled notes in the folder. Rhuaridh Gillespie. General Practitioner. Also provides cover to Arran Community Hospital and A and E department.

How did that even work?

She swallowed and took a deep breath. How bad could this be?

'How much preparation time do I have?'

There was a glint in Louie's eyes as he threw something across the desk at her. Flight details.

'A day,' he answered.

'A day?' She stood up as she said the words. 'What do you mean, a day?'

Louie just started talking as if there was nothing unusual at all about what he'd just said. 'You fly into Glasgow, car hire has been arranged—you need to drive to a place called Ardrossan to catch the ferry to Arran. The crossing takes about an hour but...' he paused as he glanced at some notes in front of him '...apparently can be hampered by the weather. So build in some extra time.'

Her brain had gone directly into overdrive. Clothes.

Equipment. What was the weather like on Arran this time of year? This was the UK, not the US. She needed to learn a bit more about their healthcare system. And what about this guy? Under normal circumstances she'd take a few days to do some background research on him—to learn what kind of a person he was—what made him tick. Anything that would give her a head start.

She shook her head. Then realised she hadn't asked one of the most important questions. 'Who is my cameraman?'

Louie gave a little cough that he tried to disguise as clearing his throat. 'Gerry.'

'Gerry?' She couldn't hide her dismay. 'Louie, he's about a hundred and five! He doesn't keep up well, his timekeeping is awful, and he always leaves half his equipment behind.'

Louie gave a half-hearted shrug. 'Give the guy a break. He needs the work. And anyway, he knows you better than most.'

She bit her lip as she picked up her bag. Maybe she was being unreasonable. He did know her better than most—he'd been there with her and Louie when she'd got that terrible call. But last time she'd worked with Gerry he'd left her sitting in the middle of a baking desert in Arizona for three hours.

'I swear if he isn't at the airport when I get there, I'm leaving without him.'

Louie waved his hand. 'Whatever.' Louie picked up his phone as she headed to the door. 'And, Kristie?'

She spun back around. 'Yeah?'

He grinned. 'Who knows—you might enjoy this.'

She didn't hesitate. She picked up a cushion from the chair nearest the door and launched it at Louie's head.

CHAPTER ONE

May

THERE WAS NO way that this amount of vomiting could be normal. Maybe it was something she'd eaten on the flight between Los Angeles and London? The chicken had looked okay. But then she'd had that really huge brownie at Heathrow Airport before the departure to Glasgow.

She groaned as her stomach lurched again and the roll of the waves threw her off balance. They weren't even out at sea any more, they were in the middle of docking at the harbour in Brodick, Arran.

'First-timer, eh?' said a woman with a well-worn face as she walked towards the gangway.

Kristie couldn't even answer.

Gerry gave her a nudge. 'Come on, they've already made two announcements telling drivers to get back into their cars. Do you want me to drive instead?'

She shook her head and took another glug of water from the bottle he'd bought her. Poor Gerry. He'd spent half of this ferry journey holding the hair from her face so she could be sick. He was more than double her age, but seemed to have weathered the journey much better than she had—even if he had twice tried to get into the car on the wrong side.

She gave him a half-hearted smile. 'Next time we get

on a flight together I'll have what you're having.' He'd popped some kind of tablet as soon as they'd boarded the flight in Los Angeles and had slept until the wheels had set down at Heathrow.

He returned a smile. 'What can I say? Years of experience.'

She watched him shuffling down the stairs in front of her to the car deck. The boat's bow was already opening, preparing for the cars to unload. Kristie ignored a few pointed glares as she made her way to their hire car and tried to squeeze back inside.

The cars in front had already moved by the time she'd started the unfamiliar vehicle and tried to remember what to do with the pedals and the gearstick.

She jumped as there was a loud blast of a horn behind her. She muttered an expletive under her breath as she started the car and promptly stalled it. The car juddered and heat rushed into her cheeks. 'Why is everything on the wrong side?'

Gerry chuckled. 'Just watch out for the roundabouts.'

She bit her bottom lip as she started the car again. The roundabout at Glasgow airport had been like an episode of the *Wacky Races*. The whole wrong-side-of-the-road aspect had totally frazzled her brain and she was sure at one point her life had flashed before her eyes.

'Arran isn't that big,' she muttered. 'Maybe they don't need roundabouts. Crazy things anyway. Who invented them? What's wrong with straight roads?'

Gerry laughed as they finally rolled off the ferry and joined the queue of traffic heading towards a road junction.

'Which way?' she asked.

'Left,' he said quickly. 'The doctor's surgery and hospital are in a place called Lamlash. It's only a few miles up the road.'

Gerry settled back in his seat as they pulled out onto

the main road. The sun was low in the sky and all around them they could see green on one side and sea on the other.

'I think I'm going to like this place,' he said with a smile, folding his hands in his lap.

Kristie blinked. Although there were a number of people around the ferry terminal, as soon as they moved further away the crowds and traffic seemed to disperse quickly. There was a cluster of shops, pubs and a few hotels scattered along what appeared to be the main street of the Scottish town, but in a few moments the main street had disappeared, only to be replaced with a winding coastal country road.

'I've never seen so much green,' she said, trying to keep her eyes fixed on the road rather than the extensive scenery.

Gerry laughed. 'You don't get out of Los Angeles often enough. Too much dry air.'

A few splotches of rain landed on the windscreen. Kristie frowned and flicked a few of the levers at the side of the wheel, trying to locate the wipers. The blinkers on the hire car flicked on and off on either side. She let out a huff of exasperation as she tried the other side.

'Road!' Gerry's voice pulled her attention back to the road as an approaching car honked loudly at her. She yanked the wheel back in an instant, her heart in her mouth. The car had drifted a little into the middle of the road as she'd tried to find the wipers. She cursed out loud as she pulled it back to the correct side of the road—which felt like the wrong side. 'Darn it. Stupid road,' she muttered.

Gerry shook his head. 'No multiple lanes here. Get with it, Kristie. Embrace the countryside.'

She pressed her lips together. She hadn't seen a single coffee shop she recognised, or any big department stores. What did people do around here? Her grip tightened on the wheel as the rain changed from a few splats to torrential within a few seconds. Her hand flicked the lever up and then down to quicken the windscreen-wiper speed. It was almost as if a black cloud had just drifted over the top of them. She leaned forward and tried to peer upwards. 'What is this? Five minutes ago the sun was shining.'

She knew she sounded cranky. But she was tired. She was jet-lagged. She wanted some decent coffee and some hotel room service. She didn't even know what time zone she was in any more.

A sign flashed past. 'What did that say?' she snapped.

'Go left,' said Gerry smoothly.

She flicked the indicator and pulled into the busy parking lot in front of her. There was a white building to their right, set next to the sea.

The rain battered off the windscreen and the trees edging the parking lot seemed to be lolling to one side in the strong winds.

Gerry let out a low laugh at her horrified face. 'Welcome to Scotland, Kristie.'

'Tell me you're joking.' He stared across the room at his colleague Magda, who had her feet up on a nearby stool and was rubbing her very pregnant belly. She sighed. 'I signed the contract ten months ago. Before, you know, I knew about this.'

'You signed a contract for filming in our practice without discussing it with me?'

She shot him an apologetic look. 'I did discuss it with you.' She leaned forward to her laptop and scrolled. 'There.' She pointed to her screen. 'Or maybe not quite discussed, but I sent you the email. I forwarded the details and the contracts. So much has happened since then.' She let her voice slow for a second.

He knew what she meant. In the last year he'd gone

from helping out at the practice as a locum to taking over from his dad when he'd died. This had been his father's GP practice, and Rhuaridh had been left in the lurch when his father had been diagnosed with pancreatic cancer and died in the space of a few weeks. Due to the difficulties in failing to recruit to such a rural post, he'd spent the last ten months, giving up his own practice in one of the cities in Scotland, packing up his father's house and selling his own, and trying to learn the intricacies of his new role. It was no wonder this piece of crucial information hadn't really stuck.

He ran his hand through his thick hair. 'But what on earth does this mean?'

Magda held up her hands. 'I'm sorry. I meant to talk to you last week when I sent them your details instead of mine—but I had that scare and just didn't get a chance.'

Rhuaridh swallowed and took a look at Magda's slightly swollen ankles. This was a much-wanted baby after seven years of infertility. Last week Magda had had a small fall and started bleeding. It had been panic stations all round, even from the team of completely competent staff in this practice and at the nearby cottage hospital. It seemed that practically the whole island was waiting for the safe delivery of this baby. There was no way he was going to put his colleague under any strain.

He sighed and sat down in the chair in front of her as he ran his fingers through his hair. 'Tell me again about this.'

The edges of her lips quirked upwards. They both knew he was conceding that she hadn't really told him properly at all.

'It's a TV show. *A Year in the Life of...*' She held out her hands. 'This one, obviously, is a doctor. It's an American company and they specifically wanted a doctor from Scotland who worked on one of the islands.'

He narrowed his gaze. 'I didn't know you wanted to be

a reality TV star.' He was curious, this didn't seem like Magda at all.

She laughed and shook her head. 'Reality TV? No way. What I wanted, and what we'll get—' she emphasised the words carefully '—is a brand-new X-ray machine for the cottage hospital, with enough funds for a service contract.'

'What?' He straightened in the chair.

She nodded. 'It's part of the deal.'

Rhuaridh frowned. How had he managed to miss this? The X-ray machine in their cottage hospital was old and overused. Even though the staff had applied to the local health board every year for an upgrade and new facilities, NHS funding was limited. While their machine still worked—even though it was temperamental—it was unlikely to be replaced. A new machine could mean better imaging, which would lead to fewer referrals to the mainland for potential surgeries. Fractures could be notoriously hard to see. As could some chest complaints. A better machine would mean more accurate diagnosis for patients and less work all round.

He looked at Magda again with newfound admiration. 'This is the reason you applied in the first place, isn't it?'

She grinned and patted her belly again. 'Give a little, get a little. You know I hate reporting on dusky X-rays. We'll have a brand-new digital system where we can enlarge things, and ping them on to a specialist colleague if we need to.' She shrugged, 'Just think of all those ferry journeys that won't need to happen.'

He nodded. Being on an island always made things tougher. Their cottage hospital only had a few available beds, which were inevitably full of some of the older local residents with chronic conditions. They had a small A and E department and a fully equipped theatre for emergencies but it was rarely used. Occasionally a visiting surgeon would appear to carry out operations on a couple of patients at a time, but they weren't equipped to carry out any kind of major surgery and any visiting consultant had to bring their whole team.

Whilst their facilities were probably adequate for their population of five thousand, every year the influx of holiday tourists during the summer months took their numbers to over twenty thousand. Slips, trips and falls made the X-ray machine invaluable. Rhuaridh had lost count of the number of times he'd had to send someone with a questionable X-ray over on the ferry to the mainland for further assessment.

'Sometimes I think I love you, Magda,' he said as he shook his head.

She wagged her finger. 'Don't tell David you said that, and just remember that while I tell you the rest.' He smiled. He'd known Magda's husband for the last ten years. He'd watched his friend battle to win the heart of the woman in front of him.

'What's the rest?' he asked as he stood up and stretched his back.

Magda bit her bottom lip. 'The filming happens for three days every month. You don't have to do anything special. They just follow you about on your normal duties. They take care of patient consent for filming. You just have to be you.'

The words were said with throwaway confidence but from the look on Magda's face she knew what was coming.

'Three days every month?'

She nodded. 'That's all.'

He pressed his lips together. It didn't sound like *That's all* to him. It sounded like three days of someone following him around and annoying him constantly with questions. It sounded like three days of having to explain to every single patient that someone was filming around him. He could kiss goodbye to the ten-minute consultation system that kept the GP practice running smoothly. He could wave a fond farewell to his speedy ward rounds in the community hospital where he knew the medical history of most of the patients without even looking at their notes.

'Three days?' He couldn't keep the edge out of his voice. He'd spent his life guarding his privacy carefully. Magda knew this. They'd trained together for six years, then jokingly followed each other across Scotland for a variety of jobs. It had been Rhuaridh who had introduced Magda to the isle of Arran off the west coast of Scotland—a place she'd fallen instantly in love with. It had been Rhuaridh who had introduced Magda to his best friend David, and his father Joe, who'd looked after the cottage hospital and GP practice on the island for thirty years. She knew him better than most. She knew exactly how uncomfortable this would make him.

She put her feet on the floor and leaned forward as best as she could with her swollen stomach. 'I know it's bad timing. I never thought this would happen.' Tears formed in the corners of her eyes. 'I always meant for it to be me that did the filming. I thought it might even be fun. Some of our oldies will love getting a moment on TV.'

He could hear the hopeful edge in her voice. He knew she was trying to make it sound better for him.

He shook his head. 'It...it'll be fine, Magda. Don't worry. You know I'll do it.' He could say the words out loud but he couldn't ignore the hollow feeling in his chest. Three days' filming every month for the next year. It was his equivalent of signing up for the ultimate torture. This was *so* not his comfort zone.

He took a deep breath. 'Okay, it's fine. You concentrate on baby Bruce. Don't worry about anything. We both know you should currently be at home, not here. Leave this with me.'

She gave a half-scowl. 'I am *not* calling my baby Bruce.'

It was a standing joke. David's family had a tradition of calling the firstborn in their family Bruce. David had missed out. He was the secondborn. Once Magda had got past the three-month mark both David and Rhuaridh had started teasing her about the family name.

He laughed. 'You know you are. Don't fight it.' He glanced at the pile of work sitting on his desk. It would take him until late into the night. With Magda going on maternity leave, and no locum doctor recruited to fill the gap, everything was going to fall to him. He was lucky. He worked within a dynamic team of advanced nurse practitioners, practice nurses and allied health professionals. He already knew they would support him as best they could.

Life had changed completely for him once his father had died. He'd felt obligated to come back and provide a health service for the people of the island when the post couldn't get filled. Unfortunately, Zoe, his partner, had been filled with horror at the thought of life on Arran. He hadn't even had the chance to ask whether she thought a long-distance relationship could work. She had been repelled by the very prospect of setting foot on the island he'd previously called home and had run, not walked, in the opposite direction.

All of that had messed with his head in a way he hadn't quite expected. He loved this place. Always had, always would. Of course, as a teenager wanting to study medicine, he'd had to leave. And that had been good for him. He'd loved his training in the Glasgow hospitals, then his time in Edinburgh, followed by a job in London, and a few months working for Doctors Without Borders, before taking up his GP training. But when things had happened and his father died suddenly? That whole journey home on the boat had been tinged with nostalgia. Coming home had felt exactly like coming home should. It had felt as if it was supposed to happen—even though the circumstances were never what he had wanted.

He moved over towards the desk and looked at Magda. 'So, when exactly does this start? In a few months?'

There was a nervous kind of laugh. 'Tomorrow,' Magda said as she stared out the window. 'Or today,' she added with a hint of panic as her eyes fixed on the woman with blonde hair blowing frantically around her face in the stiff Firth of Clyde winds. Rhuaridh's eyes widened and he dropped the file he'd just picked up.

'What?' His head turned and followed Magda's gaze to the car park just outside his surgery window.

The woman was dressed in a thin jacket and capri pants. It was clear she was struggling with the door of her car as it buffeted off her body then slammed in the strong winds. She didn't look particularly happy.

'You've got to be joking—now? No preparation time, nothing?'

Magda gave an uncomfortable swallow, her blue eyes meeting his. 'Sorry,' she whispered. 'I just got caught up in other things.'

He could sense the panic emanating from her. He felt his annoyance bubble under the surface—but he'd never show it.

His brain started to whirl. He'd need to talk to patients. Set up appropriate consultations. Make sure nothing inappropriate was filmed. He wanted to run a few questions past his professional organisation. He knew there had been some other TV series that had featured docs and medical staff, and he just wanted a bit of general advice.

A piece of paper flew out of the hand of the woman outside. 'Darn it!' Even from inside her American accent was as clear as a bell.

Magda made a little choking sound. He turned to face

her as she obviously tried to stifle her laugh. Her eyebrows rose. 'Well, she looks like fun.'

Rhuaridh pressed his lips together to stop himself from saying what he really wanted to say. He took another breath and wagged his finger at Magda. 'Dr Price, I think you owe me.'

She held out her hand so he could help pull her up from the chair. 'Absolutely.' She smiled.

Gerry seemed to be taking the wind in his stride. 'Why did we come here first?' she muttered as she opened the boot of the car to grab some of their equipment.

'Best to get things started on the right foot. Let's meet our guy, establish some ground rules, then crash.'

She gave him a sideways glance. Maybe her older colleague was more fatigued than he was admitting. She batted some of her hair out of her face. The sign outside the building read 'Cairn Medical Practice', with the names of the doctors underneath.

'Roo-ah-ree.' She practised the name on her tongue as they made their way to the main entrance. Gerry already had a camera under one arm. One thing for Gerry, he was ever hopeful.

'Roo-ah-ree.' She practised again, trying to pretend she wasn't nervous. So much was riding on this. She had to make it work. She had to make it interesting and watchable. There hadn't been background information on this doc. Apparently he'd been the last-minute replacement for someone else. And if he was anything like the majority of the people on the ferry he would be grey-haired, carry a walking stick, and be wearing a sturdy pair of boots.

The ferry. What if she still smelled of sick? She felt a tiny wave of panic and grabbed some perfume from her bag, squirting it madly around her before they went through the main entrance door.

They stepped into a large waiting area. It was empty but looked…busy. Some of the chairs were higgledy-piggledy, magazines and a few kids' toys were scattered around the tables and floor. She could see some tread marks on the carpet. This place had a well-used feel about it.

She glanced at her watch. There was no one at the reception desk. It was after six p.m. The sign on the door said that was closing time. 'Hello?' she ventured.

There was the slam of a door from somewhere and a tall ruffled, dark-haired man appeared from the back of the building. He had the oddest expression on his face. It looked almost pained.

'Hi, sorry,' he said. 'Just seeing my pregnant colleague out.' His eyes seemed to run up and down the two of them. 'You must be the TV people.'

His accent was thick, almost lilting, and it actually took her a few seconds to tune in and process his words. A frown appeared on his forehead at the delay. 'Rhuaridh Gillespie?' He lifted his hand and pointed to his chest.

Oh, my goodness. She was going to have to concentrate hard—and she didn't just mean because of the accent. He was so *not* what she expected. Instead of an old wrinkly guy, she had a lean, muscled guy with bright blue eyes and slightly too long tousled dark hair. He was wearing a light blue shirt and dress pants. And he didn't look entirely pleased to see them.

Something sparked in her brain and she walked forward, holding her hand out, knowing exactly how dishevelled she looked after their long journey. 'Kristie Nelson. It's a pleasure to meet you, Roo—' She stumbled a little. 'Dr Gillespie,' she said, praying that her signature smile would start working any moment soon.

For a while, that had kind of been her trademark. With her styled blonde locks, usually perfect makeup and 'signature' wide smile, there had been a time on local TV when she'd become almost popular. That had been the time she'd had oodles of confidence and thought her star was going to rise immensely and catapult her to fame and fortune. Instead, she'd fallen to the earth with a resounding bump.

He reached over and took her hand. It was a warm, solid grip. One that made her wonder if this guy worked out.

'Like I said, Rhuaridh Gillespie.' He leaned over and shook Gerry's hand too.

'Gerry Berkovich. Camera, lights, sounds and general dogsbody for the good-looking one.' He nodded towards Kristie.

She slapped his arm. 'As if!'

Dr Gillespie didn't even crack a smile. In fact, he barely held in his sigh. He gestured towards the nearest office. 'Come and have a seat. I've kind of been thrown in at the deep end here, so we're going to have to come to an agreement about some boundaries.'

It was the edge to his tone. She shot a glance at Gerry, who raised one corner of his eyebrow just a little. This didn't sound like the best start.

She swallowed and tried to ignore the fact she was tired, now hungry, and desperately wanted a shower and five minutes lying on a bed and staring up at a ceiling. She'd been travelling for twenty hours. She'd been in the company of other people for more than that. Sometimes she needed a bit of quiet—a bit of down time. And it didn't look like it would happen anytime soon.

Rhuaridh showed them to seats in his office.

Kristie had dealt with lots of difficult situations over the last few years in TV and moved into autopilot mode. 'I'm sure everything will be fine,' she said smoothly. 'Contracts have already been agreed—'

'Not by me,' he cut in sharply, 'And not by my patients. In fact...' he took a deep breath, lifting one hand and running it through his dark scraggy hair '... I'll need to get my professional organisation to take a look at this contract to make sure no patient confidentially will be breached inadvertently.'

He was speaking. But she wasn't really hearing. It was all just noise in her ears.

'This was all looked at—all prepared beforehand.' She could cut in too. As it went, she didn't know a single thing about the show's contracts because she'd had nothing to do with any of this. All she knew was she was on a schedule. She had three days to film enough stuff to get forty-one minutes of usable footage. Much harder than it sounded.

'I've been thrown into this. I won't do anything to compromise my patients, or my position here.' His voice was jagged and impenetrable. She could see him building a solid wall in front of himself before her very eyes. Her very tired eyes.

She'd thought he'd looked kind of sexy earlier. If this guy could do a bit of charm, the ladies would love him. But it seemed that charm and Dr Gillespie didn't go in the same sentence. 'I'm sure that—'

He stood up sharply. 'I won't move on this.'

'But we only have three days…'

Gerry gave a little cough. She turned sideways to look at him and he gave an almost invisible shake of his head.

'I'll get back to you as soon as I can. I suggest you go and check into your accommodation and try and…' he shot her a glance as if he was struggling to find the right words '…rest.'

He walked over to the door and opened it for them. This time he didn't even meet her gaze. 'I'll be in touch.'

Kristie was feeling kind of dazed. Had she just been dismissed? She wanted to stand and argue with him. Who did this guy think he was? Arrogant so-and-so. She'd travelled twenty hours for this.

But it was almost as if Gerry read her mind. He grabbed hold of her elbow as he led her back to the car.

The sky had got darker again as thick grey clouds swept overhead, followed by the obligatory spots of rain.

She opened the car and slumped into the driver's seat. Gerry started talking. 'I can shoot some of the scenery. Get a shot of the exteriors, the roads, the surgery. Maybe we could get someone to show us around the—what did they call it in the file—cottage hospital? I could even get a few shots of the ferry docking and leaving.'

'That will fill about five minutes of film when it's all edited down,' she groaned. She leaned forward and banged her head on the steering wheel. 'Why didn't I get the museum curator in Cairo? The person who is training to be an astronaut? Why did I have to get the grumpy Scottish doctor?' She thumped her head again, just to make sure Gerry understood just how frustrated she was.

'Kinda good looking, though,' he said unexpectedly.

'What?' She sat back up and shot him a weird look.

'I said, he's kind of good looking. And that cross demeanour? I think some folks might like it.'

Kristie shook her head. 'At this rate the whole first episode will have to be subtitled. Did you hear how fast he talks? And how thick that accent is?'

Gerry gave a slow appreciative nod as he folded his arms across his chest. 'He's practically got Highland warrior stamped on his forehead.' He twisted towards her and tapped one finger on his chin, looking thoughtful. 'Hey? What do you think your chances are of getting him in a kilt?'

It was no use. Her brain was clearly switching off, and Gerry's was clearly switching on. She just couldn't function.

She let out a kind of whimper. 'Blooming Arran. I need

food, a shower and a bed. Tell me you know where our hotel is.'

Gerry smiled. 'It's about a five-minute drive from here. And it's not a hotel. It's a cottage. Apparently accommodation can be tricky here. There're only a few hotels, but some holiday lets. We'll be lucky if we stay in the same place twice.'

Kristie put both hands on the steering wheel and started the engine. 'Just tell me which direction.' Her head was starting to thump. It was probably the jet-lag and a bit of dehydration. If she couldn't get something in the can in the next three days she would be toast. Her career was already dangling by a thread. Another failure against her name and Louie would be right—no one would want to work with her.

She was going to have to try all her Kristie charm on Dr Grump. Because if she didn't, who knew what could happen next?

They were sitting in his waiting room—again. Patients had already started asking questions. Some were even volunteering to be filmed. Three days of this every month for the next year?

He'd checked with his union. Apparently the TV contract was standard, and the appendix regarding patient consent was similar to one used by other TV series. As long as consent was granted and paperwork completed, there was no reason for him not to continue.

Truth was, he'd heard this news one day ago, but still couldn't bring himself to tell the TV crew. The guy—Gerry—permanently looked as if he could go to sleep at the drop of the hat, whereas his counterpart—Kristie—looked more wound up than the tightest spring.

Pam, one of the secretaries, stuck her head around the door. She had a sheaf of messages in her hand. 'Hospital called. X-ray problems again. Mrs McTaggart needs her painkillers upped. John Henderson phoned—sounded terrible—I've put him down for a house call, and…' She paused for a second, giving him a wary look. 'And I've got his permission to take the film crew.'

Rhuaridh's head flicked up from the bunch of prescriptions he'd been signing. Pam sighed. She was another member of staff that he'd inherited from his father, meaning she knew him better than most. 'You did what?'

Pam never pandered to him. 'Magda had already gone through all the patient permissions with me. So I've started getting them. Now hurry up and take that woman out of my waiting room before she spontaneously combusts.' Pam spun around and left, not giving him any chance to respond.

Rhuaridh leaned back in his chair and glanced at his watch. Nearly three p.m. He could do this. A few hours today, then all of tomorrow and he wouldn't have to see them again for another month. He tried to rationalise it in his brain. How bad could this be?

He pasted his best kind of smile on his face and walked outside.

Finally. He'd finally graced them with his presence.

There were only so many outdoor shots they could film on Arran—and Gerry had shot them all. Filler time, to use around the actual, proper filming. The thing they didn't have a single second of.

For a second yesterday, as they'd sat in the waiting room all day, she'd had half a mind to try and put a secret camera in this guy's room. It wasn't that she didn't know all the unethical issues with this, it was just that she was feeling *that* desperate.

And after two days of waiting, Rhuaridh Gillespie gave them a half-nod of his head. 'I've checked things out. We

need to go to the local hospital. You'll need to sort out
your permissions with the patients when you get there.'

She refused to let that make her mad. She'd already
spent part of the night before meeting the nurse manager
in charge at the hospital and sorting out all the paperwork
with the long-stay patients.

She hadn't let Gerry see that she'd actually been sick
outside before they'd entered. She'd been determined that
she had to get the first visit to the place over and done
with. Once they'd got inside and made the obligatory introductions she'd stuck her hands in her pockets so no one
could see them shaking. If she'd had any other choice, she
would have walked away from filming inside a hospital.
But the fact was, there wasn't another choice. It was this,
or nothing. So she'd pushed all her memories into a box
and tried to lock it up tight.

Once the horrible squirming feeling in her stomach had
finally disappeared, she'd decided that distraction was the
best technique so she'd spent some time talking with some
of the older patients, and had already decided to go back
and interview a few of them on camera.

So by the time they joined Rhuaridh in his black four-
by-four and he drove down the road to the hospital she
felt a bit better prepared and that horrible ominous sensation had diminished a little. The journey only took a
few minutes.

It became pretty clear in the first moments after they
entered the hospital that Rhuaridh wasn't going to give
them any chance to prepare, lightwise, soundwise or any-
thing-wise. It was almost as if he was determined to ignore them.

Gerry murmured, 'I can work around him.'

Kristie straightened her spine. If she didn't start to get
some decent filming soon she could kiss her career goodbye. But there was a little fire of anger burning down

inside her. She didn't let people ignore her. And she'd checked the contract, she knew exactly what Dr Gillespie was getting in return for doing this. He *owed* her three days of filming every month, and if this guy didn't start to deliver, she wouldn't hesitate to remind him.

But Kristie knew, at least for now, she should try and ease him into this filming. Maybe the guy was nervous. Maybe he was shy. Or maybe the guy was just a jerk. Part of her was mad. Did he have any idea how hard she was finding this? Obviously not. But whatever it was that was eating him, she had less than a day and a half to find out.

'So, Dr Gillespie, can you tell me about the first patient we'll be seeing?'

She could see the muscles under his white shirt tense. The ones around the base of his neck were particularly prominent. She nodded to Gerry to keep filming as Rhuaridh muttered a few unintelligible words.

'To the camera, Dr Gillespie,' she said smoothly.

He blinked and turned towards her just as Gerry flicked on their extra light. She almost stepped back. Resentment and annoyance seemed to ooze from every pore. For a second she was sure he was going to say no.

So she moved quickly. 'In fact, let's start with introductions. Face the camera, I'll introduce you, then you can tell the viewers a little about yourself.' She shot him a look, then added in a quiet voice, 'And don't mumble.'

She would never normally do things like this. Usually she would go over all the introductory questions with their subject, check their responses, and make sure everyone was comfortable before they started filming. But the fact was—on this occasion—they just didn't have the time.

Before he had a chance to object she turned to the camera and gave her widest smile. 'Hi, there, folks. It's Kristie Nelson here, and I'm your host for...' She realised her mistake almost instantly, but no one watching would notice it. Did this guy know he was going to be called a Hot Highland Doc for the next year? Maybe better to keep some things quiet, this was already an uphill struggle.

She was smooth. She'd been doing this too long. '*A Year in the Life of...*' She let her voice tail off and held both hands towards Rhuaridh. 'Our doctor. And here he is, this is Rhuaridh Gillespie and he works on the Isle of Arran. Dr Gillespie, can you tell us a little bit about your background and the work that you do?'

Rhuaridh did his best impression of a deer in the headlights. She gave him a little nudge in the ribs and he actually started.

He stared at the camera. Gerry kept it still while he stuck his head out from behind the viewfinder and mouthed, 'Go,' to him.

Rhuaridh gave the tiniest shudder that Kristie was sure only she could see before he started talking. 'Yes, hi, thanks. I'm Rhuaridh Gillespie. I grew up on this island—Arran—before leaving to train in Glasgow as a doctor, then I've worked in a number of other hospitals, and for Doctors Without Borders. I trained as a GP—a general practitioner—like my father, then came back last year to take over the practice when my father...' he paused for a split second before quickly finding a word '...retired.'

She was surprised. He was doing better than expected, even though he still looked as though he didn't want to be there.

'Can you tell the viewers a little about Arran?' she asked.

'It's an island,' he said, as though she'd just asked a ridiculous question.

She kept the smile firmly in place. 'Can you tell the viewers a little about the people here, and the hospital? What was it like growing up here?' The curses shooting across her brain stayed firmly hidden.

He gave a slow nod as if he finally understood that most people watching wouldn't have a single clue about Arran. 'Growing up here was...' his eyes looked up to the left '...fun. Free. Yeah, as a child I had a lot of freedom. Everyone knows everyone in Arran...' he gave a half-smile '...so there's not much you can get away with. But a normal day was getting on my bike and disappearing into the hillsides with my friends. The lifestyle here is very outdoors.' He gave a small frown. 'Not everyone likes that.'

She wasn't entirely sure what he meant by that but didn't push. 'And the island?' she asked again.

It was almost like his professional face slid back into place. 'The population is around five thousand people, but in the summer months that can quadruple. We have a small cottage hospital with some long-stay beds and a small A and E department. I share the work in the hospital with the other GP on the island.'

'What happens in an emergency?' asked Kristie.

He looked a little uncomfortable. 'If it's a real emergency, then we send the patient off the island by air ambulance. In other circumstances we send people by road ambulance on the ferry and on to the local district general hospital.'

'How long does that take?' She could see a dozen potential stories forming in her head.

Now he was starting to look annoyed. 'The ferry takes around an hour. The transfer from Ardrossan—where the ferry docks—and the local hospital takes around thirty minutes.'

'Wow, that could be dangerous.'

His eyes flashed. 'Not at all. We assess all our patients and make sure they are fit for the transfer before they are sent.'

'What about people needing surgeries or baby emergencies?' She knew there was another word for that but just couldn't think of it.

'Most surgeries are pre-planned and our patients will have made arrangements to go to the mainland. All pregnant women on the island are assessed by both an obstetrician and their midwife. We've had a number of planned home deliveries on the island. Any woman who has a history that would give cause for concern for her, or for her baby, has arrangements made for admission to the mainland hospital to ensure the equipment and staff required are there for her delivery. We haven't had any problems.'

Dull. This place was sounding decidedly dull. All the good stuff—the interesting stuff—got sent to the mainland. But there were a hundred documentary-style shows that covered A and E departments. How on earth was she going to make this show interesting enough for people to keep watching?

She licked her lips and turned to the computer on top of Rhuaridh's case note trolley. 'So, Dr Gillespie, let's go back. Can you tell us about the first patient we'll be seeing?'

She had to keep this moving. Interesting footage seemed to be slipping through her fingers like grains of sand on the cold beach outside. *Please let this get better.*

There was not a single thing about this that he liked. Her American accent was beginning to grate on him. 'Don't mumble' she'd had the cheek to say to him. He'd never mumbled in his life. At least, he didn't think that he had.

That spotlight had been on him as he'd done the ward round in the cottage hospital. Normally it would have taken half an hour, but her incessant questions had slowed him down more than he'd liked.

She'd kept stopping and talking in a quiet voice to her

cameraman and that had irritated him probably a whole lot more than it should have.

He was almost chanting the words in his head. *One more day. One more day.*

One of the nurses from the ward came and found him. 'Rhuaridh, there's been a message left to remind you about your home visit.'

'Darn it.' John Henderson. He still hadn't managed to drop in on him. He shook his head and grabbed his jacket and case.

'What? Where are you going?' Kristie wrinkled her nose. 'What's a home visit anyway?'

He stared at the woman standing under his nose who was almost blocking his way to the exit. He felt guilty. He'd meant to visit John before he came here, but this filming thing had distracted him in a way he hadn't been before.

He snapped, 'It's when you visit someone—at home.' He couldn't help the way he said the words. What on earth else could a home visit be?

Kristie only looked insulted for a few seconds. 'You actually do that here?'

Of course. She was from the US. It was a totally different healthcare system. They generally saw a specialist for everything. Doctors like him—general practitioners who occasionally visited sick patients at home—were unheard of.

'Of course.' He elbowed past her and moved out to his car.

'Let's go,' he heard her squeak to her colleague, and within a few seconds he heard their feet thudding behind him.

He spun around and held up his hand. 'You can't come.'

She tilted her chin upwards obstinately. 'We can.' She

turned her notes towards him. 'John Henderson, he's on the list of patients that granted permission for us to film.'

Of course. Pam had already put a system in place to keep track of all this.

He couldn't really say no—no matter how much he wanted to. He shook his head, resigned to his fate.

'Okay, get in the car but we need to go now.'

They piled into the back of his car and he set off towards the farm where John Henderson lived.

It was almost like she didn't know when to stop talking. Kristie started immediately. 'So, can you brief us on this patient before we get there?'

Rhuaridh gritted his teeth. It was late, he was tired. He didn't want to 'brief' them on John Henderson, the elderly farmer with the biggest range of health problems in the world. He was trying to work out how he hadn't managed to fit John in before the visit to the hospital. He should have. Normally, he would have. But today he'd been—distracted.

And Rhuaridh Gillespie had never been distracted before. Not even when he'd been a junior doctor juggling a hundred tasks.

He didn't speak. He could hear her breathing just behind his ear, leaning forward expectantly and waiting for some kind of answer. Eventually he heard a little sigh of frustration and she must have sat back as the waft of orange blossom scent he'd picked up from her earlier disappeared.

The road to the farm was like every road to a farm on Arran. Winding, dark, with numerous potholes and part way up a hill. This was why he needed the four-by-four.

He pulled up outside the farmhouse and frowned. There was one light inside, in what he knew was the main room. John usually had the place lit up like the Blackpool Illuminations. They liked to joke about it.

He jumped out, not waiting for his entourage to follow, knocking loudly at the front door and only waiting a few seconds before pushing it open.

'John, it's Rhuaridh. Everything okay?'

There was a whimper at his feet and his heart sank as he turned. Mac, John's old sheepdog, usually rushed to meet anyone who appeared at the farm, barking loudly, but now he was whimpering in the hall.

He bent down, rubbed the black and white dog's head. 'What's up, Mac?'

Even as he said the words he had a horrible feeling that he knew what the answer would be.

He was familiar with the old farmhouse, having visited here numerous times in the last few months. Mac stayed at his heels as he walked through to the main room. It was shambolic. Had been for the last few years, ever since John's wife had died and he'd refused any kind of help.

The sofa was old and worn, the rug a little threadbare. A few pictures hung on the walls. But his eyes fixed on the sight he didn't want to see.

'John!' He rushed across the room, already knowing it would make no difference as he knelt on the floor beside the crumpled body of the old man. Mac lay down right next to John, still whimpering as he put his head on John's back.

John's colour was completely dusky. His lips blue. 'Here, boy,' said Rhuaridh gently as he pushed Mac's head away and turned John over onto his back.

His body was still warm, probably thanks to the flickering fire. But there were absolutely no signs of life. No breathing. No heartbeat. He did all the checks he needed to, but it was clear to him that John had died a few hours before.

It didn't matter that this had been on the cards for a number of months. With his cardiac and respiratory disease John had been living on borrowed time for a while.

But the fact was Rhuaridh had loved this old crotchety guy, with his gnarled hands through years of hard work and the well-weathered, lined face.

He looked peaceful now. His face more unlined than Rhuaridh had ever seen it before. Something inside Rhuaridh ached. John had died alone. Something he'd always been afraid of. If Rhuaridh had got here earlier—if he hadn't taken so long over the hospital ward round—he might have made it in time to hold his hand for his last few breaths.

He lifted John's coldish hand and clasped it between both of his. 'I'm sorry,' he whispered before he moved and closed John's eyelids with one finger. He couldn't help the tear he had to brush away. Mac moved back and put his head on John's chest. He hadn't thought it possible for a dog to look quite as sad as Mac did now.

He pulled his phone from his back pocket and made the obligatory phone call. 'Donald, yes, it's Rhuaridh Gillespie. I've just found John Henderson. Yes, I think he's been dead for a couple of hours. You will? Thank you. I'll wait until you get here.'

He sighed and pushed his phone into his pocket then started at the sound behind him.

Gerry had his camera on his shoulder and Kristie was wide-eyed. She looked almost shocked. A wave of anger swept over him. 'Put that away. It's hardly appropriate.'

Gerry pulled the camera to one side. Kristie seemed frozen to the spot. She lifted one shaking hand towards the body on the floor. 'Is...is that it? There's...nothing you can do?' It was the first time her voice hadn't been assured and full of confidence.

'Of course there's nothing I can do,' he snapped. 'John's been dead for the last few hours.'

He didn't add the thoughts that were currently streaming through his brain. *If she hadn't delayed him at the hos-*

pital, maybe he could have been here earlier. If she hadn't distracted him at the doctor's surgery, maybe he would have made John's visit before he went to the hospital.

He knew this was all irrational. But that didn't make it go away.

Gerry's voice broke through his thoughts. 'Do you have to wait for the police?'

Rhuaridh nodded. 'They'll be here in a few minutes, and the undertaker will probably arrive at the same time.'

He turned his attention back to John and knelt down beside him again, resting his hand on John's chest. He felt odd about all of this. They'd stopped filming but it still felt like they were…intruding. And it was he who had brought them here.

Gerry seemed to have a knack of fading into the shadows, but Kristie? She stood out like a sore thumb. Or something else entirely. He'd been around plenty of beautiful, confident women in his life. What was so different about this one? She felt like a permanent itch that had got under his skin. Probably not the nicest description in the world but certainly the most accurate.

She stood to the side with her eyes fixed on the floor at first as his police colleague arrived then Craig, the undertaker. The unfortunate part of being a GP was that for he, and his two colleagues, this was semi-familiar territory.

When at last things were sorted and John's body was ready to be loaded into the undertaker's car, it was almost like the others knew and stepped back for a few seconds.

'What about Mac?' asked Donald, the police officer.

'Right.' For a few seconds Rhuaridh looked around. There was no one to take care of Mac, and they probably all knew that.

He looked over at the dog lying dolefully on the rug, his head on his paws. It didn't matter how impractical. How ridiculous. 'Give me a second.' He moved back over to John's body and slid his hand in to find the keys for the house in John's trouser pocket. Someone would need to lock up.

He stepped back to allow them to take John's body out to the hearse, then moved through to the kitchen and grabbed a bag, stuffing into it the dog's bowl and a few tins of dog food from the cupboard.

Kristie and Gerry were still hanging around in the hallway, Gerry still with the camera resting carelessly on his shoulder.

'You good?' Donald asked as Rhuaridh appeared back out of the kitchen.

He nodded and walked through to the main room. It was almost as if Mac knew because he jumped up and walked over, tail giving a few wags as he wound his body around Rhuaridh's legs.

'Come on then, old guy,' Rhuaridh said as he patted Mac's head. 'Looks like it's you and me.' He bent down and paused for a few seconds, his head next to Mac's. Mac had lived on a farm his whole life. How would he like living in a cottage by the beach? A wave of sympathy and affection flooded through him as he looked at Mac's big brown eyes. Of course he had to take this guy home.

It only took a few moments to put out the fire, flick the lights switches and lock the main door. Mac jumped into the back seat next to Gerry, who seemed quite happy to pat Mac on the drive back.

He dropped them at their rental and sped off into the dark as quickly as he could. His first day of filming couldn't have been worse. 'Please don't let them all be like this,' he murmured to Mac.

Kristie watched the car speed away. Her feet seemed frozen and she didn't even care about the brisk wind blowing around her. After a few seconds, Gerry slung his arm around her shoulders. She'd just seen her second dead body. And she couldn't work out how she felt about that—except numb. It was evoking memories that she just didn't want to recall. The little old man's house had been so... real. A few hours earlier he'd been there, and then he was just...gone.

This was exactly why she hadn't wanted to do this job. It was touching at places she kept firmly hidden, pulling at strings in her memory that she preferred not to remember. She shivered, and it wasn't from the cold.

Gerry looked at the red lights on the now far-off car. 'Funny kind of guy, isn't he?'

Anger surged inside her. 'He's got a contract. They're getting paid well for this.'

Gerry looked at her in amusement and shook his head, taking his hand off her shoulder and instead tapping the camera in his other hand.

'You haven't realised, have you?'

She shook her head. She had no idea what he was talking about.

Gerry smiled. 'That stiff-faced, crotchety doc guise that he's pulling. This? This tears it all apart.' He gave another nod of his head. 'Kristie Nelson, in here, we have TV gold.'

CHAPTER TWO

June

THE FERRY WAS much busier this time. It seemed that hordes
of schoolchildren seemed to be going on some kind of trip.

An older woman sat next to her, sipping a cup of tea.
This time Kristie had been prepared for the ferry crossing, and her anti-sickness tablets seemed to be doing the
trick. The older woman smiled. 'There's an outdoor centre. They're all going there to stay for a week. I guarantee
tonight not one of them will sleep. But after their first day
on Arran tomorrow, they'll all be sleeping by nine o'clock.'

Kristie nodded half-heartedly. She wasn't really paying
attention. Last night she'd watched the edited first show
about the Hot Highland Doc.

For want of a better word—it had been dynamite.

The editing had helped, showing the crabbit doctor—a
definitely unwilling participant in the show—turning to a
melting puddle of emotion at the death of his elderly patient. The final shot that Gerry had sneaked of him connecting with Mac the dog and saying the words, 'Looks
like it's just you and me,' would melt the proverbial hearts
of the nation when it was shown in a few weeks.

Louie couldn't contain his excitement. 'Play on the fact
he doesn't like you.'

Kristie had been a bit stung. 'What do you mean, he

doesn't like me?' She hadn't realised it was quite so obvious to anyone but her.

'The audience will love it. You against him. The sparks are tremendous.'

Kristie bit her bottom lip as the announcement came for them all to head to their cars. Last time she'd been desperate to capture anything on camera.

This time around she felt the pressure. The producers didn't just like it, they *loved* it. Apparently the limited footage they'd captured had been the most entertaining—in a heart-wrenching kind of way—of any of the other *Year in the Life of* shows. They hadn't, of course, shown John Henderson. Gerry had filmed Rhuaridh from the back, leaning over the body, without revealing anything about the identity of the patient.

He'd also filmed 'around' Rhuaridh, capturing the essence of the home and the situation, with a particular focus on Mac, and how the professionals had dealt with everything, without sticking the camera in their faces. Kristie was a tiny bit nervous what people would think about it when it finally aired—but she knew it had squeezed at even her heart.

She climbed into the car with Gerry and gave him a nod, handing him a schedule. 'I've had time to be in touch a bit more. We're spending some time in the A and E department in the cottage hospital and filming one of the regular surgeries this time.'

He gave a nod. 'Here's hoping we get something good.' He raised one eyebrow. 'No pressure, of course.'

She shot him a glare. He was being sarcastic, of course. 'Where are we staying?'

Gerry wrinkled his nose. 'We've got a bed and breakfast this time—just down the road from the surgery.' His eyes twinkled. 'Guess we won't need to live on cereal for three days this time.'

She laughed. Neither she nor Gerry was blessed with cooking skills. 'I've decided. We're eating out every night and putting it on expenses.'

He nodded in agreement, 'Oh, I can live with that.'

They settled into the bed and breakfast quickly and made their way to the surgery for their scheduled filming. It was obvious news had spread since the last time they'd been there as a number of the patients sitting in the waiting room started talking to them as soon as they appeared.

'Are you the TV people?'

'Do you want to film me?'

'When will I be on TV?'

'Oh, you're here.' Her head shot up. It was hardly the most welcoming statement. Rhuaridh was standing in the doorway of his surgery dressed in a white shirt and navy trousers. It looked like he'd caught the sun in the last few days as his skin was more tanned than before.

Her first instinct was to hear a wolf whistle in her head. If her friend Alice had been here she was sure she would have actually done it in real life. One thing was for sure—Rhuaridh Gillespie was like a good old-fashioned prom king standing right in front of her.

But then her mouth dried. For a few seconds all she could remember was how she'd felt last time she'd been around him and he'd been dealing with Mr Henderson's dead body. She tried so hard not to let the others notice her reaction. Of course, Gerry had picked up on it. But he hadn't asked any questions.

The surgery filming went fine. For the first few patients it was obvious Rhuaridh wasn't a natural in front of the camera. Eventually, though, he seemed to forget they were there. But filming blood-pressure checks, medicine reviews, chest infections and leg ulcers didn't exactly make scintillating viewing. Kristie could feel a small wave of panic start to build inside.

By the time the day had come to an end she wasn't sure they had enough for even ten minutes of not very interesting film. She was just about to clarify their arrangements for the next day when Rhuaridh's pager sounded.

He looked just as surprised as she did. He hadn't been wearing one the last time she'd been there. A deep frown creased his forehead. It took him a few seconds to look up and speak once he'd checked the message. He gave his head a little shake. 'I thought it was for the local lifeboat… but it's not…it's Magda.'

He looked around his room blankly for a few seconds. Was this a sign of panic? She would never have suspected it from Rhuaridh Gillespie—and who on earth was Magda? A wife? A girlfriend? He hadn't mentioned either last time and she couldn't help but be a tiny bit disappointed. Within another few seconds the look was gone. He strode quickly across the waiting room, grabbing his bag. Kristie stayed on his heels, waving Gerry to follow. If this was something good, she wanted to make sure they didn't miss it.

He shot her a glance as she opened the back door of his car to climb inside. She saw the words form on his lips—the words of dismissal—but she completely ignored him, turning to shout to Gerry instead, 'Let's go!'

It seemed for Rhuaridh it wasn't worth the time involved in fighting. Gerry had barely slammed the door before he took off at speed onto the main road in Lamlash. As they started to drive, his phone started ringing. He answered with a press on his steering wheel. 'Miriam, are you with her?'

'Of course. How far away are you?'

'Less than two minutes.'

'Good.' The phone went dead.

Kristie was immediately intrigued. 'Who are you visiting?'

Rhuaridh's jaw was clenched. 'My colleague, Magda. She's planned for a home delivery but things are looking complicated.'

Gerry shot her a look. There was a gleam in his eye. This would be more interesting filming than what they'd already got.

Kristie tried her best to phrase the question carefully. She obviously wanted the footage—but didn't want to get in the way if something could go wrong. Even she had a line that wouldn't be crossed.

'We didn't get to meet your colleague,' she started.

Rhuaridh cut her off. 'You should have—she was the one who signed up for the show. Her pregnancy was an unexpected but very happy event.'

Gerry gave her a thumbs-up in the back of the car. If Magda had initially signed for the show, she might not object to being filmed. There was something in the way Rhuaridh said the words. He had an obvious affection for his colleague.

They pulled up outside a large white house at the end of a long driveway. The front door was open and Kristie gestured to Gerry to get his camera on his shoulder ready to film.

They jumped out of the car and she hesitated as she heard the voices inside.

'Don't panic, Magda, let's get you out right now and I'll attach a CTG to monitor the baby. Now take a deep breath and try not to worry.'

She glanced at Gerry. Yip. He was already filming, capturing the sound inside.

Rhuaridh strode straight inside. Then stopped dead, meaning Kristie walked into the back of him.

'Oh, sorry.'

The main room of the house appeared to have undergone a complete transformation for the delivery of this baby. Right in the centre of the room was a large birthing pool. Soothing music was playing in the background, the blinds were closed and there were a few lit candles.

A heavily pregnant woman with blonde hair and a black loose wet kaftan was being helped from the pool by a worried-looking man and an older woman.

The woman looked up. 'Give me a hand, Rhuaridh.'

He stepped over quickly, taking the woman's place as she dropped to her knees and pulled a small monitor from a black case.

They eased Magda down onto the nearby sofa. Obviously no one was worried about getting it entirely wet.

'Tell me what's happening,' said Rhuaridh.

Kristie was tempted to clear her throat and remind them all that two perfect strangers were in the room, but the woman she thought was Magda looked up and waved her hand in a throwaway manner. 'Carry on,' she said as she grimaced.

'Another one?' asked the woman quickly.

Magda nodded and gripped tightly onto the man Kristie suspected was her husband.

Rhuaridh finally seemed to remember they were there. He pointed at his friends. 'Magda, David, Miriam, this is Kristie and Gerry from the TV show.'

Since Magda had already waved her hand in permission it seemed like he didn't feel the need to say anything else.

Kristie could see the way that David was looking at Rhuaridh. It was odd. She was brand new to these people but could already see a world of emotion without hearing any words. David was holding back panic, Magda had an edge of fear about her, and Miriam—who must be the midwife—had her professional face in place, while worry seemed etched on the lines on her forehead.

Rhuaridh knelt by the sofa and held Magda's hand. 'I thought you had this planned to precision.'

She patted her stomach, keeping her eyes firmly fixed on Miriam's actions as she attached the monitor. 'It seems Baby Price has his or her own plans.'

Miriam spoke in a low voice as she made the final adjustments. 'Spontaneous rupture of membrane a few hours ago. Labour has been progressing well with no concerns. Magda's around eight centimetres dilated, but she feels baby has stopped moving in the last ten minutes.'

'It's a boy,' said Rhuaridh. 'He's having a little sleep before the big event.' The hoarseness in his voice gripped Kristie around the chest. He was worried. He was worried about his friend's baby.

Magda tutted. 'We don't know it's a boy. We want a surprise.'

She was scared to make eye contact with Gerry. This was beginning to feel like a bad idea. An old man tragedy she'd almost been able to bear. Anything with a baby? No way.

Miriam flicked the switch and the monitor flickered to life. After a few seconds a noise filled the room. Kristie almost let out a cheer. Even she could recognise the sound of a heartbeat.

But the rest of the room didn't seem quite so joyous. Magda clenched her teeth as she was obviously gripped with a new contraction.

All other eyes in the room seemed fixed on the monitor. Kristie leaned forward, trying to see the number on the screen. Ninety, wasn't that good?

'What's happening?' asked Magda.

There was sense in the room of collective breath-holding. The numbers on the screen and the corresponding beat noises crept upwards.

Rhuaridh and Miriam whispered almost in unison. 'Cord prolapse.'

This was all way above Kristie's head.

Magda let out a small squeak of desperation. 'No.' As a doctor it seemed she knew exactly what that could mean even if Kristie didn't.

Rhuaridh pulled out his phone and dialled. 'Air ambulance. Obstetric emergency.' His voice was low and calm. He moved over to the corner of the room where Kristie couldn't hear him any more. By the time he'd finished, David had walked towards him.

'Tell me what's happening.'

Rhuaridh nodded. 'The cord is coming down the birth canal before, or adjacent to, the baby. It means that every time Magda has a contraction, there's a risk the cord can be compressed and affect the blood flow to your baby.'

'Our baby could die?' David's words were little more than a squeak.

Rhuaridh shook his head, but Kristie could see the tense muscles at the bottom of his neck. The tiny hairs prickled on her skin. She was useless here—no help whatsoever. What did she know about medical emergencies?

She walked over to the window and looked outside, putting her hands on her hips and taking a few breaths.

The midwife's voice cut across momentary panic. 'Magda, we're going to change your position. Kristie!' The voice was sharp—one you wouldn't hesitate to follow. 'Run upstairs to the bedroom and grab me all the pillows on the bed.'

Rhuaridh finished his call and moved over to help move Magda onto her side. Kristie did exactly what she'd been told and dashed up the stairs in the house, turning one way then the other until she found the room with the large double bed and grabbed every pillow on it. She paused for the briefest of seconds as her eyes focused on the little white Moses basket at the side of the bed. The basket that had been placed there with the hope and expectation of a beautiful baby.

She held back the sob in her throat as she ran back down the stairs and thrust the pillows towards Rhuaridh. He and Miriam moved in unison. Rhuaridh spoke in a low voice as he helped adjust Magda's position with some pillows under her left flank and her right knee and thigh pulled up towards her chest. 'The position is supposed to alleviate pressure on the umbilical cord.' His words were quiet and Kristie wasn't sure if he was explaining to her or to David.

Magda's hands were trembling slightly. She was scared and Kristie's heart went out to her. How must this feel? All of a sudden this felt like a real intrusion instead of a filming opportunity. How dared they be there right now?

Rhuaridh's gaze connected with hers. She wasn't quite sure what she was reading there. His voice seemed a little steely. 'Gerry, the air ambulance will land in the field next to the house—you might want to get that.' Gerry nodded and was gone in the blink of an eye.

She was still looking at those bright blue eyes, trying to control the overwhelming sensation of being utterly useless in a situation completely out of her area of expertise. Right now all she could do was send up a prayer that both Magda and this baby would be fine. It was amazing how quickly a set of circumstances could envelop you. Was this what every day was like for a doctor?

All of a sudden she had a new understanding of her grumpy doctor. This was a situation he could end up in any day, and today it involved a friend. She could almost sense the history in the room between them all. The longstanding friendship, along with the expectations. If something happened to Magda or this baby, things would never be the same again.

The monitor for the baby kept pinging. At least that was reassuring. Miriam and Rhuaridh had a conversation about whether another examination should be carried out. Both agreed not, though Kristie averted her gaze while

Miriam did a quick visual check to reassure that no cord was protruding.

Rhuaridh moved over next to her and she caught a whiff of his woody aftershave. 'What's gone wrong?' Kristie whispered. Magda was holding her husband's hand, her eyes fixed on the monitor that showed the baby's heartbeat.

Rhuaridh spoke in a low, quiet voice. 'Magda wasn't at high risk for anything. She'd planned for this home birth within an inch of her life. Cord prolapse is unusual, and Magda has no apparent risk factors. But, right now, every time she has a contraction, the baby's heartbeat goes down, meaning the cord is being compressed.'

'Can't you do anything?'

He shook his head. 'The cord isn't obviously protruding, so we just need to get Magda to hospital as soon as possible. This baby needs to be delivered and Magda will need to have a Caesarean section.' He ran his hand through his hair, the frustration on his face evident. 'We just don't have the facilities here for that—or the expertise.'

'How long does the air ambulance take to get here?'

'Usually not long,' he said, then looked upwards as a thud-thud-thud noise could be heard in the distance.

Kristie's heart started thudding in her chest. Maybe everything was actually going to be okay?

Magda let out a groan, and Kristie held her breath as she watched Rhuaridh and Miriam move to support her as she was hit by another contraction. All eyes were on the monitor, and although the heart rate went down, it didn't go down quite as much as it had before.

Rhuaridh glanced towards the door a few times. Kristie could see him weighing up whether to ask David to go and meet the crew or whether to go himself.

After a few seconds he squeezed Magda's hand. 'Give me a minute.' Then he jogged out the main door and across towards the field. Kristie couldn't help but follow him.

Gerry had positioned himself outside to capture the landing and the crew emerging from the helicopter.

They didn't waste any time. Within a few minutes Rhuaridh and Miriam had helped keep Magda into the correct position as they assisted her onto the trolley. The CTG monitor was swapped over for another and then Magda and David disappeared inside the helicopter before it lifted off into the air.

They all stood watching the helicopter disappear into the distance, Gerry with his camera firmly on his shoulder.

Once the helicopter finally vanished from view there were a few moments of awkward silence. They all turned and looked at the open door of the house. Miriam was first to move, walking back into the house, putting her hands on her hips and taking a deep breath.

The space felt huge and empty without Magda. The birthing pool lay with only its rippling water, monitors, blood-pressure cuff, the midwife's case and Rhuaridh's, all alongside the normal family furnishings. Pictures of David and Magda on their wedding day. The sofa with the now squelchy cushions. A multitude of towels.

'I guess we'd better clean up,' said Kristie.

She wasn't quite sure where that had come from. Cleaning up was definitely not her forte.

She bent down and lifted one of the sofa cushions, wondering if she should take it to the kitchen to try and clean it off and dry it out.

Miriam had started picking up all the midwifery equipment.

Rhuaridh appeared in front of her and grabbed the cushion. 'Leave it. We'll get it. You should just go.'

She blinked. Wondered what on earth she'd just done wrong. She'd just witnessed a scene that had almost made her blood run cold. Had she ever been as scared as this?

Yes. Probably. But that part of her brain was compart-

mentalised and knowingly put away. It was better that way.
It felt safer that way. The only time she let little parts of it
emerge was when she volunteered three nights a month on
the helpline. It was the only time she let down her guard.
Virtually no one knew about that part of her life. Louie
did. He'd been there for her when she'd got the original
phone call telling her to come to the hospital. Gerry had
been there too.

Louie had held her hand in the waiting room. He'd put
an arm around her when she'd been given the news, and
he'd stood at the door as she'd had to go and identify her
sister's body.

Her beautiful, gorgeous, fun-loving sister. She almost
hadn't recognised her on the table. Her skin had been
pale with an ugly purple mark on her neck. When she'd
touched her sister's hand it had been cold and stiff. The
scars on her sister's wrists and inside her elbows had taken
her breath away.

Everything had been new to her. She'd had no idea
about the self-harm. She'd had no idea her sister had been
depressed. Jess had hidden all of this from her—to all
intents from everyone. It had only been a long time afterwards when she'd been left to empty her sister's apartment and go through her things that she'd discovered a
frequently phoned number that was unfamiliar. The thing
that had pricked her attention most had been the number
of times that Jess had phoned—and yet had disconnected
the calls in under a minute. That's when she'd discovered
the helpline.

It was situated in their city and manned by counsellors
and trained mental health professionals, staffed twenty-
four hours a day. One visit to the centre had made her
realise she had to try and help too. She'd undergone her
training, and now manned the phone lines three nights a
month. The small hours of the morning were sometimes

the busiest in the call centre. She'd learned when to talk, and when not to. She'd learned that sometimes people just wanted to know that someone had heard them cry. Had *heard* them at all.

It always took her back to the fact that she wished Jess had stayed on the line a little longer—just once. It might have made the difference. It might have let her know she was safe to confide how she was feeling and didn't have to hide it.

Occasionally she would get a flashback to part of that first night. Hospitals were a place she'd generally avoided ever since, associating the sights and sounds with the memories of that night. It was part of the reason she'd been reluctant about this gig.

But now she was realising it was something more. Last month, with John Henderson's body, and this time, when she'd glanced at the cot upstairs—patiently waiting for its baby—she'd felt a sweep of something else. Pure and utter dread. The kind that made her heart beat faster and her breathing kind of funny.

Her heart had sunk as the helicopter had disappeared into the distance, not knowing what the outcome would be for Magda and the baby. She didn't care about the show right now. She didn't care about anything.

And all that she could see was this great hulking man standing in front of her with the strangest expression on his face. His hands brushed against hers as he closed them around the cushion, gripping it.

He gave a tug towards himself. 'I think it would be best if you go now.'

She couldn't understand. 'But the room…' She let go of the cushion and held out her hands, looking over at the birthing pool and wondering how on earth it would be emptied and taken down. 'You'll need help to clean up.'

She wanted distraction. She wanted something else to

think about. Anything to keep her mind busy until there was news about mother and baby.

'I'm sure Magda and David would prefer that their house be fixed up by friends.' He emphasised the word so strongly that she took a step backwards and stumbled, putting a steadying hand on the window frame behind her.

It was then she saw it. The flash across his face. He needed distraction just as much as she did. Probably more. He must be worried sick. Of course he was.

She'd only just met this pregnant woman. He'd known her for—how long? She wouldn't even like to guess. She knew they'd been workmates in the practice but she hadn't really had a chance to hear much more.

'I want you to go now,' he said as he turned away. 'We'll let you know how things are.'

It was a dismissal. Blunt. She wanted to grab him by the arm and yank him around, ask him who he thought he was talking to. In another life she might have.

But if she fell out with Dr Gillespie the whole show could be up in the air. So instead she pressed her lips together and looked around for her bag, grabbing it and throwing it over her shoulder, walking out the room and leaving the disarray behind her.

Gerry was standing at the door. She didn't care if the camera was on or not. 'I hate him,' she hissed in a low voice as she walked past.

Rhuaridh knew he'd just been unreasonable. He knew that Magda had agreed to the TV crew filming. But none of them had expected the outcome that had just happened.

His heart felt twisted in a hard, angry knot. Every possible scenario was running through his head right now—and not all of them were good.

He wasn't an obstetrician. The limited experience he'd had had been gained when he'd been a junior doctor. He knew the basics. He knew the basics of a lot of things. But island communities were different from most. The water cut them off from the mainland. There was no quick road to a hospital with a whole variety of specialists and equipment at his disposal.

In the last few months there had been a mountain climber with a severe head injury, a few elderly residents with hip fractures, a diver with decompression sickness, and now an obstetric emergency. All situations where he'd felt helpless—useless even. He hated that his patients needed to wait for either a ferry crossing or an air ambulance to take them where they could get the help required. He hated that he had to stand and look into their eyes, knowing that on occasion that help might actually be too late. And today, when it had been his friend and colleague, he had felt as though he was being gripped around the chest by a vice.

He'd snapped needlessly at Kristie. He knew that. But he just couldn't think beyond what would happen next for Magda, David and the baby. And until he knew that, he didn't know what came next.

Guilt swamped him. 'Kristie, wait,' he shouted as he walked out after her.

She spun around towards him. The expression in her eyes told him everything he needed to know. She was every bit as panicked and worried as he was. She was also mad. And no wonder. He knew better than to act like this. He walked over and put a hand on her shoulder. 'I'm sorry,' he said quickly. 'I'm just worried.' He glanced up at the sky. The helicopter was well out of sight. He prayed things would go well. 'I didn't mean to snap. And thank you for your help in there. I just feel so…' He struggled to say the word out loud, not really wanting to admit it.

'Helpless?' Kristie added without hesitation. He could

see her eyes searching his face. Wondering if he would agree.

He closed his eyes for a second and nodded as the rush of adrenalin seemed to leave his body all at once. 'Helpless,' he agreed with a sigh. 'I won't be able to think about another thing until I know they're both okay.'

'Neither will I,' she said quickly. Should he really be surprised? It was the first real time since she'd got here that he'd taken the time to really look at her, *really* see something other than the bolshie American TV presenter. There was something there. Something he couldn't quite put his finger on.

Her hand reached across her chest and covered the hand he had on her shoulder. He felt a jolt. It must be the warmth of her palm against his cold skin. She licked her bare lips. All her makeup had disappeared in the last few hours. She didn't need it. Something sparked in his brain. Had he really just thought that?

She squeezed his hand and spoke quietly as she held his gaze. 'Let's just do the only thing we can. Pray.'

His stomach gave a gentle flip as he nodded in agreement and looked back up at the sky. He pushed everything else away. Magda and the baby were all he could concentrate on right now. Anything else could wait.

CHAPTER THREE

July

PEOPLE WERE LOOKING at him a bit strangely, and he couldn't quite work out why. And it wasn't just the people he knew. Summer holidays had well and truly started and, as normal, the island's population had grown, bringing a stream of holidaymakers with minor complaints and medical issues to the island's GP surgery. This meant that he now had a whole host of strangers giving him strange sideways glances that turned into odd smiles.

It took one older lady with a chest infection to reveal the source.

'You're the handsome doc I saw on TV,' she said.

'What?' He was sounding the woman's chest at that point, paying attention to the auscultations of her lungs instead of to her voice.

She gave a loud tut then giggled. 'You really don't like that poor girl, do you?'

He pulled the stethoscope from his ears. 'Excuse me?'

'The pretty one. With the blonde hair. She looked shell-shocked by that death.' The woman leaned over and patted his hand. 'I'm sorry about your friend. How's Mac?'

For a few moments, Rhuaridh was stunned. Then the penny dropped like a cannonball on his head.

'You've seen the TV show?' He hadn't really paid attention to when it would air.

She grinned. 'Yes. It was wonderful. Best episode of that series yet.' She gave him a sideways glance and raised her eyebrows. 'And, yep, it's probably fair that they call you hot. But you really need to behave a bit better.'

He wasn't really paying attention to all her words. 'What do you mean—the death?'

She frowned at him, as though he were a little dense. 'Your friend. The farmer.'

'They showed that?' He felt a surge of anger. How dared they?

The old woman shook her head. 'Well, we didn't really see anything much at all. Just a pair of feet. Nothing else. It was more about...' she held her hands up to her crackly chest '...the feelings, the emotions. The love in the room.' She gave a wicked little shrug. 'And the tension. Like I said, you need to be nicer to that girl. She's very pretty, you know. She looked as though she could have done with a hug.'

Rhuaridh sat back in his chair. He was stunned. He'd kind of thought the TV show would only be shown in other countries—not this one. He hadn't expected people he met to have seen it. And he wasn't happy they'd shown the events at John Henderson's house.

The old woman sat back and folded her hands in her lap. 'Mind you, you brought a tear to my eye when you took Mac home with you. How is he, anyway? You didn't answer.'

It was almost like he was being told off. It seemed that parts of his life were now open to public view and scrutiny. Part of him wanted to see the episode—to check it didn't betray John Henderson's memory. But part of him dreaded to see himself on screen. It seemed like he might not have done himself any favours. His insides cringed.

'Mac's good,' he said on autopilot as his brain continued to whirl. 'He's settled in well.'

The old woman gave another tut and looked at him as though he didn't really know what he was doing. 'Well, are you going to write me a prescription or not? Erythromycin, please. It always works best.'

Rhuaridh picked up his prescription pad and pen. This was going to be a long, long day.

The boat was packed to the brim. There was literally not a single seat to be had, and it was lucky someone at the production company had pre-booked their car space and their rental. 'What is it?' said Gerry. 'Has the whole of mainland Scotland decided to visit the island at once?'

'Feels like it,' muttered Kristie as she was jostled by a crowd of holidaymakers. At least the sun was high in the sky and she'd remembered to take her sea sickness tablets.

She leaned on the rail as the ferry started to dock. 'The reception's been good hasn't it?'

Gerry nodded. 'I've not seen this much excitement in a while. And once they've seen the second episode? I think people will go crazy.'

Kristie blew out a long breath. The next episode was due to air in a few weeks. It was ironic really. The first episode had been all about death, and now the second was all about life. They'd improvised. Once they'd left the island, instead of heading straight back to Glasgow airport, they'd driven to the local maternity unit where they'd got Magda's permission to capture a scene with a beautiful healthy baby girl and two relieved, smiling parents. Even Kristie couldn't hide the tears at that point. But it had captured the story perfectly, and would give the viewers the happy ending they would all crave.

'What about me?' she asked Gerry. 'And what about him, what if he sees me saying I hate him?' Her stomach

twisted uncomfortably. The producer had insisted on keeping all those elements in, saying the dynamics between
her and Rhuaridh Gillespie were TV gold.

Gerry waved his hand as the gangplank was lowered
and people started filing off the boat. 'I doubt he's seen
it. And if he has? Too bad.'

They made their way down to the car. The car storage area was hot and claustrophobic. Gerry shrugged off
his jacket and tugged at his shirt. 'You okay?' she asked.

He nodded. 'Just get me out into the fresh air.'

The plans were a little different this time. They'd agreed
to focus more on Rhuaridh's role at the hospital rather
than his role at the GP surgery. It seemed harsh, but if
they hadn't had the drama with the delivery for the last
episode things might have been a little dry.

But for the first day they were going to do some background filming around the hospital. Kristie wasn't sure
how that would work out. Or how interesting it would be.
At least this time she felt a little prepared and didn't dread
it quite so much.

But she shouldn't have worried. The seventeen patients
in the cottage hospital were delighted to see her and partic-
ipate in the filming. She met an army war veteran who had
dozens of naughty stories that had her wiping tears from
her eyes. She met a young girl who was in the midst of
cancer treatment who'd come down with an infection and
was bribing the hospital kitchen staff to make her chocolate pancakes. She interviewed the hospital porter, who
was eighty and refused to retire. She met a biker who'd
come off his bike and fractured his femur. But he'd timed
it just as a visiting orthopaedic consultant was doing his
monthly clinic on Arran, so had had his surgery performed
in the equipped theatre a few hours later.

All this filming without having to deal with Dr
Grumpy—as Kristie had nicknamed him.

* * *

They'd arranged filming for a little later the next day as they'd been warned the local A and E could be quieter in the mornings. As they pulled up in the hospital car park they could already spot Rhuaridh's car—along with a whole host of others. 'I take it Friday afternoon is a busy time,' said Gerry as they got out of the car.

Kristie shrugged. 'We're trying to get away from the mundane. He's on call all weekend, so maybe we'll get something unusual.'

As they walked inside Gerry almost tripped. The waiting room was almost as busy as yesterday's ferry. He smiled. 'We might be lucky.'

Kristie looked around. 'Let's interview a few of the people waiting,' she said. The waiting room was full of a range of people. There looked like a whole host of bumps and breaks. A few kids had large eggs on their foreheads, others were holding arms a little awkwardly. Legs were on chairs, and some people were sleeping.

It didn't take long for Rhuaridh to spot them in the waiting room. His perpetual frown creased his forehead, then it was almost like he realised that had happened and he pushed his shoulders back and forced a smile on to his face. 'Kristie, Gerry, come through.'

The normally relatively quiet A and E department was buzzing inside. Names were written on a whiteboard, with times next to them. Three nurses and one advanced nurse practitioner were dealing with patients in the various cubicles.

The charge nurse, June, gave Kristie and Gerry a rundown of what was happening. She motioned to a set of rooms. 'Welcome to the conveyor belt.'

'What do you mean?'

June smiled. 'I mean that slips, fractures and falls are our biggest issue today. Everyone in the waiting room has already been assessed. We generally deal with the kids first, unless something is life threatening, then, if need be, an adult can jump the queue. But most of the people outside are waiting for X-rays, and quite a large proportion of them will go on to need a cast.' She pointed to a room that was deemed the 'plaster room' where one nurse, dressed in an apron, was applying a lightweight coloured fibreglass cast to a kid's wrist. There was another child with a similar injury already waiting outside to go in next.

Another nurse nodded on the way past. 'And I have all the head injuries. So far, nothing serious. But I have four kids and two adults to do neuro obs on for the next few hours.'

Rhuaridh walked up and touched Kristie's arm. 'Do you want to come and film a kid's assessment? He's probably got a broken wrist too, but you could capture the story from start to finish—probably in under an hour.'

Kristie couldn't hide her surprise at his consideration. She exchanged glances with Gerry. 'Well, yeah, that would be great, thanks.'

She was hoping that outwardly her calm, casual demeanour had not shifted. In truth, she could feel the beads of perspiration snaking down her back.

It was stupid. She knew it was stupid. But the A and E department was different from the ward. There was something about the smell of these places. That mix of antiseptic and bleach that sent a tell-tale shiver down her spine. She was counting her breathing in her head, allowing herself to focus on the children around her, rather than let any memories sneak out from inside.

It was working, for the most part, just as long as no one accidentally put their hand on her back and felt the damp spot.

Gerry filmed as they watched the assessment of the little boy, Robbie, who'd fallen off his bike and stuck his hand out to save his fall. Rhuaridh's initial hunch had been correct. It was a fracture that was correctable with a cast and wouldn't require surgery. He even went as far as to relieve Pam in the plaster room and put on the blue fibreglass cast himself.

As he washed his hands and the others left the room, Kristie couldn't help but ask the question that was playing around in her head.

'Why are you being so nice this time?'

He gave a cough, which turned into a bit of a splutter. 'You mean I'm not always nice?'

She choked, and tried to cover that with a cough too. By the time her eyes met his he was actually smiling. He was teasing her.

She put one hand on her hip and tilted her head. 'Okay, so you obviously know that you haven't been. What gives?'

'What gives?'

She nodded and folded her hands over her chest. She couldn't help her distinctly American expressions. It wasn't as if he didn't use enough Scottish ones of his own. Half the time she felt as if he should come with a dictionary. 'What are you up to, and why have you decided to play nice?'

He finished drying his hands and turned to face her head on. Today he was dressed a little more casually. A short-sleeved striped casual shirt and a pair of jeans.

'Someone gave me a telling-off.'

'Who?' Now she was definitely curious.

'An older woman who came to the surgery this morning. She basically told me to behave. I haven't been told that since I was six.'

She shook her head. 'I don't believe that for a second.'

He paused for a second, as if he was trying to find the right words. 'We need to talk about what's been filmed—

what it's right for you to show. But there's something else first.'

She'd just started to relax a little, but those words—'what it's right for you to show'—immediately raised her hackles. She didn't like anyone telling her what to do.

She couldn't help her short answer. 'What do you mean—what it's right for us to show?' Part of her brain knew the answer to this already. She'd had a few tiny reservations about the filming at John Henderson's house. But it had just felt too important—too big—to leave out.

She was automatically being defensive, even though she knew she might partly be in the wrong. She'd wanted to pick up the phone—not to ask his permission, just to give him a heads-up. But even though she hadn't done that, something inside her now just wouldn't let her back down. What was it with this guy? It was like he'd drawn her in, almost made her laugh, just so she might let her guard down a little then he could get into a fight with her.

The tone of her voice had obviously annoyed Rhuaridh. The smile dropped from his face and he straightened more. 'I haven't seen it,' he said sharply. 'But I'm not sure I approve of you showing film of John Henderson's death. It seems…' a crease appeared in his brow as he tried to search for the correct word '…intrusive, unnecessary.' He shook his head. 'You didn't have the correct permissions.'

Every word seemed like a prickle on her skin. 'We got permission from Mr Henderson before we visited his home, *before* he died.'

She didn't mean to emphasise the word, but she was all fired up. And as soon as the words left her mouth she realised her mistake.

The look that passed over Rhuaridh's face was unmistakeable. Complete and utter guilt. It was almost like her mouth wouldn't stop working. It was like he'd questioned her integrity and her ethics. She wouldn't let anyone get away with that. Parts of her brain were telling her to stop and think, but her mouth wasn't paying any attention to those parts.

'And we shot everything from the back. You obscured the view of Mr Henderson. The only thing that was seen was his feet. Do you really think we'd show a poor dead man on the TV show?'

'You shouldn't have shown anything at all,' snapped Rhuaridh. 'You might have gained John's permission, but to show him after he died, that's just ghoulish!'

She folded her arms across her chest. 'Don't you dare question the integrity of the show. You admitted yourself you haven't seen it—you don't even know the context in which the scenes were shown.'

'The integrity of the show? You showed a dead man!' His voice was getting louder.

'We didn't!' she shouted back. 'And you have no idea how the public reacted to it. They loved it. They didn't think it was ghoulish. They thought it was wonderful. Emotional. And sad. The whole purpose of this show is to show them something real. You can't get much more real than death.'

Those words seem to bubble up from somewhere unexpected inside her. They came out harshly, because that's what death was to her. She could remember every emotion, every thought, every feeling that had encompassed her when she'd been in that hospital room. All the things she'd been trying to keep locked in a box, deep down inside her.

For the briefest of seconds Rhuaridh looked a bit taken aback. But it seemed he was every bit as defensive as she was. 'Death is private. Death is something that shouldn't be shown in a TV show.' He stepped forward. 'If the same thing had happened to Magda's baby, would you show that too?'

His words almost took her breath away. It was the first time she'd stuttered since she'd been around him. 'W-what? N-no.' She shook her head fiercely. 'No. Of course not. What kind of people do you think we are?'

'The kind of people who intrude in others' lives, constantly looking for a story.'

An uncomfortable shiver shot down her spine. It was almost like Rhuaridh had been in the room with Louie when he'd been telling her to find a story, make a story, stir up a story to keep their part of the show the most popular. Now she was just cross.

'Why did you agree to do this anyway? You obviously don't want to be filmed. You couldn't make it any more apparent that you don't want us here. Haven't you ever watched any of the reality TV shows based in hospitals before? What did you actually expect to happen?'

He put his hand to his chest. '*I* didn't agree to this. Magda did. I had less than ten minutes' notice that you were coming. And I couldn't exactly say no, because my pregnant colleague had already signed the contract and negotiated a new X-ray machine for our department. So don't make the mistake that any of this was my idea. And what makes you think for a second I've watched any reality TV shows?' He almost spat those last words out.

The words burned her—as if what she was doing was ridiculous and worthless. Everything about this guy just seemed to rile her up in a way she'd never felt before. 'Do you think it's fun being around a guy all day who treats you like something on the bottom of their shoe?'

The A and E charge nurse, June, walked into the room. 'What on earth is going on in here? I could hear you guys at the bottom of the corridor. This is a hospital, not some kind of school playground.'

It was clear that June wasn't one to mince her words. Heat rushed into Kristie's cheeks. How humiliating. She opened her mouth to apologise but June had automatically turned on Rhuaridh.

'This isn't like you. Why on earth are you treating Kristie like this? She's only here doing a job and she spent most of yesterday on the ward talking to all the patients. They loved her. They want her to come back.'

Rhuaridh had the good grace to look embarrassed. He hung his head. It was almost odd seeing him like that, his hands on his hips and his gaze downward. He gave a low-voiced response. 'Sorry, June. We're having a bit of a difference of opinion.'

'I'll say you are. This is my A and E department and if you can't play nicely together I'll just separate you. Kristie? I hope you like kids. We've got a few in the room down the corridor who all need some kind of treatment—I've checked with the parents and you can film. Rhuaridh, I've got a potential case of appendicitis I need you to review and a couple of X-rays for you to look at.' She looked at them both. 'Now, hop to it. I've got a department to run.' June turned on her heel and strode back out the door.

For a few seconds there was silence—as if both of them were getting over their outbursts. Rhuaridh spoke first. 'You wouldn't guess she was the mother of twins, would you?'

It was so not what she'd expected to hear, and unexpected laughter bubbled at the back of her throat.

It broke the tension in the room between them.

'I'm sorry,' he continued. 'I haven't been so hospitable and I know that. I guess I felt backed into a corner. This show isn't something I would have agreed to—certainly never have volunteered for. But I can't say no. The hospital needs the new X-ray machine. You can tell that alone just by the waiting room today.' He gave a slow shake of his head as the corners of his lips actually turned upwards. 'And you seem to have really bad timing.'

She let out a laugh. 'What?'

He kept shaking his head. 'I'm beginning to wonder if you're a jinx. First the thing with John Henderson, then the thing with Magda. You always seem to be around when there's a crisis.'

'You mean you never had any crises on Arran until we started filming?' She deliberately phrased the question so he'd realise he was being ridiculous.

He sighed. 'Of course we did. But believe it or not, lots of days are just normal stuff. Nothing that dramatic or exciting, and to be honest…?' He looked away. 'I kind of like those days.'

Now she was curious. She'd done a little more research on Rhuaridh Gillespie since the last time she'd been here. She knew he'd taken over at his father's surgery when they couldn't recruit anyone to the post.

'I'm surprised to hear you say that. I thought you only came here because you had to.'

He looked up sharply, as if he hadn't expected her to know that. 'Recruitment is an issue right across the whole of Scotland. It used to be that for every GP vacancy there would be fifty applicants. Now young doctors just don't want to go into general practice. They don't want to have to own a business—run a business, and take on the huge financial debt of buying into a practice. If they even train to work as a general practitioner, they can make more money working as a locum. Then there's less pressure, less responsibility and…' he shook his head '…absolutely no continuity of care for patients.'

Kristie leaned back against the wall. 'But you trained as a general practitioner. Did you just want to work as a locum?'

He met her gaze with a thoughtful expression, as if he hadn't expected her to ask this many questions. 'I had alternative plans. At my practice in Glasgow I also worked a few days in one of the city hospitals in Dermatology. I covered outlying clinics across Glasgow, doing lots of minor surgery.'

Her mouth quirked upwards. 'You're a skin guy?'

He held out his hands. 'Biggest organ of the body. Why not?'

'And you can't do that here?'

He shrugged. 'Not as much. Sure, I can do biopsies, freeze moles with liquid nitrogen, or surgically remove anything small and suspicious. But when your population is usually around five thousand, that's not really enough people to only specialise in dermatology.'

She waited a few moments. 'So why didn't you just stay in Glasgow? Couldn't you just have left the practice here with only one doctor?'

Rhuaridh took a step back and leaned on the opposite wall. 'And leave Magda here on her own, covering the hospital and the GP practice? Leaving the community I grew up in and loved with no real service provision? What kind of person would that make me?'

It was like a bright light shining in her eyes. She could feel tiny pieces of the jigsaw puzzle slot into place.

Guilt. He'd felt responsible, and had come back to his home without really wanting to. This had a strange air of déjà vu about it. Wasn't this what had just happened with the TV series? He hadn't chosen to do this either, instead he was taking the place of his colleague unwillingly because he didn't want to let her, or the community, down. Kristie didn't doubt for one second that if he'd reneged on the contract, Arran would never get a new X-ray machine.

No wonder the guy was grumpy. Did he get to make any choices in this life?

She looked across the room into those weary blue eyes and said words she'd never have imagined herself saying. 'I guess it makes you a good person, Rhuaridh Gillespie.'

CHAPTER FOUR

August

MAC WAS LOOKING at him with an expression only a dog could give.

Rhuaridh bent down and rubbed his head. 'I'm sorry.' He meant it. He'd been neglectful. August was part of the summer season on Arran. From the end of June until the middle of August, Arran was full of Scottish, and lots of international, tourists. But come mid-August in Scotland the schools started again. Usually that would mean that things would quieten down.

But, in the UK, the English schools were still out. So, Arran was currently filled with lots of English holiday-makers. The beach had been packed all day. It seemed that croup was doing the rounds and between the surgery and the A and E department, he'd seen five toddlers with the nasty barking cough today alone. Chicken pox also seemed to be rearing its head again. Five members of one poor family were currently covered in the itchy spots.

He glanced at his watch. Kristie was due to arrive at some point and he was feeling quite...awkward.

He wasn't quite sure what had come over him last time around, and he had apologised to her, but they still had nine months of filming left. He counted in days. Twenty-seven more days around Kristie Nelson.

There was something about her. At first he'd thought it was the accent and the confidence. But he'd seen her waver on a few occasions. Her confidence was only skin deep. And that was another thing. To others, she may look like a typical anchor woman for an American TV show. Blonde, perfect teeth, hint of a tan and good figure. And somehow he couldn't help watching the way she flicked her thumb off her forefinger, or made that little clicking noise when she was thinking. It was weird. Even though he told himself she was the most annoying female on the planet, he couldn't help the way his mind would frequently drift back to something she'd said or done.

Mac nuzzled around his ankles. It snapped him back from the Kristie fog and he picked up Mac's lead and grabbed his sweater. 'Let's go, boy.' He opened the main door of his cottage and Mac bounded out towards the beach. He'd adjusted well to the move, and after a few short months it actually felt like Mac had always been there. He'd even employed a dog walker to take Mac out during the day when he was working.

The sun was dipping in the sky, leaving the beach scattered with violet evening hues. There were a few other people walking dogs, someone on a horse and a couple strolling along hand in hand.

The breeze tonight wasn't quite as brisk as it normally was. Laughter carried along the beach in the air. A group of teenagers was trying to set up a campfire.

Rhuaridh moved down closer to the firmer sand at the sea's edge. The beach ran for a few miles and Mac had got used to a long walk in the evening.

They'd only been walking for about ten minutes when he heard thudding feet behind him. He turned to take a step one way or the other and Kristie ran straight into him.

'Oh! Wow.' She stepped back and rubbed her nose.

He laughed and shook his head. 'Where did you come from?'

She was still rubbing her nose. 'I came by your house. I wanted to chat to you about the schedule tomorrow.'

'You came by my house? I wasn't expecting to see you until tomorrow.' He was surprised. He hadn't known Kristie knew where he lived—and after their last meeting, he was even more surprised she wanted to turn up at his door.

She nodded. 'We ended up swapping flights and coming a day early.'

'Does that mean you're going home a day early?'

She let out a laugh. 'Don't even try to pretend you want me around, then.'

'No.' He cringed. 'I didn't mean it like that. I'm just wondering if you wanted to swap things around.'

She stopped for a second, bending down to pat Mac, who'd bounded back to see why Rhuaridh had stopped walking. 'Hey, guy, nice to see you.'

Mac jumped up, putting two wet sandy pawprints on her jeans. He would have expected her to squirm but Kristie didn't seem bothered at all. She crouched down, letting Mac lick her hands. Kristie looked up at him. 'I thought we should maybe have a chat,' she said, biting her bottom lip.

A heavy feeling settled in his stomach. 'About last time? Yeah, we probably should.'

Her nose wrinkled. 'Not about last time,' she said. 'I thought we sorted that.'

Now he was really confused. 'Well, yeah, we sort of did, but...' He wasn't quite sure what to say next.

She straightened up, wiping her wet hands on her jeans. 'I wanted to talk to you about something else.'

'Okay.' He wasn't quite sure where this was going.

She sucked in a breath, not quite meeting his gaze. 'Let's walk.' She turned and started in the same direction he'd been headed.

'Okay,' he said again, wondering what he was getting himself into.

'You said you hadn't watched the show.'

He shook his head. 'Not my thing—no offence.'

She gave a smile, then stuck her hands in her pockets and turned to face him again. The setting sun outlined her silhouette and streaked her blonde hair with violet and pink light—like some kind of ethereal hue.

'None taken.' She cleared her throat. 'I thought I should probably let you know something.'

'What?'

'I watched the third episode before I came here. It goes out in two weeks' time.'

'And...?' He knew there must be something, why else would they be having this conversation?

She reached up and tugged at her earlobe. A sign she was nervous. He was noticing all these little things about her. Now he knew when she was angry, when she was thinking, and when she was nervous. How many other women did he know those things about?

Had he known them about his ex, Zoe? He couldn't even remember. All his memories of her had just seemed to fade into the past.

Her words came out rushed, as if she was trying to say them all before she could stop herself. 'The show's been really popular. Really popular. Partly because in the first episode it covered John Henderson's death, and in the second it introduced a beautiful baby into the world.'

He wrinkled his nose. He was thinking back to the last time she'd been here. No major events had happened.

'So what's wrong with the third episode? Not enough drama?'

She looked distinctly uncomfortable and fixed her gaze on the teenagers further down the beach. 'Nothing's wrong with it exactly. It's just changed focus a little.'

'Changed focus to what?' He was getting tired with this tiptoeing around. 'Why don't you just say what you need to?'

She pressed her lips together for a second. 'The fight we had? Gerry filmed it. He'd already captured us sparring a little in the episodes before and people had been commenting on social media about it.'

Rhuaridh's brain flashed back to the woman in the surgery, telling him he had to be nicer to Kristie. He groaned. 'Oh, no. I look like a complete and utter—'

She held up her hand and stopped him. 'My producer says it's dynamite. He says everyone is going to love it.'

'They'll love you.' Rhuaridh shook his head. 'I'm the villain. I'm the one who lost his patience.'

He could see her biting the inside of her lip.

'I'm sorry,' he said quickly.

'Don't be,' she said, equally quickly. 'The last few shows I've worked on have all been cancelled. I was beginning to be a bit of bad luck charm. In TV, that kind of reputation doesn't do you any favours.'

He stuck his hands into his pockets. 'So, you want to fight with me? Is that what you're saying?'

She pulled a face and gave a little shrug. 'Well…yes and no. It seems that a bit of tension is good for viewing—alongside all the medical stuff, of course.'

'I'm not sure fighting on screen does much for me as a doctor. I'm not normally like that.'

She gave a weak smile. 'So it's just me that drives you nuts?'

He looked out over the sea. This was the first time they'd really talked. How did he explain she might be right, without offending her—because if he couldn't understand it, how could she?

'I guess I still need to get used to someone following me around,' he said carefully. 'What are the other shows in the series?' It was a blatant attempt at changing the subject. But he was beginning to think he should have paid more attention to all the TV stuff.

'There's a museum curator in Egypt—apparently she practically doesn't let them into any room that hosts an "artefact", and the guy who is training to be an astronaut is said to be a major jerk. After the first shows they brought in someone new to follow—a guy who's trying to make his name as a country and western singer. I'm reliably informed that his singing is the worst ever heard.'

He couldn't help but laugh again. His foot traced a line in the sand. Mac had long since tired of waiting around for them both and was now chasing the tide, getting his white and black coat well and truly soaked. The smell of wet dog was going to drift all the way through the house.

'I can't imagine what they find so exciting about a doctor on an island in Scotland.'

'Maybe it's the exotic. Half the world just wants to visit Scotland and this makes them feel like they've been there.' She gave him a sideways glance. 'Or maybe they just like the grumpy doc.'

The grumpy doc. Was that what she'd nicknamed him? It wasn't the most flattering description in the world. His stomach twisted a little. He should be worrying about his reputation. He should be worrying about what people might think of him. But, strangely, the only person's opinion he was worried about right now was Kristie's. 'Why are you telling me all this?'

'I know you don't watch the series. But I thought I should forewarn you—in case, once the next episode hits, you start to get some press.'

'Bad press, you mean.'

She gave him a smile. 'Actually, no. I've told you. They love you. I was thinking more along the lines that you might get weird internet proposals, or your dating profile might explode.'

'My dating profile? You honestly think I've got a dating profile?'

She held out her hands and gave him a mischievous smile. 'Who knows?'

He shook his head as they started back down the beach. 'On an island this small I pretty much know everyone. If I had a dating profile, the whole island would know it, and anyway it's a bit hard to meet for dates when you rely on a ferry to the mainland.'

He looked at her curiously. 'Do you have one—a dating profile?'

She threw back her head and laughed. 'Are you joking? I was on TV for about ten seconds before I started getting weird emails. It seems that being on a TV show makes you fair game. Nope. I just try to meet guys the old-fashioned way.'

He looked down at her as they walked side by side. 'And how's that working out for you?' He couldn't pretend he wasn't curious.

She gave him an oblique glance. She knew. She knew the question he was asking. She held out her hand and wiggled it. 'Hmm…'

What did that mean?

She didn't say anything else so he was kind of left hanging.

'So, is everything okay for tomorrow, then?'

He nodded. 'Sure.' At that moment Mac ran up and decided to shake half of the Firth of Clyde all over them.

'Whoa!' Both of them jumped back, laughing, Kristie wiping the huge drops of water from her face and neck.

Rhuaridh took a step closer. 'Sorry.' He looked towards Mac. 'Occupational hazard, I guess.'

He reached forward without thinking. Part of her mascara had smudged just under her lower eyelid. He lifted his thumb to her cheekbone and wiped it away. Her laughter stopped as she looked up, her gaze connecting with his.

His hand froze. It was like all the breath had just been sucked from his lungs. He was so conscious of the feel of her smooth skin beneath his thumb pad. He could almost swear a tiny little zing shot down his arm.

She wasn't moving either. Her pupils dilated as he watched.

It was like every sense inside him switched on. He hadn't been paying attention. He'd been so focused on his work he'd forgotten to see what was right beside him. When was the last time he'd actually dated? Maybe once in the ten months since he'd got here. He couldn't even remember.

He couldn't remember what it was like to let a woman's scent drift around him like it was now. To look into a pair of eyes that were looking right back at him.

There was a shout behind them and both of them jumped back. It was only one of the teenagers carrying on.

But the moment was gone. Kristie looked a little embarrassed and wiped her hands down on her jeans. 'I'd better get back,' she said quickly. 'Gerry and I need to chat about the filming tomorrow.' She started to walk quickly down the beach, then turned once to look at him. 'I'll see you tomorrow.'

The words seem to hang between them, as if she was willing him to add something else. But he gave a quick nod. 'Sure.'

Kristie broke into a jog back down the beach. He couldn't help but stare at her silhouette. Mac bounded up and sat at his feet, looking up at him quizzically.

If there was mental telepathy between a human and a dog, Mac was currently calling him an idiot.

He kicked the sand at his feet. 'I know, I know,' he said as he shook his head and stuck his hands in his pockets.

He pushed his thoughts from his head. She was from LA. She worked on a TV show. He was crazy to think she might actually be interested in some guy from Arran. His ex had been quick to tell him that Arran was a dull, boring rock in the middle of nowhere. What could it possibly have to interest some woman who was probably two minutes from Hollywood? He stared out as the sun drew even closer to the horizon, sending warming streaks across the sky. He sighed. 'Let's go, Mac,' he said as he turned and headed back to the cottage.

Kristie dressed carefully. For the first time since she'd come to the island she wore a dress. It was still summer here—even though it was much cooler than LA. Her hair didn't usually give her much trouble, so she just ran a brush through it as usual. Her makeup took her no more than five minutes. She'd even applied it once in a dark cupboard with no light.

Gerry gave her a smile as she emerged from her room in their rental. 'Special occasion?'

She shook her head, and pretended she didn't notice the rush of heat to her cheeks. What on earth was she doing? Maybe she'd just imagined that moment on the beach. Maybe it had been nothing at all. She'd only wanted to warn him about the hype. Or had she?

Truth was, she never really watched herself on TV much. It seemed too egotistical. But watching the episode between her and Rhuaridh had brought all those emotions back to the surface. She couldn't ever remember a guy getting under her skin the way Rhuaridh Gillespie had. And on the way over on the ferry this time she'd been nervous. Something else that was unusual for her.

Maybe it was the apparent popularity of the show. She'd

already had a few interview requests. Last night when she'd logged onto her social media account she'd seen over four hundred comments about the show. What would happen when the third show went out?

Gerry was leaning against the wall. He looked paler than normal. 'Okay?' she asked.

'Sure,' he said. 'Just a bit of indigestion. It's my age.'

She gave a nod and headed to the stairs. They were filming at the surgery today, covering one of the paediatric clinics and immunisation clinics.

Screaming babies. Just her kind of thing. Not.

Gerry fumbled in his pocket and some lollipops landed on the floor. Kristie bent and picked them up. 'Since when did you like candy?'

He tapped the side of his nose. 'It's my secret weapon. It's in case we have unco-operative kids at the clinic today.'

She shook her head and held up one of the bright red lollipops. 'It's a pure sugar rush. No way will they let you hand these out. Think of the tooth decay.'

He winked. 'I'm wiser than you think. They're sugar-free.' He started walking down the stairs in front of her. 'Don't let it be said that an old guy doesn't have any new tricks.'

'What about the additives?' She stared at the colour again.

He shrugged in front of her. 'Can't think of everything.'

She shook her head and stuck some in the pocket of her dress. She could always eat them herself.

The clinic was chaos. It was a mixture of development checks, immunisations and childhood reviews.

Most of the mothers were delighted at the prospect of their child being filmed, so permissions were easy.

Rhuaridh was wearing a pale pink shirt today and dark trousers. She hated the fact he always looked so handsome. He moved through the waiting room easily, picking up babies and toddlers and carrying them through to the examination room, all while chatting to their mothers. He seemed at ease here. It was as if he'd finally decided to accept they'd be around and was doing what they'd asked him to do right from the beginning—ignore them.

But it made Kristie's insides twist in a way she didn't like.

Some of babies squealed. She didn't blame them, getting three jabs at once was tough. She didn't have much experience around kids or babies, so watching Ellen, the health visitor, do the development checks was more interesting than she'd thought.

She watched the babies follow things with their eyes, weight bear on their legs, and lift their heads up in line with their bodies. The older ones could grab things, sit up and balance on their own, and babble away quite happily.

Her favourite was a little boy just short of two years old. He came into the room with the biggest frown on his face. When Ellen tried to persuade him to build some bricks, say a few words or draw with a crayon he had the same response to everything. 'No.' His mother looked tired and sat with another baby on her lap, apologising profusely for her son's lack of co-operation.

Ellen took some measurements and laughed and turned to Kristie. 'As you can see, he has a younger sister. I've been in the house a dozen times and know he can do all these things—if he wants to.'

Kristie stopped smiling at the little guy and turned her attention to the mum. She had dark circles under her eyes and looked as if she might burst into tears. Kristie's first reaction was to open her mouth and move into counselling mode but before she could, Ellen gave an almost imperceptible nod of her head towards Kristie and Gerry, and they backed out of the room.

Kristie stood against the wall for a few minutes and just

breathed. She had no idea what was going on with that woman, but her own thoughts immediately raced back to her sister. The last few volunteer shifts on the helpline had been quiet. She'd almost willed the phone to ring, then had felt guilty for thinking that. In the end, she'd used the time in an unexpected way.

She'd started writing. She wasn't sure what it was at first, but it had started to take shape into a piece of fiction—a novel, based on her experience with her sister and how suicide affected everyone. Her sister's death had impacted on every part of her life. She'd watched the life drain from her mother and father and their health deteriorate quickly, with them eventually dying within a few months of each other.

Burying three family members in a short period of time had messed with her head so much she found it hard to form new relationships. Hard to find hope to invest in a future that might get snatched away from her. Of course, thoughts like those were irrational. She knew that. But she also knew that the last few men she'd met she'd kept at arm's length. Whether she'd wanted to or not.

She sighed as the door opened again and Ellen crossed the hall to Rhuaridh's room with a slip of paper in her hand.

Kristie's mouth dried as the health visitor took charge of the children, then let the mother go and see Rhuaridh on her own.

She couldn't help herself but follow Ellen to where she was bouncing the baby on her knee and entertaining the toddler, who'd now decided to draw pictures.

'Is she okay?'

Ellen looked up. 'It's likely she has postnatal depression. We screen all new mums twice in the first year. I've visited Jackie at home a lot. She's had two very colicky babies. Lack of sleep is tough.'

Kristie rubbed her hands up and down her arms, instantly cold. That piece of paper. That assessment that they do on all new mums—why hadn't there been something like that for her sister? Would it have worked? Would it have picked anything up?

Maybe she was putting hope in something that didn't exist. But just the thought—that there was a simple screening tool that would have picked up something...

'Do you use it for other people?'

Ellen looked up. She'd started building a pile of bricks on the floor with the toddler. 'The postnatal depression scale? No, it's designed specifically for women who've just had a baby. We've used it for years, though, and I think it's very effective. Even if it just starts a conversation between me and the mum.'

'But you took her through to see Rhuaridh?'

Ellen looked over Kristie's shoulder. 'This is very personal. I have to ask that you don't film anything about this case.'

Kristie nodded. 'Of course not.'

'In that case, the final question in the tool—it's about self-harm. It asks if the mum has ever felt that way. If she answers anything other than no, I always need to have a conversation with the GP.'

Kristie felt her voice shake. 'So, what do you do for mums who feel like that?'

Ellen gave her a thoughtful look. 'It all depends on the mum. Some I visit more, every day if I have to. Some I get some other support—like a few hours at nursery for one, or both of their kids. Some Rhuaridh will see. He might decide to start them on some medication, or to refer them to the community mental health nurse, or even to a consultant. Whatever will help the mum most.'

Kristie leaned back against the wall, taking in everything that was being said. The mum was in with Rhuaridh for a while. By the time she came out, she was wiping her eyes but seemed a bit better. It was as if a little spark had appeared in her eyes again. Maybe she finally felt as if someone was listening.

Kristie waited until the clinic was finished then found Rhuaridh while he was writing up some notes.

'That mum? What did you do for her?'

He looked a little surprised by her question but gestured for her to close the door. 'Sit down,' he said.

She took a deep breath and sat down on the chair next to him. 'I talked to her,' he said quietly.

'That's it?' She couldn't hide how taken aback she felt.

'And I listened,' he added.

'But her questionnaire…' she began.

He held up his hand. 'Her questionnaire is just a little bit of her. It's a snapshot in time. I listened. I listened to how she was feeling and talked to her and let her know that some of this is normal for a new mum. She's beyond tired. She hasn't had a full night's sleep in two years. How do you think that would impact on anyone's mental health?'

'But you let her leave…' Her voice trailed off, as her mind jumped ahead.

'I let her leave with an assurance of some support systems in place. While she was here, she phoned her sister and asked her to take the kids overnight. She's coming back to see me again tomorrow and we'll talk again.'

'Oh.' Kristie sagged into the chair a little. Her stomach still churned.

There was so much here that was tumbling around in her brain. She knew that most of the thoughts she was having weren't rational—they were all tinged by her own experience. That desperate sense of panic.

She took a few breaths and tried to put her counselling head on. The one she used three nights a month. Rhuaridh had taken time to talk to the mother and acknowledge her feelings—usually the single most important act someone could do. Then he'd arranged follow up and support. Just like she would hope and expect from a health professional.

Rhuaridh leaned forward and put his hand over hers. 'Kristie, is everything all right?'

And for the first time in her life she wasn't quite sure how to answer. Should she tell him? Should she let him know she worked as a counsellor and what she'd been through herself?

Her mouth was dry. He was looking at her with those bright blue eyes—staring right at her as though he could see right down to her very soul. To all the things she kept locked away tight. Part of her wanted to tell him. Part of her wanted to share.

But something was stopping her. Something wouldn't let her open her mouth and say those words. So before she could think about it any longer, she got up and rushed out.

CHAPTER FIVE

September

'YOU'VE NEVER WATCHED?'

Rhuaridh shook his head as Magda cradled baby Alice. She gave him a curious smile. 'I can't believe it. You should. I have to admit, I'm almost a little jealous.'

'Of what?'

He was drinking a large cup of coffee while he compared a few notes with her on a few of their chronically ill patients. On Arran, a doctor would never really be off duty, and Magda was far too nosy not to want to discuss some of their long-term cases.

'Of you.' She waved one hand while she fixed her gaze back on her fair-haired daughter while she screwed up her nose and gave a sigh. 'But no. If I'd been in the show that wouldn't have worked anyway.'

Rhuaridh put down his cup and held out his hands. 'Give me my goddaughter and tell me what on earth you're talking about.'

Magda stood up and put Alice into his arms, before settling back and putting her feet up on the sofa. 'It's all about the chemistry.'

'Chemistry? I thought you didn't like chemistry. You always complained about it when we were students.'

She shook her head and looked at him as if he was

completely dumb. 'Not school chemistry. *Chemistry*. You know…between a man and a woman. Phew! If I need to teach you about the birds and bees I'm going to question whether you should be working as a doctor.'

He shifted in the chair, realising where this was going to go. He shook his head and Alice wrinkled her face. He stopped moving. He knew who was in charge here.

He spoke quietly. 'I've no interest in watching myself on TV. I know everything that's happened—not all of which I'm entirely proud of.'

She gave a sigh. 'You know. They edit things. And they've edited the show for the drama. To be honest, I'm surprised we've not got women heading to Arran by the boatload.' She raised one eyebrow. 'They always seem to catch your good side.'

'Do I have a bad side?' he teased.

But it was almost as if Magda was still talking to herself. 'Then again, most of the women would know they wouldn't get a look in. The chemistry between you and Kristie…' she kissed her fingertips then flicked out her fingers '…is just off the scale.' She gave him a smile. 'You're doing so much better than the others in the show. I can't even watch the country and western singer. And the astronaut is possibly the most arrogant person on and off the planet.'

His mind was spinning. Was everyone who was watching thinking the same thing about him and Kristie? He felt like some teenage boy under scrutiny. *He* hadn't even really worked out what was going on between them.

He liked her. He knew he liked her. But anything more just seemed…ridiculous.

But was it?

Alice made a little noise in his arms. Magda closed her eyes. 'She didn't sleep a wink last night.'

'Didn't she?'

Rhuaridh looked around and glimpsed the pram near the doorway. 'Do you want me to take her for a walk? Mac is mooching around outside anyway. I was planning on taking him for a walk.'

'Would you?' As she said the words she snuggled down further into the sofa. 'Just an hour would be great.'

Rhuaridh smiled and settled Alice into the pram, closing the door as quietly as he could behind him.

Mac gave him a look. Rhuaridh wagged his finger. 'Don't get jealous, old one. Just get in line. We've got a new boss now.'

'Really?'

Rhuaridh nearly jumped. Kristie was standing behind him with a bag in her hand.

'Where did you come from?'

She grinned. 'LA. You know, America.' She made signals with her hands. 'Then a plane and a boat.'

'Okay, okay, I get it.'

She was wearing a pair of black and white checked trousers and a black shirt tied at her waist. Her hair was loose about her shoulders and she seemed totally at ease as she leaned over him and looked into the pram. 'I came to see my favourite girl, but I see you've already kidnapped her. Whaddya say we share?'

Rhuaridh gripped the pram a little tighter as he smiled back. 'Ah, but this is my goddaughter. And this is the first time I've actually managed to kidnap her.'

Kristie made the little clicking noise she always did when she was thinking. He leaned a little closer and caught a whiff of her light zesty perfume. 'To tell you the truth, I think Mac's a little jealous.'

Kristie dropped to her knees and rubbed Mac's head, bending down to put her head next to his. 'Poor boy. Is he neglecting you again?' She wrapped her hand around

Mac's lead. 'How about we take turns? I'll take Mac, then swap you on the way back.'

Rhuaridh gave a nod and they started to walk down towards the town. The weather was bright with just a little edge in the air. Kristie chatted constantly, telling him about plane delays and double-booked accommodation. It didn't take long for her to turn the conversation back to work. 'Have you seen that young mum again?'

Rhuaridh gave her a sideways glance. Last time he'd seen Kristie she'd been more than a little preoccupied about the case. She'd rushed out the room when he'd asked her if something was wrong, and the next day she'd left to go back to LA. He hadn't seen her since.

He'd been curious about why she'd been so concerned. He'd had enough experience in life to know when to tread carefully. People didn't come with a label attached declaring their past life experiences.

'I've seen her quite a lot—so has Ellen, the health visitor. She's talking, and I don't think she's going to feel better overnight, but I think if we have adequate support systems in place, and an open-door policy, I think she'll continue to make improvements. Ellen has visited her at home a lot—talked through how she's feeling about things. They've even been out walking together—like we are today.'

He gave her another glance. He thought he knew what the next answer would be. 'You haven't included anything in the filming, have you?'

Kristie shook her head. 'Absolutely not. It's mainly just footage from the immunisation clinic and the baby clinic.'

He gave a nod and then changed tack. 'So, what are you and Gerry going to do tonight about food?'

She blinked. 'What do you mean?'

'The place you've booked into after the mix up—they

didn't tell you, did they? Their kitchen is out of order. Something to do with an electricity short.'

Kristie let out a big sigh. 'Darn it. I never even asked. We just said we needed beds for the next few days after the mix-up at the other place.'

She nudged him as they kept walking. 'Okay, so give me the lowdown on all the local places.' She wrinkled her nose. 'Though I'm not sure about Gerry. He's been really tired. I think the jet-lag is hitting him hard this time.'

Rhuaridh gave her a cheeky kind of grin. 'Well, if you can promise me that you actually eat, I'll show you my favourite place in town.'

'What do you mean—if I actually eat?'

He laughed. 'You're from LA. Don't you all just eat green leaves and the occasional bit of kale or spinach?'

Now she laughed too. 'You heard about that new diet?' She shuddered. 'Oh, no. Not for me. Anyhow, I'm a steak kind of girl.'

'You are?' He actually stopped walking and looked at her in surprise.

She pointed to her chest. 'What? I don't look like a steak girl?'

He couldn't help but give her an appreciative gaze. 'If steak's what you like, I know just the place.'

She glanced around. They were right in the heart of Brodick now. There were a number of shops on the high street, a sprinkling of coffee shops and a few pubs.

'Cool. Which one is it?'

He turned the pram around. 'It's back this way.'

Quick as a flash, Kristie came alongside and bumped him out of the way with her hip, taking his place at pushing the pram. 'Don't try and steal my turn. You got the way out. I get the way back.' She bent over the pram and stroked the side of Alice's face. 'She's just a little jewel, isn't she?'

He was surprised at the affection in her voice. 'You like kids?'

'I love kids.' She shrugged. 'Not all of them like me, right enough.'

He stopped walking. 'Where did you pick that up?'

'What?' There was a gleam in her eye.

'"Right enough". It's a distinctly Scottish expression.'

She lifted one hand from the pram and counted off on her fingers. 'I was trying it out for size. Everyone uses it in the surgery. I'm also looking for opportunities to use *drookit, minging* and...' She wrinkled her brow. 'What's the one that Mr McLean who comes to the surgery always uses?'

Rhuaridh burst out laughing. 'Wheesht?'

'That's it!' she said, pointing her finger at him. *'Wheesht.'*

It sounded strange in her American accent. But he liked it. He liked it a lot.

She started walking again. 'There's another one I've heard. It might even be used to describe you sometimes.' She gave him a nod of her head.

'I dread to think. Hit me with it.'

This time the glance she gave him was part mysterious, part superior. 'Crabbit,' she said triumphantly.

Part of him was indignant, part of him wanted to laugh. 'Crabbit? Me?' He pointed to his chest. 'No way. No way could I ever be described as crabbit. I'm the nice guy. The fun-loving squishy kind of guy.' He gestured down to Alice. 'The kind of guy who takes his goddaughter for a walk to give his friend a break.' He raised his eyebrows at her. 'Beat that one, LA girl.'

She folded her arms across her chest, letting momentum carry the pram for a few seconds. 'That sounds like a challenge.'

'It is.' He'd never been one to back down from a challenge.

He swooped in and grabbed the pram handle. 'Ms Nelson, I believe you just neglected your duty. I think I should take over again.'

Before she could protest he nodded towards the pub at the other side of the road. 'Billy's Bar. Best steaks in town. They even do a special sauce for me.'

'What kind of sauce?'

'I could tell you. But I'd have to kill you. It's a secret I'll take to my grave. But if you come along with me tonight, I'll let you have some.' The words were out before he really had a chance to think about them.

'Dinner with the doctor,' she mused out loud. 'Just exactly how good are these steaks?'

'Better than you've ever tasted. The cows bred in the Arran hills are special. More tender.'

There was a smile dancing across her lips. 'Okay, then.' She gave him a cheeky wink. 'But only because I might want to put the steak on film.'

Part of him was elated. Part of him was put out. It had been a casual, not-really-thought-about invitation. But things had seemed to be heading in this direction. But now, had she only said yes because she wanted to film their dinner? Was this something to try and get more viewing figures?

Because that hadn't even crossed his mind.

Kristie kept chatting again. It seemed she had a gift for chat. And she didn't seem to slow down for a second. They were almost back at Magda's house when Rhuaridh's page sounded.

He took one glance and grabbed his phone. 'Something wrong?' she asked, taking over the pram-pushing again.

He nodded. Listened carefully to the person at the end of the phone before cutting the call. In the blink of an eye he swooped up little Alice, dropping a kiss on her forehead before running inside with her. Kristie was still fumbling with the pram in the doorway as he came back outside.

'Leave it,' he said, running past her. 'And phone Gerry. Tell him to meet us at the wilderness centre.'

Kristie's head flicked one way then the other, as if she should work out what to do next. He was in the car already and, reaching over, flung open the passenger door. 'Now, Kristie!' he yelled.

Her hands were refusing to do what they were told as she tried to phone Gerry. It took three attempts to finally press the correct button. Rhuaridh was driving quicker than she'd ever seen him. He'd already phoned the cottage hospital and given some instructions to the staff.

It seemed that there was only one ambulance on Arran and it was on its way too.

'What's the wilderness centre?'

'It's an experiential learning place. Adults and kids come and learn to mountain climb, hike, swim, canoe, camp, fish and a whole host of other things.'

'So...' She was almost scared to ask. 'What's happened?'

'There's been an accident. There's a waterfall in the hills. One of the instructors and one of the kids have been hurt.'

He turned up a track that led up one of the nearby hills. Now she understood why he had a four-wheel drive. The terrain was rugged. 'Will the ambulance get up here?'

He nodded. 'You haven't seen it yet, have you?'

She shook her head.

'It's not a regular ambulance because of the terrain it has to cover, well, that and the fact a high number of our injuries are around the foot of Goat Fell—'

'Goat Fell?' she interrupted.

He pointed off to the side. 'Arran's highest mountain,

more than eight hundred metres tall. Really, really popular with climbers, and it is a real climb. Especially at the end. Some people don't really come equipped for it and end up injuring themselves.'

'Okay,' she murmured. She looked to where he pointed. She couldn't even see the top of the mountain as it was covered with low-hanging clouds.

They were climbing higher, going through trees and bushes. 'Where is this place?'

'Another few minutes.' He gave her an anxious kind of glance, his voice steady. 'Until the ambulance gets here you might need to give me a hand. Are you okay with that?'

Her response was quicker than he expected. 'It's only hospitals that spook me.'

'What?'

He caught one quick glimpse of her face before he had to look back at the path. For a split second he thought she might be cracking a joke, but her expression told him otherwise.

He swore he could see the pathways firing in his own brain. He'd thought she'd been a little unsettled in the hospital. Just something off—something he couldn't quite put his finger on.

'Why are you spooked by hospitals?'

It was totally not the right time to ask a question like that. And speeding up a hill towards an accident scene was not the right place to give an answer. Of course he knew that. But how could she expect him not to ask?

'Past experience,' she replied in a tight voice. 'One I'd rather not talk about.'

He couldn't help his response. 'You must have loved the thought of coming here.'

They reached the crest of the hill and veered down towards the valley where the waterfall lay.

She shot him a wry expression. 'Let's just say I really wanted the museum in Egypt or the astronaut. Lucky old me.'

His gut gave a twist. As they approached the waterfall site he could see an array of people, all dressed in wet-weather gear, crowded around a man on the ground.

He had to let this go right now. He had a job to do.

'Will you be okay to help?' he asked again. For the next few minutes at least he might need to count on Kristie for help. If she couldn't help, she might well be a hindrance and he'd ask her to stay in the car.

Her voice was tight and she glanced at her phone. He reached over and grabbed her hand. 'Be honest.'

She stared for the briefest of seconds at his hand squeezing hers. 'I'll be fine,' she said without meeting his gaze. 'Gerry's messaged. He's just behind us. He was at the hospital and hitched a ride in the ambulance.'

Rhuaridh nodded. He had to take her at her word. He had to trust her. And hopefully it would only be for a few minutes.

'I'll grab the blue bag, you grab the red,' he said as he jumped from the car.

He walked swiftly to the group of people. One of the instructors was on the ground with a large laceration on his head. From one glance Rhuaridh could see that his breathing was a little laboured. But that was the point. At least he was breathing.

'Where's the other casualty?'

A teenage boy pointed to the bottom of the roaring waterfall. 'Under there. He jumped from the top.'

Rhuaridh's heart gave a little leap. 'Under *there*?'

'Not under the water. Under the waterfall. He says he can't feel his legs so no one wanted to move him.'

Rhuaridh was already stripping off his shoes and jacket. He pulled a monitor from one bag, bent over and stuck the three leads on the first guy's chest. It only took a few seconds to check the readings. He knelt down beside the guy, pulled his stethoscope out and made another check. Lungs were filling normally, no sign of damage. 'What happened?' he asked the nearest kid.

'Ross and Des went into the water as soon as Kai jumped and went under. Des got Kai and pulled him into the cave but when Ross tried to climb the rock face he slipped and hit his head on the way down.' The young boy talking gulped, 'A few of us jumped in and pulled him out. He hasn't woken up at all.'

Rhuaridh pulled a penlight from his pocket and checked Ross's pupils, then completed a first set of neuro obs. It was first-line assessment for any head injury. He scribbled them down and handed them to Kristie.

He handed Kristie a radio. 'You keep these.'

'Where are you going?' There was a definite flash of panic in her eyes.

A teenage girl, her face streaked with tears, tugged at his sleeve. 'The other instructor is with Kai. He stayed with him after Ross got hurt, trying to help.'

Rhuaridh started rummaging through the kitbags. He tucked the other radio into his belt. There was no doubt about it—he was going to get very wet.

He bent over next to Kristie, checking the monitor again. He kept his voice low. 'Keep an eye on his breathing. It seems fine and his heart rate is steady. He's given himself quite a bang on the head. If he starts to wake up, just keep him steady on the ground. If he's agitated or confused, radio me straight away.'

Rhuaridh wouldn't normally leave an unconscious patient, but right now he'd no idea of the condition of the child under the waterfall. As the only medic on site he had to assess both patients. He put his hand on Kristie's shoulder. 'The ambulance crew should be here in a few minutes.' He could tell she was nervous, but she lifted her own hand and put it over his.

'Go on, Rhuaridh. Go and check on the kid. We'll be fine.'

Rhuaridh gave a few instructions to some of the other teenagers around. Most were quiet, a few looked a bit shocked but had no injuries. 'Stay with Kristie, she'll let me know if there's any problems.'

He waded into the water. Cold. It was beyond cold. This waterfall was notorious for the temperature as it was based in a valley with little sunlight. By the time he'd waded across to the middle of the pool the water had come up over his waist and to the bottom of his ribs, making him catch his breath.

The instructor had been wearing a wetsuit that would keep his temperature more steady—hopefully the teenager would be too.

The spray from the waterfall started to soak him. He knew this place well enough. There was a ridge on the rocks the falls plummeted over. It was the only way to get access to the cave under the falls and the only way to access that ridge was to wade through the water and try and scale the rock face.

He had nothing. No climbing equipment. No wetsuit. Not even a rope.

He heard a painful groan. Even though the noise from the falls was loud, he could hear it echoing from the cave. He moved sideways, casting his eyes over the rock face, looking for a suitable place to start.

It had been years since he'd been here. As a teenager he'd been able to scale this rock with no problems. It had practically been a rite of passage for any kid that lived on the island. But that had been a long time ago, when he'd probably been a lot more agile than he was now.

The first foothold was easy, his bare foot pushing him

upwards. He caught his hands on the rocks above and pulled himself up, finding a position for the second foot.

'Careful, Doc,' shouted one of the kids.

He moved left, nearer the falls. There was a trick to this, trying to keep hold of the wall, which got more and more slippery by the second as he edged closer. The weight on his back from the backpack and red portable stretcher was affecting his balance, making him grip all the tighter. His knuckles were white as he waited for the right second to duck his head and jump through the falls to the cave behind.

As he jumped he had a millisecond of panic. What if the injured kid was directly in his path? But as he landed with a grunt behind the falls he realised he was clear. He fell roughly to the side, the equipment on his back digging sharply into him.

It took his eyes a few seconds to adjust. It wasn't quite dark in here. Light still streamed through the waterfall.

'About time,' said Des, the instructor, cheekily. He was sitting next to the injured boy, who was lying on the floor of the cave.

The cave was larger than most people would expect, and the grey rock had streaks of brown and red. There was almost room for a person to stand completely upright, and definitely enough room for six or seven people to sit within the cave. This place had been one of the most popular hideouts when Rhuaridh had been a kid and half the island had scraped their initials into the rock. He'd half a mind to flash his torch over the rock to find his own.

Rhuaridh caught the brief nod from Des. They'd been at school together years ago. He moved closer to the boy. 'Kai? How are you? I heard you jumped off the waterfall.'

His eyes were scanning up and down Kai's body. There was an angry-looking projection underneath the wetsuit covering his left foreleg.

He touched Kai's shoulders. 'One of your friends said you couldn't feel your legs, is that still true?'

'I wish!' said Kai loudly as he groaned again.

Des caught Rhuaridh's eye. 'He said at the beginning he couldn't feel his legs but that was literally only for a few moments. He's been feeling pain in his leg ever since, and for obvious reasons I've not moved him.'

Rhuaridh nodded. He knew exactly what he'd find if he cut Kai's wetsuit open. The only question was whether the bone was protruding from the skin. Right now, it was covered by the wetsuit and still protected.

Rhuaridh turned around and tugged the portable stretcher free from its packaging and started opening it out. There was no way Kai would be able to walk or swim anywhere.

Des had worked as an instructor at the wilderness centre for years and was experienced enough to need little direction. He helped unfold the stretcher while Rhuaridh took some time to assess Kai. He held his hands above the injured leg. 'Okay, I promise I'm not going to touch that bit. But I am going to take a look.' He pulled a torch from his backpack and checked the skin colour. 'Can you wiggle your toes?'

Kai grimaced but wiggled his toes while letting out a low yelp.

'Allergic to anything?'

Kai shook his head.

'How old are you?'

'Fourteen.'

'Any medical conditions I should know about? Or any regular medicines you need to take?'

Kai shook his head to both questions.

'Do you know how much you weigh?'

'Why?'

'I'm going to give you something to ease the pain. We're

going to have to help you onto the stretcher, then carry you out through the waterfall. There's no other way out of here.'

Kai shook his head. 'No way. I can't stand the water pounding on my leg.'

Rhuaridh pulled out some kit. 'There's a metal hoop that fits on top of the stretcher. This plastic can go over the top of the hoop. It will keep the water off your leg, and hopefully protect you.' He looked at the water cascading past his shoulder. 'There *is* no other way out of here. We can get you in the stretcher, but we couldn't manoeuvre it upright to slide you through the space at the side.'

He shook his head as he looked at it. 'I had to imitate a spider to get in here, and I still got soaked by the waterfall on the way in.' He turned to Des. 'You've been around here just as long as me. Can you think of any other way to get him out?'

Des shook his head too. 'Not a chance. He's almost the same size as you and me. There's no way we could manoeuvre him. We just need to go straight through the waterfall.'

Rhuaridh calculated how much pain relief to give Kai and administered it quickly. 'We'll give it some time to take effect before we get you onto the stretcher.'

The radio at his waist crackled. 'Rhuaridh? Rhuaridh, are you there?'

Kristie's voice echoed around the cave. 'Who's that?' asked Des.

Rhuaridh pulled the radio from his waistband. 'What's up, Kristie?'

'They're not here yet and he's starting to wake up.'

'The ambulance crew haven't arrived?' He was surprised. He'd expected them to arrive a few minutes after he left.

'No.' Her voice sounded kind of strained. 'Gerry's here.

He got dropped back at our car and came himself. Apparently the ambulance had to stop at a road accident. They've taken the people to the hospital.'

Rhuaridh shook his head. Typical. Everything happened at once. The ambulance hadn't been used at all in the last week and now two simultaneous calls.

'Kristie, tell me the numbers on the monitor.'

There was silence for a few seconds, then her voice came through. 'The P is eighty-six. That's his pulse, isn't it?'

'That's fine. What's the other one?'

'It's ninety-seven.'

'That's his oxygen saturation. That's good. It means his breathing and lungs are okay.'

'Uh-oh.'

Rhuaridh sat up on his knees. 'What do you mean, "uh-oh"? Kristie?'

There was a crackle. Then a rumble of voices—all muffled. It was hard to hear anything with the constant background roar of falling water. Rhuaridh exchanged a look with Des. He'd never met the other instructor at the centre. Throughout the year many instructors from different countries came to help at the centre—Des was the only real constant. 'Your guy. Anything I should know about him?'

Des's brow wrinkled. 'Ross?' He shook his head. 'Don't think so. He's been here about three weeks. Worked in a similar place in Wales.'

'Any medical history?'

Des pulled a face. 'To be honest, I can't remember. But if there had been anything major it would be on his initial application form.'

Rhuaridh knew that all the paperwork for the centre would be up to date. Des's wife dealt with that. But he also knew that Des wouldn't recall a single thing about it. He'd never been a paper person.

'Rhuaridh!' The shout came through the crackling radio and made all three in the cave start.

'Kristie, what's wrong?'

Even though it was difficult, he was on his feet, crouching in the cave. Staring at the rushing water that was currently between Kristie and himself.

'He's thrashing about. I think he's having some kind of seizure, what do I do?'

He could hear the panic in her voice. He signalled with his head to Des, who immediately pulled the prepared stretcher alongside Kai, knowing they would have to get out of there quickly.

'Do you know the recovery position?' he radioed to Kristie.

'W-hat?'

'His side. Turn him on his left-hand side. Get Gerry or some of the older kids to help you if need be. Once he's on his side pull up his right leg slightly and bring his right arm over so his hand is on the ground in front of him.'

And then there was nothing. No reply. No chatter. Just silence as his stomach churned. Either Ross's head injury had caused agitation and Kristie was mistaken, or he was having a full-blown seizure—neither of which were good signs. Kai would already need to be sent to the mainland for surgery. Now it looked like Ross would need to be airlifted. The nearest head injury unit was in Glasgow—it would take too long to get there by ambulance and ferry.

'Ready, Doc?'

Des had moved to Kai's head and shoulders, ready to slide the lad onto the stretcher. Rhuaridh bent down straight away. 'Sure. Kai, your painkiller should have started working by now. We're going to slide you over onto the stretcher. It should only be a bit uncomfortable, and once you're on the stretcher the metal hoop will mean that nothing will touch your leg.'

He was trying hard to stay very calm, all while his brain wondered how Kristie was doing. He'd left her out there. He knew she wasn't medically qualified at all, but he'd felt duty bound to come and assess his other patient. Would he have left her out there if he'd known the ambulance would be so long?

His mouth was dry. He couldn't help but remember that momentary glance in her eyes when she'd told him hospitals freaked her out. He'd wanted to ask more, but there hadn't been time. He was drawn to this woman. He liked her. He couldn't ignore the flicker of attraction that seemed to permeate the air around them. But the truth was he barely knew her.

He was moving on autopilot. 'Ready?' he asked Kai.

The teenage boy screwed up his face and Des held him by the shoulders and Rhuaridh gently took the weight off his legs. The movement was swift, with only a minor yelp from Kai. Des helped move the plastic casing quickly over the stretcher, zipping it closed, protecting the rest of Kai's body and only leaving his face exposed.

'Who is going first?' Des asked as he eyed the cascading waterfall. Each of them was going to have to step through it carrying the stretcher.

'I'll do it,' said Rhuaridh quickly. He tried the radio again. 'Kristie, how are you? How is Ross? Have you got him in the recovery position?'

There was an agonising pause.

'I think so. But he's still…twitching.'

'I'll be right there.' He could hear the tension in her voice. He wanted to jump straight through the waterfall and be by her side. But he was a doctor. He was so used to taking the emotion out of things and doing the duty he was bound to—like now, when he had to try and take care of two injured patients. Where was that darned ambulance?

Before he had chance to let his brain churn any more he signalled to Kai and Des. 'Are we ready?'

They nodded. Rhuaridh looked at Kai. 'When I give you the signal, take a deep breath. I'll have the front end of the stretcher and we'll literally just need to walk through the waterfall. You know the pond isn't particularly deep. This isn't dangerous. Just a few moments of pounding water around your ears.'

Kai nodded. 'I've been through it once when Des pulled me back in here. I'll be okay. Let's get this over with.'

Rhuaridh put the rest of the equipment back in the rucksack and put it on his back. He jumped down into the pool with the waterfall directly at his back. The noise was deafening, so he used signals to grab the stretcher above his shoulders and gesture to Kai. Des was ready and they moved swiftly through the waterfall and back out into the pool. Water cascaded over them, but it only took a few seconds to be free of the noise and clear their noses and mouths.

From the crest of the hill he could see a flash of bright green. The paramedics had finally arrived. Most of the kids were still crowded around the sides of the pool. They waded slowly across, setting Kai down gently as his friends surrounded him. One of the paramedics knelt beside him, and the other joined Rhuaridh at Kristie's side.

Her eyes were glinting with fear. 'He's literally just stopped shaking. He seemed to wake up for a few seconds, thrashing his legs and arms out, then he started shaking again.'

There was a red mark on the side of her cheek.

'Did you get caught by his arm?' asked Rhuaridh.

She shook her head. 'I'm fine. It doesn't matter.'

But it did to Rhuaridh.

It only took a few moments to assess Ross and to arrange an air ambulance for him. His pupil reactions were sluggish now and it was obvious the knock to the head had been harsh. He needed proper assessment in a specialist centre.

Rhuaridh then took time to recheck Kai before loading him up in the ambulance with the paramedics, ready for transfer for surgery.

By the time the ambulance had left with both patients, Des had gathered the teenagers together to take them back to the wilderness centre. Gerry was still chatting to a few that he'd caught on film.

Kristie was standing at the side, dirt smudged on her cheek and on the knees of her trousers. Rhuaridh reached out, took her hand and led her off to the side, pulling her down next to him on a large overturned tree trunk that had fallen over years before.

'Are you okay? I'm sorry that I left you.'

She gave a small shake of her head, fixing her gaze on the view ahead.

He hadn't let go of her, enclosing one of her slim hands in both of his. She moved her gaze to meet his.

He held his breath. He couldn't help it. All he could focus on was the blue of her eyes. The hand he held between his was trembling slightly and he gave it a squeeze. 'I didn't mean to leave you alone so long. I thought the ambulance would only be a few minutes.'

Her voice was quiet. 'You had to go and check on the boy. I know that.' She gave a weak smile, 'You're a doctor. It's your job.'

'But it's not yours,' he replied, his voice hoarse.

She'd been shaking. She was pale. Pieces were falling into place. Now he understood why she'd seemed distracted in the hospital. He'd thought she either wasn't that interested or had just had her mind on other things.

She'd been nervous. She'd been scared. And he'd missed it.

'Why don't you tell me why you don't like hospitals, Kristie?'

She licked her lips and shook her head. 'It's not something we need to talk about.'

She looked him straight in the eye and pulled her hand free from his, lifting it to touch his cheek. 'You just scaled part of a rock face and walked through a waterfall, Dr Gillespie. Some people might call that superhero material.'

'What would you call it?' The words were out instantly. Instinct. His gut reaction to that question. Because he really wanted to know the answer. He wanted to know exactly what Kristie Nelson thought about him.

If he'd thought for a few more seconds he'd have realised she'd just avoided his question. The one that might get to the heart of who she was.

'I haven't quite decided yet,' she whispered, the edges of her mouth turning upwards. 'But things are looking up.'

Her hand on his skin was making his pulse race. His eyes went instinctively to her mouth. The mouth he wanted to kiss.

He moved forward, all rational thoughts leaving his brain as his lips firmly connected with hers. She reacted instantly, leaning in towards him and sliding one hand up the side of his neck. He knew she needed comfort. He knew she needed reassurance. This seemed so obvious, so natural and it looked like Kristie thought so too.

Her skin was cold, but her lips were warm. Sweet. Responsive. She didn't seem to mind they were sitting on a log in the middle of the damp countryside. She didn't seem to mind at all, and as her hand raked through his hair he could almost feel the temperature rising around them.

But little alarms were going off in his brain, like red flags frantically waving. How could he kiss her when he knew there was something else affecting her?

He took a deep breath. He reluctantly pulled back. For a

moment, neither of them spoke—just stared at each other as if they couldn't quite believe what had just happened.

Rhuaridh pressed his lips together for a second, doing his best to collect his thoughts. The ones he was currently having involved sweeping Kristie up into his arms, into his car and away from this whole place. But she'd said something. She'd revealed a part of herself that she hadn't before and every instinct told him that he had to try and peel back more of Kristie's layers.

'Wow,' she said softly as a hint of a smile touched her lips.

'Wow,' he agreed. His timing was all wrong. He looked at her steadily, keeping his voice even. 'Kristie, I do think we need to talk.'

There was a flash of momentary confusion in her eyes. He could almost see the shutters going down again, as if she knew what was about to come next.

He kept going. 'I think the reason you don't like hospitals is important. I think, when I work with someone, if something significant has happened in the past that affects how they feel or think about something, I should know. I should know not to expose them to a situation that they might find hard.'

She pulled her hand back as if she'd been stung. 'Is that what we're doing, working together?'

It was the way she asked the question—as if those words actually hurt—that made him catch his breath. He could hear it in her voice. The unspoken question. Was that all it was? Particularly after that kiss...

But she didn't wait for an answer. She just brushed off her trousers, stood up and walked away...for the second time.

CHAPTER SIX

October

SHE CLOSED HER social media account. *Will they? Won't they?* seemed to be everywhere she looked. She'd even been invited on a talk show to discuss her blossoming 'relationship' with Rhuaridh Gillespie, the world's hottest Highland doc.

'I'm going to kill you, Gerry,' she muttered.

He was staring out of the ferry window at the thrashing sea, rubbing his chest distractedly. 'No, you're not. You've got the most popular show on the network. You love it.'

'I don't have time to love it. I can't get a minute of peace.' She rubbed her eyes and leaned against the wall.

'What's wrong?' he asked.

She sighed. 'There was a call last night.' She rubbed her hands up both arms. It was cold. Scotland was much colder than LA, but that chill had seemed to come out of nowhere. 'It was hard. I don't know if I helped. I've spent the whole journey wondering if…' Her voice trailed off.

Gerry touched her shoulder. 'Don't. You volunteer. You counsel. You're the person who listens in the middle of the night when someone needs to talk. You do the best that you can. That's all you can do.'

She put her head back on the wall. Fatigue sweeping over her. 'I know that. But I can't help but worry.'

'You don't look that great,' said Gerry.

She closed her eyes for a second. 'I don't feel that great. I forgot to take my seasickness tablets. I'll be fine when we land.'

The truth was she was nervous, and a little bit sad. She wasn't quite sure what to say to Rhuaridh. She'd felt the connection. And she was sure he had too.

Didn't their kiss prove it? But that had been fleeting. Rhuaridh had stopped it almost as soon as it had started. And then he'd pressed about the thing she didn't want to talk about. Wasn't ready to talk about.

And it had haunted her for the last month. Her head even felt fuzzy right now. She loosened the scarf she'd wound around her neck. It was irritating her. They'd started filming earlier, following up on Ross, the instructor with the head injury last month, who'd had emergency surgery. He was staying in Glasgow, recovering well, even though he was pale with a large part of his hair now missing. The young boy, Kai, had his leg in a cast but took great delight in showing them just how fast he could get about on his crutches.

Thank goodness those two parts of filming were wrapped up. It would mean they would need less footage whilst on Arran. She closed her eyes, part of her not wanting to spend too much time in Rhuaridh's company and part of her aching for it.

She was so confused right now. And who was making all that noise? She shivered, pulling her coat closer around her. Rhuaridh. Sometimes thinking about him made her angry, sometimes it made her feel warm all over. Her mind would drift back to that second on the beach...then that second sitting in the woods together. Her life currently felt like a bad young adult romance novel.

'Kristie. Kristie.' Someone was shaking her. 'We need to go. Here, give me the keys. I'll drive.'

'What? No?' She stood up and promptly swayed and sat back down. Had she actually fallen asleep?

Gerry was looking at her oddly. 'You're sick,' he said, holding out his hand for the car key. 'I'll drive. It's the same place as last time.'

She thought about saying no. She knew Gerry didn't like driving 'abroad', as he put it. But she was just so darned tired. She pushed the keys towards him. 'Okay, just once. And don't crash.'

'Kristie? You need to drink something.'

She moved, wondering why the bed felt so lumpy, trying to turn around, but her face met an unexpected barrier. She spluttered and opened her eyes. Dark blue was facing her. What?

She pushed herself back, trying to work out why there was a solid wall of dark blue in the bedroom in the cottage.

The voice started again. 'Kristie? Turn back this way. You need to drink something.'

Her brain wasn't making sense. Was she dreaming?

She moved back around again. Opening her eyes properly. They took a moment to focus. Directly ahead was a flickering orange fire. She pushed herself up, the material underneath her unfamiliar, velvety to touch. She looked down. She wasn't in her bed in the cottage. In fact, she didn't recognise this place at all. 'What? Wh…where am I?'

A face appeared before her. One she couldn't mistake. 'Rhuaridh?'

He nodded and knelt at the side of what she presumed must be his sofa. 'Here.' He held a glass of water with a straw. 'Will you drink something?'

Her throat felt dry and scratchy. She grabbed the straw and took a drink of the cold water. Nothing had ever tasted so good.

She moved, swinging her legs so she was sitting up

right. 'Ooh…' Her head felt as if she'd been pushed from side to side.

'Careful. You haven't sat up for over a day.'

She blinked and took a few breaths, looking down at the large, soft white T-shirt she was wearing, along with an unfamiliar pair of grey brushed-cotton pyjama bottoms.

'Whose are these? And…' she looked about again '…how did I end up here?'

Rhuaridh pulled a face. 'The clothes? I guess they're yours. I had to buy emergency supplies for you. And you ended up here because Gerry panicked. He couldn't wake you up or get you out the car after you landed from the ferry. Your temperature was through the roof and you were quite confused.'

'I was?' She hated that she couldn't remember a single thing about this. 'But…you're busy. You don't have time to look after someone.' She was suddenly very self-conscious that she staying in the doctor's house.

He shrugged. 'I'm the doctor. It's what I do.'

Her head was feeling a little straighter. She tugged at the T-shirt self-consciously. 'What's been wrong with me?'

'You've had some kind of virus.'

'You're a doctor, and that's all you can tell me?' she asked, without trying to hide her surprise.

'Yes,' he said as he smiled. 'Your temperature has gone up and down as your body has fought off the virus. It made you a bit confused at times. You needed sleep to give your body a chance to do the work it had to.'

'Why didn't you send me to hospital?'

'Because you didn't need to go to hospital. You needed complete rest, simple paracetamol and some fluids.' He stood up. 'And some chicken soup—which I've just finished making. I'll go and get you some.'

He walked away towards the kitchen then ducked back

and gave her a cheeky wink. 'You gave me five minutes of panic, though—you had a bit of a rash.'

She stared down in horror, wondering where on earth the rash had been—and how he had seen it.

All of a sudden she realised that someone had changed her into these clothes and put her others somewhere else. She looked around the room. It was larger than she might have expected. Comfortably decorated with a wooden coffee table between her and the flickering fire, the large navy-blue sofa and armchairs. At the far end of the room next to one of the windows was a dining table and chairs, with some bookshelves built into the walls. Part of her wanted to sneak over and check his reading materials.

Rhuaridh appeared a few moments later carrying a tray. The smell of the soup alone made her stomach growl. He laughed as he sat down next to her, his leg brushing against hers.

He slid the tray over towards her. There was a pot of tea, a bowl of chicken and rice soup that looked so thick she could stand her spoon in it, and some crusty bread and butter.

'Aren't you having some?' she asked, conscious of the fact she'd be eating in front of him. He nodded. 'Give me a sec.' He walked back through to the kitchen then joined her on the sofa as she took her first spoonful of soup.

It was delicious. Not like anything they had in LA. Soup wasn't that popular there. But she'd noticed in Scotland a whole variety of soups seemed a staple part of the diet. 'You actually made this?'

He nodded. 'From an old recipe of my dad's. I can make this one, Scotch broth, lentil and bacon, and tomato.' He frowned as he was thinking. 'I can also make mince and potatoes, stovies, steak pie, and chicken and leek pie. After that? My menu kind of falls off a cliff.'

'Okay, is this where I admit I only know what part of that menu is?'

She was starting to feel a little more alive. Now she'd woken up and orientated herself, she wasn't quite so embarrassed by what had happened. Rhuaridh had looked after a million patients. He was a doctor. It was his job.

She kept on spooning up the soup. 'I think this is the best thing I've ever tasted,' she admitted. 'You'll need to teach me. I can't make anything like this. In fact, avocado and toast is about my limit.'

'What do you eat in LA?'

She grinned. 'Avocado and toast. And anything else that I buy in a store.'

She liked the way he laughed. Deep and hearty.

It didn't take long to finish the soup. She sighed and leaned back on the sofa. 'That was great.'

His hand brushed against hers as he moved the tea on the table in front of her and lifted her soup bowl. It made her start.

'I wonder… I know it's been an imposition having me here, but could I use your shower before I get ready to go back to my own cottage?'

He pointed to the staircase. 'There's a spare room with an en suite bathroom at the top of the stairs. Some of your things are in there. I only brought you down here when you were so cold—so the fire could heat you.'

He'd carried her. He'd carried her down here. The intimacy of the act made her cheeks blaze unexpectedly.

As Rhuaridh made his way back to the kitchen, she practically ran up the stairs. Sure enough, the white bedclothes were rumpled and there was a bag with her clothes at the side. Her stomach flip-flopped. She grabbed what she could and headed to the shower.

He'd spent the last day worrying about her. When Gerry had turned up at his door, it had taken him all his time to assess her to reassure himself that there was nothing serious going on.

The sigh that Gerry had finally let out when Rhuaridh had told him that it was likely she had some kind of virus her body was fighting off had filled the room. He'd sent Gerry back to the rental, advising him that he'd watch over her.

Against his spare white bedding she'd looked pale, her normal tan bleached from her skin, and her temperature had been raging. He'd had to strip her clothes off, then try and dose her with some paracetamol whilst she'd been barely conscious.

He'd known it would pass. He'd known it was part and parcel of the body fighting off a virus—and sleeping was the best thing she could do. But it didn't stop him settling into a chair in the corner of the room and spending an uncomfortable night there, watching over Kristie.

Next day he'd run out to the nearest shop to buy her something to wear as the virus ran its course and she went from hot to cold. He'd had a heart-stopping minute when he'd pulled back the bedclothes and seen the red rash all over her abdomen. But it had faded just as quickly as it had appeared and he'd pulled the pyjamas onto her.

Now she was awake and showering—and would probably want to leave. And he was struck by how sorry he was about that. He'd never shared this cottage with anyone. Since he'd moved to Arran he hadn't brought anyone back to this space. Mac was watching carefully from the corner. He'd come over and sniffed at Kristie a few times, then nudged her in the hope she'd wake up and bring him food. When that hadn't happened he'd slumped off to the corner again.

It had been over a year since Rhuaridh had lived with someone. The penthouse flat that he'd shared with Zoe in one of the central areas of Glasgow didn't have the charm of this old cottage. Its plain white walls and sterile glass now seemed to Rhuaridh like some kind of indicator of their relationship. Zoe had liked living with a colleague who was doing well. Someone she thought might 'go places'. Of course, that had all come to a resounding crash when he'd told her his intention to return home to Arran as a general practitioner.

He couldn't remember the strength of his feelings back then. If Zoe had been sick, would she even have wanted Rhuaridh to take care of her—the way he had Kristie? It was likely not. There were no similarities between the two women. Zoe didn't have the warmth that Kristie did. Even when Kristie was sick, she'd still occasionally reached out and squeezed his hand.

There was something about that connection. That taking care of someone. Letting them share the space that was essentially yours. Somehow with Kristie it didn't feel intrusive. It just felt…right. He'd never experienced that with Zoe. Instead, he'd just felt like part of her grand plan. One that had come to a resounding halt when he'd said he was moving back to Arran. Rejection always hurt. That, and the feeling of not being 'enough' for someone. He had none of that from Kristie. Instead, it felt like they were pieces of the same puzzle—albeit from thousands of miles apart—that just seemed to fit together. And it didn't matter that long term it all seemed impossible, because right now was all he wanted to think about.

Rhuaridh turned as Kristie came back down the stairs. Her damp hair was tied up, her cheeks looked a bit pinker and she'd changed into the clothes that Gerry had stuck in a bag and brought around yesterday. 'Stole some of your deodorant,' she said apologetically. 'Gerry's idea of toiletries seems to be only a toothbrush.'

'No worries,' he said casually. He pointed to the table.

'I made some more tea. I thought you wouldn't be ready for anything more sociable.'

She eyed the tea and accompanying plate of chocolate biscuits. 'That's about as sociable as I can manage,' she said as she sat back on the sofa and tucked her legs underneath her. 'Hey, Mac,' she said, calling the dog over and rubbing his head, 'I'm sorry, have I been ignoring you?' She bent down and dropped a kiss on his head. 'Promise you it wasn't intentional.'

She let Rhuaridh pour the tea and hand her a cup before he sat down next to her again. The pink T-shirt she was wearing made her look more like herself.

'I'm glad you're feeling better,' he said. And he meant it.

She sipped her tea. 'I'm so sorry. I've really put you out. What about work?'

He looked at her and gave a gentle shake of his head. 'It's Sunday. You arrived late on Friday night and there's been a locum on call at the hospital this weekend.'

Her eyes widened as she realised what those words meant. Her hand flew to her mouth. 'Your first weekend off? Oh, no. I'm so sorry. You must have had plans.'

He shrugged. 'I guess you changed them for me.'

She blinked. Her eyes looked wet. 'I'm sorry,' she whispered, her voice a bit croaky.

'Don't be. You brightened up our weekend. Mac's getting bored with me anyhow. He likes the change of company.'

She gave him a curious glance. 'Do you normally bring patients back to your house?'

He paused, knowing exactly how this would sound. 'There's a first time for everything.'

Her breathing faltered and that made his own hitch. He wondered if she'd say something else but instead she sighed and leaned back against the sofa again. 'We've missed filming. We won't have time to get much more.'

'Gerry didn't seem too worried. To be honest, after his initial moment of panic, he almost seemed relieved. I think the guy might need a bit of a break.'

'You've spoken to Gerry?'

'He's been round a few times.' He didn't add that Gerry might have filmed her while she'd slept. That was for Gerry to sort out. According to Gerry, a host's consent was implicit, it was built into their contract—no matter what the situation.

She shuffled a little on the sofa and rested her head on his shoulder. 'We got some footage before we got here. You know about Kai and Ross?'

He was surprised. He hadn't realised they were being so thorough. 'I knew that you followed up on Magda and the baby, but I didn't know you'd followed up on all the other patients too.'

She lifted her head and looked him in the eye. 'Of course. The viewers love it. They want to know if everyone is okay. Haven't you realised that human beings are essentially nosy creatures and want to know everything?'

He could answer that question in so many ways. He could laugh. He could crack a joke. But he didn't.

He'd looked after Kristie for the last twenty-four hours. And at so many points in that time he'd wished he didn't only get to spend three days at a time with her. He'd wished all their time wasn't spent filming. He'd prefer it if it could just be them, without anyone else, no patients, no cameras.

So he didn't make a joke because this was it. This was the time to ask the question he should have asked before.

'Why don't you tell me?' he said gently.

'Tell me what?'

'Tell me why you don't like hospitals.' He could see it instantly. The shadow passing over her eyes.

She swallowed and stared into the fire for a few moments, then reached up and brushed her hand against her damp hair. She wasn't looking at him. He could see he'd lost her to some past memory. Maybe it was the only way she could do this.

'I don't like hospitals because I had to go there...' her voice trembled '...when my sister died.'

The words cut into him like a knife. Now he understood. Now he knew why he could always tell that something was amiss.

'It's everything,' she continued. 'The lights, the smell, the busyness, and even the quiet. The overall sound and bustle of the place.' Now she turned to meet his gaze and he could see just how exposed she was. 'And it doesn't matter where in the world the hospital is because, essentially, they're all the same. And they all evoke the same memories for me.'

He was nodding now as he reached out and took one of her hands in his, intertwining their fingers. 'This job?' she said, as she dipped her head. 'It was the absolute last one that I wanted. I wanted the Egyptian museum. I wanted the astronaut's life. Not because I thought they were more exciting, just because I knew they wouldn't bring me to a hospital. And you—' she looked straight at him '—were always going to do that to me.'

He kept nodding. He was beginning to understand her a little more. Just like he wanted to. But she hadn't answered the most important question. 'What happened to your sister, Kristie?'

She blinked, her eyes filled with tears. 'I don't talk about it,' she whispered. 'Hardly anyone knows.'

'You don't have to tell me. I want you to trust me, Kristie. I want you to know that I'm your friend.' Friend? Was that what you called someone he'd kissed the way he'd kissed her?

He was treading carefully. He had to. He could tell how

delicate this all was for her. Holding hands was as much as she could handle right now and he knew that.

She closed her eyes and kept them that way. 'My sister was unwell. She'd been unwell for a long time, and…' a tear slid down her cheek '…felt that no one was listening. She took her own life.'

The words finished with a sob and he pulled her forward into his arms.

He didn't speak. He knew there was nothing he could say right now that would help. She'd told him hardly anyone knew and she didn't really talk about it, so this had been building up in her for a long time. Pain didn't lessen with time, often it was amplified. Often it became even more raw than it had been before.

He hated Kristie feeling that way, so he stayed there and he held her, stroking her hair and her back softly until she was finally all cried out.

'I'm sorry,' he whispered.

She lifted her head and tilted her face towards his. 'You said we were friends,' she said hoarsely. 'Are we friends? Because what I'm feeling… I don't feel that way about a friend.'

He could feel his heart thudding in his chest. It was almost as if she'd been reading his mind for the past two months—ever since they'd sat on that log together. Since they'd shared that kiss. 'How do you feel?'

She reached up and touched the side of his face. 'How many people have you looked after in your house?' she asked.

'None.'

'How many people have you made chicken soup for?' She tilted her head and smiled at him.

He couldn't help but return that smile. 'None.'

She slid her hand up around his neck. 'Then I'm

going to take it for granted that all of this…' she paused '…means something.'

'I think you could be right,' he whispered as he bent forward and finally put his lips on hers.

And all of sudden everything felt right.

CHAPTER SEVEN

November

'I'M SORRY, MISS. That's the just the way is it. We've cancelled the ferries for the rest of today. We can't take them
out in a storm like this. We'd never get docked on the other
side, it's not safe for the passengers or the crew.'

She could feel panic start to creep up her chest.

'But you'll sail tomorrow, won't you?'

He shook his head. 'Not likely. The storm's forecast to
be even worse tomorrow. And it's to last the next day too.
It could be Thursday before the ferries are sailing again.'

She couldn't breathe. She couldn't miss filming—not
because of the show but because, if she didn't film, she
didn't get to spend time with Rhuaridh. The guy she'd been
counting down the last four weeks for. The guy she'd been
texting every day. And most nights.

Gerry shook his head. 'Louie won't be happy with this.
We'll need to use whatever unused footage we have.' He
made a bit of a face and walked away.

The man at the ferry terminal gave her a shrug. 'Sorry,
it only usually happens around twice a year. Storms get
so bad no one can get off or on the island.'

'But there must be another way? A smaller boat? A
helicopter? What if there's a medical emergency?'

The man gave her a look. 'To take a smaller boat out in

this weather would be suicide. As for emergencies, everyone on the island knows that this can sometimes happen.
If the doc can't fix it, it can't be fixed.'

She stepped back. He'd got her with that word. *Suicide*.
She'd been desperate. She'd been ready to run around the
harbour to try and charter a smaller boat. But she wouldn't
do that now. Not after that word.

She looked out through the glass at the ferry terminal. She couldn't even see Arran on the horizon, just the
mass of grey swirling storm, and hear the thud of the
pouring rain.

Another month without seeing Rhuaridh again?

It had never seemed so long.

CHAPTER EIGHT

December

HE WAS WAITING at the ferry terminal. It was ridiculous. She would be driving the hire car but he still wanted to see her. Two months. Two months since their second kiss.

Sometimes he felt guilty, thinking he'd taken advantage. But from the stream of messages they'd exchanged since then, there had been no indication that she thought that.

Was it possible to actually get to know someone better by text, email and a few random video chats? Because it felt like it was. He'd learned that Kristie's favourite position was sitting on her chair at home, in her yoga pants, eating raisins.

She'd learned that he was addicted to an orange-coloured now sugar-free fizzy drink that some people called Scotland's national drink. He didn't let many people know that. She'd also laughed as she'd watched him try to follow a new recipe and increase his limited kitchen menu, and fail dismally.

It was only when he was standing on the snow-covered dock that he realised he'd no idea what car she would be driving this time. But she spotted him first, flashing her headlights and pulling to a stop next to him in the car park.

'Hey!' She jumped out of the car with a wide smile on

her face. At first she looked as if she was about to throw her arms around him, but something obviously stopped her as she halted midway and looked a bit awkward. Instead, she held out her hands. 'Snow,' she said simply as she looked about.

She lifted her chin up towards the gently falling snow, closing her eyes and smiling as she spun around.

Gerry got out of the car and looked mildly amused.

'You've never seen snow before?' asked Rhuaridh.

'Of course I haven't,' she said, still spinning around. 'I live in LA. It's hardly snow central.'

Rhuaridh looked over at Gerry. 'What about you?'

Gerry shook his head. 'Don't worry about me. I spent three months filming in Alaska. I *know* snow.'

Rhuaridh smiled as he kept watching Kristie. He'd never realised this would be her first experience of snow. 'It's not even lying properly,' he said. 'Give it another day and we might actually be able to build a snowman or have a snowball fight.'

'Really?' She stopped spinning, her eyes sparkling.

He nodded. 'Sure. Now come on, I'm taking you two guys to dinner in the pub just down the road. Let's go.'

'Good for me,' said Gerry quickly, climbing back into the car.

Kristie stepped up in front of him. 'You don't have to do that,' she said, still smiling.

She was so close he caught the scent of her perfume. It was different, something headier. 'But I want to.' He slid his hand behind her, holding her for the briefest of seconds. 'I might have missed having you around.'

'Good.' She blinked as a large snowflake landed on her eyelashes. 'Let's keep that up.'

Part of her was excited and part of her was laced with a tiny bit of trepidation. Louie was massively excited. It seemed he'd taken over production of the episode where she'd been unwell and had included footage of Rhuaridh looking after her, interspersed with a few repetitions of their previous interactions.

It wasn't her favourite episode because it felt so intrusive. The whole episode was literally dedicated to the relationship between them, rather than the life of a Highland doc. But Louie had argued his case well. 'The viewers have been waiting for this. They want it. And what else have we got to show them this month? You didn't exactly do any filming on the island, we were lucky Gerry actually filmed anything at all.'

She knew in a way he was right. But when she'd taken on this role, she hadn't realised the story would become about her too.

Watching the scenes where Rhuaridh had been looking after her had brought a lump to her throat. He was so caring. So quietly concerned. It was a side of him she hadn't seen before. And the way that he'd looked at her at times had made her heart melt. Thank goodness Gerry hadn't been around to film their kiss. She hadn't told him about either of the times they'd kissed. He was already looking at her a bit suspiciously—as if he suspected something— so she didn't plan on revealing anything more.

The pub that Rhuaridh took them to was warm and welcoming, panelled with wood. Every table was taken and the pub was full of Christmas decorations—twinkling lights, a large decorated tree and red and green garlands underneath the bar. Rhuaridh insisted they all eat a traditional Scottish Christmas dinner—turkey, stuffing, roast potatoes, tiny sausages, Brussels sprouts and mashed turnip all covered in gravy. 'This is delicious,' said Gerry. 'A bit more like our Thanksgiving dinner. But I like it. I could eat more of this.'

Kristie leaned back and rubbed her stomach, groaning. 'No way. I couldn't eat another single thing.'

Rhuaridh was watching them both with a smile on his face. 'Well, I'm still trying to make up for the fact you spent a few days here eating hardly anything.'

'Are you trying to take care of me, Dr Gillespie?' she teased.

He shook his head. 'No way. You're far too difficult a patient.' There was a twinkle in his eyes as he said the word. He glanced at Gerry, obviously not wanting this conversation to become too personal. 'What are your plans for filming this time? Do we need to make up for lost time?'

Kristie shifted a little uncomfortably, not quite sure how to tell him about the episode that would go out in a few weeks, but Gerry got in there first. 'Don't worry,' he said with a wave of his hand, 'we've got that covered. We had some old unused footage and just mixed it with the fact that Kristie was pretty much out of action.'

'Oh, okay.' Rhuaridh seemed to accept the explanation easily. 'So what about this time?'

Kristie had given this some thought. 'We've got quite a bit of footage of some of the patients in the cottage hospital. Christmas is a big deal. I know we're not actually here for Christmas Day, but it might be nice if we could get some film of how the staff deal with patients who they know will have to stay in hospital for Christmas.'

Rhuaridh lifted his eyebrows. 'You mean, you actually want some heart-warming stuff for Christmas instead of some kind of crisis?'

Gerry laughed. 'If you can whip us up a crisis we'll always take it, but I think we were going to try and keep with the season of goodwill. On a temporary basis, of course.'

Rhuaridh looked carefully at Kristie. 'Do you feel okay about filming in the hospital?'

Gerry's eyebrows shot upwards. He had no idea that

she'd shared her secret with the doc. Kristie cleared her throat awkwardly, trying to buy a bit of time. But she could come up with nothing. It seemed that honesty might be for the best.

'He knows about Jess. I told him.'

She couldn't decipher the look Gerry gave her. 'Okay, then,' he said simply.

She took a few moments. She'd thought about this when Louie had suggested it. Everything previously had seemed like a diktat—it had been required for the show so she'd had to grit her teeth and get on with it. She'd been so fixated on how she felt about hospitals, deep down, that she hadn't taken the time to reconsider how her perspective might have changed a little. 'We're talking about the older patients who are too sick to get home. You know I met some of them before?'

Rhuaridh nodded.

She smiled as things seemed to click in her mind. 'I actually really enjoyed talking with some of them. They're not patients. They're people. People who've lived long, very interesting lives and have a hundred tales to tell. Maybe we should try and film an update on a few of the people we've spoken to before—and maybe we should ask them about Christmases from years gone by. How did people normally celebrate Christmas on Arran? Are there any special traditions?'

Rhuaridh and Gerry exchanged a glance and looked at her, then at each other again.

Gerry leaned over the table. 'What do you think's happened to her?'

'I think she's turned into some kind of Christmas holiday movie. You know—the kind that play on that TV channel constantly at Christmas.'

Kristie laughed and nudged both of them. 'Stop it, you guys. Maybe I'm just getting into the spirit of things. First time I've seen snow. First time I've been in a place that's cold at Christmas. All my life I've spent my Christmases in sunshine next to a pool. Give a girl a break. I'm just getting in the mood.'

As soon as she said the words she felt her cheeks flush. She hadn't quite meant it to come out like that. Gerry didn't seem to notice, but she knew that Rhuaridh did as he gave her a gentle nudge with his leg under the table.

'It's settled, then,' said Gerry as he raised his pint glass towards them. 'Tomorrow we go be festive!'

Arran in the snow was truly gorgeous. He hadn't paid much attention before because snow in winter was the norm here. But somehow, seeing it through Kristie's eyes gave him a whole new perspective on how much the whole island looked like a Christmas-card scene.

Now, as he looked out of the window as they pulled up at the hospital, he took a deep breath and let himself love everything that he could see. He always had loved this place, but the break-up with Zoe had left him living under an uncomfortable cloud. Her words had continued to echo in his head.

'It's an island in the middle of nowhere. There's not a single thing to do on that place. How anyone can stay there more than one night is beyond me. I'd be bored witless in the first week.'

Those words had continued to wear away at him. The place where he'd grown up and loved hadn't been good enough for the woman he'd loved at that time. *He* hadn't been good enough for her.

His loyalties had felt tested to their limit. The loyalties and love he had for the place he'd called home, and his loyalties to his profession, his future dreams, and the woman he'd lived with.

For the first time he actually realised what a blessing it had been that things had come to a head.

He'd always wondered if the move to Arran again was just a temporary move—to fill the gap until someone else could be recruited for the GP surgery. But in the last two months things had changed and he couldn't help but wonder if the TV show was the cause of that.

For the first time in for ever there had been applicants for the GP locum weekend cover posts that had been advertised for as long as Rhuaridh had been here. That was why he'd had cover the last time Kristie had been here. Other GPs were taking an interest in Arran. He'd had some random emails, one asking about covering Magda's maternity leave, and another from a doctor who wanted to complete his GP training on the island. That had never happened before.

Before, he'd felt he was stuck here.

Now he knew he was choosing to stay here. And that made all the difference.

Kristie had a piece of red tinsel in her hair. 'Are we going in, or are we sitting here?'

He smiled. 'Let's go. I'm going to review a few patients while we're here.'

Gerry tagged behind a little, almost like he was giving them a bit of space. Rhuaridh wondered just how much the cameraman suspected. He'd been so tempted to give Kristie a kiss when she'd first arrived that he wondered if Gerry had noticed that.

Rhuaridh watched as Kristie entered the hospital. Her footsteps faltered a little but she held her head up high and ran her hand along the wall as she entered the building. It was like she was using it to steady herself. He paused for a second, then stopped worrying about who was around and who would see.

She'd shared with him why she was antsy around hospitals. She'd shared a part of herself. He walked alongside her and took her other hand in his, giving it a squeeze. She looked down—surprised—then squeezed back. He didn't say anything. He didn't have to.

They carried on down the corridor.

They were only in the hospital for a few minutes before one of the nursing assistants grabbed Kristie and persuaded her to help put up some more decorations.

'We can't put them in the clinical areas, but we can put them at the entrance and in the patients' day room.'

'No tree on the ward?' he heard Kristie say. She looked quite sad.

Rhuaridh shook his head. 'Infection control issues. Also allergies—they harbour dust. Health and safety too—they could be a fire risk.'

'Phew.' Kristie let out a huge sigh. 'How do you remember so many interesting rules and regulations?' She rolled her eyes. 'And here was me thinking that Christmas decorations would have a place in hospitals—to improve mental health, lift spirits, and to help orientate some of the older patients to time and place.'

He raised his eyebrows. 'Touché. What have you been reading?'

'Lots.' She smiled. 'I'm not just a pretty face.' Her words hung there as they smiled at each other, then she glanced over her shoulder as the nursing assistant appeared with another box. 'Or just an objectionable reporter,' she added quickly.

He pointed to the half-erected tree. 'This has been here for as long as I have. And, Ms Objectionable Reporter, the stuff you say about lifting spirits and orientating to time and place is right. But...' he paused '...our biggest issue in this season is winter vomiting—also known as norovirus. If we end up with that?' He held up his hands and shook his head. 'There's a huge outbreak cleaning protocol, and something like this would have to be taken down and disposed of if it had been in a clinical area.' He gave a shrug. 'Better safe than sorry.'

She picked up a piece of sparkling green tinsel and draped it around his neck. 'Aw, it's a shame. Maybe you could impersonate the Christmas tree instead?'

'Ha-ha. Now, don't you have patients to film?'

'Don't you have patients to see?'

The nursing assistant's head turned from side to side, smiling at the flirtation and teasing going on before her very eyes. 'Glad to see you two are finally getting on,' she said under her breath.

It gave Rhuaridh a bit of a jolt and he nodded and strode towards the ward. 'Catch up if you can,' he shouted over his shoulder.

He spent the next hour reviewing patients, writing prescriptions and watching Kristie out of the corner of his eye. She seemed easier, relaxed even. By now everyone was used to Gerry hovering around in the background with the camera.

It was nice to see her that way. She had a long conversation with one of the older men who was recuperating after a hip operation. She tried a few Christmas carols with a couple of the female patients. She helped put out cups of tea and coffee, and was particularly interested in the range of cakes that appeared from the hospital kitchen.

'It's like a baker's shop,' she said in wonder.

The nurse near her nodded. 'We find that often appetites are smaller when patients get older. Our kitchen staff are great. The cook was even in earlier, asking people what their favourites were. That's why we have Bakewell tarts, Empire biscuits and fairy cakes.'

Rhuaridh heard Kristie whisper, 'Don't you get into trouble about the sugar?'

The nurse shook her head. 'Not at this point. Calories

are important. Look around. Most of our patients are underweight, not overweight. We'd rather feed them what they like than look at artificial supplements.'

Kristie flitted from one patient to the next, squeezing hands and making jokes. Occasionally he glimpsed a far-off look in her eye that didn't last long. The patients loved her.

But the more he watched, the more he had nagging doubts. He couldn't pretend he didn't like her. The whole world could see that he did. But was the whole world also laughing at him? After all, what would a gorgeous girl from LA find interesting about a Scottish island? There were no TV studios, no job opportunities. Most of the time during winter half the island shut down. There was no cinema. No department stores—only a few local shops. There was one slightly posher hotel with a swimming pool, gym and spa but there wasn't a selection to choose from. And there were only two hairdressers on the entire island. Kristie had already told him she loved trying different places.

Zoe's words echoed around his head. Boring. Dull. Nothing to do.

He hadn't been able to maintain a long-term relationship with a woman in Glasgow just over fifty miles away. How on earth could he even contemplate anything with a woman from LA—five thousand miles away? He must be losing his marbles.

Just at that moment, Kristie leaned forward and pressed her head against that of one of the older, more confused patients. He could see she was talking quietly to him. His hands were trembling, and Kristie put her own over his, squeezing them in reassurance. She pointed to the Christmas tree through the doors. She was orientating him to time and place.

And that was it. A little bit of his heart melted. Did it

really matter if this would come to nothing? Maybe it was time for him to start living in the here and now.

And the here and now for him was that Kristie would still be visiting for three days a month for the next four months. And if that was all he'd get, he'd be a fool to let it slip through his fingers.

Her anxieties were slowly but surely beginning to melt away. She would always hate hospitals. They would always have that association for her. But somehow, this time, things felt different.

Different because she knew Rhuaridh had her back.

If she needed a minute—if her heart started racing or her breathing stuck somewhere inside her chest—she didn't need to hide it or pretend it was something else entirely. And the weird thing was that none of those things had actually happened.

Maybe it was Bill, the older man, who'd distracted her completely. In a lucid moment he'd just told her about his wife dying fifteen years before and how much it had broken his heart. Then he'd started to gently sing a Christmas carol they'd loved together. Kristie had joined in and when, a few moments later, he'd become confused and panicky, she'd taken his hand and reassured him about where he was, who he was, and what he was doing there.

This could be her. This could be Rhuaridh. This could be anyone that she knew and loved. No one knew what path lay ahead for them, and if she could give Bill a few moments of reassurance and peace then she would.

Rhuaridh came over and placed a warm hand on her shoulder. 'I've just finished. Do you have some more people to film?'

She shook her head. 'Gerry's looking tired. I think we've done enough today. We'll come back tomorrow and finish then.'

Rhuaridh gave a nod. 'Okay. The snow's got a bit thicker since yesterday. We might be able to scrounge up a few snowballs. Are you game?'

She wrinkled her nose. 'Game? What does that mean?'

He laughed. 'It's like a challenge. It means are you ready to do a particular action—like making snowballs.'

Now she understood. She took a few minutes to say goodbye to Bill, then joined Rhuaridh. 'Okay, then, I'm game.'

Gerry joined them outside, and grabbed the car keys while they plotted. The hospital grounds were large, with a grassy forecourt lined with trees.

'Why go anywhere else?' asked Kristie. She zipped up her new red winter jacket—which would never see the light of day in LA. She kicked at the thick snow on the ground. 'Let's just have our snowball fight here.' She put her hands on her hips and looked around, her breath steaming in the air in front of her. 'Or maybe we should start with a snowman. I've always wanted to build a snowman.'

Rhuaridh pulled some gloves out of his pocket. Kristie winced. Gloves. She'd forgotten about gloves. He walked closer. 'Did you forget the most essential tool for playing with snow?'

She grimaced, hating to start on the back foot. 'Maybe.'

He handed his gloves over. 'Here, use mine.'

She grinned. 'Doesn't you being a gentleman give me an unfair advantage?'

His eyes gleamed. He leaned forward, his lips brushing against the side of her face as he whispered in her ear. 'Yeah, but that would only count if I thought you might actually win.'

'That's fighting talk.' She gave him her sternest glare but she knew he was teasing.

He nodded. 'It is. So let's start. First to make a snowman wins.'

She looked across at the wide snow-covered lawn and wagged her finger encased in the thick gloves. 'We split this straight down the middle. Don't try and steal my snow.'

'Your snow?'

'Absolutely. This is *my* snow.' She gave him a wary nod. 'I'm the guest.'

'You are, aren't you?' He bent down and scooped some of the snow into his bare hands. 'I haven't told you, have I?'

She frowned. 'Told me what?'

'I might have a bit of a competitive streak. Go!' Something streaked across the dark sky towards her, hitting her squarely on the shoulder and splattering up into her face.

She choked for a second as Rhuaridh's deep laugh rang across the night air. He didn't waste any time. He ran straight into the middle of his patch and started trying to pack snow together.

She shook the snow off her hair and out of her face. 'Cheat! I'll get you for that.'

'Keep up!' he shouted over his shoulder.

She didn't waste any time, running to her own patch of snow and trying to pack it like Rhuaridh was doing. After a few minutes she had pressed enough together to form a giant snowball that she could start rolling across the grass to make it bigger. She couldn't hide her delight. Within a few minutes she was out of breath. Pushing snow was harder than she could ever have imagined.

She looked up. Rhuaridh was making it look so easy. Ratfink.

She kept going, loving the whole experience of being in the snow. Before long she had a medium-sized snow-ball, just about big enough to be a body.

Rhuaridh had already positioned his in the middle of

the green and was rolling another. She ran to catch up, ignoring the fact hers already looked a bit smaller than his.

If he thought he had a competitive edge, he had nothing on her.

She stopped for a moment, distracted by seeing him blow on his hands for a few seconds. Just watching him gave her a little thrill. His dark hair, which always looked as if it just about needed cutting, his broad shoulders and long legs. Jeans suited him—though she'd never say it out loud. Even from here she could see the deep concentration on his face as he went back to rolling the second ball for the snowman's head. It gave her the opening she needed. She pulled together her first small snowball and threw it straight at him. It landed right at his feet.

He looked up and smiled. 'Given up already? What's happened to your snowman?'

'I've taken pity on you,' she said quickly, not wanting to admit that she'd no idea how, if she rolled a second ball of snow, she'd actually get it on top of the snowman. She grinned and grabbed some more snow, trying her best to shape a snowball and throw it at him. But it seemed she didn't quite have the technique and it disintegrated in mid-air.

'Seems like you LA girls need some snow training,' he said as he strode towards her. He was laughing at her.

She tried again then started to laugh too when it didn't quite work. 'What is it? Do they teach Scottish kids how to make a snowball at birth?'

He shook his head. 'Much earlier. We learn in the womb. It's a survival skill.'

He was right next to her, his tall frame standing over her. She dusted off the gloves and looked up, taking a step closer. She wanted to hold her breath, to stop steam appearing between them. His hair was in front of his deep blue eyes—and they were fixed on hers. Behind him was the backdrop of the navy sky speckled with stars, followed by the snow-covered outline of the cottage hospital. Right now, it felt like being on a Christmas card.

He lifted one hand and touched the side of her cheek, his cold finger made her jump, and they both laughed. 'Red looks good on you,' he said huskily.

'Does it?' She couldn't help it, she stepped forward. She just couldn't resist. It was as if there was a magnet, pulling them together. They were already close but this removed the gap between them. His other hand went instantly to her waist.

He gave a little tug at the scarf around her neck. 'I guess I should say it now.'

She swore her heart gave a jump. 'Say what?'

His cold finger traced a line up her neck, and across her lips. Teasing her.

His head dipped down towards her. 'It's a little early.'

Yip, her heart had forgotten how to beat steadily.

'Early for what?' she whispered.

He pulled something out of his pocket. She recognised it. It was plastic, green and white, slightly bent, and had come from the decoration box in the hospital.

'What are you doing?' she asked.

'This,' he said, 'is mistletoe. And I thought it was time to say Merry Christmas and introduce you to the Scottish tradition.'

She slid her arms around his waist as her smile grew wider. 'And what tradition might that be?'

His lips lowered towards hers. 'The one of kissing under the mistletoe.'

His lips weren't as cold as his hands and the connection between them sent a little shockwave through her body. Last time they'd kissed had been in his front room. It had been comfortable. Warm. And had felt so right.

This was what she'd been waiting for. This had been the

thing that had teased in her dreams for the last two months. Expectation was everything. And Rhuaridh Gillespie was meeting every expectation she'd ever had.

Because kissing the hot Highland doc was like standing in a field full of fireworks. And if things got any hotter, they'd light up the entire island.

CHAPTER NINE

January

'IT'S DYNAMITE! WHY didn't you tell me you two were an item?'

'What?' Kristie rubbed her eyes.

'The film. The backdrop of snow. The two of you silhouetted outside the hospital, kissing. The public will die for this. I tell you, once this goes out, you'll have any job that you want. What *do* you want? A talk show? More reporting? How about something fun, like a game show?'

For the briefest of seconds she felt a surge of excitement. Louie was telling her she could have her pick of jobs. How long had she waited to hear those words?

But her stomach gave a flip and she tried to mentally replay what he'd said.

Her voice cut across his as he kept talking. She could almost feel the blood drain from her body. 'What do you mean—the kiss? The silhouette?'

'You and Gerry must have planned that. Tell me you planned it. It couldn't have been more photogenic. I guarantee you that someone will put that picture on a calendar next year.'

Dread swept over her. 'Is that what you think of me? That I *planned* to kiss Rhuaridh?'

'Best career move ever,' came Louie's prompt reply.

Now she was sitting bolt upright in bed. They'd caught the last ferry to Arran the night before and when she'd gone to Rhuaridh's cottage there had been no one home— not even Mac.

She hadn't managed to see the last lot of the footage. Gerry had some excuse about technical issues. Now she knew why. She'd kill him. She'd kill him with her bare hands.

She stumbled out of bed, her feet getting caught in the blankets. For a few seconds she blinked then glanced at her watch. It was still dark outside. Shouldn't it be daytime? She kept the phone pressed to her ear as she walked over and drew back the curtains, flinching back at the thick dark clouds and mist.

'Don't you dare use that footage. I've not seen it. And I didn't agree to it being used.'

'Of course you did,' said Louie quickly. 'It's in your contract.'

'*Please*, Louie.' She didn't know whether to shout or burst into tears. She'd try either if she thought they might work. 'I let you get away with using my sick footage. But not this stuff. It's not fair on me. And it's not fair on Rhuaridh.'

'Oh, it's not fair on Rhuaridh?' Louie's voice rose and Kristie knew his eyebrows had just shot upwards. 'Well, it's pretty obvious that you like him now. But just remember, you have a job to do. And don't forget exactly what he's getting in return for us filming. And anyway, by the end of all this neither of you two will need to work. You'll spend the next few years touting yourselves around the talk shows. The public will *love* this.'

Her heart plummeted. Everything she'd felt about the kiss, the anticipation, the expectation, the longing, and the electricity—the whole moment had stayed in her mind like some delicious kind of dream. But now it seemed tarnished. It seemed contrived and unreal. She sagged down onto her bed. She'd wanted to keep the kiss to herself. She'd wanted that intensely personal moment to remain between her and Rhuaridh. Because that's the way it should be. Her perfect Christmas kiss.

'Gotta go,' Louie said quickly. 'Got another call. Try and catch another kiss on film—or maybe have a fight. That could really kick the figures up.'

The phone clicked. He was gone.

Her brain was spinning. She'd planned to get up this morning and put the new clothes on she'd bought to meet Rhuaridh. She had the whole thing pictured in her head. The checked pinafore she'd picked up that almost looked tartan, along with the thick black tights and black sweater—again clothing she'd never have a chance to wear in LA. It was amazing how a few days in Scotland a month had started to change her wardrobe. She'd never had much use for chunky tights, warm clothing and thick winter jackets. She even had a few coloured scarves, gloves and hats.

Now the pinafore hanging over the back of the chair in the room seemed to be mocking her. Her jaw tightened. She grabbed yesterday's jeans and shirt, pulling them on in two minutes flat, and marched across the hall towards Gerry's room. She couldn't hide the fact she was anything other than mad.

'You filmed us? You filmed us and you didn't tell me?' She had burst straight through the door—not even knocking.

Gerry was standing with his back to her, the camera at his shoulder. He spun around and swayed. She stepped forward to continue her tirade but the words stuck somewhere in her throat. Gerry's skin was glassy. She couldn't even describe the colour. White, translucent, with even a touch of grey.

Even before she got a chance to get any more words out, Gerry's eyes rolled and he pitched forward onto the bed.

'Gerry!' she yelled, grabbing at him and fumbling him round onto his back. She knelt on the bed and shook both his shoulders. But his eyes remained closed.

She tried to remember what she'd seen on TV. She felt around for a pulse, not finding anything at the neck but eventually finding a weak, thready pulse at his wrist. She squinted at his chest. Was he breathing? It seemed very slow.

She grabbed her phone and automatically pressed Rhuaridh's number. He answered after the second ring. His voice was bright. 'Kristie, are you—?'

'Help. I need help. It's Gerry. He's collapsed at the bed and breakfast we're staying in.'

She could hear the change in his tone immediately, almost like he'd flicked a switch to go into doctor mode. 'Kristie, where is he?'

'On the bed.' She was leaning over Gerry, watching him intently.

'Was there an accident?'

'What? No. He just collapsed.'

'Is he breathing?'

She paused, eyes fixed on Gerry's chest. 'I… I think so.'

'Has he got a pulse?'

'Yes, but it's not strong…and it's not regular.'

'Kristie, I'm getting in the car. Pam has phoned for the ambulance. Which B and B are you at?'

She glanced over her shoulder to find the name on the folder on the bedside table, reciting the name to Rhuaridh.

'I'll be five minutes. Shout for help. Get someone to stay with you, and tell them to make sure the front door is open.'

It was the longest five minutes of her life. When Rhuaridh appeared at the door, at the same time as the ambulance crew, she wanted to throw her arms around him.

She moved out of the way as they quickly assessed Gerry, then moved him onto a stretcher. Gerry seemed to have regained consciousness, although his colour remained terrible. She darted around to the side of the bed and grabbed his hand. 'Why didn't you tell me you didn't feel well?' she asked.

He shook his head and as he made that movement, parts of her brain sprang to life. The way his colour hadn't been great the last few months, his indigestion, his tiredness.

A tear sprang to her eye. She'd missed it. She should have told him to get checked out. But she'd been too preoccupied with herself, too occupied with the show—and with Rhuaridh—to properly look out for her colleague.

Rhuaridh pulled some bottles from his bag and found two separate tablets. 'Gerry,' he said firmly. 'I need you to swallow these two tablets. It's important. Can you do that for me?'

One of the ambulance crew handed him a glass of water with a straw. 'C'mon, mate, let's see if you can manage these.'

After a few seconds Gerry grimaced then managed to swallow down the tablets. Rhuaridh opened Gerry's shirt and quickly attached a monitor to his chest.

Kristie reached out and touched his shoulder. 'Gerry, I'm sorry, please be okay.'

Gerry's eyes flickered open. 'Hey,' he said shakily. 'Remember the camera.' He gave a crooked smile. 'Don't want to miss anything.' His eyes closed again and Kristie felt herself moved aside as the ambulance crew member reached for the stretcher.

She gulped then grabbed the car keys as Rhuaridh turned towards her. 'What's wrong?' she whispered.

Rhuaridh's voice was low. 'I think he's had a heart attack. I'll be able to confirm it at the hospital.'

She nodded as a tear rolled down her cheek.

'Hey,' he said softly as he picked up his bag. His other hand reached up and brushed her tear away. 'Don't cry. We'll get things sorted.'

'Doc?' A voice carried from outside the door. One of the ambulance crew stuck his head back inside. 'We might have a problem.'

He was stuck between trying to reassure Kristie and trying to reassure himself.

The weather was abysmal. No helicopter could land on Arran or take off in the next few hours. It seemed he was it.

This happened. This was island life. Thankfully it didn't happen too often, but in the modern age lots of people didn't really understand what living on an island meant.

Kristie was pacing outside as Rhuaridh read Gerry's twelve-lead ECG and rechecked his observations. Normally people with a myocardial infarction would be transported to hospital and treated within two hours. But those two hours were ticking past quickly and Gerry had no hope of reaching a cardiac unit.

Most people with this condition would end up in a cardiac theatre, with an angiogram and stent inserted to open up the blocked vessel. But there was no specialised equipment like that on Arran.

There were monitoring facilities and Gerry was currently attached to a cardiac monitor in one of the side rooms with an extra nurse called in to observe him closely for the next twenty-four hours.

Kristie couldn't stop pacing. He hated to see how worried she was, but the truth was he couldn't give her the guarantee she so desperately needed—that Gerry would be fine.

Rhuaridh put down the phone after talking to one of the consultants in Glasgow. Emergency situations called for emergency treatment.

'What's happening?' Kristie was at his side in an instant.

He ran his fingers through his hair. 'Bloods and ECG confirm it. Gerry's had a massive heart attack. If he was on the mainland he'd go to Theatre to get the vessel cleared and probably have a stent put in to try and stop it happening again.'

It seemed she knew where this conversation would go. 'But here?'

'But here I've given him the first two drugs that should help, and now we'll need to do things the more old-fashioned way and give him an IV of a drug that should break up the clot.'

She frowned. 'Why don't you still just do that? It sounds better than Theatre.'

He gave a slow nod. He had to phrase this carefully. 'Studies show the other way is better. But as that isn't an option, this is the only one we have.'

'That doesn't sound good.' Her voice cracked.

Rhuaridh put his hand on her arm. 'It takes an hour for the treatment to go in, then we have to monitor him carefully. There can be some side-effects, that's why we've called an extra nurse in to monitor Gerry all day and overnight.'

Kristie's head flicked from side to side. 'Right, where can I stay?'

He tried not to smile. He knew she would do this. 'You can stay with me. I'm going to have to stay overnight too. We'll pull a few chairs into one of the other rooms close by. Miriam, the nurse, can give me a shout if she needs me.'

He looked down at her white knuckles gripping the camera in her hand. 'What are you going to do with that?'

She took a few breaths as if she were thinking about it, then she lifted her chin and looked at him. 'I'm going to do Gerry's job. I'll film it.'

There was something in her eyes that struck him as strange. 'Are you okay?'

Her jaw was tight. 'If Gerry was the one out here, he would film. He told me back at the B and B.' She nodded as if she was processing a few things. 'And I'll film you. You can explain what a heart attack is and what the medicines are that you've given Gerry.' She paused for the briefest of seconds then added, 'Then you can talk about the weather and why we can't leave. I'll ask you a few questions about that.'

He tilted his head to the side. What was wrong with Kristie? Something just seemed a little...off. He understood she was worried about her colleague. Maybe this was her way of coping—to just throw herself into work.

He gave a cautious nod. 'Of course we can do an interview. But give me a bit of time. I'm going to set up the IV with Miriam and have a chat with Gerry.'

She pressed her lips together and swung the camera up onto her shoulder. 'Carry on. I'll capture what I can.'

Just as he'd finally managed to get used to Gerry constantly hovering in the background with a camera, now everything was flipped on its head and Kristie hovering with a camera was something else entirely. Initially he'd found Gerry's filming intrusive, and probably a bit unnecessary. But Kristie's? That was just unnerving. Gerry had an ability to be unnoticeable and virtually silent. Now he was constantly aware of the scent of Kristie drifting from behind him and the noise of her footsteps on the hospital floor.

Where Gerry had felt like a ghost, Kristie was more like a neon light.

And things were certainly illuminating. It turned out

Gerry had been harbouring a history of niggling indigestion and heaviness in his arms and a constant feeling of tiredness. Trouble was, Gerry had worked out himself that all the signs were pointing to cardiac trouble—but instead of seeking treatment he'd kept quiet, out of fear of losing his job.

Rhuaridh wasn't there to judge. Healthcare and insurance in the US was completely different from healthcare in the UK.

He turned to speak to Kristie just in time to notice a big fat tear slide down her cheek. Her eyes were fixed on Gerry's pale face as he lay with his eyes closed on the hospital bed, surrounded by flashing monitors and beeping IVs.

Something inside him clenched. This was her worst nightmare. Of course it was. She hated hospitals and now she was forcing herself to stay to be with Gerry. He knew in his heart that any suggestion he made about her leaving would fall on deaf ears. Rhuaridh slid his arm around her shoulders and pulled her towards him. 'You okay?'

She shook her head then rested it on his shoulder. 'I was mad at him. I went across to his room to shout at him.'

Rhuaridh tilted his head towards her. 'Why on earth did you want to shout at Gerry? You two seem to get on so well. You complement each other.'

She hesitated for a second then pulled a face. 'If I tell you why I was mad, you might get mad too.'

Rhuaridh shook his head. He had no idea what she was talking about. 'Okay, I feel as if I missed part of the conversation here.'

Her eyes lowered, her hands fumbling in her lap. Her voice was sad when she spoke. 'I found out Gerry filmed us kissing outside the hospital in December. I didn't know. He didn't say a word to me. And now my producer, Louie, has seen it, and loves it, so it's going to be in the next episode of the show, no matter how much I begged him not to use it.'

For the first time since she'd got here Rhuaridh felt distinctively uncomfortable. He didn't actually care about being filmed kissing Kristie. What he did care about was the fact she didn't seem to want anyone else to know. All those previous thoughts that he'd pushed away rushed into his head. Why would a girl like Kristie be interested in a guy from a Scottish island?

He took a deep breath and said the words he really didn't want to. 'What's wrong with us kissing?'

Her head turned sharply towards his. 'It's private. It's not something I want to share with the world.'

She was looking at him as if he should understand this. But his stomach was still twisting. His brain was sparking everywhere. He was looking at this woman in a new way. A way that told him she could easily break his heart.

He'd kind of shut himself off from the world since he'd come to Arran—focusing on work had seemed easier than realising he might never get the opportunity to meet someone to share his life with. And even though he knew things were ridiculous and completely improbable, even the fact that he'd thought about Kristie in that context had meant that he'd finally started to open himself up a little again. But it seemed he couldn't have timed things worse.

'We were in a public place,' he said carefully. 'That isn't so private.'

For a millisecond he might have been annoyed with Gerry—just like he had been in the beginning, questioning everything they filmed and the ethics behind it.

But Kristie had already told him. She needed this show to be a hit. If she didn't want the world to know they'd kissed, then at least part of him could be relieved she wasn't playing him.

She looked wounded by his words, her hand flew up to her chest. 'But it's private to me,' she said empathically.

He leaned forward, looking into those blue eyes and then whispering in her ear, 'Kristie, I don't care if the world knows we're kissing.' And he meant it. He glanced at Gerry on the bed. They still didn't know how this would all turn out for Gerry. If he had medical insurance he'd get shipped home once his treatment was complete. But chances were Rhuaridh wouldn't see him again anytime soon. Gerry might not be fit enough to travel like he had been.

He had to admire the canny old rogue. He'd seen the opportunity to film and taken it. Something flashed into Rhuaridh's head. Something he hadn't really processed earlier.

'Gerry asked you to film—and you did. We don't know how this is going to play out yet, Kristie.' He was serious. The IV drug Gerry was currently on could cause heart arrhythmias. It could also lead to small clots being thrown off while the heart was trying to re-perfuse. There were no guarantees right now. 'I'm not sure this is footage you should use.'

He left the words hanging in the air.

She blinked and her body gave a tremble. When she spoke her voice was shaky, 'I'm a terrible person. You know I want Gerry to be okay, don't you?'

He nodded and she continued, 'And I was still angry when he asked me to start filming, so I just automatically did. I've left the camera running at times without actually being behind it. I'm not even sure exactly what's been shot.'

Rhuaridh slid his hand over hers. 'I know what you're thinking. You need to take a breath. Take a moment. If Gerry is fine, then you've covered his work. You can show what happens to people in an island community when there's no possibility of getting off the island. This is a fact of life here. Gerry's had an alternative treatment for his heart attack. We hope it will work. If it does, you have footage.' He squeezed her hand. 'If it doesn't, then you stay some extra days and we'll shoot something else.'

He was trying to give her an alternative. The last thing he wanted was for her to be forced to use footage that would prove to be heartbreaking for her. He whispered again. 'No one needs know it's there.'

She shook her head. 'But it is. Our cameras don't need to go back to the studio to be uploaded. Everything uploads automatically to our server. Even if I don't want to use it, Louie probably will.'

'Surely he's not that heartless? You told me he was the guy that held your hand while you were at the hospital.' He leaned forward. 'Footage of us kissing? That's nothing. But if something happens to Gerry? No way. He couldn't use that. He wouldn't use that.' Rhuaridh wasn't quite sure who he was trying to convince. Her or himself.

She leaned back in against his shoulder and put her hand up on his chest. 'I hope so,' she whispered in reply, as both of their eyes fixed on the pulse, pulse, pulse of Gerry's monitor.

CHAPTER TEN

February

TRAVELLING WITH SOMEONE else felt all wrong. Thea was nice enough, but clearly obsessed. She had around one hundred Scottish travel books and couldn't seem to understand there wasn't time to drive around all the rest of Scotland before they got the ferry to Arran. It seemed she hadn't quite grasped the size of Scotland, or the terrain. By the time they docked in Arran, Kristie had a full-blown migraine.

The last few days at the helpline had been hard. Someone had called and kept hanging up after a few minutes. Every time it had happened, Kristie's thoughts flooded back to her sister. This could be someone like Jess. Someone who needed to be heard but couldn't find the words.

She'd struggled with it so much but she dealt with her feelings by continuing to work on the book she'd started writing a couple of months before. It had been years since she'd tried to write things. Last time she'd done this she'd been in college. But all of that had been pushed aside as her course work had taken priority. Now this story seemed to be shaping itself. All of it was fiction. None of it was based on a real person. Instead, it was an amalgamation of years of experiences. But it all felt real to Kristie. Even though this show was the thing the whole world was excited about, this story was the thing that kept her awake at night—that, and thinking of a hot Highland doc.

She'd also had over a thousand social media messages today alone. Since the kiss had been shown, her social media presence had erupted even more than before. Her conversations with Rhuaridh had continued. He'd been hit with just as many messages as she had—more, probably. And he was feeling a bit shell-shocked by it all. But Rhuaridh seemed able to pull his professional face into place and use his job as a protective shield.

She looked up just in time to meet the glare of an elegant-looking woman with gleaming dark brown hair. She looked out of place on the Arran ferry in her long wine-coloured wool coat, matching lipstick and black high heels. Kristie frowned. Why on earth would that woman be glaring at her?

'Will he be waiting for you at the dock? Should I film that?' Thea asked. Kristie started at Thea's voice and turned just in time to catch Thea shooting her a suspicious look. 'And this thing—it is real? Or is it all just made up for the camera? I have to admit I'm kind of curious.'

Kristie was more than a little stunned. 'You think it's fake?'

Thea was still talking. 'I mean, let's just say I'm asking in principle, because—let's face it—he is *hot*.'

A surge of jealousy swept through Kristie. 'You think Rhuaridh is *hot*?' She said the words almost in disbelief.

Thea threw back her head and laughed. 'Oh, honey, the whole world thinks he's hot.'

Now she wasn't just jealous. Now she was mad. Rhuaridh Gillespie was hers. She could picture herself as a three-year-old stamping her foot. Very mature.

And still Thea kept talking. Did the woman ever shut up? 'And anyway, you're from LA, he's from—what is it called again? Arran? How's that ever gonna work? He might as well be on the moon. I mean, let's face it, in a few months you won't be getting paid to come here any more. I bet these flights cost a small fortune.'

A horrible sensation swept over Kristie. She'd always known this—it's not like she was stupid. But she'd tried not to think about it.

The horn sounded as the boat docked, the sound ricocheting through Kristie's head. She winced and stood up. 'Come on,' she growled at Thea.

Her heart gave a leap as she pulled into the car park of the GP surgery. Rhuaridh was standing outside, waiting for her, his thick blue parka zipped up against the biting wind.

Thea let out a sound kind of like a squeak as Kristie jumped out of the car and ran towards him. She couldn't help it. Four weeks was just too long. Rhuaridh dropped a kiss on her nose and wrapped his arm around her. 'What's the update on Gerry?' he asked straight away.

She gave a sigh. 'Good, but not so good. He's started cardiac rehab classes and is making some progress. He's tired. I think he's frustrated that things are taking longer than he hoped. He's been assured he should make a good recovery, but just has to show some patience.' She pulled a face. 'And the TV channel won't cover his travel insurance until he's been signed off as fit by the doctor. And, to be honest, I think that will take a few months.'

The way Rhuaridh nodded made her realise that he'd known this all along—even if she hadn't. He leaned forward and touched her cheek with his finger. 'You okay? You look tired.'

'I am.' She glanced sideways over her shoulder. 'Thea—

I'll introduce you to her in a sec—is exhausting. My head is thumping.'

He paused for a second, giving Thea, who already had the camera on her shoulder, a quick wave. 'And the next show?'

Kristie let out another sigh. Maybe she was more tired than she'd thought. 'The show is going out with Gerry as the star and you and I as background footage. Gerry's fine about it.'

'And are you?'

'I guess I should be happy we're not as front and centre this time. But we're still there. The camera was running at the hospital and it's caught us sitting together, holding hands.'

'I can live with that.' It was as if he chose those words carefully.

She met his gaze, ignoring the way her hair was whipping around her face in the wind. 'So can I.' She couldn't help the small smile that appeared on her face. There was just something about being around Rhuaridh. Not only did he make her heart beat at a million miles a second, he was also her comfort zone. Her place.

She leaned forward and rested her head against his chest for a second. 'Kristie?' he said.

Although she'd told him about her sister, she'd never got round to telling him about the helpline. Things were playing on her mind. She needed a chance to talk to him—but she wanted to do that when they were alone.

She lifted her head. 'Can we go to the pub tonight for dinner?' Tonight was only a couple of hours away. She could wait that long.

'Of course.' He nodded. She watched as he painted a smile on his face and put his hand out towards Thea. 'Gerry, you've changed a little,' he joked. 'Welcome to Arran.'

* * *

Three hours later they finally had some peace and quiet. Even though the pub was busy, they were tucked in a little nook at the back where no one could hear them talk.

Rob, the barman, had just brought over their plates of steaming food, steak pie for Rhuaridh and fish for Kristie. Rhuaridh lifted his fork to his mouth and halted.

Kristie followed his gaze. The elegant woman from the boat was crossing the pub, heading directly towards their table. Every head in the room turned as she passed, her wool coat now open, revealing a form-fitting black dress underneath. She was easily the best-dressed woman in the room and she knew it.

Kristie's skin prickled. She could sense trouble. Rhuaridh looked almost frozen as the woman approached.

Kristie tilted her head, pretending she felt totally at ease. 'Can I help you?'

The woman looked down her nose at Kristie. For all her elegance, she wasn't half as pretty when she was sneering at someone. 'Oh, the American.' She said the words as if Kristie were some kind of disease.

Years of experience across cutthroat TV shows meant that Kristie was more than prepared for any diva behaviour. She gave her most dazzling smile. 'I'm afraid you have me at a disadvantage. Who are you?' The words were amiable enough, but Kristie knew exactly how to deliver them. The implication of 'not being important enough to know' emanated from her every pore.

There was a flash of anger in the woman's eyes but Rhuaridh broke in. 'Kristie, this is Zoe.'

'Zoe?'

The woman straightened her shoulders. 'Zoe Brackenridge. Rhuaridh and I are...' a calculating smile appeared on her lips '...very good, old friends.'

The ex. It was practically stamped on her forehead. But Kristie wasn't easily bested.

Zoe seemed to dismiss her, turning her attention to Rhuaridh. 'Rhuaridh, do you think we could go back to the cottage? I think we need to have a private chat.'

'I'm not quite sure there's room enough for three,' said Kristie quickly. Too quickly, in fact, she was in danger of letting this woman make her lose her cool.

But it seemed that Rhuaridh had limited patience too. 'What are you doing on Arran, Zoe? I thought you hated the place.' His gaze was steely.

There was a tiny flicker in the woman's cheek. She wasn't unnerved. She was angry. She looked Rhuaridh straight in the eye, 'Like I said, we need to talk.'

'We talked some time ago. I think you said everything you needed to.'

Zoe leaned forward and touched Rhuaridh's arm, leaving her hand there. Kristie resisted the temptation to stab her with her fork. 'Rhuaridh, I'm sure there are some things we could catch up on.'

'Like what?'

Kristie almost choked. She'd never heard Rhuaridh be that rude before. Funnily enough, she kind of liked it.

Now Zoe was starting to show some signs of frustration. 'I think we have a lot of things to catch up on. One of the consultants I'm working with was enquiring about you—there could be a job opportunity in Glasgow. It would be perfect for you.' She looked over her shoulder. 'Get you away from this island. Now you've done that show, you should be able to recruit someone else for here. Get your career back on track. Get your life back on track.'

Rhuaridh stood up, his dinner untouched, and reached out for Kristie's hand. 'You've watched the show?'

Kristie felt as if she'd been catapulted back into high school. This seemed like teenage behaviour. Rhuaridh had never really talked about the relationship he'd had with Zoe, but in Kristie's head she could see Zoe watching the show, seeing how captivated the world was with Rhuaridh, and realising exactly what she'd let go. Now she'd shown up like some high school prom queen back to claim her king.

Zoe rolled her eyes, then settled her gaze on Kristie. It was distinctly disapproving. 'It doesn't exactly show you in the best light.' She waved her hand. 'And as for that title...' She gave a shudder and touched his shoulder. 'I think it's time a friend helped you get back to where you should be.'

Kristie ground her teeth. Did this woman even know how condescending she sounded? But she didn't get a chance to say anything. Rhuaridh stepped up right in front of the woman.

He stood there for a few seconds. Zoe cast Kristie a triumphant glance that was short-lived. Rhuaridh spoke in a low voice. 'Let me be clear. We don't have anything to talk about. And you've just rudely interrupted dinner between me...' he paused for the briefest of seconds '...and my girlfriend.'

It was like someone had sucked the air out of her lungs. *Girlfriend*. She liked that word. She liked it a lot.

'Goodbye, Zoe,' he finished as he gave Kristie's hand a tug and pulled her with him as he headed to the door, leaving some money on the bar. 'Sorry about dinner,' he muttered as he kept walking.

She ignored her empty stomach as she cast a look over her shoulder. Zoe looked stunned. It was probably her best look.

'Beans on toast,' said Rhuaridh. 'Fine dining. The staple diet of most Scottish students.'

Kristie raised her eyebrows at him. 'I think we could

have got away with taking the plates. No one would have noticed.'

He let out a sigh. She hadn't said a word in the car back to the cottage. It was as if she knew he needed some time to sort out his head. He couldn't believe Zoe had turned up here. There had been a few random emails that he hadn't replied to. But he would never have expected her to show up in the place she'd shown so much contempt for.

There had always been a side to Zoe that hadn't exactly been complimentary—one she tried to keep hidden. Zoe, at heart, was competitive. Whether that was in her career, in her love life, or in her finances. And it was the 'at heart' part that annoyed him most.

He'd been deluged with messages from every direction. Even though he still hadn't watched the show, he couldn't fail to notice its impact. Zoe's competitive edge must be cursing right now. She wasn't here really because she regretted her actions or her words. No, she was here because she wanted a bit of the limelight. This wasn't an act of love. This was an act of ambition.

Kristie pressed her lips together as she picked up her plate and walked over to the sofa. It was clear her mind was somewhere else.

'I'm not sure what you and Thea have planned for footage for this month's filming. I imagine Thea will need to find her way around the surgery and hospital for now so I've not scheduled anything in particular. But I've arranged for filming in the school to happen next month,' he said quickly, trying to pull her away from whatever was giving her that pained expression. 'There's a whole host of immunisations coming up. They're handled by the nurse immunisation team, but I generally try to go along in case there are any issues.'

'What kind of issues?'

'There are usually a few fainters. The odd child who

might have a panic attack. Consents are all done before we get there, and all the children's medical histories have been checked.'

'Mmm…okay.'

He put his plate down. 'Kristie, what did you want to talk about earlier?'

She pushed her plate away and pulled her legs up onto the sofa, turning to face him with her head on her hand. She gave her head a shake. 'I'm just tired. It's nothing.'

'It's not nothing. It's something. Tell me.'

She gulped. He could see her doing that so reached out and took her hand. After a few minutes she finally spoke. 'I told you about my sister. But what I didn't tell you was that after she died I contacted the helpline she'd phoned a few times and volunteered. The calls she made were short. She always disconnected. But I felt as if I wanted to do something.' She ran her other hand through her hair. 'I couldn't get it out of my head that when she'd been feeling low, the place she'd called was there, not me.'

Her voice started to tremble. 'And I realised that I could be that person at the end of the phone for someone else. So I volunteered, they trained me, and I've been manning the phone three times a month for the last few years.'

He'd listened carefully. He knew there was more.

'So what's wrong?'

She stared down at her hands. 'The last few nights, someone has been phoning, staying on the line for less than a minute then hanging up. I know that's what Jess did.' Her voice cracked. 'And I can't help but wonder if I'm failing them, just like I failed Jess.'

Rhuaridh didn't hesitate, he pulled her into his arms. 'You didn't fail your sister, Kristie, and you haven't failed this person either. They've called. They've got to take the decision to speak. Sometimes people call six or seven times before they pick up the courage to speak. All you can do is be there. All you can do is answer and let them know that you're prepared to listen whenever they want to speak.'

'But what if offering to listen isn't enough?' Her wide blue eyes were wet with tears.

His heart twisted in his chest. He could see just how desperate she was to save any other family from the pain she'd suffered. He could see just how much she wanted to help.

He put his hands at either side of her head. 'Kristie Nelson, you are a brilliant big-hearted person. But you have to accept that there are some things in this life we can't control—no matter how much we want to. All we can do... is the best that we can. I know that's hard to accept. But we have to. Otherwise the what-ifs will eat us up inside.'

He leaned forward and rested his head against hers. They stayed like that for the longest time. At first he could see the small pulse racing at the bottom of her neck, but the longer they stayed together, the more her body relaxed against his, and the more her breathing steadied and eased. He wanted to give her that space and time to gather her thoughts—just like he was gathering his.

She took another breath. 'There's more,' she said quietly.

'What?'

She licked her lips. 'These last few months I started working on something—a book.'

He was momentarily confused. 'A book?'

She nodded. 'It's fiction. But it's based on Jess, and what happens when a member of your family commits suicide. The impact it has on all those around. It's about a tight-knit family and a group of old high school friends. How they all second-guess themselves wondering if they could have done something—changed things—and how they have to learn to live and move on.'

He pulled back and looked at her, amazed. 'Wow, that sounds…incredible.' He reached forward and brushed back a strand of hair from her face. 'Can I read it?'

She looked surprised. 'Do you want to?'

'Of course. Now. Do you have it?'

A smile danced across her lips as she stood up and crossed the room, picking up her laptop. 'It's still in the early stages. There might be spelling mistakes—grammatical errors.'

He shook his head and held out his hands. 'I don't care. Just give it to me.'

He bent over the bright screen and started reading as she settled beside him.

Three hours later it was the early hours of the morning. Kristie's manuscript. It was beautiful, touching and from the heart. And it smacked of Kristie. Every word, every nuance had her unique stamp on it. He brushed a tear from his eye and nudged her. She'd fallen asleep on his shoulder.

'Kristie, wake up.' He gave her a shake and she rubbed her tired eyes.

'You've finished?'

He nodded and she bit her bottom lip. 'What did you think?'

He held out his hand. 'I think it's brilliant. It's heartbreaking. It's real. You have to finish this. *This* is what you should be doing, Kristie. This is so important. I *felt* for every one of the people in this story. You have to get this out there.'

Her eyes sparkled. 'You think so? Really?'

He nodded. 'Without a doubt. You have a gift as a writer. Do it. I believe in you. Once an agent sees this, they'll snatch it up with both hands.'

A smile danced across her lips. He could see the impact his words were having. The fact he believed in her ability to tell this story. It felt like pieces of their puzzle were just slotting into place.

He couldn't believe that Zoe had shown up today. He'd never seen someone look so much like a fish out of water. But it was almost as if a shadow had been lifted off his shoulders. She'd always intimated that Arran was less, and he was less for being here. He'd compromised his career and his life. And for a time those thoughts had drip-dripped into his self-conscious.

But tonight was like shining a bright light on his life. Everything was clear for him. He was exactly where he wanted to be, and with the person he wanted to be with. Zoe's visit—instead of unsettling him—had actually clarified things for him. He didn't care about the distance between him and Kristie. He had no idea how things would play out. All he knew was that he wanted to think about the here and now. With her.

It was almost as if their brains were in accord. Kristie lifted her head and gave him a twinkling smile. 'I just remembered something you said tonight.'

'What?'

'Girlfriend, hey?' she said as she slid her arms around his neck.

His voice was low as his hands settled on her waist. 'I just remembered something you said too. I heard you tell her the cottage wasn't big enough for three,' he said as his lips danced across the skin on her neck. 'You made it sound like you were staying here.'

'Oh, I am.' She smiled as she pulled him down onto the sofa and made sure he knew exactly how things were.

CHAPTER ELEVEN

March

Don't get too comfortable. Miss LA will get just as sick of the place as any normal human would. How can smoggy hills compare to the glamour of Hollywood? Your success is just your fifteen minutes of fame. You should be asking yourself where your career will be in five years' time. That's what's important.

RHUARIDH SHOOK HIS head and deleted the email. It was sad, really. Zoe was trying to provoke a reaction from him and the truth was he felt nothing. He wasn't interested in her or in anything she had to say.

He looked out the window towards the hills. Were they smoggy? Maybe. Goatfell was covered at the top by some clouds. But Kristie had already said she wanted to climb it with him. Every time she visited she seemed a little more fascinated by Arran and wanted to see more. Her attitude was the complete opposite of Zoe's and that made him feel warm inside. She didn't see Arran as the last place on earth she wanted to visit—she might not want to ever stay here but when she was here, she made it seem like an adventure. And he'd take that.

He picked up the case he had ready to go to the high school. The immunisation team would be setting up right now and he'd arranged to meet Kristie and Thea there as they came straight off the first morning ferry. Chances were they'd be tired—they'd been travelling all night, but a delayed flight had caused them a few problems.

The local school was only a few minutes away. The whole place was buzzing. The immunisation team never failed to amaze him by how scarily organised they were. One of the nurses met him just as Thea burst through the door with her camera at the ready. 'Wait for me,' she shouted.

He shook his head and looked down at the list of children the nurse wanted him to give a quick review. Nothing much to worry about. Kristie stepped in behind Thea. Her cheeks flushed pink and her skin glowing. Every pair of eyes in the room turned towards them.

'Hey,' she said self-consciously, tugging at a strand of her hair.

'Hey,' he replied.

What he wanted to do was kiss her. But he didn't want to do it in front of an audience. As soon as the thought crossed his brain the irony struck him. Thanks to Gerry, the whole world had already seen them kiss.

Kristie slipped into professional mode. Interviewing a few of the nurses, watching the kids come in for their vaccinations and capturing a few of them on camera too.

Everything was going smoothly until one of the teachers came in, white-faced. 'Dr Gillespie. I need some help.' Rhuaridh didn't recognise him. He must be one of the supply teachers.

Rhuaridh looked up from where he was finishing talking to a child with a complicated medical history. 'Can it wait?'

The teacher shook his head. 'No, it definitely can't.' He was wringing his hands together and the worry lines across his forehead were deep.

Rhuaridh was on his feet in a few seconds. Thea was still filming on the other side of the room, so Kristie followed Rhuaridh and the teacher up some stairs to the second floor of the school.

The teacher had started tugging at his shirtsleeve. 'I don't know what to do. She's been up and down. Apparently her father died last year and the school has been worried about her. Sometimes she just walks out of class. But today—she's barricaded herself into one of the rooms. Her friend told us that she said she wanted to kill herself. To join her dad.'

Rhuaridh heard Kristie's footsteps falter behind him. He turned around and raised his hand. 'Maybe you should let me handle this.'

He could see the strain on her face, but didn't get a chance to say anything further as the teacher stopped in front of one of the rooms. 'Here,' he said. 'I've tried everything.'

'Is it Jill Masterton?' Rhuaridh asked. He knew everyone on the island—so unless someone new had just moved over, the only teenager he knew who had lost her father in the last year was Jill.

The teacher nodded. 'I've been talking to her for the last half-hour. I didn't think she was serious. I just thought it was attention-seeking. But…but then she said some other stuff, and I realised…' he shook his head '…whatever it was I was saying just wasn't helping.'

Rhuaridh could see the stress on the teacher's face. 'Have you contacted her mum?'

He nodded. 'She's on the mainland, waiting to catch the first ferry back.'

Rhuaridh took a deep breath. He didn't know this girl well. He hadn't seen much of her in the surgery. He turned to the teacher. 'Do you have any guidance teachers or counsellors attached to the school?'

The teacher shook his head. 'I'm only temporary. I came to cover sick leave. The guidance teacher—you probably know her, Mary McInnes—had surgery on her ankle. She's not expected back for a few months.'

Of course. He should have remembered that. He ran his fingers through his hair. 'Has she told you anything at all?'

The teacher now tugged at his tie. It was clear he was feeling out of his depth. 'She won't speak to me at all. But she doesn't know me. And the teachers that she does know haven't had any reply. Last time someone tried to speak to her she said if anyone else came she would jump out of the window.'

There was a nagging voice of doubt in Rhuaridh's head. He hadn't seen this young girl since he'd got back here. She wouldn't remember him at all. When he'd left the island she'd been barely a baby. He held out his hands. 'I'm a doctor. I can speak to her. But I'm not a psychiatrist, or a psychologist. I don't want to make anything worse. Particularly if she's already made threats.'

'Do you have any other counsellors on the island?' Kristie stepped forward. The teacher shook his head.

She put her hand on her chest. 'Then let me.' She turned to Rhuaridh. 'You know that I've been trained. Let me talk to her. Maybe I can relate. I lost someone I loved too, plus I understand what it's like to be a teenage girl.'

'I don't want you to be out of your depth,' he said quietly. He was thinking about her being upset the other week when the caller to the helpline wouldn't speak.

'I want to try,' she said determinedly.

Rhuaridh turned back to the teacher. 'Maybe we should wait. Maybe we should tell her that her mum is on her way back over on the ferry. Has anything else been happening in the school we should know about—any bullying?'

The teacher shrugged. 'I'm sorry. I just don't know. Nothing obvious.'

Rhuaridh let out a sigh. He was torn. Torn between looking after the girl behind the door and putting the woman he loved in a position of vulnerability.

There was so much at risk here, so much at stake. How would this affect Jill and Kristie if things didn't work out? What if Jill reacted to something that Kristie said—the impact on both could be devastating. He was so torn. He wanted to fix this himself—but he wasn't sure that he could. Maybe Jill would react better to a woman, particularly one who might understand her loss. Ahead of him was the closed door. It was symbolic really—demonstrating exactly how the young girl in there felt. He glanced from the panicked temporary teacher and the determined woman in front of him, his head juggling what was best for everyone. There was a hollow echo in his head.

Kristie straightened up. She'd had enough of this. Enough of waiting. He was trying to protect her—she got that. But she didn't need protection.

On the ferry on the way over here today, all she'd thought about was how much she wanted to see Rhuaridh. How much she wanted to be in his arms. For the last four weeks she'd started to dream in Technicolor—and the dreams didn't just include Rhuaridh, they also included this place. Arran, with its lush green countryside, hills and valleys, and surrounding stormy seas. Even though she'd had a dozen job offers now and enough money in the bank to pay the bills for a while, her love of TV was definitely waning. The book she'd started writing had taken on a life of its own. Rhuaridh's encouragement had meant the world to her, and after that the words had just seemed to flow even easier. She'd shown it to Louie, who'd shown it to another friend who was a literary agent. The agent had offered representation already. It was almost like her world had shifted, shaping her future. And the one thing she'd been sure of was that her heart was leading the charge. Could she think about a life in Scotland? She hadn't really considered things. Would she be able to walk away from her TV career, and her work with the helpline?

She swallowed and turned to both men. 'I'm going to do this.'

She walked up to the door and stood close, trying to think of the best way to appeal to Jill. Kids were all over social media right now. Maybe she should try the *you-might-know-me* approach?

She gave the door a gentle rap with her knuckles. 'Jill, it's Kristie Nelson. You know, from the TV show? I've come to talk to you.'

She could hear sobbing inside the room. The kind that made the bottom fall out of her stomach. 'I don't want to talk to anyone.'

Kristie leaned her head back against the door, trying to think like a teenager these days. Her head was still in the social media zone. Their life revolved around social media. She pulled out her phone and did a search for Jill. Sure enough, it only took seconds to find her. Her online profile had a few selfies, and a few older pictures that showed a little girl laughing, sitting on her father's knee. It made her heart pang.

'How are you feeling?' she started.

'How do you think I'm feeling?' came the angry shout.

Good. She'd had another reply. Her main goal now was to keep Jill talking.

'I know about your dad, Jill. I know how sad you're feeling. Do you want to talk? Because I'm here. I'm here to listen to you.'

The sobs got more exasperated. 'How can you know how I'm feeling? How can you know what's in my head? Have you lost your dad?'

Kristie turned around and slid down the door so she

was leaning against it. She may as well get comfortable. She wanted Jill to know that she was there to stay—there to listen. 'I've lost both of my parents,' she answered quietly. 'And I lost my sister three years ago. And I think about her every single day and the fact she's not here. And sometimes it catches me unawares—like when I see something I know she'd like and I can't show it to her, or when I hear something that makes me laugh and I can't pick up the phone and tell her.'

There was silence for a few seconds then she heard a noise. Jill was moving closer to the door. 'Three years?' she breathed.

'Honey, these feelings will get better with time. You won't ever forget, and some days will be sadder than others, but I promise you, you can learn to live with this. You just need to take it one day at a time. You just need to breathe.'

She could feel empathy pouring out of her as she tried to reach out to the teenager behind the door. The teenager who thought that no one could understand.

The voice was quiet—almost a whisper. 'It would have been my dad's birthday today. He would have been forty-five.' Kristie's heart twisted in her chest. Of course. A birthday for someone who'd been lost. The roughest of days.

She heard the strangled sob again. All she wanted to do was put her arms around this hurting young girl. 'I get it,' she said steadily. 'Birthdays are always hard. I'm not going to lie to you. I've cried every birthday, Thanksgiving and Christmas that my sister hasn't been here.' She took a deep breath. 'Just know that you're not alone, Jill. Other people have gone through this. They understand. You just need to find someone to listen. Someone you feel as if you can talk to. Do you have someone like that?'

The reply was hesitant. 'It should be my mum. But I can't. I can't talk to her because she's so upset herself. She cries when she thinks I can't hear.' There was another quiet noise. Kristie recognised it. Jill had sat down on the opposite side of the door from her. It gave her a sense of hope.

'Okay, I get it. What about if we find someone who is just for you? Someone you can talk to whenever you need to?'

'Th-that might be okay... But...'

'But?' prompted Kristie.

'I don't want to have to go somewhere. To see someone.'

'Would you talk to someone on the phone? Have you tried any of the emotional support helplines around here?'

'M-maybe.'

Kristie sucked in her breath. 'Did you talk?'

There was silence for a few seconds. 'No.'

Tears were brimming in Kristie's eyes.

'I... I just wasn't ready.'

Kristie rested her head on her knees. One of the things that Rhuaridh had said before clicked into place in her mind. About all you can do is the best that you can. She wiped her tears again. 'Are you ready now?' she asked.

'I... I think so...'

'Jill, can I come in?'

There was the longest silence. Then a click at the door. Kristie cast a glance over her shoulder to where the teacher and Rhuaridh were standing. Her heart twisted in her chest. He hadn't believed in her. And for a few seconds it had felt like a betrayal—like the bottom had fallen out of her world. But she would deal with that later. Right now, she was going to do the best that she could.

'Kristie...' The voice came from behind her.

But she just shook her head, opened the door and closed it behind her.

He sat there for hours. First talking to the teacher, then to Jill's frantic mother, who'd practically run all the way from the ferry. He'd managed to get hold of a children's mental health nurse who would come and see Jill tomorrow from the mainland. This wasn't something that could be fixed overnight.

Kristie finally emerged from the classroom with her arm around Jill's shoulder. Jill threw herself into her mother's arms and Kristie waited to talk to both mother and daughter together. Just like he would expect a professional counsellor to do.

She'd been a star today. And he knew she'd been scared. He knew she'd had to expose part of herself to connect with the teenager. And words couldn't describe how proud he was of her right now.

He stood to the side until he was sure she had finished talking, then joined her to let Jill and her mother know the plans for the next day.

The rest of the students had now been sent home so the school was quiet, silence echoing around them. Rhuaridh lifted his hand to touch Kristie's cheek. 'I can't believe you did that,' he said quietly.

She met his gaze. 'I had to. She needed someone to talk to—someone to listen—and I could be that person.'

'I'm so proud of you. I know this must have been difficult.'

Something jolted in his heart. He hadn't wanted to say these words here, but he had to go with the feelings that were overwhelming him. 'I love you, Kristie. I've spent the last few months loving you and was just waiting for the right time to tell you.' He held up one hand, 'And even though it's a completely ridiculous and totally unromantic place, the right time is now.'

He couldn't stop talking. 'And I know it's ridiculous because we live on different continents and both have jobs and careers. I don't expect you to pack up and live here. In fact, the last thing I'd want is for you to come here and resent me for asking you to. But I had to tell you. I had to tell you that I love you and you've stolen a piece of my heart.' He lifted his hand to his chest.

She blinked and he could see the hesitation on her lips and his heart twisted inside his chest. He'd taken her by surprise. She hadn't been expecting this.

For a few seconds she said nothing. He'd said too much.

All his insecurities from Zoe's desertion flooded back into his brain as if he'd just flicked a switch. Her look of disdain and disapproval. Kristie's face didn't look like that—hers was a mixture of panic and…disappointment? She was disappointed he'd told her he loved her?

He was a fool. He should never have said anything. He'd just been overwhelmed with how proud he was of her that he'd obviously stepped across a whole host of boundaries he hadn't realised were there.

There was a laugh beside them and he pulled his hand back sharply.

'Oh, the Hot Highland Doc. I'd heard you were in the school.'

Rhuaridh turned to the teacher who'd just walked up beside them. 'What?'

The teacher just kept smiling. 'The kids talk about you all the time.'

He shook his head, thinking he hadn't heard correctly. 'What did you call me?'

'The Hot Highland Doc. It's a great title, isn't it? Better than the Conscientious Curator or the Star-struck Astronaut. Pity the geography is off.'

She gave a shrug and kept walking on down the corridor.

Rhuaridh tried to process the words. He spun back to face Kristie. 'She's joking, right?'

Kristie looked a little sheepish. 'I… I didn't have any

say in it.' They were the first words she'd said since he'd told her he loved her.

He stepped back and looked down at himself. 'Hot Highland Doc? That's how you've described me to the world? Of all the ridiculous descriptions…' He shook his head again. 'And we're nowhere near the Highlands!'

He was overreacting. He knew that. But right now he felt like a fool.

A few things clicked in his brain, comments he'd heard people say but hadn't really picked up on at the time. 'I can't believe you'd let them do that.' Then something else crossed his mind. 'I can't believe you didn't warn me.'

Kristie breathed. The air was stuck somewhere in her throat. He'd just told her he loved her, then almost snatched it back by inferring they could never work. It was like giving her a giant heart-shaped balloon then popping it with a giant pin.

Her stomach was in knots. For a few seconds there she'd thought the world was perfect and their stars had aligned, but then Rhuaridh had kept talking. Was he talking himself out of having a relationship with her? Had she only been pleasant company while the filming was going on?

It was as if every defence automatically sprang into place. 'It's not up to me to tell you. The TV series hasn't exactly been a secret. Most of the island watches it. If you weren't such a social media recluse you would have picked up on it in the first month.'

Her brain was jumbled right now. Everything felt so muddled.

'Was any of this real for you? You tell me you love me one second, then tell me how ridiculous our relationship is in the next? Who does that? What kind of a person does that sort of thing?' The words were just spilling out in anger. No real thought because all she could feel right now was pain. All the things she'd considered for a half a second seemed futile now. Coming to Arran? Accepting the book deal and giving up the TV job? How on earth could she leave LA? She was crazy for even considering anything like that.

There was a flash of hurt in his eyes then his jaw clenched.

The anger kept building in her chest, turning into hot tears spilling down her cheeks.

She stepped back and looked him straight in the eye. Her words were tight. 'And…we're done. Goodbye, Rhuaridh.' She had to get out of there. She had to get out of there now.

Her pink coat spun out as she turned around and strode down the corridor. Her heart squeezed tight in her chest, part hurt, part anger. Why on earth had she thought for even a second that this might work?

He watched her pink coat retreating, trying to work out what the hell had just happened. He'd told her he loved her and she'd walked away.

There was a movement at the end of the corridor. A camera. Thea.

It appeared he'd just been starring in his own worse nightmare.

Fury gripped his chest. He put his hands on his hips for a few seconds, staring down as he took a few deep breaths.

This had all been for nothing. He'd been crazy to think they could ever make this work.

Then he straightened his back and walked in the opposite direction.

CHAPTER TWELVE

April

'I QUIT.'

'You can't quit. The show has just been syndicated.'

'For once, Louie, listen to what I tell you. I quit. I'm not setting foot on that island again.'

'Your contract says you are.'

'So sue me.'

Kristie slammed the phone down just as it buzzed. She turned it over.

Can we talk?

She stared at the name. Rhuaridh. Her hand started to shake.

NO.

She typed it in capital letters.

Last time he'd been this tired he'd been a junior doctor on a twenty-four-hour shift. He'd been delayed at both Glasgow then London airports. The heat hit him as soon as he set foot on the tarmac in Los Angeles. Most people in the UK drove cars with gears. Rhuaridh had never driven an automatic and hadn't quite realised it almost drove himself, meaning when he put the car into reverse in the car park at the airport, he almost took out the row of cars behind him.

He was torn between trusting the air-conditioning and just putting down the window to let some air into the car. It was dry. Scratchy dry.

He hadn't slept a wink on the flights. He'd been too busy thinking about the way they'd left things. Once he'd calmed down he'd tried to find her, but it seemed that she and Thea had caught the first ferry off the island.

He'd spent a few days replaying everything in his head. Trying to work out why things had gone so wrong.

Rhuaridh didn't want to call. He hadn't really wanted to text either, he just wanted to see her. He wanted to be in the same room as her. He wanted to talk to her.

He'd only sent the text once he'd landed, when he'd had a crazy second of doubt that he'd look like some kind of madman turning up at her door uninvited.

His brain wobbled at the number of lanes on the highway. At this rate he'd be lucky to make it there at all. Being called the Hot Highland Doc at least a dozen times between Arran and Los Angeles now seemed like some kind of weird irony. For the first time in his life complete strangers had recognised him. He'd been asked for autographs and selfies. People had asked him to speak so they could hear his accent. And there had been lots of questions about Kristie.

Most people had been completely complimentary— but he was sure that was because there was a lag time of six weeks between filming and the finished episode being shown. Once they saw the next episode that was scheduled—which would surely contain their fight and Kristie walking away—he was pretty sure he'd be toast the world over.

But here was the thing. He wasn't worried about the rest of the world. He was only worried about her.

He pulled up outside an apartment complex in the Woodland Hills area of Los Angeles. It looked smart. Safe.

He lifted his chin and pushed every doubt away. It was time. Time to put his heart on the line and tell this woman—again—just how much he loved her. Just how much he was prepared to do to make things work between them. She might still hate him but he had to try. And he could only try his best.

There was a rumble outside her apartment door, followed by a buzz. Was she expecting a delivery? She didn't think so.

Kristie looked down. She'd been wearing this pink slouchy top and grey yoga pants for the last two days. She hadn't even opened the blinds these last few days. She was officially a slob. She shrugged and headed to the door, pulling it open to let the bright Los Angeles sunshine stream into her apartment.

She squinted. Looked. And looked again. Her breath strangled somewhere inside her. Was she finally so miserable that she was seeing things?

'Hey.' The Scottish lilt was strong. She couldn't be imagining this. 'I thought we should talk.'

Her hand went automatically to her hair, scrunched up in a dubious ponytail. She didn't have a scrap of makeup on her face. Every imaginary meeting between them she'd had in her mind these last few days had been nothing like this.

'Can I come in?' She blinked and looked behind him. Three large cases.

'What are you doing?'

'I'm…visiting,' he said cautiously.

She automatically stepped back. 'I just texted you.'

'I know.' He smiled.

She shook her head. 'I said I didn't want to talk.'

'And if you don't then I'll leave,' he said steadily. 'But I've flown five thousand miles. Can we have five minutes?'

She gestured to her sofa. 'Five minutes.' She moved quickly, picking up the empty wrappers from the cookies and chips that were lying on the coffee table.

Rhuaridh sat down heavily. He'd flown five thousand miles to talk to her.

Her brain was spinning.

She'd replayed their last moments over and over in her head. She'd always known he'd object to the title of the show—*she'd* even objected to it when she'd initially heard it. But because he didn't go on social media, or the streaming network, she'd always secretly hoped he wouldn't find out. She'd been lucky. Up until last week. And the timing had been awful because by that point she'd felt so hurt and angry that she hadn't felt like explaining—hadn't felt like defending the show.

'How's Jill?' she asked.

He nodded. He was wearing jeans and a pale blue shirt that were distinctly rumpled. He gave her a thoughtful smile. 'It's baby steps. And everyone knows that. But she said I could let you know how she's doing. She's seen the CAMHS nurse and a counsellor. Two days ago she told me that she'd phoned the number in the middle of the night when her head was spinning, she couldn't get back to sleep and she'd felt so alone. She told me she'd cried, and that the woman at the end of the phone had spoken softly to her until she'd fallen asleep again.'

Tears pricked at Kristie's eyes. 'It sounds like it's a start.'

'Everything has to start somewhere,' he replied. It was

the way he said those words, the tone, that made her turn to face him. 'And so do we.'

He sighed and ran his fingers through his hair. 'Kristie, I'm sorry, I feel as if this all spun out of control and I still can't really work out why. Except...' he paused for a second '... I probably put my foot in my mouth.' He didn't wait for her to reply before he continued. 'The one thing that I know, and I know with all my heart, is that I love you, Kristie. I don't want to be without you. And I don't care where we are together, just as long as we get a chance to see if this will work.'

His words made her catch her breath.

He kept talking. 'I hated how we left things.' He shook his head. 'I hate that we fought over...nothing. I love you. I can't bear it when you're sad. I can't bear it when you're feeling down. I just want to wrap my arms around you and stop it all.' He gave a wry laugh, 'And, yes, I know it's ridiculous. I know it's probably really old-fashioned.' He put his hand on his chest. 'But I can't help how I feel in here.'

He took a breath. 'When I told you that I loved you and you didn't reply, I made a whole host of assumptions. Then my mouth started talking and my brain didn't know how to stop it. I thought it was crazy to dare to hope we could be together. It's what I wanted, but how selfish would I be to ask you to pack up your whole life for me? To move from your home, and your career, to be with a guy you'd spent a few days a month with?

'So...' he gestured towards the cases '...because I'm so hopeless with words I decided to try something different.'

She stared at him, her voice stuck somewhere in her throat.

'So...' he paused and she could tell he was nervous '... I decided that actions speak louder than words. That's why I've packed everything up. Magda is due back at work and we've got a locum for the next few months.' He shook his head. 'The irony of doing the show is that we had about twenty people apply. So...' he met her gaze '...if you're willing to talk, if you're willing to give things a try, just tell me. Tell me where your next job is, and this time I'll come to you. Because I love you, Kristie. I'll love you to the ends of this earth.'

She stared at him. Trying to take in his words. 'You'd move here? To be with me?'

'Of course. I'd do anything for you, Kristie—whatever it takes.'

She sagged back a little further into the sofa, then turned her head to face him. His words were swimming around her brain—the enormity of them. Her heart was swelling inside her chest. Those tiny fragments of doubt that had dashed through her mind when he'd made the suggestions about moving had evaporated. She raised one eyebrow, curiously. 'What makes you think I don't like Arran?'

He shot her a suspicious glance and counted off on his fingers. 'Er...maybe the weather. The ferries. Or lack of them. No supermarkets, no malls.'

She leaned towards him. 'Maybe I like all that. Maybe I like waking up in a place where the view changes daily. Maybe I like a place where most people know each other's names.'

He sat forward. It was obviously not what he was expecting to hear and she could see the hopeful glint in his eyes. 'Can I have more than five minutes?' he whispered.

She licked her lips and took a breath. If this was real, if she wanted this to be real, she had to be truthful—she had to put all her cards on the table.

'I've been angry these last few days. Angry with myself and angry with you. When I came to Arran I wanted to tell you that I loved you too. And when you told me first, then added about how it was all crazy and we could never work…it was like giving me part of my dream then stealing it all away again.'

He grimaced.

'I wanted you to ask, Rhuaridh. I wanted you to do exactly what you're here to do now, for me, without the big gesture. All I wanted you to do was to ask me to stay. To ask me to choose you, and to choose Arran.'

He blinked, a mixture of confusion and relief sweeping over his face. 'I thought that would be selfish. Conceited even, to ask you to give everything up.'

'Just like what you've done for me now?' She held her hands out toward his cases.

He let out a wry laugh and shook his head, reaching over to intertwine his fingers with hers. 'It seems that we both crossed our wires when we were really heading for parallel paths.'

She gave a slow nod of her head. 'I want you to know that I've made a decision.'

He straightened a little. 'What kind of decision?'

'A take-a-chance-on-everything life, love, career decision.'

He opened his mouth to speak but she held up her hand. 'I love you, Rhuaridh. The whole world could see it before I could. I started to dream about getting on that ferry, reaching Arran and never leaving again. I've started to like rain. And I definitely love snow. And my job?' She pulled a face and held up her hands. 'It used to be everything, but it's not been that for a long time. Not since Jess died. My family died. Not since I started volunteering at the helpline.' She looked at him nervously. 'I've had enough of TV. No matter what they offer me right now, the only offer I'm going to take is the book deal.'

'You have a book deal?' His eyes widened. 'That's brilliant!'

She looked up into his eyes. 'You gave me the push I

needed, you made me write the book in my heart. And you were right. There's been a bidding war. The publishers love it.'

He stopped for a second and tilted his head. 'Is that the only offer you're going to take?'

She licked her lips. 'That depends.'

'Depends on what?' He'd shifted forward, it was like he was hanging on her every word. Funny, handsome, grumpy, loyal Rhuaridh—her own Scotsman—was hanging on her words.

'I came to Arran to tell you I wanted to stay.' She rested her hand against her heart. 'That I'd lived my last few months in Technicolor. It was the life I'd always wanted. I'd found a man I loved and a place I thought I could call home.' She shook her head. 'I know the title of the show is ridiculous. Of course it's ridiculous. It's a TV show. But honestly? At the time I didn't think it was worth the fight. And...' she pressed her lips together for a second '... I honestly hoped you wouldn't find out.'

He reached over and touched her face. 'Kristie, I don't care about the TV show. I love you. I flew all this way to tell you that. Please forgive me. I'll move anywhere in the world with you. But if Arran's where you want to be, then nothing would make me happier.' The glint appeared in his eyes again. 'Mac will never forgive me if I don't bring you home. He hasn't looked at me since you left.'

She smiled. 'Mac is missing me?'

'He's pining. Like only an old sheepdog can. The only look he gives me these days is one of disgust.'

She edged a little closer. 'Well, when you put it like that, I don't want to see Mac suffer.'

His arms slid around her waist as her hands rested on his shoulders. 'I mean, every dog should have two parents.' Her hands moved up into his hair.

His lips brushed the side of her ear. 'I absolutely agree.' He looked at the three large suitcases at the doorway. 'Now, are you going to help me get those cases home?'

EPILOGUE

One year later

THE BRIDE'S THREE-QUARTER-LENGTH dress rippled in the breeze as she walked towards him clutching orange gerberas in one hand and Mac's lead in the other.

It felt as if the whole island had turned up for this event. The local hotel had hired three separate marquees to keep up with the numbers but whilst the sun was shining they'd decided to get married outside so everyone could see.

Rhuaridh's heart swelled in his chest. Kristie's hair wasn't quite so blonde now, her skin not quite so tanned, but he'd never seen anything more beautiful than his bride. Her grin was plastered from one side of her face to the other.

He leaned over, winking at Gerry, who sat on a chair nearby holding a camera, capturing the ceremony for them, then turned back and held out his hands towards his bride's. 'Now, no fancy moves, no running out on me.'

Her eyes sparkled. 'We're on an island. There's nowhere to go and...' she winked '... I'm not that good a swimmer. I guess you'll have to keep me.'

He slid his arms around her waist. 'Oh, I think I can do that.'

He bent towards her as Gerry shouted, 'Hey! Wait up! It's too early for a kiss.'

The celebrant laughed as Kristie slid her hands around his neck. 'What do you think?' she whispered, her lips brushing against his skin and her blue eyes continuing to sparkle.

Mac let out an approving bark and the whole congregation laughed too.

'Oh, it's never too early for a kiss,' said Rhuaridh, as he tipped his bride back and kissed her while the whole island watched.

* * * * *

COMING SOON!

We really hope you enjoyed reading this book.
If you're looking for more romance
be sure to head to the shops when
new books are available on

Thursday 26th September

To see which titles are coming soon, please visit
millsandboon.co.uk/nextmonth

MILLS & BOON

FOUR BRAND NEW STORIES FROM
MILLS & BOON MODERN

The same great stories you love,
a stylish new look!

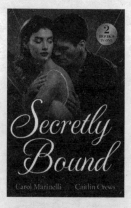
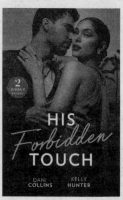
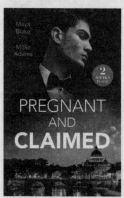

OUT NOW

MILLS & BOON

LET'S TALK

Romance

For exclusive extracts, competitions and special offers, find us online:

f MillsandBoon

X @MillsandBoon

⊙ @MillsandBoonUK

♪ @MillsandBoonUK

Get in touch on 01413 063 232

Afterglow Books is a trend-led, trope-filled list of books with diverse, authentic and relatable characters, a wide array of voices and representations, plus real world trials and tribulations. Featuring all the tropes you could possibly want (think small-town settings, fake relationships, grumpy vs sunshine, enemies to lovers) and all with a generous dose of spice in every story.

♪ @millsandboonuk

⊙ @millsandboonuk

afterglowbooks.co.uk

#AfterglowBooks

For all the latest book news, exclusive content and giveaways scan the QR code below to sign up to the Afterglow newsletter:

SCAN ME

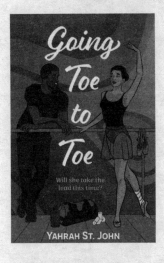

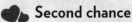
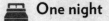

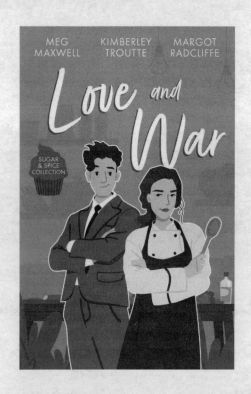

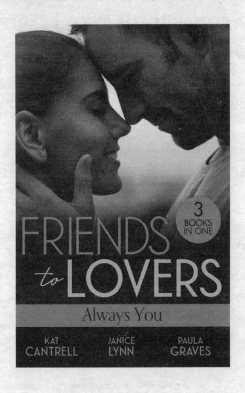

MILLS & BOON

THE HEART OF ROMANCE

A ROMANCE FOR EVERY READER

MODERN

Prepare to be swept off your feet by sophisticated, sexy and seductive heroes, in some of the world's most glamourous and romantic locations, where power and passion collide.

HISTORICAL

Escape with historical heroes from time gone by. Whether your passion is for wicked Regency Rakes, muscled Vikings or rugged Highlanders, awaken the romance of the past.

MEDICAL

Set your pulse racing with dedicated, delectable doctors in the high-pressure world of medicine, where emotions run high and passion, comfort and love are the best medicine.

True Love

Celebrate true love with tender stories of heartfelt romance, from the rush of falling in love to the joy a new baby can bring, and a focus on the emotional heart of a relationship.

HEROES

The excitement of a gripping thriller, with intense romance at its heart. Resourceful, true-to-life women and strong, fearless men face danger and desire - a killer combination!

From showing up to glowing up, these characters are on the path to leading their best lives and finding romance along the way – with plenty of sizzling spice!

To see which titles are coming soon, please visit

millsandboon.co.uk/nextmonth

MILLS & BOON
HEROES
At Your Service

Experience all the excitement of a gripping thriller, with an intense romance at its heart. Resourceful, true-to-life women and strong, fearless men face danger and desire – a killer combination!

Eight Heroes stories published every month, find them all at:

millsandboon.co.uk